EVERYMAN,

I WILL GO WITH THEE,

AND BE THY GUIDE,

IN THY MOST NEED

TO GO BY THY SIDE

EVERYMAN'S POCKET CLASSICS

# PARIS STORIES

EDITED BY SHAUN WHITESIDE

EVERYMAN'S POCKET CLASSICS
Alfred A. Knopf New York London Toronto

THIS IS A BORZOI BOOK
PUBLISHED BY ALFRED A. KNOPF

This selection by Shaun Whiteside first published in Everyman's Library, 2016
 Published in the United States by Alfred A. Knopf, a division of Penguin Random House LLC, New York, and in Canada by Penguin Random House Canada Ltd., Toronto. Distributed by Penguin Random House LLC, New York. Published in the United Kingdom by Everyman's Library, 50 Albemarle Street, London W1S 4BD and distributed by Penguin Random House UK, 20 Vauxhall Bridge Road, London SW1V 2SA.

www.randomhouse.com/everymans
www.everymanslibrary.co.uk

ISBN: 978-1-101-90756-6 (US)
978-1-84159-620-4 (UK)

A CIP catalogue reference for this book is available from the British Library

Typography by Peter B. Willberg

Typeset in the UK by Input Data Services Ltd, Bridgwater, Somerset

Printed and bound in Germany by GGP Media GmbH, Pössneck

# PARIS STORIES

# Contents

# PREFACE

'WE'LL ALWAYS HAVE PARIS,' Bogart tells Bergman at the end of *Casablanca*, establishing Paris once and for all as the romantic capital of the world, a position that the city continues to hold even today. This may account for its status as the world's leading tourist destination, with its iconic landmarks, its boulevards and pavement cafés, its impeccable chic and, for Anglo-Saxon visitors at least, its dashing suggestions of freedom and, for some, impropriety. As I hope I show in this selection, there is of course much more to Paris than the tourists see. I have opened in the Paris of the early Renaissance, where Rabelais' giant Gargantua, perched on the towers of Notre Dame, cheerfully relieves his bladder on the horrified crowd below, to stress another side of the city – its robust, outrageous satirical streak, its disdain for convention and decorum.

Eighteenth-century travellers like Laurence Sterne enjoyed teasing their readers with accounts of lax morals and brazen forwardness unimaginable at home – no doubt stirring many curious souls to make the journey themselves, or dream forlornly of doing so. Vivid accounts of the Revolution stress the potential for violence that lay beneath the city's surface. And its great anatomists, the realist novelists of the nineteenth century, captured in almost photographic detail the archetypal city not only of the elegant upper classes who set the tone for the rest of Europe, but of the multitudes who toiled in the streets down below. The vibrant city of the twentieth century is a place of both gleeful artistic experiment and existential gloom, attracting both the gilded and the lost.

I hope that in this collection I have captured some of Paris's great variety, its seamier side, the world of the *petites gens*, as well as its glitter, its glamour, its keen intelligence and its sexy, seductive allure. There is romance here, yes, but there is also cynicism, satire and revolt, and a refusal to be dragged down for long by history's darker turns. 'He who contemplates the depths of Paris is seized with vertigo. Nothing is more fantastic. Nothing is more tragic. Nothing is more sublime.' So wrote Victor Hugo. I will raise a glass of champagne to that.

Shaun Whiteside

FRANÇOIS RABELAIS

From

# GARGANTUA AND PANTAGRUEL

1534

Translated by Sir Thomas Urquhart and Pierre Le Motteux

## *How Gargantua was sent to Paris, and of the huge great Mare that he rode on; How she destroyed the Oxe-flies of the Beauce.*

IN THE SAME season *Fayoles*, the fourth King of *Numidia*, sent out of the countrey of *Africk* to *Grangousier*, the most hideously great Mare that ever was seen, and of the strangest forme, (for you know well enough how it is said, that *Africk* alwayes is productive of some new thing:) she was as big as six elephants, and had her feet cloven into fingers, like *Julius Caesar*'s horse, with slouch-hanging eares, like the goats in *Languedoc*, and a little horne on her buttock; she was of a burnt sorel hue, with a little mixture of daple gray spots, but above all she had a horrible taile; for it was little more or lesse, then every whit as great as the Steeple-pillar of St. *Mark* beside *Langes*: and squared as that is, with tuffs and *ennicroches*, or haire-plaits wrought within one another, no otherwise then as the beards are upon the eares of corne.

If you wonder at this, wonder rather at the tails of the *Scythian* Rams, which weighed above thirty pounds each, and of the *Surian* sheep, who need (if *Tenaud* say true,) a little cart at their heeles to beare up their taile, it is so long and heavy. You female Lechers in the plaine countreys have no such tailes. And she was brought by sea in three Carricks and a Brigantine unto the harbour of *Olone* in *Thalmondois*. When *Grangousier* saw her, Here is (said he) what is fit to carry my sonne to *Paris*. So now, in the name of God, all will be well, he will in times coming be a great Scholar, if it were not (my masters) for the beasts, we should live like Clerks: The next morning (after they had drunk, you must understand) they took their journey; *Gargantua*, his Pedagogue *Ponocrates*, and his traine, and with them *Eudemon* the young Page, and because the weather was faire and temperate, his father caused to be made for him a paire of dun boots, *Babin* calls them buskins: Thus did they merrily passe their time in travelling on their high way, alwayes making good chear, and were very pleasant till they came a little above *Orleans*, in which place there was a forrest of five and thirty leagues long, and seventeen in breadth, or thereabouts. This forrest was most horribly fertile and copious in dorflies, hornets and wasps, so that it was a very Purgatory for the poor mares, asses and horses: But *Gargantua*'s mare did avenge herself handsomly of all the out-rages therein committed upon beasts of her kinde, and that by a trick whereof they had no suspicion; for as soon as ever they were entred into the said forest, and that the wasps had given the assault, she drew out and unsheathed her taile, and therewith skirmishing, did so sweep them, that she overthrew all the wood alongst and athwart, here and there, this way and that way, longwise and sidewise, over and under, and felled every where the wood with as much ease, as a mower doth the grasse, in such sort that never since hath ther been there, neither wood, nor *Dorflies*: for all the countrey was thereby reduced to a plain champain-field: which *Gargantua* took great pleasure to behold, and said to his company no more but this, *Je trouve beau ce*, I finde this pretty; whereupon that countrey hath been ever since that time called *Beauce*: but all the breakfast the mare got that day, was but a little yawning and gaping, in memory whereof the Gentlemen of *Beauce*, do as yet to this day break their fast with gaping, which they finde to be very good, and do spit the better for it; at last they came to *Paris*, where *Gargantua* refresh't himself two or three dayes, making very merry with his folks, and enquiring what men of learning there were then in the city, and what wine they drunk there.

## *How Gargantua payed his welcome to the Parisians, and how he took away the great Bells of our Ladies Church.*

SOME FEW DAYES after that they had refresh't themselves, he went to see the city, and was beheld of every body there with great admiration; for the People of *Paris* are so sottish, so badot, so foolish and fond by nature, that a jugler, a carrier of indulgences, a sumpter-horse, or mule with cymbals, or tinkling bells, a blinde fidler in the middle of a crosse lane, shall draw a greater confluence of people together, then an Evangelical Preacher: and they prest so hard upon him, that he was constrained to rest himself upon the towers of our Ladies Church; at which place, seeing so many about him, he said with a loud voice, I beleeve that these buzzards wil have me to pay them here my welcom hither, and my *Proficiat*: it is but good reason, I will now give them their wine, but it shall be only in sport; Then smiling, he untied his faire *Braguette*, and drawing out his *mentul* into the open aire, he so bitterly all-to-bepist them, that he drowned two hundred and sixty thousand, foure hundred and eighteen, besides the women and little children: some neverthelesse of the company escaped this piss-flood by meer speed of foot, who when they were at the higher end of the University, sweating, coughing, spitting, and out of breath, they began to swear and curse, some in good hot earnest, and others in jest, *Carimari, Carimara: Golynoly, Golynolo*: by my sweet Sanctesse, we are wash't in sport, a sport truly to laugh at, in *French Par ris*, for which that city hath been ever since called Paris, whose name formerly was *Leucotia*, (as *Strabo* testifieth, *lib, quarto*) from the Greek word *λευκότης*, whitenesse, because of the white thighs of the Ladies of that place. And forasmuch as at this imposition of a new name, all the people that were there, swore every one by the Sancts of his parish, the *Parisians*, which are patch'd up of all nations, and all pieces of countreyes, are by nature both good *Jurers*, and good *Jurists*, and somewhat overweening; whereupon *Joanninus de Barrauco libro de copiositate reverentiarum*, thinks that they are called *Parisians*, from the *Greek* word *παῤῥησία,* which signifies boldnesse and liberty in speech. This done, he considered the great bells, which were in the said tours, and made them sound very harmoniously, which whilest he was doing, it came into his minde, that they would serve very well for *tingling Tantans*, and *ringing Campanels*, to hang about his mares neck, when she should be sent back to his father, (as he intended to do) loaded with *Brie* cheese, and fresh herring; and indeed he forthwith carried them to his lodging. In the mean while there came a master begar of the Fryers of *S. Anthonie*, to demand in his canting way the usual benevolence of some hoggish stuffe, who, that he might be heard afar off, and to make the bacon, he was in quest of, shake in the very chimneys, made account to filch them away privily. Neverthelesse, he left them behinde very honestly, not for that they were too hot, but that they were somewhat too heavy for his carriage. This was not he of *Bourg*, for he was too good a friend of mine. All the city was risen up in sedition, they being (as you know) upon any slight occasion, so ready to uproars and insurrections, that forreign nations wonder at the patience of the Kings of *France*, who do not by good justice restrain them from such tumultuous courses, seeing the manifold incoveniences which thence arise from day to day. Would to God I knew the shop, wherein are forged these divisions, and factious combinations, that I might bring them to light in the confraternities of my parish. Beleeve for a truth, that the place wherein the people gathered together, were thus sulfured, hopurymated, moiled and bepist, was called *Nesle*, where then was, (but now is no more) the Oracle of *Leucotia*: There was the case proposed, and the inconvenience shewed of the transporting of the bells: After they had well *ergoted pro* and *con*, they concluded in *Baralipton*, that they should send the oldest and most sufficient of the facultie unto *Gargantua*, to signifie unto him the great and horrible prejudice they sustain by the want of those bells; and notwithstanding the good reasons given in by some of the University, why this charge was fitter for an Oratour then a Sophister, there was chosen for this purpose our Master *Janotus de Bragmardo*.

## *How Janotus de Bragmardo was sent to Gargantua, to recover the great bells.*

MASTER *Janotus*, with his haire cut round like a dish *a La caesarine*, in his most antick accoustrement *Liripipionated* with a graduates hood, and, having sufficiently antidoted his stomack with Oven-*Marmalades*, that is, bread and holy water of the Cellar, transported himself to the lodging of *Gargantua*, driving before him three red muzled beadles, and dragging after him five or six artlesse masters, all throughly bedaggled with the mire of the streets. At their entry *Ponocrates* met them, who was afraid, seeing them so disguised, and thought they had been some maskers out of their wits, which moved him to enquire of one of the said artlesse masters of the company, what this mummery meant? it was answered him, that they desired to have their bells restored to them. As soon as *Ponocrates* heard that, he ran in all haste to carry the newes unto *Gargantua*, that he might be ready to answer them, and speedily resolve what was to be done. *Gargantua* being advertised hereof, called apart his Schoolmaster *Ponocrates*, *Philotimus* Steward of his house, *Gymnastes* his Esquire, and *Eudemon*, and very summarily conferred with them, both of what he should do, and what answer he should give. They were all of opinion that they should bring them unto the goblet-office, which is the Buttery, and there make them drink like Roysters, and line their jackets soundly: and that this cougher might not be puft up with vain-glory, by thinking the bells were restored at his request, they sent (whilest he was chopining and plying the pot) for the Major of the City, the Rector of the facultie, and the Vicar of the Church, unto whom they resolved to deliver the bells, before the *Sophister* had propounded his commission; after that, in their hearing, he should pronounce his gallant Oration, which was done, and they being come, the Sophister was brought into a full hall, and began as followeth, in coughing.

## *The Oration of Master Janotus de Bragmardo, for recovery of the bells.*

HEM, HEM, *Gudday* Sirs, *Gudday & vobis* my masters, it were but reason that you should restore to us our bells; for we have great need of them. *Hem, hem, aihfuhash*, we have often-times heretofore refused good money for them of those of *London* in *Cahors*, yea and of those of *Bordeaux* in *Brie*, who would have bought them for the substantifick quality of the elementary complexion, which is intronificated in the terrestreity of their quidditative nature, to extraneize the blasting mists, and whirlwindes upon our Vines; indeed not ours, but these round about us; for if we lose the *piot* and liquour of the grape, we lose all both sense and law. If you restore them unto us at my request, I shall gaine by it six basketfuls of sauciges, and a fine paire of breeches, which will do my legs a great deal of good, or else they will not keep their promise to me. Ho by gob *domine*, a paire of breeches is good, *& vir sapiens non abhorrebit eam*. Ha, ha, a paire of breeches is not so easily got, I have experience of it my self. Consider, *Domine*, I have been these eighteen dayes in *metagrabolising* this brave speech, *Reddite quæ sunt Caesaris, Caesari, & quae sunt Dei, Deo. Ibi jacet lepus*, by my faith, *Domine*, if you will sup with me in *cameris*, by cox body, *charitatis nos faciemus bonum cherubin; ego occidit unum porcum, & ego habet bonum vino*: but of good wine we cannot make bad Latine. Well, *de parte Dei datè nobis bellas nostras*; Hold, I give you in the name of the facultie a *Sermones de utino*, that *utinam* you would give us our bells. *Vultis etiam pardonos? per diem vos habebitis, & nihil payabitis*. O Sir *Domine*, *Bellagivaminor nobis*; verily, *est bonum vobis*. They are useful to every body, if they fit your mare well, so do they do our facultie; *quae comparata est jumentis insipientibus, & similis facta est eis, Psalmo nescio quo*; yet did I quote it in my note-book *& est unum bonum* Achilles, a good defending argument, *hem, hem, hem, haikhash*; for I prove unto you that you should give me them. *Ego sic argumentor. Omnis bella bellabilis in Bellerio bellando, bellans bellativo, bellare facit, bellabiliter bellantes: parisius habet bellas; ergo gluc*. Ha, ha, ha, this is spoken to some purpose; it is *in tertio primae*, in *Darii*, or elsewhere. By my soul, I have seen the time that I could play the devil in arguing, but now I am much failed, and henceforward want nothing but a cup of good wine, a good bed, my back to the fire, my belly to the table, and a good deep dish. *Hei domine*, I beseech you, *in nomine Patris, Filii, & Spiritûs sancti*, Amen, to restore unto us our bells: and God keep you from evil, and our Lady from health; *qui vivit & regnat per omnia secula seculorum. Amen.* Hem, *hashchehhawksash, qzrchremhemhash, verùm enim vero, quandoquidem, dubio procul, aedepol, quoniam, ità certè, medius fidius*; A Town without bells is like a blinde man without a staffe, an Asse without a crupper, and a Cow without Cymbals; therefore be assured, until you have restored them unto us, we will never leave crying after you, like a blinde man that hath lost his staffe, braying like an Asse without a crupper, and making a noise like a Cow without Cymbals. A certain Latinisator, dwelling near the Hospital, said since, producing the authority of one *Taponnus*, I lie, it was *Pontanus* the secular Poet, who wish't those bells had been made of feathers, and the clapper of a foxtail, to the end they might have begot a chronicle in the bowels of his braine, when he was about the composing of his carminiformal lines: but, *Nac petet in petetac tic torche Lorgne*, or *Rot kipipur kipipot put pantse malf*, he was declared an Heretick; We make them as of wax. And no more saith the deponent. *Valete & plaudite. Calepinus recensui.*

## *How the Sophister carried away his cloth, and how he had a suite in law against the other Masters.*

THE SOPHISTER HAD no sooner ended, but *Ponocrates* and *Eudemon* burst out in a laughing so heartily, that they had almost split with it, and given up the ghost, in rendering their souls to God: even just as *Crassus* did, seeing a lubberly

Asse eate thistles; and as *Philemon*, who, for seeing an Asse eat those figs which were provided for his own dinner, died with force of laughing; together with them Master *Janotus* fell a laughing too as fast as he could, in which mood of laughing they continued so long, that their eyes did water by the vehement concussion of the substance of the braine, by which these lachrymal humidities, being prest out, glided through the optick nerves, and so to the full represented *Democritus Heraclitising*, and *Heraclitus Democritising*. When they had done laughing, *Gargantua* consulted with the prime of his retinue, what should be done. There *Ponocrates* was of opinion, that they should make this faire Orator drink again, and seeing he had shewed them more pastime, and made them laugh more then a natural soule could have done, that they should give him ten baskets full of sauciges, mentioned in his pleasant speech, with a paire of hose, three hundred great billets of logwood, five and twenty hogsheads of wine, a good large down-bed, and a deep capacious dish, which he said were necessary for his old age. All this was done as they did appoint: only *Gargantua*, doubting that they could not quickly finde out breeches fit for his wearing, because he knew not what fashion would best become the said Orator, whether the martingal fashion of breeches, wherein is a spunghole with a draw-bridge, for the more easie caguing: or the fashion of the Marriners, for the greater solace and comfort of his kidneys: or that of the *Switsers*, which keeps warm the *bedondaine* or belly-tabret: or round breeches with streat cannions, having in the seat a piece like a Cods taile, for feare of over-heating his reines; all which considered he caused to be given him seven elles of white cloth for the linings. The wood was carried by the Porters, the Masters of Arts carried the sauciges and the dishes, and Master *Janotus* himself would carry the cloth. One of the said

Masters, (called *Jesse Bandouille*,) shewed him that it was not seemly nor decent for one of his condition to do so, and that therefore he should deliver it to one of them: Ha, said *Janotus*, *Baudet*, *Baudet*, or, Blockhead, Blockhead, thou dost not conclude *in modo & figura*; for loe, to this end serve the suppositions, *& parva Logicalia: pannus, pro quo supponit? Confusè* (said *Bandouille*) *& distributivè*. I do not ask thee (said *Janotus*,) Blockhead, *quomodo supponit*, but *pro quo*? It is, *Blockhead*, *pro tibiis meis*, and therefore I will carry it, *Egomet, sicut suppositum portat appositum*; so did he carry it away very close and covertly, as *Patelin* the *Buffoon* did his cloth. The best was, that when this cougher in a full act or assembly held at the *Mathurins*, had with great confidence required his breeches and sauciges, and that they were flatly denied him, because he had them of *Gargantua*, according to the informations thereupon made, he shewed them that this was *gratìs* and out of his liberality, by which they were not in any sort quit of their promises. Notwithstanding this, it was answered him, that he should be content with reason, without expectation of any other bribe there. Reason: (said *Janotus*,) we use none of it here, unluckie traitors, you are not worth the hanging: the earth beareth not more arrant Villains then you are, I know it well enough; Halt not before the lame; I have practised wickednesse with you: By Gods rattle I will inform the King of the enormous abuses that are forged here, and carried underhand by you, and let me be a Leper, if he do not burn you alive like *Sodomites*, Traitors, Hereticks and Seducers, enemies to God and vertue. Upon these words they framed articles against him: he on the other side warned them to appear: In summe, the Processe was retained by the Court, and is there as yet. Hereupon the *Magisters* made a vow, never to *decrott* themselves in rubbing off the dirt of either their shoes or clothes: Master *Janotus* with his Adherents, vowed never to blow or snuffe their noses, until judgement were given by a definitive sentence; by these vows do they continue unto this time both dirty and snottie; for the Court hath not garbeled, sifted, and fully looked into all the pieces as yet. The judgement or decree shall be given out & pronounced at the next *Greek* Calends, that is, never: as you know that they do more then nature, and contrary to their own articles: the articles of *Paris* maintain, that to God alone belongs infinitie, and nature produceth nothing that is immortal; for she putteth an end and period to all things by her engendered, according to the saying, *Omnia orta cadunt, &c.* But these thick mist-swallowers make the suits in law depending before them both infinite and immortal; in doing whereof, they have given occasion to, and verified the saying of *Chilo* the *Lacedemonian*, consecrated to the Oracle at *Delphos*, that misery is the inseparable companion of law-debates: and that pleaders are miserable; for sooner shall they attain to the end of their lives, then to the final decision of their pretended rights.

LAURENCE STERNE

From

# A SENTIMENTAL JOURNEY THROUGH FRANCE AND ITALY

1768

# PARIS

WHEN A MAN can contest the point by dint of equipage, and carry all on floundering before him with half a dozen lackies and a couple of cooks – 'tis very well in such a place as Paris – he may drive in at which end of a street he will.

A poor prince who is weak in cavalry, and whose whole infantry does not exceed a single man, had best quit the field; and singalize himself in the cabinet, if he can get up into it; – I say *up into it* – for there is no descending perpendicular amongst 'em with a *'Me voici! mes enfans'* – here I am – whatever many may think.

I own my first sensations, as soon as I was left solitary and alone in my own chamber in the hotel, were far from being so flattering as I had prefigured them. I walked up gravely to the window in my dusty black coat, and looking through the glass saw all the world in yellow, blue, and green, running at the ring of pleasure. – The old with broken lances, and in helmets which had lost their vizards; – the young in armour bright which shone like gold, beplumed with each gay feather of the east, – all, – all, tilting at it like fascinated knights in tournaments of yore for fame and love. –

Alas, poor Yorick! cried I, what art thou doing here? On the very first onset of all this glittering clatter thou art reduced to an atom; – seek, – seek some winding alley, with a tourniquet at the end of it, where chariot never rolled or flambeau shot its rays; – there thou mayest solace thy soul in converse sweet with some kind grisette of a barber's wife, and get into such coteries! –

– May I perish! if I do, said I, pulling out the letter which I had to present to Madame de R—. – I'll wait upon this lady, the very first thing I do. So I called La Fleur to go seek me a barber directly, – and come back and brush my coat.

## THE WIG. PARIS.

WHEN THE BARBER came, he absolutely refused to have any thing to do with my wig: 'twas either above or below his art: I had nothing to do but to take one ready made of his own recommendation.

– But I fear, friend! said I, this buckle won't stand. – You may immerge it, replied he, into the ocean, and it will stand. –

What a great scale is every thing upon in this city! thought I. – The utmost stretch of an English periwig-maker's ideas could have gone no further than to have 'dipped it into a pail of water.' – What difference! 'tis like Time to Eternity!

I confess I do hate all cold conceptions, as I do the puny ideas which engender them; and am generally so struck with the great works of nature, that for my own part, if I could help it, I never would make a comparison less than a mountain at least. All that can be said against the French sublime, in this instance of it, is this: – That the grandeur is *more* in the *word*, and *less* in the *thing*. No doubt, the ocean fills the mind with vast ideas; but Paris being so far inland, it was not likely I should run post a hundred miles out of it, to try the experiment; – the Parisian barber meant nothing. –

The pail of water standing beside the great deep, makes, certainly, but a sorry figure in speech; – but, 'twill be said, – it has one advantage – 'tis in the next room, and the truth of the buckle may be tried in it, without more ado, in a single moment.

In honest truth, and upon a more candid revision of the matter, *The French expression professes more than it performs*.

I think I can see the precise and distinguishing marks of national characters more in these nonsensical *minutiae* than in the most important matters of state; where great men of all nations talk and stalk so much alike, that I would not give ninepence to choose amongst them.

I was so long in getting from under my barber's hands, that it was too late to think of going with my letter to Madame R— that night: but when a man is once dressed at all points for going out, his reflections turn to little account; so taking down the name of the Hôtel de Modene, where I lodged, I walked forth without any determination where to go; – I shall consider of that, said I, as I walk along.

## THE PULSE. PARIS.

HAIL, YE SMALL sweet courtesies of life, for smooth do ye make the road of it! like grace and beauty, which beget inclinations to love at first sight: 'tis ye who open this door and let the stranger in.

– Pray, Madame, said I, have the goodness to tell me which way I must turn to go to the Opéra Comique? – Most willingly, Monsieur, said she, laying aside her work. –

I had given a cast with my eye into half a dozen shops, as I came along, in search of a face not likely to be disordered by such an interruption: till at last, this, hitting my fancy, I had walked in.

She was working a pair of ruffles, as she sat in a low chair, on the far side of the shop, facing the door.

– *Tres volontiers*, most willingly, said she, laying her work down upon a chair next her, and rising up from the low chair she was sitting in, with so cheerful a movement, and so cheerful a look, that had I been laying out fifty louis d'ors with her, I should have said – 'This woman is grateful.'

You must turn, Monsieur, said she, going with me to the door of the shop, and pointing the way down the street I was to take, – you must turn first to your left hand, – *mais prenez garde* – there are two turns; and be so good as to take the second – then go down a little way and you'll see a church: and, when you are past it, give yourself the trouble to turn directly to the right, and that will lead you to the foot of the Pont Neuf, which you must cross – and there any one will do himself the pleasure to show you. –

She repeated her instructions three times over to me, with the same goodnatur'd patience the third time as the first; – and if *tones and manners* have a meaning, which certainly they have, unless to hearts which shut them out, – she seemed really interested that I should not lose myself.

I will not suppose it was the woman's beauty, notwithstanding she was the handsomest grisette, I think, I ever saw, which had much to do with the sense I had of her courtesy; only I remember, when I told her how much I was obliged to her, that I looked very full in her eyes, – and that I repeated my thanks as often as she had done her instructions.

I had not got ten paces from the door, before I found I had forgot every tittle of what she had said; – so looking back, and seeing her still standing in the door of the shop, as if to look whether I went right or not, – I returned back to ask her, whether the first turn was to my right or left, – for that I had absolutely forgot. – Is it possible! said she, half laughing. 'Tis very possible, replied I, when a man is thinking more of a woman than of her good advice.

As this was the real truth – she took it, as every woman takes a matter of right, with a slight curtsy.

– *Attendez!* said she, laying her hand upon my arm to detain me, whilst she called a lad out of the back shop to get ready a parcel of gloves. I am just going to send him, said she, with a packet into that quarter, and if you will have the complaisance to step in, it will be ready in a moment, and he shall attend you to the place. – So I walk'd in with her to the far side of the shop: and taking up the ruffle in my hand which she laid upon the chair, as if I had a mind to sit, she sat down herself in her low chair, and I instantly sat myself down beside her.

– He will be ready, Monsieur, said she, in a moment. – And in that moment, replied I, most willingly would I say something very civil to you for all these courtesies. Any one may do a casual act of good nature, but a continuation of them shows it is a part of the temperature; and certainly, added I, if it is the same blood which comes from the heart which descends to the extremes (touching her wrist) I am sure you must have one of the best pulses of any woman in the world. – Feel it, said she, holding out her arm. So laying down my hat, I took hold of her fingers in one hand, and applied the two forefingers of my other to the artery. –

– Would to heaven! my dear Eugenius, thou hadst passed by, and beheld me sitting in my black coat, and in my lack-a-day-sical manner, counting the throbs of it, one by one, with as much true devotion as if I had been watching the critical ebb or flow of her fever. – How wouldst thou have laugh'd and moralized upon my new profession! – and thou shouldst have laugh'd and moralized on. – Trust me, my dear Eugenius, I should have said, 'There are worse occupations in this world *than feeling a woman's pulse.*' – But a grisette's! thou wouldst have said, – and in an open shop! Yorick –

– So much the better: for when my views are direct, Eugenius, I care not if all the world saw me feel it.

## THE HUSBAND. PARIS.

I HAD COUNTED twenty pulsations, and was going on fast towards the fortieth, when her husband, coming unexpected from a back parlour into the shop, put me a little out of my reckoning. – 'Twas nobody but her husband, she said; – so I began a fresh score. – Monsieur is so good, quoth she, as he pass'd by us, as to give himself the trouble of feeling my pulse. – The husband took off his hat, and making me a bow, said, I did him too much honour – and having said that, he put on his hat and walk'd out.

Good God! said I to myself, as he went out, – and can this man be the husband of this woman!

Let it not torment the few who know what must have been the grounds of this exclamation, if I explain it to those who do not.

In London a shopkeeper and a shopkeeper's wife seem to be one bone and one flesh: in the several endowments of mind and body, sometimes the one, sometimes the other has it, so as, in general, to be upon a par, and totally with each other as nearly as man and wife need to do.

In Paris, there are scarce two orders of beings more different: for the legislative and executive powers of the shop not resting in the husband, he seldom comes there: – in some dark and dismal room behind, he sits commerce-less, in his thrum nightcap, the same rough son of Nature that Nature left him.

The genius of a people, where nothing but the monarchy is *salique*, having ceded this department, with sundry others, totally to the women, – by a continual higgling with customers of all ranks and sizes from morning to night, like so many rough pebbles shook long together in a bag, by amicable collisions they have worn down their asperities and sharp angles, and not only become round and smooth, but will receive, some of them, a polish like a brilliant: – Monsieur *le Mari* is little better than the stone under your foot.

– Surely, – surely, man! it is not good for thee to sit alone: – thou wast made for social intercourse and gentle greetings; and this improvement of our natures from it I appeal to as my evidence.

– And how does it beat, Monsieur? said she. – With all the benignity, said I, looking quietly in her eyes, that I expected. – She was going to say something civil in return – but the lad came into the shop with the gloves – *A propos*, said I; I want a couple of pairs myself.

## THE GLOVES. PARIS.

THE BEAUTIFUL GRISETTE rose up when I said this, and going behind the counter, reach'd down a parcel and untied it: I advanced to the side over against her: they were all too large. The beautiful grisette measured them one by one across my hand. – It would not alter their dimensions. – She begg'd I would try a single pair, which seemed to be the least. – She held it open; – my hand slipped into it at once. – It will not do, said I, shaking my head a little. – No, said she, doing the same thing.

There are certain combined looks of simple subtlety, – where whim, and sense, and seriousness, and nonsense, are so blended, that all the languages of Babel set loose together, could not express them; – they are communicated and caught so instantaneously, that you can scarce say which party is the infector. I leave it to your men of words to swell pages about it – it is enough in the present to say again, the gloves would not do; so, folding our hands within our arms, we both lolled upon the counter – it was narrow, and there was just room for the parcel to lay between us.

The beautiful grisette looked sometimes at the gloves, then sideways to the window, then at the gloves, – and then at me. I was not disposed to break silence: – I followed her example: so, I looked at the gloves, then to the window, then at the gloves, and then at her, – and so on alternately.

I found I lost considerably in every attack: – she had a quick black eye, and shot through two such long and silken eyelashes with such penetration, that she look'd into my very heart and reins. – It may seem strange, but I could actually feel she did. –

It is no matter, said I, taking up a couple of the pairs next me, and putting them into my pocket.

I was sensible the beautiful grisette had not asked above a single livre above the price. – I wish'd she had ask'd a livre more, and was puzzling my brains how to bring the matter about. – Do you think, my dear Sir, said she, mistaking my embarrassment, that I could ask a *sous* too much of a stranger – and of a stranger whose politeness, more than his want of gloves, has done me the honour to lay himself at my mercy? – *M'en croyez capable?* – Faith! not I, said I; and if you were, you are welcome. So counting the money into her hand, and with a lower bow than one generally makes to a shopkeeper's wife, I went out, and her lad with his parcel followed me.

RESTIF DE LA BRETONNE

From

# LES NUITS DE PARIS

1792

Translated by Linda Asher and Ellen Fertig

# MASSACRES
## September 2 to 5, 1792

AUGUST 10 HAD revived the Revolution and brought it to its peak; September 2, 3, 4 and 5 cast a brooding horror over it. Those dreadful events must be described impartially, and the writer must remain cool while he makes his reader shudder. No breath of passion must stir him; otherwise, he becomes a demagogue instead of a historian.

On Sunday at six or seven o'clock I went out, unaware as usual of what was happening. I set off for my island – that beloved Île Saint-Louis, from which a villain had forced the residents to oust me. Ah, how evil a man without breeding can be! In this tranquil refuge, where I entered unobserved, I heard nothing except for a domestic who was saying to another through the window: 'But, Catherine, that sounds like the alarm ringing! Is something else happening?' Catherine answered, 'I guess so. Master says to lock up.' I moved on, without seeming to listen. I did not walk around the island completely; I left by the Pont Marie and the Port au Blé. There was dancing there. I found that reassuring. When I reached the large restaurant with the stairs, at the end of the port, I saw more dancing. But just then a passer-by exclaimed, 'Will you stop your dancing! They're doing another kind of dance in some places!' The dancing stopped. I went on, with a heavy heart; without knowing exactly why, I followed the quays – Pelletier, Gèvres, Mégisserie or Ferraille – and I reached the Café Robert.

I knew a little man there, of Swiss extraction but born

in Paris, who always knew what was going on in his neighborhood, the Théâtre-Français section . . . 'They're killing them in the prisons,' he told me. 'It began with my district, at the Abbaye. They say it started with a man put in the stocks at the Grève yesterday who said he didn't give a d— for the nation, and other insults. People got excited; they took him up to the Hôtel de Ville, and he was condemned to be hanged. He had said, earlier, that the prisons were full of people who thought as he did, and that they'd get their chance soon enough, that they had weapons, and that they would be left behind in the city when the volunteers went off . . . The result is that today crowds gathered in front of the prisons, forced the doors, and they're killing everyone who's in for anything but debts.' I became very upset and frightened as I listened to little Fragnières; the picture he described, however, was far from the truth. After I had read the newspapers I asked him if he was going my way. For I was frightened. 'Gladly,' he replied, 'but let us go by the Abbaye. Then I'll take you to your door.'

We set out together. Everything seemed in a kind of stupor in the noisy rue Dauphine, which still bore that name. We went as far as the prison gate without difficulty. There we found a group of spectators in a circle; the killers were at the gate, both inside and out. The judges were in the guardroom. The prisoners were brought before them. They were asked to give their names. The records of their arraignment were studied. The nature of the charge against them decided their fate. An eyewitness told me that often the killers inside pronounced the sentence before the judges did. A tall man, cool and sober in manner, was brought before them; he was accused of hostility and of aristocracy. They asked him whether he was guilty. 'No, I have done nothing; only my feelings were under suspicion, and in the three months I have been in prison they have found nothing against me.' At his words, the judges inclined toward clemency, but a voice cried in the Provençal accent, 'An aristocrat! Off with him – to the Force! To the Force!'

'So be it, to the Force, then,' the man replied, 'I shall not be any guiltier for having changed prisons!' (He was unaware, the poor wretch, that the phrase 'to the Force!' uttered at the Abbaye meant the death sentence; just as the cry 'to the Abbaye,' pronounced in the other prisons, sent a victim to the slaughterhouse.) He was shoved outside by the man who had shouted, and he passed through the fatal gateway. He was astonished by the first sword-thrust, but then he dropped his hands and let himself be killed, without a gesture of protest . . .

I who could never bear the sight of blood – imagine my state when I found myself pushed right under the swords by that inquisitive Fragnières! I was shaking! I felt I was getting weak and threw myself to one side. A shrill scream from a prisoner more sensitive to death than the others instilled me with a wholesome rage, which strengthened my legs enough to leave the place. I did not see the rest . . .

The killing had started at the Châtelet by then; the crowd moved on to the Force. But I did not go with them; I was hoping to escape these horrors by staying home. I went to bed. A sleep made fitful by the fury of the carnage yielded me only troubled rest, often interrupted by a terrified start. But that was not all. Toward two o'clock I heard a bunch of savages pass beneath my window, none of whom seemed to speak with a Parisian accent; they all sounded unfamiliar to me. They were singing, roaring and howling. In the midst of it all, I heard: 'Let's go to the Bernardins! Let's go to Saint-Firmin!' (Saint-Firmin was a priests' residence; the galley slaves were at the Bernardins at the time.) A few of these killers were shouting: 'Long live the nation!' One of them – whom I would have liked to see in order to behold the hateful soul in his detestable face – was shouting furiously: 'Long live death!' I do not have this second-hand; I heard it myself, and shuddered at it. They meant to kill both the convicts and the Saint-Firmin priests. Among the latter was Abbé Gros, an ex-delegate to the Constituent Assembly, once my priest at Saint-Nicolas-du-Chardonnet, at whose home I had dined with two ladies from Auxerre. He reproached me that evening, in fact, for having expressed some disapproval of priestly celibacy in *La Vie de Mon Père*. Among the killers Abbé Gros saw a man with whom he had had some connection. 'Ah, my friend, so you're here too! Well – and what do you all want here at this hour?'

'Oh,' the man replied, 'we have come for no good ... You've been decent to me ... But why did you retract your oath?' The man turned his back on the priest, as the kings and Richelieu did to their victims, and gave a signal to his companions. Abbé Gros was not stabbed, he was granted a kinder death; they threw him out of the window. His brain splattered ... he did not suffer ... I shall say nothing of the convicts. Those poor wretches saw an end put to lives that even they could not regret. But earlier in the evening, another horrendous scene – one I did not see, of which I was unaware at the time – had taken place at the Carmelite monastery near the Luxembourg garden. For a few days all the non-juring clergy, arrested either at the city tollgates or during house-visit night, had been brought together there. The bishop of Arles had joined them voluntarily to console and encourage his brethren. And do not think for a moment that I am taking the side of the fanatic priests just because I have related this moving incident! They are my sworn enemies – in my eyes the most despicable beings. No, no, I do not grieve for them! They have done too much harm to the country; earlier, by their scandalous behavior which removed all restraint from the people; later, by their scheming. There is nothing either good or evil in the will of the Society: when a Society, or its majority, wishes something that calls down war and vengeance upon the nation, it is a monster! He who hopes to avenge God and His religion is an impious apostate, a mad blasphemer, claiming to act as God's protector. God loves but one thing: order. It is order which is His protection, and order is always found in the will of the majority; the minority is always in the wrong, even if it is morally right. It takes only common sense to see this truth. The priests fancy their creed is essential; they are wrong; what is essential is fraternal love. They violate it, even in saying mass. All evil is done to us, here below, by the fools – specious reasoners, false and obstinate minds – for these are what constitute the immense mob of fools . . . But I digress.

The killers entered the monastery at about five o'clock. The priests had no suspicion of the fate that awaited them, and several engaged themselves in conversation with the new arrivals, whom they believed to be an escort that was to accompany them to their destination. One of them, probably bribed, offered to save the bishop of Arles. The bishop did not deign to listen to him. 'But, I tell you Monsieur l'abbé, I mean what I say –' Another killer, who had not understood his words, came over to play a vicious game with his victim by pulling at his hair, wig or ear: 'Come now, don't act like a child, Monsieur l'abbé!' (A famous remark, once made to a sham priest climbing the scaffold.) This evidently was too much for the bishop, for he answered: 'What did you say, you scum?' I report this according to someone who heard it. These words were answered by a sword-thrust which felled the bishop; he was finished off. Another priest called the executioners 'scum' as well. He took more than twenty slashes, repeating all the while, 'Scum! Scum! Scum!' Two or three escaped, probably out of the goodness of some killers' hearts.

The killers were at the Conciergerie, at the Force. They killed at those two prisons, and at the Châtelet, all through the night. It was at the Conciergerie that Montmorin de Fontainebleau died, and perhaps Montmorin the minister. During that awful night the people played the role of the lords of earlier times, who in the silence and darkness of night slaughtered so many victims, innocent or guilty! It was the people who ruled that night and, through the hideous sacrilege on the part of those agitators, turned despot and tyrant.

Let us rest for a moment. Other scenes await us on the morning of the third at the Force . . .

I rose from my bed, in a frenzy of fear. The night had not refreshed me at all; it had set my blood aflame. I went out. I listened. I followed the crowds running to see the 'disasters' – for that was their term. As I passed the Conciergerie I saw a killer I was told was a sailor from Marseilles, whose wrist was swollen from overexertion. I went on. The front of the Châtelet was lined with mounds of corpses. I started to run off. And yet I followed the crowds. I reached rue Saint-Antoine at the end of rue des Ballets just as a poor wretch, who had seen the man in front of him get killed, set off at top speed as he emerged from the doorway instead of stopping dead in his tracks. A man who was not among the killers but one of those unthinking machines, of which there are so many, stopped him with a pike in the stomach. The poor creature was caught by his pursuers and slaughtered. The man with the pike remarked to us, unruffled, 'I didn't know they meant to kill him.'

This prelude had almost sent me home, when I was struck by another scene. I saw two women come out: one whom I have come to know since as the interesting Mme. de Saint-Brice, lady in waiting to the erstwhile prince royal; and a young woman of sixteen: she was Mlle. de Tourzel. They were led into the Saint-Antoine church. I followed them. I looked at them closely, as much as their veils would allow. The girl was weeping. Mme. de Saint-Brice was comforting her. They were kept prisoner there. I left after a while; I could not go back . . . I returned to the end of rue des Ballets. There I saw two other women climbing into a carriage, and in a low voice someone told the driver, 'To Sainte-Pélagie.' I may be mistaken, but I believe it was the municipal councilman Tallien who gave the order.

There was a pause in the slaughter: something was happening inside . . . I talked myself into thinking that it was finished. Then a woman appeared, white as a sheet, supported by a doorkeeper. Brusquely she was told: 'Shout "Vive la nation!"'

'No! No!' she said. She was forced up onto a pile of corpses. One of the killers seized the doorkeeper and pulled him away. 'Please,' the pitiable woman cried, 'don't hurt him!' She was told again to shout 'Vive la nation!' She refused with disdain. With that, a killer grabbed her, tore off her dress and slit her belly open. She fell, and was finished off by the others. Never in my life had I imagined such atrocity. I wanted to run away but my legs failed. I fainted. When I came to, I saw the blood-soaked head. I was told that they had washed it, curled it, mounted it on the point of a pike and paraded it under the Temple prison windows. Futile cruelty! It could not be seen from there. That unlucky woman was Mme. de Lamballe. On my way home I had the satisfaction of seeing Mme. de Saint-Brice being escorted back to her parents' house, along with Mlle. de Tourzel. They were trembling; the fate of d'Angremont, Laporte and Durosoi had frightened everyone connected with the court.

The massacre continued. On my way I learned from a rather trustworthy stranger, who testified to it, that the dregs of Paris had mingled with the killers in order to help their comrades escape from prison. They had control both inside and out, so that they were masters of life and death. Occasionally, when several of these felons came along in succession, and the killers grew impatient with nothing to do, these scoundrels would murder an innocent man, unbeknownst to the judges, and so it happened that several patriots were slaughtered. I returned home, wracked with sorrow and weariness, probably because I had had no real rest for so long.

Have I forgotten anything of that terrible night and the day that followed it? I cannot tell! It is too distressing for me to turn my memory back upon those atrocious deeds, deeds nonetheless ordered by someone, ordered in cold blood, without the knowledge of Mayor Pétion or Minister Roland. Then who ordered them? The cowards are in hiding. They dare not show themselves. But we can see them behind the veil that conceals them. If they believe they did right, as their spokesmen insinuate, then let them come forward and set forth their reasons! We will lament their error, and perhaps enlighten them!

What, then, was the true motive for this butchery? Many people think it was actually done so that the volunteers, when they set out for the frontiers, would not have to leave their wives and children at the mercy of criminals whom the tribunals might acquit and release, whom evildoers might help to escape, and so on. I wanted to learn the truth, and I may perhaps have discovered it in the end. There was only one purpose – to eliminate the non-juring priests. Some even wanted to eliminate all priests. Now, it was felt that there was still some religious fanaticism, and that such an act, directed explicitly against the priests and against them alone, would arouse certain people. Far from fulfilling the purpose, deportation would only put the priests in the position of an emigrant community possibly more threatening than if they remained. What was to be done with them? Eliminate them. If it had been possible to do this by some means other than killing them, they would not have been killed. So they were killed, and, to camouflage that illegal action, the prison affair was devised . . .

HONORÉ DE BALZAC

From

# A HARLOT HIGH AND LOW

1838–47

Translated by Rayner Heppenstall

# A PARISIAN LANDSCAPE

THE RUE DE Langlade, like the adjacent streets, runs between the Palais Royal and the rue de Rivoli. This part of one of the smartest districts of Paris will long preserve the contamination it received from those hillocks that were the middens of old Paris, topped with windmills. These narrow streets, dark and muddy, where trades are carried on which do not care about external appearance, take on at night a mysterious physiognomy and one full of contrasts. Coming from the bright lights of the rue Saint Honoré, the rue Neuve des Petits Champs and the rue de Richelieu, where there are always crowds and where are displayed the masterpieces of Industry, Fashion and the Arts, any man to whom Paris at night is unknown would be seized with gloom and terror as he plunged into the network of little streets which surround that brightness reflected in the sky itself. Thick shadow succeeds upon a torrent of gaslight. At wide intervals, a pale street-lamp casts its smoky and uncertain gleam, not seen at all in some of the blind alleys. Passers-by walk quickly and are uncommon. The shops are shut, those still open are of unsavoury character: a dirty wine-shop without lights, a linen-draper's selling eau de Cologne. An unwholesome chill folds its damp mantle about your shoulders. Few carriages pass. Notable among these sinister spots are the rue de Langlade, the opening of the Passage Saint Guillaume and various street turnings elsewhere. The municipal Council has never yet found means to cleanse this great leper-house, for prostitution long ago established its headquarters there.

Perhaps it is fortunate for Parisian society that these alleys should retain their foul aspect. Passing that way in the daytime, nobody could imagine what all those streets become at night; they are scoured by singular creatures who belong to no world; white, half-naked forms line the walls, the darkness is alive. Female garments slink by walking and talking. Half-open doors suddenly shout with laughter. Upon the ear fall those words which Rabelais claimed to have frozen and which now melt. Strumming music comes up between the flagstones. The sound is not vague, it means something: when it is raucous, that is a human voice; but if it contains notes of music, there is no longer anything human about it, only a whistling sound. Blasts on a whistle are indeed frequently heard. Provocative, mocking, the click of heels approaches and recedes. All these things together make the mind reel. Atmospheric conditions are changed in this region: it is hot in winter and cold in summer. But, whatever the weather, nature there offers the same curious spectacle: this is the fantastic world of the Berliner Hoffmann. Sent to inspect it, the meticulous clerk would no longer credit his senses once he had returned by the same turnings to decent streets in which there were passers-by, shops and light to see by. More disdainful or more easily shamed than the kings and queens of earlier times, who were not afraid to concern themselves with the courtesans in their cities, modern administration and politics dare no longer look this plague in the face. True, what is done must change with time and place, and measures which affect individual liberty are always a delicate matter; but a degree of breadth and boldness might be displayed in purely material schemes to do with air, light and building. The moralist, the artist and the wise administrator will regret the old Wooden Galleries of the Palais Royal where the sheep were folded which appear wherever strollers go by; and is it not better for strollers to loiter where they are? What happened? Today the most brilliant stretches of the boulevards cannot be enjoyed in the evening by families for what should have been enchanted outings. The Police have failed to make a proper use of what are nevertheless called Passages, to spare the public way.

The girl crushed by a jest at the Opera ball had been living, for the past month or two, in the rue de Langlade, in a house of ignoble appearance. Ill-plastered against the wall of a much larger house, this construction without either breadth or depth, lighted only from the street, yet rises to a prodigious height, recalling the stick up which a parrot climbs. Each floor consists of a two-roomed apartment. The house is served by a narrow staircase against the outer wall, whose course may be traced from outside by fixed lights which feebly illuminate it within and on each landing of which stands a sink, one of the most horrible peculiarities of Paris. The shop and the living quarters immediately above it then belonged to a tinsmith, the owner lived on the first floor, the four floors above were occupied by well-behaved seamstresses to whom the owner and caretaker were indulgent because of the difficulty of letting a house so oddly constructed and situated. The neighbourhood had become what it was by reason of the fact that it contained so many just such houses, of no use to serious Commerce and thus able to be exploited only by unacknowledged, precarious or undignified trades.

## INTERIOR AS FAMILIAR TO SOME AS UNKNOWN BY OTHERS

AT THREE O'CLOCK in the afternoon, the caretaker, who had seen Mademoiselle Esther brought back half-dead by a young man at two o'clock in the morning, had just been holding counsel with the grisette on the top floor, who, before taking a carriage to some party of pleasure, had evidenced disquietude about Esther, from whom she had heard no movement. No doubt Esther was still asleep, but she ought not to have been. Alone in her lodge, the caretaker wished she had been able to go up to the fourth floor, where Mademoiselle Esther lodged. Just as she decided to leave her lodge in charge of the tinsmith's son, the said lodge being a mere recess in the wall off the tinsmith's landing, a cab arrived. A man enveloped from head to foot in a cloak, with the evident intention of concealing his costume and station, got out and asked for Mademoiselle Esther. This wholly reassured the caretaker, to whom it fully explained the silence and tranquillity of the recluse. As the visitor climbed the steps above her lodge, the caretaker noticed silver buckles on his shoes and fancied she had glimpsed the black fringe of the sash about a cassock; she went down and asked the cabman, who replied without speaking, in a manner the caretaker understood. The priest knocked, received no answer, heard a quiet sighing from within, and shouldered the door open with a vigour doubtless to be attributed to the power of Christian charity, though in another man it might have seemed mere habit. He hurried through to the second room, and there saw, before a Virgin in coloured plaster, poor Esther not so much kneeling as collapsed in a heap with hands together. The 'little milliner' was dying. Cinders in the grate told the story of that dreadful morning. The hood and mantle of the domino lay on the floor. The bed had not been slept in. The poor creature, stricken to the heart with a mortal wound, had without doubt arranged all on her return from the Opera. The wick of a candle, set hard in the sconce of a candlestick, showed how completely Esther had been absorbed in her last reflections. A handkerchief soaked with tears proved the sincerity of the despair of this Mary Magdalene, whose classic pose was that of the harlot without religion. This final repentance made the priest smile. Inexpert at dying, Esther had left the inner door open without calculating that the air in the two rooms needed a greater quantity of coal to make it unbreathable; the fumes had merely dazed her; colder air from the staircase now brought her slowly back to an appreciation of her woes. The priest remained standing, lost in gloomy meditation, untouched by the divine beauty of the young prostitute, watching her first movements as though it had been some animal. His eyes travelled from the barely animate body to objects in the room with apparent indifference. He studied the furnishings of this room, whose cold, worn red tiles were barely hidden by a wretched, threadbare carpet. An old-fashioned cot in painted wood, surrounded by curtains of yellow-brown calico with a dull-red rose-pattern; a single armchair and two painted wooden chairs, covered with the same calico, with which also the windows were curtained; a grey wallpaper speckled with flowers, blackened and greasy with age; a mahogany work-table; the fireplace cluttered with kitchen utensils of the cheapest kind, two large bundles of firewood broken apart, a stone mantelpiece on which a few glass ornaments stood, with bits of jewellery and scissors; a card of dirty thread, white, scented gloves, a delicious hat propped on the water jug, a Ternaux shawl stuffing a crack in the window, an elegant dress hanging on a nail, a little, uncomfortable sofa without cushions; broken clogs and pretty shoes, laced half-boots fit for a queen, china plates chipped and cracked, the remains of a meal among cutlery of German nickel, the silverware of the Parisian poor; a basket full of potatoes and dirty linen, a clean gauze bonnet on top; a hideous wardrobe, its glass doors open, empty, on its shelves a selection of pawnshop tickets: such was the array of joyous and dismal, wretched and expensive objects which met the eye. These luxuries among the broken fragments, this household so appropriate to the Bohemian life of the limp, half-dressed wench sunk down like a horse dead in its harness, pinned by a broken shaft, caught in the reins, did this curious spectacle give the priest pause? Did he say to himself that at any rate that lost creature was acting disinterestedly to love a rich young man and at the same time live in such poverty? Did he ascribe the disorder in the room to a disordered life? Was his feeling one of pity, or of fear? Was his charity stirred? Whoever had seen him, arms folded, forehead creased with thought, tight-lipped, eye scathing, would have thought him possessed by contradictory impulses and thoughts in which a gloomy distaste and baleful intentions predominated. He was, certainly, insensible to the pretty, round breasts half-flattened against the knees and the delicious forms of a crouching Venus revealed beneath the black material of the skirt, so tensely was the dying woman coiled upon herself; the abandon of this head, which, seen from behind, displayed its white, supple, vulnerable nape, the beautiful shoulders of a nature boldly developed, did not move him; he did not raise Esther up, he did not seem to hear the heart-breaking inhalations by which the return to life was accomplished: it needed a dreadful sob and the terrifying look which the girl cast upon him before he deigned to raise her and carry her to the bed with an ease which betrayed prodigious strength.

'Lucien!' she murmured.

'Love returns, the woman is not far behind,' said the priest with a sort of bitterness.

The victim of Parisian depravity then perceived her

rescuer's style of dress, and said, with the smile of a child grasping at something long desired: 'I shan't die, then, without being reconciled to heaven!'

'You will be able to expiate your faults,' said the priest, bathing her forehead with water and holding under her nose a vinegar bottle he found in a corner.

'I feel life not leaving but flowing back into me,' she said after receiving the priest's attentions and expressing her gratitude to him with expressions of unaffected simplicity.

This engaging pantomime, which the Graces themselves, bent on pleasing, could scarcely have bettered, might have been thought at least partly to explain the girl's curious nickname. ['the Torpedo']

'Do you feel better?' asked the ecclesiastic, giving her a glass of sugar and water to drink.

The man seemed to know his way about households of this kind, he knew where everything was. He had made himself at home. This gift of being everywhere at home belongs only to kings, light women and thieves.

VICTOR HUGO

From

# LES MISÉRABLES

1862

Translated by Christine Donougher

## From THE BOWELS OF LEVIATHAN

### *Bruneseau*

PARIS'S SEWER WAS legendary in the Middle Ages. In the sixteenth century Henri II attempted a survey that came to nothing. Not a hundred years ago, Mercier tells us, the sewer system was abandoned, and left to itself to survive as best it could.

That was ancient Paris, consigned to disputes, indecision and uncertainty. For a long time it was quite stupid. Later, '89 showed how cities come to their senses. But in the good old days the capital had little idea. It did not know how to manage its affairs either morally or materially, and was no more capable of sweeping away filth than abuses. Everything was an obstacle, everything was debatable. The sewer, for example, followed no route. People could no more find their bearings down there than they could understand each other in the city. Above ground the unintelligible, below ground the unchartable. Beneath the confusion of tongues was the confusion of tunnels. Underlying Babel was the Labyrinth.

Sometimes the Paris sewer took to overflowing, as though this unappreciated Nile were suddenly seized with anger. There were, disgusting to relate, inundations of sewerage. At times, this stomach of civilization failed to digest properly, resulting in a reflux from the cloaca into the city's gullet, and Paris got an after-taste of its own excreta. There was something to be said for these bouts of remorse on the part of the sewer. They were warnings – taken very badly, in fact. The city was outraged that its filth should be so bold, and would not tolerate its return. Flush it away more effectively.

The inundation of 1802 is still a vivid memory to Parisians in their eighties. The filth spread crosswise over Place des Victoires, where the statue of Louis XIV stands. It entered Rue St-Honoré by the two manholes in the Champs-Élysées, Rue St-Florentin by the St-Florentin drain, Rue Pierre-à-Poisson by the Sonnerie drain, Rue Popincourt by the Chemin-Vert drain, Rue de la Roquette by the Rue de Lappe drain. It filled the gutter running down the middle of Rue des Champs-Élysées to a depth of well over twelve inches. And, to the south, the outlet into the Seine backed up, sending it into Rue Mazarine, Rue de l'Échaudé and Rue des Marais, where after covering a hundred and twenty yards it stopped just a few paces short of the house where Racine had lived, showing greater respect for the seventeenth-century poet than for the king. It reached its maximum depth in Rue St-Pierre, where it rose three feet above the flagstones of the gutter, and its maximum expanse in Rue St-Sabin, where it stretched over two hundred and sixty yards.

At the beginning of this century the Paris sewers were still a place of mystery. Filth will never be well thought of, but in this instance such was its ill-repute that it was regarded with dread. Paris knew in some confused way that there was underneath it a terrible cavern. People spoke of it as of that monstrous pit of Thebes teeming with fifteen-foot-long centipedes and that might have served Behemoth for a bathtub. The sewermen's great boots never ventured beyond certain well known points. It was still very close to the time when waste-carts, on top of which Sainte-Foix fraternized with the Marquis de Créqui, discharged their loads directly into the sewers. As for any flushing, responsibility for that task was entrusted to downpours of rain, which clogged rather than cleared. Rome still allowed its waste dump a little poetry, calling it the Gemonian Steps. Paris insulted its cloaca and called it the Stink-Hole. Science and superstition concurred in their horror. The Stink-Hole was no less loathsome to hygiene than to legend. Paris's bogeyman flourished under the fetid vault of the Mouffetard drain. The corpses of the Marmousets had been thrown into the Barillerie drain. Fagon had attributed the terrible malignant fever of 1685 to the great long stretch of the Marais open drain, which remained uncovered in Rue St-Louis, almost opposite the sign of the Gallant Messenger, until 1833. The mouth of the Rue de la Mortellerie drain was famous for the vermin that came out of it. With the sharp points of its iron grating suggestive of a row of teeth, it was like a dragon's maw in that deadly street, breathing hell over men. The popular imagination enlivened the grim Parisian sump with who knows what hideous mixture of infinitudes. The sewer was bottomless. The sewer was a barathrum. The idea of exploring these leprous regions did not even occur to the police. To probe this unknown, to fathom this darkness, to go exploring this abyss – who would have dared? It was terrifying. Yet someone did volunteer. The sewer had its Christopher Columbus.

One day in 1805, during one of the emperor's rare appearances in Paris, the minister of the interior, some Decrès or Crétet or other, attended the master's *petit lever.* The sound of their swords being trailed after them by all those extraordinary soldiers of the great Republic and the great Empire could be heard from Place du Carrousel. Napoleon's doorway was choked with heroes, men from the Rhine, the Escaut, the Adige and the Nile, companions of Joubert, Desaix, Marceau, Hoche, Kléber, Fleurus balloonists, Mainz grenadiers, Genoa bridge-builders, hussars the Pyramids had gazed on, artillerymen bespattered by Junot's cannon-ball, cuirassiers who had taken by assault the fleet lying at anchor in the Zuyderzee. Some had followed Bonaparte across the bridge at Lodi, others had been with Murat in the trenches at Mantua, others had gone ahead of Lannes along the sunken road at Montebello. There in the courtyard of the Tuileries was the whole army of that time, represented by a section or a unit, guarding Napoleon in his sleep. And it was the magnificent epoch when the Grand Army had Marengo behind it and Austerlitz ahead of it. 'Sire,' the minister of the interior said to Napoleon, 'yesterday I saw the most intrepid man in your Empire.' 'What man was that?' said the emperor brusquely. 'And what has he done?' 'Sire, he's intending to do something.' 'And what is that?' 'To visit the sewers of Paris.'

This man existed, and his name was Bruneseau.

## *Unknown Details*

THE VISIT TOOK place. It was a formidable campaign, a nocturnal battle against pestilence and asphyxiation. It was at the same time a journey of discovery. A few years ago one of the survivors of this expedition, an intelligent workman, very young at the time, was still recounting some of the curious details that Bruneseau felt obliged to leave out of his report to the prefect of police, as a discredit to the administrative style. Disinfection procedures were very rudimentary in those days. Bruneseau had hardly gone beyond the first intersections of that subterranean network when eight of the twenty workmen refused to go any further. The operation was complicated. The visit involved cleaning. So there was cleaning to be done, and at the same time surveying: noting water inlets, counting gratings and outlets, detailing the branch structure, indicating the currents where the waters divided, identifying the respective perimeters of the various sewage basins, probing the smaller drains grafted on to the main drain, measuring the maximum height of each drain and the width, at the base of the vault as well as at floor level, and lastly plotting the level of every water inlet relative to both drain floor and street. Progress was arduous. It was not uncommon for the ladders descending into the sewers to plunge into three feet of sludge. The lamps guttered in the miasmic fumes. Every now and then a sewerman was carried out unconscious. At certain points, a precipitous drop. The ground had given way, the paving had collapsed, the drain had turned into a soak-pit. There was nothing solid left. A man suddenly disappeared. He was rescued with the greatest difficulty. On the advice of Fourcroy they lighted, at regular intervals, in duly sanitized locations, big wire-mesh containers filled with resin-soaked tow. The wall was covered in some places with gnarled fungi that looked like tumours. The very stone itself seemed diseased in this unbreathable atmosphere.

In his exploration Bruneseau followed the direction of the flow. At the head of the two Grand-Hurleur channels he deciphered on a projecting stone the date 1550. This stone marked the furthest that Philibert Delorme, charged by Henri II with visiting Paris's subterranean network, had reached. This stone was the sixteenth century's mark on the sewer. Bruneseau found the seventeenth century's handiwork in the Ponceau drain and the Rue Vieille-du-Temple drain, vaulted between 1600 and 1650, and the eighteenth century's handiwork in the western section of the collector channel, which was enclosed and vaulted in 1740. These two vaultings, especially the one that was less old, of 1740, were more cracked and decrepit than the masonry of the orbital sewer, which dated from 1412, when the Ménilmontant fresh-water brook was elevated to the rank of Paris's main sewer, a promotion similar to that of a peasant appointed chief valet to the king, something like Gros-Jean transformed into Lebel.

In a few places, particularly beneath the court of justice, were identified what were thought to be the cavities of ancient dungeons actually built into the sewer. Hideous oubliettes. An iron neck-collar hung in one of these cells. They were all walled up. There were some bizarre finds, including the skeleton of an orang-utan that had vanished from the Jardin des Plantes in 1800, a disappearance probably connected with the famous and indisputable apparition of the devil in Rue des Bernardins in the last year of the eighteenth century. The poor devil had ended up drowning in the sewer.

Beneath the long arched corridor that ends at Arche-Marion, a perfectly preserved rag-picker's basket excited the admiration of the experts. Everywhere, the sludge, which the sewermen had learned how to deal with intrepidly, abounded in valuable objects, gold and silver jewellery, precious stones, coins. Any giant that had sifted this cesspool would have had the riches of centuries in his sieve. Where the two branches of Rue du Temple and Rue Ste-Avoye divided, a curious Huguenot copper medal was found, showing a pig wearing a cardinal's hat on one side and a wolf with a tiara on its head on the other.

The most surprising discovery was made at the entrance to the main sewer. This entrance had once been closed off by a grating, of which nothing but the hinges remained. From one of these hinges, arrested there in its passage, no doubt, hung a dirty shapeless rag, fluttering in the dark, not quite completely disintegrated. Bruneseau brought his lantern up close and examined this tattered oddment. It was of very fine batiste, and discernible in one corner, less frayed than the others, was a heraldic coronet embroidered above these seven letters: LAVBESP. The coronet was the coronet of a marquis, and the seven letters stood for 'Laubespine'. It was realized that what they had before their eyes was a piece of Marat's shroud. Marat in his youth had had an amorous intrigue. It was around the time that he held the post of physician to the household of the Comte d'Artois. From that affair with a great lady – a matter of historical record – he was left with this bedsheet. Casualty of fate, or souvenir. At his death, this being the only linen of any fineness that he had in his house, it was used to wrap his body. In cerements that had known carnal pleasure old women had shrouded for burial the tragic Friend of the People.

Bruneseau passed on. That rag was left where it was, just as it was. Out of contempt or respect? Marat deserved both. And besides, the mark of destiny that it bore was enough to make anyone hesitate to touch it. In any case, burial things are best left in the place they themselves have chosen. In short, it was a strange relic. A marquise had slept in it. Marat had rotted in it. It had been through the Panthéon and ended up with the rats in the sewer. This remnant of the bedchamber, whose every fold Watteau would once have joyfully depicted, had come to be worthy of Dante's steady gaze.

The visit to Paris's underground waste-disposal network lasted a full seven years, from 1805 to 1812. Along the way Bruneseau designated, directed and brought to completion some major works. In 1808 he lowered the floor of the Ponceau and, creating new routes everywhere, in 1809 he extended the sewers under Rue St-Denis to the Fontaine des Innocents, in 1810 under Rue Froid-Manteau and La Salpêtrière, in 1811 under Rue Neuve-des-Petits-Pères, Rue du

Mail, Rue de l'Écharpe, Place Royale, and in 1812 under Rue de la Paix and Chaussée-d'Antin. At the same time he had the whole network disinfected and sanitized. In the second year of his work Bruneseau was joined by his son-in-law Nargaud.

So it was that at the beginning of this century the old society attended to its hidden underside and put its sewers to rights. At least that was one thing cleaned up.

Full of twists and turns, creviced and fissured, in need of repaving, potholed, suddenly veering off at bizarre angles, rising and descending without any logic, fetid, feral, fearsome, steeped in darkness, its flagstones and walls scarred and gashed, horrendous – looking back, that is what Paris's ancient sewer was like. Tunnels branching off in every direction, ducts criss-crossing, junctions, multiple intersections, radial-patterned like mining trenches, with dead ends, blind alleys, saltpetre-lined vaults, foul sumps, scabrous seepings from the walls, dripping ceilings, blackness – nothing equalled the horror of this old waste-disposal crypt, Babylonian alimentary canal, cavern, catacomb, alley-riddled abyss, gigantic burrow where in the mind's eye that enormous blind mole, the past, is seen prowling through the shadows in filth that was once magnificence.

This, we repeat, was the sewer of old.

## *Present-day Progress*

TODAY THE SEWER is clean, stark, straight, as it should be. It almost realizes the ideal of what is meant in England by the word 'respectable'. It is decent and drab; well laid out; you might almost say 'well turned out'. It has the look of a tradesman who has come up in the world. It is almost light enough to see. The sludge observes a decorum. At first sight it might easily be mistaken for one of those underground passageways that were once so common and so useful to fleeing monarchs and princes, in the good old days 'when the people loved their kings'. The present sewer is a fine sewer, where the pure style prevails. Driven out of poetry and having apparently taken refuge in architecture, the classic rectilinear alexandrine verse seems inherent in every stone of this long and palely shadowed vault. Every drain is an arcade. The Rue de Rivoli is emulated, even in the sewer. The fact is, if the geometrical line has a place anywhere it is certainly in a city's sewerage system. Here, everything must conform to the shortest route. The sewer has acquired a certain official status nowadays. Even police reports, in which it sometimes figures, are no longer disrespectful when referring to it. The words that characterize it in administrative language are formal and dignified. What used to be called a 'passage' is now called a 'gallery'. What used to be called a 'hole' is now called an 'inspection chamber'. Villon would no longer recognize his old bolt-hole. This network of cellars has its immemorial population of rodents, pullulating more than ever. From time to time a seasoned old sewer-rat dares to show its head at the window and observes the Parisians. But even these vermin are tamed, satisfied as they are with their subterranean palace. The sewer has nothing of its earlier barbarism. The rain that used to foul the sewer now flushes it. But do not be too trusting. Noxious fumes still inhabit it. It is more hypocritical than irreproachable. The Prefecture of Police and the health commission have done their best, but despite all the sanitization measures it exudes a faintly suspect smell, like Tartuffe after confession.

What we can agree on is that since, all things considered, mucking-out is a tribute the sewer pays to civilization, and from that point of view Tartuffe's conscience is an advance on the Augean Stables, there has certainly been some improvement in Paris's sewer system.

GUSTAVE FLAUBERT

From

# A SENTIMENTAL EDUCATION

1869

Translated by Robert Beldick and revised by Geoffrey Wall

ONE MORNING IN December, on his way to attend a lecture on procedure, he thought he noticed more animation than usual in the rue Saint-Jacques. Students were rushing out of the cafés or calling to each other from house to house through the open windows; shopkeepers were standing out on the pavement, watching uneasily; shutters were being closed; and when he reached the rue Soufflot he saw a large crowd assembled round the Panthéon.

Youths in groups of anything from five to twelve were strolling around arm in arm, occasionally going up to larger groups which were standing here and there; at the far end of the square, against the iron railings, men in smocks were holding forth, while policemen were walking up and down beside the walls, their three-cornered hats cocked to one side and their hands behind their backs, making the pavement ring with the sound of their heavy boots. Everybody wore a mysterious, anxious expression; clearly something was in the air; and on each person's lips there was an unspoken question.

Frédéric found himself standing next to a fair-haired young man with a pleasant face, who sported a moustache and a little beard like a dandy of the age of Louis XIII. He asked him what all the excitement was about.

'I've no idea,' the other replied; 'and neither have they. It's a habit of theirs nowadays. It's a good joke, isn't it!'

And he burst out laughing.

The petitions for reform which had been circulated among the National Guard, together with the Humann census and other events, had led during the past six months to inexplicable demonstrations.

Indeed, these now took place so often that the newspapers no longer mentioned them.

'All this lacks form and colour,' Frédéric's neighbour continued. 'I do trow, honoured sir, that we have degenerated. In the good old days of Loys the Eleventh, nay even of Benjamin Constant, there was more of a rebellious spirit among the scholars of the town. I deem them as meek as sheep, as stupid as gherkins, and by my troth, well fitted to be grocers. And this is what folks call the Youth of the Schools.'

He spread his arms out wide, like the actor Frédéric Lemaître in *Robert Macaire.*

'Youth of the Schools, I give you my blessing!'

Then, speaking to a rag-picker, who was poking around among some oyster shells outside a wine-merchant's shop:

'You, my good man – are you a member of the Youth of the Schools?'

The old man turned a hideous face towards him, in which, in the midst of a grey beard, a red nose and two stupid, bleary eyes could be distinguished.

'No! You look to me rather like "one of those men of criminal appearance who can be seen, in various groups of people, scattering money in handfuls". Oh, scatter away, venerable greybeard! Corrupt me with the treasures of Albion! *Are you English?* I do not reject the gifts of Artaxerxes! Let us talk a little about the Customs Union.'

Frédéric felt somebody touch him on the shoulder, and turned round. It was Martinon, looking astonishingly pale.

'Well,' he said with a deep sigh, 'another riot!'

He was afraid of getting involved, and was very sorry for

himself. Men in smocks he found particularly worrying, because they were sure to belong to secret societies.

'What secret societies?' said the young man with the moustache. 'That's just an old dodge of the Government's, to scare the middle classes.'

Martinon begged him to lower his voice, for fear of the police.

'You mean to say you still believe in the police? Come to that, Monsieur, how do you know that I'm not a police spy myself?'

And he looked at him in such a way that Martinon, thoroughly upset, failed to see the joke at first. The crowd was pushing them back, and all three of them had been forced to climb up on to the little staircase which led, by way of a corridor, into the new amphitheatre.

Soon the throng split up of its own accord; several people bared their heads; they were greeting the famous professor, Samuel Rondelot, who, wrapped in his thick frock-coat, raising his silver-rimmed spectacles in one hand, and wheezing asthmatically, was ambling along on his way to give his lecture. This man was one of the great jurists of the nineteenth century, rivalling even Zachariae and Ruhdorff. Although he had recently been raised to the peerage, this had not altered his behaviour in the slightest. He was known to be poor, and was greatly respected.

Meanwhile, on the far side of the square, some people started shouting:

'Down with Guizot!'

'Down with Pritchard!'

'Down with the traitors!'

'Down with Louis-Philippe!'

The crowd surged forward, and, pressing against the closed door of the courtyard, prevented the professor from going any further. He stopped at the foot of the staircase. Soon he could be seen on the lowest of the three steps. He spoke; a loud murmur drowned his voice. A popular figure a moment before, he was hated now, for he represented authority. Every time he tried to make himself heard the shouting began again. With a sweeping gesture he urged the students to follow him. He was greeted with general uproar. He shrugged his shoulders contemptuously and disappeared down the corridor. Martinon had taken advantage of his position to vanish at the same time.

'What a coward!' said Frédéric.

'He's a sensible fellow,' the other replied.

The crowd broke into applause. They regarded the professor's retreat as a victory. People were looking out of every window. Some started singing the 'Marseillaise'; others suggested marching to Béranger's house.

'To Laffitte's!'

'To Chateaubriand's!'

'To Voltaire's!' yelled the young man with the fair moustache. The policemen tried to push their way through the crowd, saying as gently as they could:

'Move along, gentlemen, move along now.'

Somebody shouted:

'Down with the butchers!'

This insult had become customary since the troubles in September. Everybody took it up. They hissed and jeered at the guardians of the law, who began to turn pale. One of them could not stand it any longer, and seeing a boy who had come too close to him and was laughing in his face, he gave him such a violent shove that he fell on his back five yards away, in front of the wine-merchant's shop. Everybody drew away, but almost immediately the policeman himself was on the ground, felled by a sort of Hercules whose hair protruded like tangled string from under an oil-cloth cap.

After standing for a few minutes on the corner of the rue Saint-Jacques, he had suddenly dropped a large cardboard box he was carrying, in order to throw himself at the policeman; and now, holding him prostrate beneath him, he was punching him in the face with all his might. The other policemen came running up. The big fellow was so strong that it took at least four of them to overpower him. Two shook him by the collar, two others pulled him by the arms, and a fifth pounded him in the small of his back with one knee, and all of them called him a brigand, a murderer, and a rioter. With his chest bare and his clothes in tatters, he protested his innocence; he had not been able to stand by and see a child struck down.

'My name is Dussardier! I work for Messieurs Valincart Frères, laces and fancy goods, rue de Cléry. Where's my cardboard box? I want my box!'

He kept repeating:

'Dussardier! . . . rue de Cléry. My box!'

However, he calmed down and, with a stoical air, allowed himself to be marched off in the direction of the guardhouse in the rue Descartes. A stream of people followed him. Frédéric and the young man with the moustache walked immediately behind him, full of admiration for the shop-assistant and in a state of great indignation at the brutality of the authorities.

The further they went, the thinner the crowd became.

Every now and then the policemen looked round and glared ferociously; and once the rowdy characters could find nothing more to do, and the inquisitive nothing more to see, they gradually drifted away. Passers-by looked Dussardier up and down and indulged in loud and insulting comments.

One old woman, standing on her doorstep, even shouted that he had stolen a loaf; this injustice added to the exasperation of the two friends. At last they arrived at the guardhouse. There were only about twenty people left. The sight of the soldiers was enough to disperse them.

Frédéric and his companion boldly asked to see the man who had just been taken to the cells. The sentry threatened to lock *them* up if they persisted. They demanded to see the officer in charge in their capacity as law-students, refused to give their names, declaring that the prisoner was a fellow pupil of theirs.

They were shown into a bare room with four benches placed against walls of smoke-blackened plaster. A hatchway opened at the far end. Dussardier's robust face appeared. With his dishevelled hair, his honest little eyes, and his square-tipped nose, he looked rather like a good-natured dog.

'Don't you recognize us?' said Hussonnet.

This was the name of the young man with the moustache.

'But . . .' stammered Dussardier.

'Oh, stop playing the fool,' the other went on. 'Everybody knows that you're a law-student like ourselves.'

In spite of the winks they gave him, Dussardier failed to grasp their meaning. He seemed to reflect for a moment, and then suddenly asked:

'Have they found my box?'

Frédéric, discouraged, raised his eyes to the ceiling. Hussonnet replied:

'Ah, you mean the box you put your lecture notes in! Yes, yes! Don't you worry about it!'

They started their dumb show again. Dussardier finally realized that they had come to help him; and he kept quiet, not wanting to compromise them. Besides, he felt a sort of shame at seeing himself raised to the social rank of a student, on a par with these young men who had such white hands.

'Do you want to send a message to anybody?' asked Frédéric.

'No, thank you, nobody.'

'But what about your family?'

He hung his head without answering; the poor fellow was a bastard. The two friends were astonished by his silence.

'Have you got anything to smoke?' Frédéric went on.

Dussardier felt his clothes, then took out of the depths of his pocket the debris of a pipe, a splendid meerschaum pipe, with an ebony stem, a silver lid, and an amber mouthpiece.

For three years he had been working on this pipe to make it a masterpiece. He had taken care to keep the bowl constantly encased in a chamois leather sheath, to smoke the pipe as slowly as possible, never putting it down on a marble surface, and to hang it up every night beside his bed. Now he shook the broken pieces in his hand, the nails of which were bleeding; and, with his chin sunk on his chest and his eyes staring, he gazed at these ruins of his happiness with a look of ineffable melancholy.

'What if we gave him some cigars?' whispered Hussonnet, reaching towards his pocket.

Frédéric had already put a full cigar-case on the edge of the hatch.

'Take these. Goodbye, and keep your chin up!'

Dussardier threw himself on their two outstretched hands. He clasped them in a sort of frenzy, his voice broken with sobs.

'What? . . . For me? . . . For me? . . .'

Evading his expressions of gratitude, the two friends left

the guardhouse, and went to lunch together at the Café Tabourey, in front of the Luxembourg.

While he was cutting his steak, Hussonnet informed his companion that he worked for several fashion magazines and designed advertisements for *L'Art Industriel.*

'Jacques Arnoux's business,' said Frédéric.

'You know him, do you?'

'Yes. No . . . I mean, I've seen him, I've met him.'

He asked Hussonnet casually if he ever saw his wife.

'Now and then,' the Bohemian replied.

Frédéric did not dare to go on asking questions; this man had just assumed a position of immense importance in his life; he paid the bill for their lunch without the other raising the slightest objection.

Their sympathy was mutual; they exchanged addresses, and Hussonnet cordially invited him to accompany him as far as the rue de Fleurus.

They were in the middle of the garden when Arnoux's employee, holding his breath, twisted his face into a horrible grimace and started crowing like a cock, whereupon all the cocks in the neighbourhood replied with prolonged cock-a-doodle-doos.

'It's a signal,' said Hussonnet.

They stopped near the Théâtre Bobino, in front of a house which was approached by way of a passage. In an attic window, between pots of nasturtiums and sweet-peas, a young woman appeared, bareheaded, in her underwear, leaning on the roof-gutter.

'Good-day, my angel, good-day, my duck,' said Hussonnet, blowing kisses to her.

He kicked open the gate and disappeared.

Frédéric waited the rest of the week for him. He did not dare to go to Hussonnet's lodgings, for fear of appearing impatient to have his hospitality repaid; but he searched for him all over the Latin Quarter. One evening he met him, and took him to his room on the Quai Napoléon.

They talked for hours, opening their hearts to one another. Hussonnet hankered after the fame and profits of the theatre. He collaborated on musical comedies which were never produced, had ideas galore, and wrote the words for songs: he sang one or two for Frédéric's benefit. Then, catching sight of a volume of Hugo and another of Lamartine in the bookcase, he launched into a sarcastic attack on the Romantic school. Those poets had neither common sense nor grammar, and anyway they were not French! He prided himself on knowing his language and criticized the finest phrases with that cantankerous severity, that pedantic taste which characterizes frivolous-minded people when they come face to face with serious art.

Frédéric was offended; he felt like breaking off relations. Why should he not risk, here and now, the question on which his happiness depended? He asked the young writer if he could take him to Arnoux's house.

Nothing could be simpler, and they agreed to meet next day.

EDMOND AND JULES DE GONCOURT

From

# JOURNALS

1871

Translated by Robert Baldick

## Thursday, 25 May

ALL DAY LONG, the guns and rifles have gone on firing. I spent the day walking round the ruins of Auteuil, where the damage and destruction is such as might have been caused by a whirlwind.

Carriages kept going by along the road from Saint-Denis to Versailles, taking back to Paris people whose stay in the country had made them positively archaic.

Paris is decidedly under a curse! After a drought lasting a whole month, there is now a wind of hurricane force blowing across the burning city.

## Friday, 26 May

Today I was walking beside the railway line near Passy station when I saw some men and women surrounded by soldiers. I plunged through a gap in the fence and found myself at the edge of the road on which the prisoners were waiting to be taken to Versailles. There were a great many prisoners there, for I heard an officer say to the colonel, as he handed over a piece of paper: 'Four hundred and seven, including sixty-six women.'

The men had been split up into lines of seven or eight and tied to each other with string that cut into their wrists. They were just as they had been captured, most of them without hats or caps, and with their hair plastered down on their foreheads and faces by the fine rain that had been falling ever since this morning. There were men of the people there who had made themselves head coverings out of blue check handkerchiefs. Others, drenched to the skin by the rain, were holding thin overcoats tight across their chests, with a bulge where they were carrying a hunk of bread. They came from every class of society: hard-faced workmen, bourgeois in socialist hats, National Guards who had not had time to change out of their uniforms, and a couple of infantrymen with ghostly-white faces – stupid, fierce, indifferent, mute figures.

There was the same variety among the women. There were women wearing kerchiefs next to women in silk gowns. I noticed housewives, working-girls, and prostitutes, one of whom was wearing the uniform of a National Guard. And in the midst of them all there stood out the bestial head of a creature whose face was half-covered with an enormous bruise. Not one of these women showed the apathetic resignation of the men. There was anger and scorn on their faces, and many of them had a gleam of madness in their eyes.

Among these women, there was one who was singularly beautiful, with the implacable beauty of a young Fate. She was a girl with dark, curly hair, steely eyes, and cheekbones red with dried tears. She stood frozen as it were in a defiant posture, hurling insults at officers and men from a throat and lips so contracted by anger that they were unable to form sounds or words. Her mute, twisted mouth masticated abuse without being able to spit it out. 'She's just like the girl who stabbed Barbier!' a young officer said to one of his friends.

Everyone was ready to go when pity, which can never entirely abandon man, induced some of the soldiers to hold out their water-bottles to the women, who with graceful movements turned their heads and opened parched mouths to drink, at the same time keeping a wary eye on the scowling face of an old gendarme. The signal for departure was given and the pitiful column moved off on its journey to Versailles under a watery sky.

Sunday, 28 May

Driving along the Champs-Élysées in a cab, I saw, in the distance, legs running in the direction of the great avenue. I leaned out of the window. The whole avenue was filled by a huge crowd between two lines of troopers. I got out and joined the people running to see what it was. It was the prisoners who had just been taken at the Buttes-Chaumont, walking along in fives with a few women in their midst. 'There are six thousand of them,' a trooper in the escort told me. 'Five hundred were shot on the spot.' At the head of this haggard multitude a nonagenarian was walking along on trembling legs.

Despite all the horror one felt for these men, one was saddened by the sight of this dismal procession, in the midst of which one could see some soldiers, army deserters, who had their tunics on inside out, with their grey cloth pockets hanging by their sides, and who seemed to be already half stripped for the firing-squad.

I met Burty in the Place de la Madeleine. We walked along the streets and boulevards, suddenly crowded with people who had emerged from their cellars and hiding-places, thirsting for light and sunshine, and wearing on their faces the joy of liberation. We went to collect Mme Burty, whom we persuaded to come out for a stroll. While Burty, who had suddenly been stopped in the street by Mme Verlaine, was discussing ways and means of concealing her husband, Mme Burty told me a secret which Burty had kept from me. One of his friends on the Public Committee, whose name she did not mention, had told

Burty, four or five days ago, that the Government no longer had control over anything and that they were going to enter all the houses in Paris, confiscate the valuables they contained, and shoot all the householders.

I took leave of the Burtys and went to see how much of Paris had been burnt by the Federates. The Palais-Royal has been burnt down, but the pretty façades of the two wings overlooking the square are intact; money will have to be spent on reconstructing the interior. The Tuileries need to be rebuilt along the garden and overlooking the Rue de Rivoli.

There is smoke everywhere, the air smells of burning and varnish, and on all sides one can hear the hissing of hosepipes. In a good many places there are still horrible traces of the fighting: here a dead horse; there, beside the paving-stones from a half-demolished barricade, a peaked cap swimming in a pool of blood.

The large-scale destruction begins at the Châtelet and carries on from there. Behind the burnt-out theatre, the costumes have been spread out on the ground: carbonized silk in which, here and there, one catches sight of the gleam of golden spangles, the sparkle of silver.

On the other side of the embankment, the Palais de Justice has had the roof of its round tower decapitated. There is nothing left of the new buildings but the iron skeleton of the roof. The Prefecture of Police is a smouldering ruin, in whose bluish smoke the brand-new gold of the Sainte-Chapelle shines brightly.

By way of little paths made through barricades which have not yet been demolished, I eventually reached the Hôtel de Ville.

It is a splendid, a magnificent ruin. All pink and ash-green and the colour of white-hot steel, or turned to shining agate where the stonework has been burnt by paraffin, it looks like the ruin of an Italian palace, tinted by the sunshine of several centuries, or better still like the ruin of a magic palace, bathed in the theatrical glow of electric light. With its empty niches, its shattered or truncated statues, its broken clock, its tall window-frames and chimneys still standing in mid-air by some miracle of equilibrium, and its jagged silhouette outlined against the blue sky, it is a picturesque wonder which ought to be preserved if the country were not irrevocably condemned to the restorations of M. Viollet-le-Duc. The irony of chance! In the utter ruin of the whole building there shines, on a marble plaque intact in its new gilt frame, the lying inscription: *Liberty, Equality, Fraternity.*

### Monday, 29 May

Posted up on all the walls I see MacMahon's proclamation announcing that it was all over at four o'clock yesterday afternoon.

This evening one can hear the movement of Parisian life starting up again, and its murmur like a distant tide: the hours no longer fall into the silence of the desert.

### Wednesday, 31 May

There are tricolours in every window and on every carriage. The cellar ventilators of all the houses have been blocked up again. Across the paving-stones which are being replaced, the people of Paris, dressed in their travelling-clothes, are swarming in to take possession of their city once more.

All is well. There has been neither compromise nor conciliation. The solution has been brutal, imposed by sheer force of arms. The solution has saved everyone from the dangers of cowardly compromise. The solution has restored its self-confidence to the Army, which has learnt in the blood of the Communards that it was still capable of fighting. And finally, the bleeding has been done thoroughly, and a bleeding like that, by killing the rebellious part of a population, postpones the next revolution by a whole conscription. The old society has twenty years of peace before it, if the powers that be dare what they are free to dare at the moment.

### Saturday, 10 June

Dined this evening with Flaubert, whom I had not seen since my brother's death. He has come to Paris to find some information for his *Tentation de Saint Antoine*. He is still the same, a writer above all else. This cataclysm seems to have passed over him without distracting him for one moment from the impassive making of books.

### Saturday, 1 July

At the Gare du Nord, prisoners of war were arriving back from Germany. Pale faces, thin bodies in greatcoats too big for them, faded red cloth and worn grey cloth: this is the sight to which the trains from Germany are treating Paris every day.

They walked along with little sticks in their hands, bent under grey canvas kitbags. Some of them were dressed in German breeches, and others were wearing a cloth cap in the place of the peaked cap they had left on some battlefield. Poor fellows! When they were turned loose, it was a pleasure to see them straighten up, it was a pleasure to hear their worn soles tread the pavements of Paris with a brisk, eager step.

The Princess received me with that liveliness which is peculiar to her and which she puts into her handshake. She took me for a stroll in the park and started telling me about herself, about her stay in Belgium, about her sufferings in exile. She told me that for a long time she could not understand what was happening to her in Belgium, but that she knows now: she was present there in body but completely absent in mind, so completely indeed that she used to wake up in the morning thinking that she was in her Paris house. When I congratulated her on her good health, she said: 'Oh, it hasn't always been like that! There was a bad period, a peculiar period, during which my jaws set so hard, after all that I had been through, that sometimes I really had difficulty in eating anything.'

She spoke to me too of the Emperor, whom she had seen again, and whom she characterized as an *impersonal being*, a man whose fall did not seem to have affected him.

### Sunday, 9 November

Flaubert told me today of the unexpected good fortune which had come to the 'Présidente', who had received a bond to the value of fifty thousand francs a year, two days before the Siege: a gift from Richard Wallace, who had slept with her in the past and had told her: 'You'll see, if ever I become a rich man, I'll remember you.'

He told me too about a Chinese envoy who had arrived in Paris during our Siege and our Commune, in the midst of our cataclysm, and to whom somebody had remarked:

'You must find all this extremely surprising.'

'No, not at all', he had replied. 'You are young, you Westerners, you have hardly any history to speak of . . . It has always been like this . . . The Siege and the Commune are everyday events for the human race . . .'

Flaubert invited me to stay for dinner, and afterwards he read to me from his *Tentation de Saint Antoine*. My first impression: the Bible, the Christian past, brought up to date in the Horace Vernet manner, with the addition of Bedouin and Turkish bric-à-brac. My second impression: a huge book of notes on Antiquity forced into the stupid machinery of a spectacular play, with a good many sheets of the compilation refusing to go through the mill.

## 1875

### Monday, 25 January

The Flaubert dinners are unlucky. Coming away from the first, I caught pneumonia. Today, Flaubert himself was missing: he is confined to bed. So there were only four of us: Turgenev, Zola, Daudet, and myself.

We talked first of all about Taine. While we were trying to define the deficiencies and imperfections of his talent, Turgenev interrupted us to say with his usual originality of mind and soft, warbling voice: 'The comparison is not a flattering one, gentlemen, but allow me to compare Taine to a pointer I once owned; he quartered, he pointed, he went through all the motions of a hunting dog to perfection; only he had no sense of smell. I was obliged to sell him.'

Zola was tucking into the good food, and when I asked him whether by any chance he was a glutton, he replied: 'Yes, it's my only vice; and at home, when there isn't anything good for dinner, I'm miserable, utterly miserable. That's the only thing that matters; nothing else really exists for me. You know what my life is like?'

And his face clouding over, he launched out on the story of his misfortunes. It is strange what a whiner that fat, pot-bellied young fellow is, and how quickly he falls into a melancholy mood. He had begun painting the gloomiest of pictures of his youth, of the vexations of his everyday life, of the insults that were heaped upon him, of the suspicion with which he was regarded, and of the sort of quarantine established around his work, when Turgenev remarked: 'How peculiarly French! One of my Russian friends, a great thinker, said to me the other day that the Jean-Jacques Rousseau type was a French type and that it was to be found only in France . . .'

Zola, who had not listened to what Turgenev had said, went on with his jeremiad; and when we pointed out that he had no reason to complain, and that he had come a long way for a man who was not yet thirty-five, he exclaimed: 'Do you want me to be absolutely frank with you? You'll take me for a child, but never mind! I shall never be decorated, I shall never receive any kind of honour in recognition of my talent. For the public I shall always be a pariah, yes, a pariah!'

And he repeated four or five times: 'A pariah!'

We tease the realist about his appetite for bourgeois honours. Turgenev looked at him for a moment with a kind of fatherly irony, and then came out with this charming fable: 'Zola, on the occasion of the emancipation of the serfs, an event in which you know that I played a certain part, Count Orloff, who is a friend of mine and at whose wedding I had been best man, invited me to dinner at the Embassy. I may not be the foremost Russian writer in Russia, but in Paris, seeing that there aren't any others, you'll grant that I must be. Well, that being the case, do you know where I was placed at table? I was given the forty-seventh place; I was placed *after* the pope, and you know how we despise priests in Russia!'

And a little Slavonic smile appeared in Turgenev's eyes by way of conclusion.

Zola was in a talkative mood. The portly young fellow, full of childish naïvety, the greed of a spoilt trollop, and a slightly socialistic envy, went on telling us about his work, about his daily output of a hundred lines, about his cenobitism, his quiet home life, with no other distraction in the evenings but a few games of dominoes with his wife or a visit from a few fellow southerners. In the midst of all this, he forgot himself so far as to confess that at bottom his greatest pleasure, his greatest satisfaction, consisted in feeling the power and influence that he exerted over Paris through the medium of his prose; and he said this in an unpleasant tone of voice, the revengeful tone of voice of a poor devil who had known years of poverty.

During the realist novelist's bitter confession, Daudet, who was slightly tipsy, kept reciting dialect ballads from the south to himself, and seemed to be gargling with the sweet music of that sunny poetry.

Wednesday, 17 February

This evening Dumas was dining at the Princess's. The new Academician tried his best to behave like an ordinary mortal and to humiliate his colleagues as little as possible with his triumph.

After dinner, he began to talk very interestingly about the way a theatrical success was organized, and at one point, turning towards Flaubert and myself, he said in a voice in which profound contempt was combined with something akin to pity: 'You fellows, you don't realize the importance, for the success of a play, of the composition of the first-night audience; you have no idea of all that has to be done . . . For instance you have to make sure that there are friends and admirers sitting around the four or five members every club sends along on those occasions, because they are anything but enthusiastic theatre-goers. And if you don't see about this, and about that . . .' And he taught us a great many things of which we were totally ignorant and which, now that we know them, we shall never be able to put into practice.

Sunday, 28 February

At Flaubert's, we were enthusing over the poetry of the Englishman Swinburne when Daudet exclaimed:

'Incidentally, I've heard that he's a homosexual. There are the most extraordinary stories told about his stay at Étretat last year . . .'

'Further back than that, a few years ago,' said young Maupassant, 'I saw something of him for a little while.'

'Why, yes,' said Flaubert; 'didn't you save his life?'

'Not exactly,' replied Maupassant. 'I was walking along the beach when I heard the shouts of a drowning man, and I waded into the water. But a boat had beaten me to it and had already fished him out. He had gone for a bathe dead drunk. But just as I was coming out of the water, soaked to the skin right up to the waist, another Englishman, who lived in the neighbourhood and was Swinburne's friend, came up to me and thanked me warmly.

'The next day I received an invitation to lunch. It was a strange place where they lived, a sort of cottage containing some splendid pictures, with an inscription over the door which I didn't read on that occasion, and a big monkey gambolling around inside. And what a lunch! I don't know what I ate; all I can remember is that when I asked the name of some fish I was eating, my host replied with a peculiar smile that it was meat, and I could not get any more out of him! There was no wine, and we drank nothing but spirits.

'The owner of the place, a certain Powell, was an English lord, according to people at Étretat, who concealed his identity under his mother's maiden name. As for Swinburne, picture a little man with a forked chin, a hydrocephalous forehead, and a narrow chest, who trembled so violently that he gave his glass St. Vitus's dance and talked like a madman.

'One thing annoyed me straight away about that first lunch, and that was that now and then Powell would titillate his monkey, which would escape from him to rub up against the back of my neck when I bent forward to have a drink.

'After lunch the two friends opened some gigantic portfolios and brought out a collection of obscene photographs, taken in Germany, all life-size and all of male subjects. I remember one, among others, of an English soldier masturbating on a pane of glass. Powell was dead drunk by this time, and kept sucking the fingers of a mummified hand which was used, I believe, as a paperweight. While he was showing me the photographs, a young servant came in, and Powell promptly closed the portfolio.

'Swinburne speaks very good French. He has an immense fund of learning. That day he told us a lot of interesting things about snakes, saying that he sometimes watched them for two or three hours at a time. Then he translated some of his poems for us, putting tremendous spirit into the translation. It was very impressive. Powell is no ordinary man either: he has brought back a collection of fascinating old songs from Iceland.

'The whole household, in fact, intrigued me. I accepted a second invitation to lunch. This time the monkey left me in peace; it had been hanged a few days before by the little servant, and Powell had ordered a huge block of granite to put on its tomb, with a basin hollowed out on top in which the birds could find rainwater during periods of drought. At the end of the meal they gave me a liqueur which nearly knocked me out. Taking fright, I escaped to my hotel, where I slept like a log for the rest of the day.

'Finally I went back there for one last visit, to find out the truth, to make certain whether or not I was dealing with perverts or homosexuals. I showed them the inscription over the door, which read: *Dolmancé Cottage*, and asked them whether they were aware that Dolmancé was the name of the hero of Sade's *Philosophie dans le Boudoir*. They answered in the affirmative. "Then that is the sign of the house?" I asked. "If you like," they replied, with terrifying expressions on their faces. I had found out what I wanted to know, and I never saw them again.'

ÉMILE ZOLA

From

# L'ASSOMMOIR

1880

Translated by Margaret Mauldon

THREE WEEKS LATER, at about half-past-eleven on a lovely sunny morning, Gervaise and Coupeau the roofer were having a brandied plum together at Père Colombe's bar, the Assommoir. Coupeau had been smoking a cigarette outside on the pavement when Gervaise crossed the road after delivering some laundry; he'd made her come in with him and now her big square laundry basket lay beside her on the ground, behind the little zinc table.

Père Colombe's Assommoir stood at the corner of the Rue des Poissonniers and the Boulevard de Rochechouart. The sign bore the single word 'Spirits' written in tall blue letters right across it. There were some dusty oleanders growing in two half-barrels at the entrance. The enormous counter with its rows of glasses, its water vat and its pewter measures stretched along to the left of the entrance, and the vast room was decorated all round with huge casks painted pale yellow and highly varnished, with hoops and spigots of shining copper. Higher up were shelves displaying bottles of liqueurs, jars of brandied fruit and carefully arranged flasks of all kinds; they concealed the walls, reflecting their vibrant splashes of apple green, pale gold and soft reddish-brown in the mirror behind the counter. But the real attraction of the place, standing beyond an oak balustrade in the glassed-in rear courtyard, was the still, which the customers could see working, with its long-necked alembics and its tubes coiling down into the ground, a veritable devil's kitchen in front of which boozing workmen would hang about and day-dream.

Now, at this stage of the lunch hour, the Assommoir was empty. Père Colombe, a stout man of forty wearing a sleeved waistcoat, was serving a little ten-year-old girl who'd asked for four sous' worth of spirits in a cup. Sunshine flooded in through the door, warming the wooden floor which was permanently wet with the spit of smokers. And from the counter, from the casks, from the entire room, a smell of spirits rose up, an alcoholic vapour which seemed to make even the dust-motes spinning about in the sunlight dense and drunken.

Coupeau, meanwhile, was busy rolling a fresh cigarette. He looked spick-and-span in his smock and little peaked cap of blue cloth, and his white teeth gleamed when he laughed. With his protruding lower jaw, slightly flattened nose and fine brown eyes, his face reminded you of a cheerful, good-natured dog. His thick curly hair stood up on its own. At twenty-six, his skin was still soft. Opposite him Gervaise, in a black cloth jacket, her head bare, was finishing her plum, holding it by its stem with her fingertips. They were sitting close to the street, at the first of the four tables set alongside the casks in front of the counter.

When the roofer had lit his cigarette, he put his elbows on the table and, leaning forward, gazed for a moment in silence at the young woman's pretty face. That morning, her fair skin had the milky transparency of fine porcelain. Then, referring to something private between them, he asked simply, keeping his voice low:

'So it's no? You're sayin' no?'

'But of course it's no, Monsieur Coupeau,' Gervaise replied calmly, with a smile. 'You're not going to start on about that here, surely. And you did promise to be sensible, didn't you … If I'd known, I'd have refused your offer of a drink.'

He said nothing more, and went on leaning close, staring at her with bold, inviting tenderness, entranced by the corners of her lips, tiny pale pink corners, slightly wet, which revealed the bright red of her mouth when she smiled. Nevertheless she didn't draw back, but continued looking unruffled and affectionate. After a silence, she spoke again:

'I'm sure you don't really mean it. I'm an old woman, I am; I've a great big boy of eight … Whatever would we do together?'

'Lor',' murmured Coupeau with a wink. 'Same as everyone else!'

But she answered, with a gesture of irritation: 'Oh! If you think it's always fun … It's clear you've never had to run a home. No, Monsieur Coupeau, I've got to stick to what matters. Fun and games don't get you anywhere, you know. I've two mouths to feed at home, and they're hearty eaters, let me tell you! How d'you suppose I'll ever manage to bring up me little chicks if I spend me time larking about? And then, well it's like this, me bad luck's really taught me a lesson. You know, when it comes to men, I just don't fancy 'em any more. It'll be a good while before I'm caught again.'

She explained herself dispassionately, sounding very wise and calm as if she were talking about something to do with laundering, like why she wouldn't starch a shawl. You could see she'd worked it all out in her head, after long and careful thought.

Coupeau kept repeating tenderly:

'You're makin' me very unhappy, very unhappy …'

'Yes, I can see that,' she replied, 'and I'm very sorry on your account, Monsieur Coupeau. You mustn't take it amiss. If I wanted a bit of that, lord, I'd sooner it was with you than anyone else. You seem like a nice chap, you're kind. We'd try it out together, wouldn't we, and see how long it lasted. I'm not being stuck-up, I'm not saying it couldn't have happened . . . Only, what would be the point, since I don't want to? I've been at Madame Fauconnier's for a fortnight now. The kids are at school. I've a job, I'm quite happy . . . Best leave things as they are, eh?'

She bent down for her basket.

'You're keeping me chatting, when they'll be expecting me at Madame's . . . You'll find someone else, Monsieur Coupeau, of course you will, someone prettier than me, who won't have a couple of brats to drag about.'

He was looking at the clock set in the mirror. He made her sit down again, exclaiming: 'Wait a bit! It's only twenty-five to twelve! . . . I've still twenty-five minutes. Surely you're not afraid I'll do something silly – we've got the table between us . . . Come on, d'you hate me so much you won't even have a little chat?'

Not wishing to be unkind, she put her basket down and they talked like old friends. She'd had her lunch before setting out with the laundry and he'd bolted down his soup and beef that day so he could watch for her. While answering his questions in a pleasant way Gervaise kept looking through the windows, between the jars of brandied fruits, at all the activity in the street, which was amazingly crowded with people now it was the lunch hour. Along the two pavements, jammed into the narrow space between the houses, came an endless rush of striding feet, swinging arms and jabbing elbows. The latecomers, workmen who hadn't been let out on time, raced along with giant strides, their faces bad-tempered and hungry, and went into the baker's across the road, reappearing with a pound loaf under their arm before going into the Veau à deux têtes, three doors further on, for the six-sous set meal. Next to the baker there was also a fruiterer who sold fried potatoes and mussels with parsley, and a continuous stream of working girls in long aprons emerged carrying bags of chips and cups of mussels; other girls – pretty, bare-headed, dainty-looking – were buying bunches of radishes. Leaning forward, Gervaise could see another shop, a pork-butcher's, crowded with people, where children came out holding, wrapped in greasy paper, a breaded chop, a sausage or a piece of hot black pudding. Meanwhile, along the road which even in fine weather was always slimy with black mud because of the trampling throng, little groups of workers were already coming out of the eating houses and setting off in twos and threes; sluggish with food, they dawdled about, slapping their open palms on their thighs, calm and slow amid the jostling of the crowd.

A group had gathered at the door of the Assommoir.

'What about it, Bibi-la-Grillade,' asked a croaky voice, 'ain't you goin' to stand us a round o' rotgut?'

Five workmen came in and stood by the bar.

'Hey, here's that old crook Colombe,' continued the voice. 'Now we want the real old stuff, mind, and in proper glasses, not thimbles!'

Père Colombe was serving them placidly. Another lot of three workmen arrived. The overalls would gather slowly into groups at the pavement corner, stop there for a little while, then push their way between the dust-grey oleanders into the bar.

'Don't be silly! What a dirty mind you have!' Gervaise was saying to Coupeau. 'Of course I loved him ... Only, after the horrible way he left me ...'

They were talking about Lantier. Gervaise hadn't seen him again; she believed he was living with Virginie's sister, at La Glacière, at that friend's who was supposed to be starting a hat factory. In any case, she'd no intention of chasing after him. At first she'd been dreadfully hurt and had even thought of throwing herself into the river but now she'd made herself see sense and felt it was all for the best. If she'd stayed with Lantier she mightn't have been able to bring up her kids, he went through money so fast. He could come and see Claude and Étienne, she wouldn't kick him out. Only, as far as she was concerned, she'd sooner be chopped into little bits than let him touch her with the tip of his finger. She said all this very decisively, like a woman who has her whole life clearly planned, while Coupeau, still driven by his desire for her, kept making jokes and dirty remarks out of everything, asking her the crudest questions about Lantier, but so cheerfully and with such a gleaming white smile that she never even thought of taking offence.

'I bet you knocked him about,' he said finally. 'Oh, you're a bad 'un! You beat everybody up.'

She interrupted him with a long laugh. Still, it was true, she *had* beaten up that hulking great Virginie. That day, she'd have been more than happy to strangle somebody. She began laughing even more when Coupeau explained that Virginie was so mortified at having displayed everything she'd got, she'd left the neighbourhood. Gervaise's face, however, still kept its childlike sweetness; she showed him her chubby little hands, declaring she wouldn't harm a fly; she only knew about beating up because she'd been at the receiving end herself so damn often. That started her talking about her girlhood in Plassans. She'd never been one for the men; men bored her; when Lantier had taken her, at fourteen, she thought that was nice because he said he was her husband and it was like playing house. Her only weakness, she assured him, was being very soft-hearted, liking everybody, getting desperately fond of people who then put her through endless misery. So, when she loved a man, she wasn't interested in all that nonsense, what she dreamt of was simply living together happily ever after. When Coupeau started to snigger and mentioned her two kids, whom she certainly hadn't hatched out under the bolster, she rapped him on the knuckles, adding that of course she was made the same way as other women; only it was wrong to imagine women were always mad keen on you-know-what; women were taken up by their homes, they worked their fingers to the bone in the house and went to bed at night too worn out not to fall asleep straight away. Besides, she was like her mother, a tireless worker who'd died in harness after serving as beast of burden to Père Macquart for over twenty years. She was still very thin, while her mother had had a pair of shoulders on her broad enough to stave in a door, but just the same she took after her in the way she got desperately fond of people. And even her bit of a limp came from the poor woman, whom Père Macquart was forever beating half to death. Time and again her mother had told her about the nights when Macquart came home blind drunk and made love so brutally that he almost broke her bones, and certainly she, Gervaise, with her gammy leg, must have been started on one of those nights.

'Oh, it's hardly anything, it doesn't show at all,' said Coupeau, to please her.

She shook her head; she knew quite well it showed; she'd be bent double by the time she was forty. Then with a little laugh she added gently:

'You've funny tastes, to fancy a girl who limps.'

So then, leaning closer to her with his elbows still on the table, he became less guarded in his flattery, as if trying to make her drunk with words. But she went on shaking her head, not letting herself be tempted, although she found that coaxing voice beguiling. She listened to him with her gaze fixed on the street, apparently absorbed once more by the ever-increasing crowds. Now, in the empty shops, they were sweeping up; the fruiterer was taking the last panful of fried potatoes off the stove and the pork-butcher was tidying up the jumble of plates on his counter. Groups of workmen were emerging from all the eating houses; great strapping fellows with beards were pushing and slapping each other about, playful as kids, their heavy nailed boots making a scraping noise as they went sliding over the cobbles; others, their hands deep in their pockets, were enjoying a quiet smoke, blinking their eyes as they gazed at the sun. They poured on to the pavement, the roadway, the gutters, streaming out of open doorways like a slow-running tide, coming to a stop amid the passing carts, making a trail of workmen's overalls and smocks and old coats which looked all faded and colourless in the rays of golden light which filled the street. Factory bells could be heard in the distance; however the workmen weren't hurrying but kept stopping to relight their pipes; then, after calling to each other from bar to bar, they finally made up their minds to get back to work and slouched off, dragging their feet. Gervaise amused herself watching three men, one tall and two short, who stopped and turned round every few paces; in the end they came back down the street, heading straight for Père Colombe's Assommoir.

'Well now,' she murmured, 'those three must be proper lazy-bones!'

'Hey,' said Coupeau, 'I know the tall one, it's Mes-Bottes, a pal o' mine.'

The Assommoir had filled up. People were talking very loudly, sometimes shouting to break through the hoarse rumble of voices. At times a fist would bang down on the counter and make the glasses ring. The drinkers were crowded together, standing in little clusters with their hands crossed on their bellies or tucked behind their backs; over by the casks there were some groups who had to wait a quarter of an hour before being able to order their drinks from old Colombe.

'Why, if it isn't old nose-in-air Cadet-Cassis!' shouted Mes-Bottes, giving Coupeau a great whack on the shoulder. 'Quite the gent, what with 'is cigarettes and 'is fancy shirts! So, we're trying to make an impression are we, standing the lady friend a little treat?'

'Hey! Piss off!' answered Coupeau, very put out.

But the other just laughed. 'Right! Very snooty, aren't we, mate? Well, once a moron always a moron . . .'

He turned his back, after staring at Gervaise with a frightful leer. She drew away, rather scared. The atmosphere, thick with pipe-smoke, alcohol fumes and a strong smell of male bodies, was making her choke and she began to cough a bit.

'Oh, drinking's foul!' she muttered.

And she told him that years ago, in Plassans, she used to drink anisette with her mother, but one day it had nearly killed her, so now she couldn't bear to touch spirits.

'Look,' she said, pointing at her glass, 'I ate me plum, but I'm leaving the syrup because it would make me ill.'

Coupeau couldn't understand either how people could swallow spirits by the glassful. There was no harm in having the odd plum. But as for rotgut, absinthe and all that other muck – thanks very much, they could keep it! His mates could chaff him as much as they liked, he stayed outside when those piss-tanks dropped into the boozer. Old man Coupeau, who'd been a roofer like him, had bashed his head in when he fell on to the pavement of the Rue Coquenard from the eaves of number 25, one day when he'd had a few, and the memory of that kept 'em all sober in his family. Whenever he himself went along the Rue Coquenard and saw the spot, he'd sooner drink water out of the gutter than have a glass of wine in a bar, even if it was free. He ended by remarking:

'In our line of business, you need steady legs.'

Gervaise had picked up her basket. However she didn't get up, but held it on her lap, with a far-away, dreamy look on her face as if the young workman's words had stirred in her some dimly-felt thoughts about life. And she went on slowly, with no apparent transition:

'My God! I'm not ambitious, I don't ask for much . . . My ideal would be to get on with me work in peace, always have something to eat and a nice little place to sleep – you know, just a bed, a table and two chairs, that's all . . . Oh! I'd also like to be able to bring up me kids to be decent folk, if I could . . . There's another ideal I have, and that's not to be beaten, if I ever took up with anyone again; no, I wouldn't want to be beaten . . . And that's all, really, that's all I want.'

She considered, searching her mind for other wishes but could find nothing else that was important. Nevertheless she did go on, after a little hesitation:

'Oh yes, at the end, you might want to die in your own bed . . . After slogging away all me life, I'd really like to die in me own bed, at home.'

Gervaise got up. Coupeau, who strongly approved of what she'd been saying, was already on his feet, for he was worried about the time. But they didn't leave immediately; she was full of curiosity to see the big copper still which was working away under the transparent glass roof of the little courtyard at the back, behind the oak barrier. Coupeau, who'd followed her, explained how it worked, pointing out the different parts of the machine and showing her the huge retort from which came a trickle of crystal-clear alcohol. The still, with its weirdly-shaped containers and its endless coils of piping, had a gloomy look about it; there was no steam escaping from it, and you could just hear a kind of breathing, like a subterranean rumbling, coming from deep within; it was as if some midnight task were being glumly performed in broad daylight by a strong, taciturn worker. Meanwhile, Mes-Bottes, with his two mates, had come over and was leaning on the oak balustrade, while they waited for a free spot at the counter. His laugh sounded like a pulley that needed greasing as, nodding his head, he gazed fondly at the boozing machine. Christ almighty! wasn't she a sweetheart! There was enough in that great big copper belly to keep your whistle wetted for a whole week! He'd have liked it, he would, if they'd solder the end of the tubing between his teeth, so he could feel the rotgut – still warm, it'd be – filling him up, flowing on and on right down into his heels, like a little stream. Lor'! he'd never have to budge again, it'd be a bleeding good exchange for the thimbles that rat Colombe dished out! His pals were all laughing and declaring that that sod Mes-Bottes didn't half have the gift of the gab. The still worked silently on, with no flame visible, no cheerful play of light on its lack-lustre copper surface, sweating out its alcohol like a slow-flowing but relentless spring which would eventually flood the bar-room, spill over the outer boulevards and inundate the vast pit that was Paris. Gervaise gave a shudder and stepped back; trying to smile, she murmured:

'I know it's silly, but that machine really gives me the shivers . . . Drink always gives me the shivers . . .'

Then, coming back to her cherished vision of perfect happiness:

'Well, aren't I right? It'd be so much better to work, put food on your table, have a little place of your own, bring up your kids and die in your own bed . . .'

'An' not get beaten,' added Coupeau cheerfully. 'But I'd

never beat you, I wouldn't, if only you'd say yes, Madame Gervaise ... You needn't be scared, I never drink, an' anyway I love you too much. Come on, how 'bout tonight, let's keep each other's tootsies warm.'

He'd lowered his voice and was murmuring in her ear as, holding her basket in front of her, she made her way through the crowd. But she went on refusing, shaking her head several times. Nevertheless she did turn round to smile at him, and seemed pleased that he didn't drink. She'd certainly have said yes to him if she hadn't promised herself never to take up with a man again. At last they reached the door and went out. Behind them the Assommoir was still packed, with the hoarse rumble of voices and the fumes from all those rounds of booze wafting out into the street. They could hear Mes-Bottes calling Colombe a dirty swindler and accusing him of only half filling his glass. He himself was a real brick, one hell of a fellow, as good as they came. The boss could go fuck himself, he wasn't going back to that dump of a workshop, he felt like having a wander. And he suggested to his two companions that they go to the Petit bonhomme qui tousse, a boozer near the Barrière Saint-Denis, where you could get it neat.

'Ah! You can breathe here,' said Gervaise, when they were on the pavement. 'Well, goodbye and thank you, Monsieur Coupeau ... I'd better hurry.'

She was going along the boulevard. But he'd taken her hand and was keeping it in his, saying:

'Why don't you come with me, round by the Rue de la Goutte-d'Or, it's hardly out of your way at all ... I've got to drop by my sister's before I go back to work ... We can keep each other company.'

In the end she accepted, though she did not take his arm, and they walked slowly up the Rue des Poissonniers side by side.

GUY DE MAUPASSANT

# A PARISIAN AFFAIR

1881

Translated by Siân Miles

IS THERE ANY keener sense known to man than woman's curiosity? There is nothing in the world she would not do in order to satisfy it, to know for certain, to grasp and possess what has hitherto remained in her imagination. What would she not do to achieve that? When her impatient curiosity is at its height, she will shrink from nothing, and there is no folly to which she will not stoop, no obstacle she will not overcome. I refer, of course, to the really feminine woman, the sort who on the surface may appear quite reasonable and objective, but whose three secret weapons are always in a high state of readiness. The first is a kind of watchful, womanly concern for what is happening around her; the second, even more deadly in its effect, is guile disguised as common decency; and the third is the exquisite capacity for deception and infinite variety which drives some men to throw themselves at her feet, and others off the parapets of bridges.

The one whose story I want to tell you about was a little provincial woman who had led until then a boringly blameless life. Her outwardly calm existence was spent looking after her family, a very busy husband and two children whose upbringing, in her hands, was exemplary in every way. But her heart was ravaged by an all-consuming, indefinable desire. She thought constantly about Paris and avidly read all the society pages in the papers. Their accounts of receptions, celebrations, the clothes worn, and all the accompanying delights enjoyed, whetted her appetite still further. Above all, however, she was fascinated by what these reports merely hinted at. The cleverly phrased allusions half-lifted a veil beyond which could be glimpsed devastatingly attractive horizons promising a whole new world of wicked pleasure.

From where she lived, she looked on Paris as representing the height of all magnificent luxury as well as licentiousness. Throughout the long, dream-filled night, lulled by the regular snoring of her husband sleeping next to her on his back with a scarf wrapped round his head, she conjured up the images of all the famous men who made the headlines and shone like brilliant comets in the darkness of her sombre sky. She pictured the madly exciting lives they must lead, moving from one den of vice to the next, indulging in never-ending and extraordinarily voluptuous orgies, and practising such complex and sophisticated sex as to defy the imagination. It seemed to her that hidden behind the façades of the houses lining the canyon-like boulevards of the city, some amazing erotic secret must lie.

And she herself was growing old. She was growing old, never having known a thing about life beyond the hideously banal monotony of regularly performed duties which, by all accounts, was what happily married life consisted of. She was still pretty. The uneventful life she lived had preserved her like a winter apple in an attic. Yet she was consumed from within by unspoken and obsessive desires. She wondered if she would die without ever having tasted the wicked delights which life had to offer, without ever, not even once, having plunged into the ocean of voluptuous pleasure which, to her, was Paris.

After long and careful preparation, she decided to put into action a plan to get there. She invented a pretext, got herself invited by some relatives and, since her husband was unable to accompany her, left for the city alone. The alleged discovery of some long-lost friends living in one of its leafy suburbs enabled her as soon as she arrived to prolong her stay by a couple of days or rather nights, if necessary. Her search began. Up and down the boulevards she walked, seeing nothing particularly wicked or sinful.

She cast her eye inside all the well-known cafés, and each morning her avid reading of the *Figaro*'s lonely hearts' column was a fresh reminder to her of the call of love. But she found nothing that might lead her to the great orgies she imagined actresses and artists enjoyed all the time. Nowhere could she discover the dens of iniquity about which she had dreamed. Without the necessary 'Open Sesame' she remained debarred from Ali Baba's cave. Uninitiated, she stood on the threshold of the catacombs where the secret rites of a forbidden religion were performed. Her petty bourgeois relatives could offer her an introduction to none of the fashionable men whose names buzzed in her ears. In despair, she had almost decided to give up when, finally, happy chance intervened.

One day, as she was walking down the Chaussée d'Antin, she stopped to look at the window of a shop selling Japanese *bibelots* in such gay, cheerful colours as to delight the eye. She was looking thoughtfully at its amusing little ivories, its huge oriental vases of vivid enamelwork and its strange bronzes, when she heard from within the voice of the proprietor. With low, reverential bows, he was showing a fat, bald-headed little man with grizzled stubble the figure of a pot-bellied Buddha, the only one of its kind, or so he claimed.

With each of the merchant's utterances, the famous name of his customer sounded like a clarion call in her ears. The other browsers, young ladies and elegant gentlemen, cast oblique, highly respectful glances in the direction of the well-known author who was absorbed in his examination of the figure. One was as ugly as the other. The pair might have been taken for brothers.

'To you, Monsieur Jean Varin,' the shopkeeper was saying, 'I'll let it go for 1,000. Cost, in other words. To anyone else, it would be 1,500. My artist customers mean a lot to me. I like to offer them a special price. Oh yes, they all come to me you know, Monsieur Jean Varin ... Yesterday, for example, Monsieur Busnach bought an antique goblet from me ... and the other day ... you see those candlesticks over there, aren't they lovely? Sold a pair like them to Monsieur Alexandre Dumas ... and I mean ... that piece you've got there ... if Monsieur Zola saw that, it'd be gone in five minutes, I can assure you, Monsieur Varin ...'

The writer hesitated, undecided. He was obviously attracted to the figure but not the price. Had he been standing quite alone in the middle of a desert, he could not have been more oblivious of the interest he was arousing. Trembling, she went in. Young, handsome, elegant or not, it was nevertheless Jean Varin himself and on Jean Varin alone she now fixed a bold gaze. Still struggling with himself, he finally replaced the figure on the table.

'No,' he said, 'it's too expensive.'

The merchant redoubled his efforts.

'Too expensive, Monsieur Jean Varin? But you know it's worth two thousand if it's worth a franc!'

Sadly, as he continued to gaze into the enamelled eyes of the figure, the man of letters replied, 'I'm sure it is. But it's too expensive for me.'

At this, wildly daring, she stepped forward and said: 'Supposing *I* were to ask. What would it be to me?'

Surprised, the merchant replied: 'Fifteen hundred, Madame.'

'I'll take it.'

The writer, who until then had been totally unaware of her presence, turned round quickly and at first somewhat coldly looked her up and down. Then he cast more of a connoisseur's eye over her. She was charming, vibrant and suddenly lit up by the flame which had till this second been dormant within her. After all, a woman who snaps up a curio at 1,500 is not exactly run-of-the-mill.

With exquisite delicacy in her movement, she turned to face him now and said in a trembling voice, 'I'm so sorry, Monsieur. I'm afraid I rather rushed in. Perhaps you had not yet decided.'

He bowed. 'I had indeed, Madame.'

In a voice shaking with emotion she said: 'If you should ever change your mind, either today or at some later time, it shall be yours. I bought it solely because you liked it.'

Visibly flattered, he smiled. 'But how on earth do you know who I am?' he inquired. She listed his works and expressed with some eloquence her admiration of them. Leaning his elbows on a piece of furniture he settled down to a conversation, weighing her up all the while with his penetrating gaze.

New customers had come into the shop and from time to time the merchant, delighted with such living testimony to the excellence of his stock, called from one end of the shop to the other: 'There you are, you see, Monsieur Jean Varin! What about that then?' Everyone looked over and she felt a thrill of pleasure at being seen chatting on such intimate terms with one of the great and the good.

Dizzy with success, she felt like a general about to make one supremely daring attack. 'Monsieur,' she said, 'would you do me a great, a very great favour? Will you let me give you this figure as a keepsake from a woman of ten minutes' acquaintance who has the most ardent admiration for you?'

He refused. She insisted. Laughing happily, he resisted yet again, but she was determined.

'In that case, I shall take it to your home straight away. Where do you live?'

He refused to give his address but having acquired it from the merchant as she paid, she rushed off to find a fiacre. The writer ran to catch her up, unwilling to expose himself by accepting this gift from a total stranger, and, with it, who knew what sort of obligation. Reaching her just as she was jumping into the cab, he flung himself in and nearly fell on top of her as it jolted into motion. He sat down beside her, more than a little embarrassed.

She was quite intractable. His protests and pleas fell on deaf ears. As they arrived at the door, she set out her conditions.

'I shall agree not to leave it with you if, throughout the whole of today, you will carry out all my wishes.'

The whole thing sounded so extraordinarily amusing that he accepted.

'Now,' she said. 'What would you normally be doing at this time of day?'

After a little hesitation, he said: 'I'd be going for a walk.'

In a firm tone she ordered, 'To the Bois!'

And off they went. After this, he had to tell her the names of all the women people were talking about, especially the flighty ones, and give her every intimate detail he could about where they lived, how they spent their days, and all their wicked little ways.

It was now getting towards evening time.

'What do you usually do at this sort of time?' she asked.

Laughing, he replied, 'I go for a glass of absinthe.'

They went into a large boulevard café where he was a regular and met all his colleagues. He introduced them to her. She was wild with joy. And in her head, there echoed ceaselessly the words 'At last! At last!'

Time passed. 'Is this when you normally dine?' she asked.

'Yes, Madame,' he replied.

'Then, Monsieur, let's go and dine,' she said.

Emerging from the Café Bignon, she asked, 'What do you normally do in the evening?'

He looked at her steadily.

'It depends. Sometimes I go to the theatre.'

'Well then, Monsieur, let's go to the theatre.'

He was recognized by the management at the Vaudeville who found seats for them straight away. To crown it all, she was seen by the entire audience, sitting by his side in the first row of the balcony.

After the show, he kissed her hand gallantly and said, 'It only remains, Madame, for me to thank you for a delightful . . .'

She interrupted. 'What is it you do at this time of night?'

'What do I do? You mean what do I . . .? Well I go home, of course.'

'In that case, Monsieur, let us go to your home,' she said, laughing shakily.

Not a word more was spoken. From time to time a shiver ran through her, half of terror, half of delight. She was in an exquisite agony, torn between the desire to run away and her determination, in her heart of hearts, to stay and see it through.

As they mounted the stairs, her feelings nearly overcame her and she leaned heavily on the banister while he wheezed on ahead, carrying a taper.

As soon as she was in the bedroom, she undressed quickly, slid wordlessly into bed and, huddling up against the wall, waited.

She was as unsophisticated, however, as only the lawful wife of a country solicitor can be, while he was as demanding as a pasha with three tails. They did not get on at all well. Not at all.

Afterwards, he fell asleep. The night hours passed silently save for the ticking of the clock as, motionless, she thought of her conjugal nights at home.

By the yellow light of a Chinese lantern, she looked in dismay at the tubby little man beside her, lying on his back with the sheet draped over his hot-air balloon of a belly.

While he snored like a pipe-organ, with comic interludes of lengthy, strangulated snorts, the few hairs he possessed, exhausted by the onerous responsibility of masking the ravages of time on his balding skull during the day, now stood perkily on end. A dribble of saliva flowed from the corner of his half-open mouth.

When dawn finally broke, light fell through a gap in the drawn curtains. She got up, dressed noiselessly and had just managed to ease the door open when the latch grated. He woke up and rubbed his eyes. It took a few seconds for him to recover his senses, when the whole affair came flooding back into his mind.

'Oh . . . so . . . you're leaving then, are you?' he asked.

'Well . . . yes,' she stammered, 'it's morning.'

He sat up in bed.

'Look . . .' he said, 'let *me* ask something for once, will you?'

As she made no reply, he went on, 'I don't understand what you've been up to all this time . . . since yesterday. Come on . . . tell me what you're up to . . . I can't work it out . . .'

Gently, she drew closer, blushing like a young girl.

'I always wanted to know what it was like to be . . . wicked . . . and actually . . . it turns out to be not all that much fun . . .'

She ran from the room, flew down the staircase and flung herself out into the street.

Down it an army of sweepers was sweeping. They swept the pavements and the cobblestones, driving all the litter and filth into the stream of the gutter. With the same regular movement, like reapers in the field, they swept up all in a wide semi-circle ahead. And as she ran through street after street, still they came to meet her, moving like puppets on a string with the same, mechanical, mowing movement. She felt as though something inside her, too, had now been swept away. Through the mud, down to the gutter and finally into the sewer had gone all the refuse of her over-excited imagination.

Returning home, the image of Paris swept inexorably clean by the cold light of day filled her exhausted mind, and as she reached her room, sobs broke from her now quite frozen heart.

VILLIERS DE L'ISLE-ADAM

# THE UNKNOWN WOMAN

1883

Translated by Robert Baldick

*For Madame la Comtesse de Laclos*

The swan remains silent all its life in order to sing well a single time.

*Old proverb*

The holy child whom a beautiful line of verse turns pale.

ADRIEN JUVIGNY

THAT EVENING, THE whole of Paris society was at the Italian Opera for a performance of *Norma*. It was the farewell appearance of Maria Felicia Malibran.

The entire house, at the last strains of Bellini's prayer, *Casta diva*, had risen to its feet and was applauding the singer in a glorious din. Flowers, bracelets, and crowns were thrown on to the stage. A feeling of immortality surrounded the august artiste, who was close to death and fading away under the impression that she was singing.

In the middle of the orchestra stalls, a young man whose face revealed a proud, determined spirit was clapping until he burst his gloves, to show the passionate admiration he felt.

Nobody in Parisian society knew this theatregoer. He did not look like a provincial, but a foreigner. Sitting in that orchestra stall, in clothes which were rather new, but impeccably cut and with a dull sheen, he would have appeared well-nigh bizarre if it had not been for his air of mysterious, instinctive elegance. Examining him, one would have been tempted to look around him for space, sky, and solitude. It was extraordinary, but is not Paris the city of the Extraordinary?

Who was he and where did he come from?

He was an untamed youth, an aristocratic orphan – one of the last of this century – a melancholy nobleman from the north who had escaped, three days before, from the shadows of a manor in Cornouailles.

His name was the Comte Félicien de la Vierge; he was the proprietor of the Château de Blanchelande, in Lower Brittany. A burning thirst for life and curiosity about the wonderful hell of Paris had suddenly fired that huntsman in his remote home. He had set off, and here he was. His presence in Paris dated only from that morning, so that his big eyes were still shining.

It was the first evening of his youth! He was twenty years old. It was his entry into a world of brilliance, forgetfulness, commonplaces, gold, and pleasure. And *by chance* he had arrived just in time to hear the farewell of her who was leaving.

A few moments had sufficed for him to accustom himself to the splendour of the auditorium. But at La Malibran's first notes, his soul had started; the auditorium had disappeared. Familiarity with the silence of the woods, the hoarse wind of the rocks, the sound of the water on the stones of torrents, and the solemn approach of dusk had educated this proud young man in poetry; and in the timbre of the voice he was listening to, it seemed to him that the soul of those things was imploring him from afar to return.

Just as, in a transport of enthusiasm, he was applauding the inspired artiste, his hands suddenly stopped, and he remained motionless.

In one of the boxes a young woman of great beauty had

just appeared. She was looking at the stage. The delicate, noble lines of her dimly perceived profile were obscured by the red shadows of the box, like a Florentine cameo in its locket. Pale and all alone, with a gardenia in her dark hair, she rested her hand, whose shape revealed an illustrious lineage, on the balcony. In the bodice of her black silk dress, veiled with lace, a sickly jewel, an admirable opal, doubtless in the likeness of her soul, shone inside a ring of gold. A lonely figure, indifferent to the audience, she seemed to be lost in the invincible charm of the music.

Chance, however, ordained that she should turn her gaze vaguely towards the crowd; at that moment, the young man's eyes and hers met for a second, long enough to shine and grow dim.

Had they known each other before? . . . No. Not on this earth. But let those who can tell where the Past begins decide where those two creatures had already possessed one another, for that solitary glance had persuaded them, once and for all, that their lives had not begun in the cradle. Lightning shows up, in a single flash, the foaming breakers of the nocturnal sea, and, on the horizon, the distant lines of the silvery waves: similarly the impression made on that young man's heart by that swift glance was not graduated; it was the intimate, magical revelation of a world unveiled. He closed his eyes, as if to hold prisoner the two blue gleams which had lost themselves within them. Then, in an attempt to resist that oppressive giddiness, he looked up again at the unknown woman.

Once more she pensively turned her eyes towards his, as if she had read the thoughts of that uncouth suitor and had found them perfectly natural. Félicien felt himself turn pale; that glance gave him the impression of a pair of arms languidly meeting around his neck. It had happened! That woman's face had just been reflected in his mind as in a familiar mirror, had taken form there, had recognized itself there, had fixed itself there for ever under the magical influence of well-nigh divine thoughts.

He was experiencing the first, unforgettable love.

Meanwhile the young woman, opening her fan, whose black lace was touching her lips, seemed to have withdrawn once again into her reverie. Now anybody would have said that she was exclusively absorbed in the melodies of *Norma*.

On the point of raising his opera-glasses towards the box, Félicien felt that this would be an unseemly act.

'Seeing that I love her!' he said to himself.

Impatient for the end of the act, he gave himself up to his thoughts. How was he to speak to her, to learn her name? He knew nobody he could ask. He could consult the register of the Italian Opera the next day – but what if it were a box taken just for that evening? It was getting late; the vision was going to disappear. Well, his carriage would follow hers, that was all . . . It seemed to him that there was no other solution. Afterwards he would think of something. Then he said to himself, in his sublime innocence: 'If she loves me, she will notice and give me some clue.'

The curtain fell. Félicien hurried out of the opera house. Once he was under the peristyle, he started walking up and down in front of the statues.

His valet came up to him, and he gave him some whispered instructions; the man withdrew into a corner, where he stood waiting attentively.

The vast noise of the ovation given to the singer gradually died down, like all the triumphal noises of this world. The audience started coming down the great staircase. Félicien, his eyes fixed on the top of the stairs, between the two marble vases from which streamed the dazzling river of the crowd, waited.

Of the radiant faces, the gowns, the flowers on the girls' brows, the ermine capes, the splendid flood of people flowing past him under the lights, he saw nothing.

And the whole of that concourse soon melted away, little by little, without the young woman appearing.

Had he let her escape without recognizing her? No, that was impossible. An old footman in a powdered wig, covered in furs, was still standing in the foyer. On the buttons of his black livery shone the parsley leaves of a ducal coronet.

All of a sudden, at the top of the deserted staircase, *she* appeared! Alone! A slim figure in a velvet cloak, with her hair hidden beneath a lace mantilla, she rested her gloved hand on the marble banister. She noticed Félicien standing beside a statue, but did not appear to pay any further attention to his presence.

She came slowly down the stairs. The footman went up to her and she said a few words to him in a low voice. He bowed and promptly made off. The next moment a carriage could be heard driving away. Then she came out. Still alone, she went down the outer stairs of the theatre. Félicien scarcely took the time to tell his valet:

'Go back to the hotel by yourself.'

A moment later he was in the Place des Italiens, a few paces away from the lady; the crowd had already disappeared down the surrounding streets; the distant echo of the carriages was growing fainter.

It was a crisp, starry October night.

The unknown woman was walking along very slowly as if unaccustomed to being on foot. Should he follow her? He decided that there was nothing else he could do. The autumn wind brought him the faint amber perfume which came from her, and the long-drawn rustling of the silk on the asphalt.

At the corner of the Rue Monsigny she paused for a second to take her bearings, and then walked on, as if it were a matter of indifference to her, as far as the deserted and dimly lit Rue de Grammont.

Suddenly the young man stopped; a thought occurred to him. Perhaps she was a foreigner!

A carriage might pass by and carry her off for ever! He would pace the city streets without ever finding her again!

To be parted from her for ever by the accident of a street, of a moment which might last all eternity! What a horrifying prospect! This thought so disturbed him that he cast aside all considerations of propriety.

Passing the young woman at the corner of the dark street, he turned round, went horribly pale, and, leaning against the iron pillar of a street lamp, he bowed to her. Then with a sort of magnetic charm emanating from his whole person, he said very simply:

'Madame, you know that I saw you this evening for the first time. As I am afraid that I might never see you again, I must tell you . . .' – here he nearly fainted – '. . . that *I love you*!' he concluded in a low voice, 'and that if you pass me by I shall die without saying those words to anybody else.'

She stopped, raised her veil, and gazed intently at Félicien.

'Monsieur,' she replied after a brief silence, in a voice whose purity revealed the remotest intentions of the mind, 'Monsieur, the feeling responsible for your pallor and your bearing must indeed go deep, for you to regard it as sufficient justification for what you are doing. Consequently I do not feel at all offended. Pull yourself together, regard me as a friend.'

Félicien was not surprised at this reply; it seemed natural to him that his ideal should give him an ideal answer.

The situation was one, in fact, in which both had occasion

to remember, if they were worthy of it, that they were among those who make the proprieties and not those who observe them. For what the common herd calls the proprieties is only a mechanical, servile, and almost ape-like imitation of what has been vaguely practised by creatures of a lofty nature in ordinary circumstances.

In a transport of ingenuous affection, he kissed the hand she offered him.

'Will you give me the flower you have been wearing in your hair all evening?'

The unknown woman silently removed the pale flower from under the lace and gave it to Félicien.

'Goodbye now,' she said, 'and for ever.'

'Goodbye?' he stammered. 'Then you don't love me? . . . Oh, you are married!' he exclaimed suddenly.

'No.'

'You are free! Oh, heavens!'

'Forget me, all the same! You must, Monsieur.'

'But in one moment you have become my very heartbeat! How can I live without you? The only air I want to breathe is yours! I don't understand what you mean. Forget you; how can I?'

'A terrible misfortune has overtaken me. It would be useless to tell you about it, for it would make you mortally unhappy.'

'What misfortune can separate those who love each other?'

'This one.'

Saying this, she closed her eyes.

The street stretched away into the distance, absolutely deserted. A gateway leading into a little enclosure, a sort of melancholy garden, was wide open beside them. It seemed to be offering them its shade.

Félicien, like an irresistible, adoring child, drew her beneath this dark archway, putting his arm round a waist which accepted his embrace.

The intoxicating feeling of the warm, firm silk moulding her body filled him with a feverish longing to clasp her in his arms, to carry her off, to lose himself in her kiss. He resisted. But giddiness robbed him of the power of speech. He summoned up only these indistinct, stammered words:

'Heavens, how I love you!'

Then the woman laid her head against the breast of the man who loved her, and said in a voice of bitter despair:

'I cannot hear you! I could die of shame! I cannot hear you! I would not be able to hear your name! I would not be able to hear your dying breath! I cannot hear the beat of your heart which I can feel against my forehead and my eyelids! Can't you see the horrible suffering which is killing me? . . . I am . . . oh! . . . I am *deaf*.'

'Deaf?' exclaimed Félicien, overwhelmed with amazement and trembling from head to foot.

'Yes, for years past. And all the medical skill in the world is incapable of awakening me from this horrible silence. I am as deaf as the sky and the tomb, Monsieur. It is terrible, but it is the truth. So leave me.'

'Deaf?' repeated Félicien, whom this unimaginable revelation had left distracted, thunderstruck, unable even to think of what he was saying. 'Deaf?'

Then, all of a sudden, he exclaimed:

'But this evening, at the Italian Opera, you applauded the music!'

He stopped, realizing that she could not hear him. The thing suddenly became so horrifying that it brought a smile to his lips.

'At the Italian Opera?' she replied, smiling herself. 'You

forget that I have had time to study the external appearance of a good many emotions. Am I the only one? We belong to the station in life which fate allots to us, and it is our duty to live up to it. That noble woman who was singing surely deserved some supreme tokens of admiration? Besides, do you think that my applause was very different from that of the most enthusiastic *dilettanti*? I was a musician in the old days!'

At these words Félicien looked at her, rather bewildered and still trying to smile.

'Oh!' he said, 'are you making fun of a heart which loves you to desperation? You say that you cannot hear and yet you answer me!'

'Alas,' she said, 'the trouble is that you think that what you are saying is peculiar to you, my dear friend. You are sincere, but your words are new only for you. For me you are reciting a dialogue of which I have learnt all the answers in advance. For years now, it has always been the same for me. It is a part in which all the phrases are dictated and enforced with truly dreadful precision. I know it so well that if I agreed to commit the crime of joining my distress, even for a few days, to your destiny, you would find yourself constantly forgetting the baneful confession I have just made to you. I can assure you that I should take you in completely, neither more nor less than any other woman. I should even be incomparably more real than reality. Remember that circumstances always dictate the same words and that the features always match them to some extent! I should guess so accurately that you would find it impossible to believe that I could not hear you. Let us think no more about it.'

This time he felt frightened.

'Oh!' he said, 'what bitter words you are entitled to utter! . . . But if that is how things stand, I want to share with you, even eternal silence if need be. Why do you want to shut me out from that misfortune? I would have shared your happiness! And our souls can make good the deficiencies of all that exists.'

The young woman started, and she looked at him with shining eyes.

'Will you give me your arm and walk a little way along this dark street?' she said. 'We will imagine that it is a walk full of trees, spring, and sunshine. I too have something to tell you which I will never say again.'

The two lovers, their hearts in the grip of a mortal sadness, walked along, hand in hand, like a pair of exiles.

'Listen to me,' she said, 'you who can hear the sound of my voice. Do you know why I felt that you did not offend me? And why I answered you? . . . Admittedly it is only natural that I should have acquired the ability to read, in a man's features and attitudes, the feelings which determine his actions; but it is quite another matter that I should sense, with an equally profound and as it were infinite precision, the value and quality of those feelings as well as their intimate harmony in the person speaking to me. When you took it upon yourself, just now, to commit that appalling breach of manners, I was perhaps the only woman in the world who could understand, at that very moment, its real significance.

'I answered you because it seemed to me that I could see shining on your brow that mysterious sign which reveals those whose thought, far from being obscured, dominated, and gagged by their passions, enhances and deifies all the emotions of life and brings out the ideal contained in all the feelings they experience. My dear friend, let me tell you my secret. The fate, at first so hard to bear, which has afflicted my physical being, has become for me a liberation from countless tyrannies. It has freed me from that intellectual deafness of which most other women are victims.

'It has made my soul sensitive to the vibrations of the eternal things of which creatures of my sex usually know only the travesties. Their ears are closed to those wonderful echoes, those sublime reverberations. So that the keenness of their hearing affords them nothing but the ability to perceive just what is instinctive and external in the purest and most delicate pleasures. They are the Hesperides, guardians of those enchanted fruits of whose magic value they are forever ignorant! I, alas, am deaf ... but what of them? What do they hear? Or rather, what do they listen to among the words addressed to them, apart from the confused noise which matches the facial expressions of the person speaking to them? So that heedless, not of the apparent meaning of each word, but of its profound, revealing *quality*, of its *true* meaning, in fact, they are content to see a flattering intention in it which is ample for them. It is what they call "real life" with one of those smiles ... Oh, you'll see, if you go on living! You'll see what mysterious oceans of innocence, conceit, and base frivolity are hidden beneath that delicious smile! Just try to convey to one of those women the depths of dark, divine, captivating love, strewn with stars like Night itself, which creatures of your nature experience! If your expressions filter as far as her brain, they will be distorted in it, like a pure spring passing through a swamp. So that in reality that woman *will not have heard them.* "Life is incapable of fulfilling those dreams," they say, "and you ask too much of it." As if life were not made by the living!'

'Oh, God!' murmured Félicien.

'Yes,' his unknown companion went on, 'a woman cannot escape from that natural condition, intellectual deafness, except perhaps by paying an inestimable price, as I have done. You imagine that women have a secret, because they express themselves only through actions. Priding themselves on this secret, which they do not know themselves, they enjoy giving the impression that it is possible to discover it. And many a man, flattered by the thought that he is the long-awaited discoverer, ruins his life by marrying a stone sphinx. Not one of them can rise *beforehand* to the thought that if a secret, however terrible it may be, is *never* revealed, it might as well not exist.'

The unknown woman broke off.

'I am in a bitter mood this evening,' she went on. 'This is why: I no longer envied those women what they possess, having seen the use which they make of it – and which I would probably have made of it myself! But here you are, you, whom I would have loved so much in the past! . . . I can see you . . . I can understand you . . . I can recognize your soul in your eyes . . . you offer it to me, *and I cannot take it from you*!'

The young woman buried her head in her hands.

'Oh!' replied Félicien in a low voice, with tears in his eyes. 'I can at least embrace your soul in the breath of your lips! Understand me! Let yourself live! You are so beautiful! The silence of our love will make it more sublime and ineffable, and my passion will be enhanced by all your suffering, all our melancholy . . . Dear creature, married to me for ever, come and let us live together.'

She gazed at him with eyes which were also bathed in tears, and, putting her hand on the arm encircling her, she said:

'You are going to tell me yourself that it is impossible! Listen! I want to finish explaining myself, now, for you will never hear me again . . . and I do not want to be forgotten.'

She spoke slowly and walked along with her head resting against the young man's shoulder.

'Live together, you say . . . You forget that after the first raptures, life takes on an intimate character in which the need to express oneself precisely becomes inevitable. That is a solemn moment! And it is the cruel moment when those who have married without paying heed to their words receive the irreparable punishment for giving so little attention to the *quality* of the real, indeed, unique, meaning which those words acquired from those who uttered them. "We have no illusions left," they tell each other, thinking that they can thus conceal, behind a trivial smile, the painful contempt which they really feel for their sort of love – and the despair it causes them to admit it to themselves.

'For they are unwilling to acknowledge that they possess only what they wanted to possess! They find it impossible to believe that – apart from Thought, which transfigures all things – everything in this world is illusory. And that every passion, accepted and conceived in sensuality alone, soon becomes more bitter than death for those who have given themselves up to it. Look passers-by in the face, and you will see if I am mistaken. But tomorrow, when that moment came for us . . . I should have your gaze, but not your voice! I should have your smile, but not your words! And I can tell that you do not talk like other people.

'Your simple, primitive soul must express itself with a well-nigh absolute vigour. And so the gradations of your feelings cannot be revealed except in the very music of your words. I would be aware, of course, that you are permeated with my image, but the form which you give me in your thoughts, the way in which you picture me, and which can be expressed only in a few words chosen every day – that form without precise lines and which, thanks to those same divine words, remains vague and tends to melt into the Light and pass into that infinity which each of us carries in his heart – that one and only reality, in fact, is something I shall never know! No!

To think that I should be condemned never to hear that ineffable music, hidden in a lover's voice, that murmur full of marvellous inflexions, which envelops a woman and makes her turn pale! Oh, he who wrote on the first page of a sublime symphony: "This is how Fate knocks at the door" had known the voices of musical instruments before suffering the same affliction as I.

'He remembered them as he composed! But how am I to remember the voice with which you have just said to me for the first time: "I love you"?'

Listening to these words the young man had become downcast; what he felt was sheer terror.

'Oh!' he cried. 'But you are opening up in my heart abysses of anger and misery! I stand on the threshold of paradise and I have to close the door of happiness on myself! Are you the supreme temptress? It seems to me that I can see shining in your eyes a kind of pride at having filled me with despair.'

'Come, now!' she replied. 'I am the woman who will not forget you! How can one forget words one has guessed at but not heard?'

'Alas, Madame, you are wantonly killing all the youthful hopes I had placed in you? But if you will live with me, we will conquer the future together! Let us love one another bravely! Come to me!'

With an unexpected feminine gesture, she gently pressed her lips against his, in the darkness, for a few seconds. Then she said to him with a sort of weariness:

'My dear friend, I tell you that it is impossible. There are melancholy hours when, irritated by my infirmity, you would seek the opportunity to make it more obvious. You would not be able to forget that I cannot hear you ... nor to forgive me for it, I assure you. You would be led, inevitably, *to stop speaking to me*, to stop pronouncing a single syllable in my presence! Your lips alone would tell me: "I love you", but the vibration of your voice would not disturb the silence. You would even be reduced to writing to me, which would hurt me. No, it is impossible! I refuse to spoil my life for a half of love. Although I am a virgin, I am the widow of a dream, and I want to remain unsatisfied. I tell you, I cannot take your soul in exchange for mine. Yet you were the man destined to possess my being! . . . And it is for that very reason that it is my duty to deny you my body. I am taking it away. It is my prison! May I be liberated from it before long! I do not want to know your name . . . *I do not want to read it!* . . . Farewell! . . . Farewell! . . .'

A gleaming carriage stood a few yards away, at the corner of the Rue de Grammont. Félicien vaguely recognized the lackey he had seen under the peristyle of the Italian Opera when, at a sign from the young woman, a manservant lowered the carriage's folding steps.

She let go of Félicien's arm, darted away like a bird, and got into the carriage. The next moment everything had vanished.

Monsieur le Comte de la Vierge set off again the following day for his lonely Château de Blanchelande . . . and he has never been heard of since.

Admittedly he could pride himself on having met, straight away, a forthright woman *who had the courage of her convictions.*

J. K. HUYSMANS

# THE FOLIES-BERGÈRE

1880

From

# PARIS SKETCHES

Translated by Brendan King

# I

AFTER YOU'VE ENDURED the shouts of programme-sellers and the solicitations of boot-blacks offering to polish your shoes, after you've passed through the ticket-barrier where, standing amid a group of seated gentlemen and assisted by a chain-wearing usher, a young man sporting a ginger moustache, a wooden leg and a red ribbon takes your ticket, the stage curtain finally comes into view, cut across the middle by the ceiling-like mass of the balcony. You can see the lower part of the cloth, and, in front of it, the two grilled eyes of the prompt-boxes and the horse-shoe of an orchestra pit full of heads, an uneven and shifting field where, against the dull gleam of bald heads and the glossy pomaded hair of the men, the hats of the women stand out, their feathers and their flowers sprouting in profusion on all sides.

A great hubbub rises from the gathering crowd. A warm haze, mingled with exhalations of every kind and saturated with the acrid dust that comes from carpets and chairs when you beat them, envelops the hall. The smell of cigars and women becomes more noticeable; gas lamps, reflected from one end of the theatre to the other by mirrors, burn more dimly; it is only with difficulty that you can move about, and only with difficulty that you can make out, through the dense ranks of bodies, an acrobat on stage who is methodically devoting himself to some gymnastic exercises on the fixed bar.

For a moment, through a gap formed by two shoulders

and two heads, you catch a glimpse of him, bent double, his feet braced and clamped to the bar, accelerating in a circular motion, turning furiously until he loses human form, spitting out sparks like those catherine wheels that whirl round, fizzing, in a shower of gold; then, little by little, the music which has been spinning round with him slows its spiralling pace and, little by little, the form of the acrobat reappears, his pink, gold-braided tights, shaking less energetically now, sparkle only here and there, and then, back on his feet, the man waves to the crowd with both hands.

## II

*For Ludovic de Francmesnil*

THEN, AS YOU ascend to the upper gallery of the hall, amid women whose long trains rustle as they snake up the steps, climbing a staircase where the sight of a plaster statue holding a gas-lit torch in its hand immediately reminds you of the entrance of a brothel, the music engulfs you in your turn, feebly at first, then loudly and more distinctly at the next turn of the stairs. A blast of hot air hits you in the face and there, on the landing, you see the opposite sight to that downstairs, a completely reversed image, the curtain falling from the top of the proscenium, cut in the middle by the red ledge of the open boxes curving in half-moons round the balcony suspended a few feet beneath them.

An usherette, her pink ribbons fluttering over a white bonnet, offers you a programme which is a marvel of an art-form that is at once both spiritualist and positivist: phoney Indian cartomancers, a lady who calls herself a palmist and a graphologist, a hypnotist, clairvoyants, soothsayers who tell fortunes using coffee grounds, pianos and ocarinas for hire, job lots of maudlin music for sale, all this for the soul; advertisements for sweets, for corsets and suspenders, radical cures for intimate afflictions, a unique treatment for diseases of the mouth, all this for the body. Only one thing disconcerts: an advert for a sewing machine. It's easy to understand why there's one for a fencing-school, there are a lot of stupid men about! But the 'Silent Wonder' and the 'Singer' aren't tools you ordinarily associate with the working girls who come here; unless this advert was placed here as a symbol of respectability, as an inducement to chaste labours. It is perhaps, under a different form, one of those moral tracts that the English distribute to lead creatures of vice back to virtue.

Imagination is decidedly a very good thing: it allows you to credit people with ideas even more stupid than those they undoubtedly already have.

## III

*For Léon Hennique*

THEY ARE OUTRAGEOUS and they are magnificent as they march two by two round the semicircular floor of the auditorium, powdered and painted, eyes drowned in a smudge of pale blue, lips ringed in startling red, their breasts thrust out over laced corsets, exuding waves of opoponax which they disperse by fanning, and which mingles with the strong aroma of their underarms and the subtle scent of a flower expiring on their bust.

You watch, entranced, as this gaggle of whores passes rhythmically by, against a dull red backdrop broken only by windows, like wooden merry-go-round horses that twirl in slow-motion to the sound of an organ around a bit of scarlet curtain embellished with mirrors and lamps; you watch their thighs churn under dresses the bottoms of which are edged by white petticoats that flounce, like eddies of foam, under the hem of the material. You gasp as you follow the skill with which these women's backs slide between the bellies of men who, coming in the opposite direction, open and close again around them, revealing a glimpse, through the gaps between the men's heads, of the backs of their chignons, lit on each side by the golden gleam of a piece of jewellery, by the flash of a gemstone.

Then you tire of this interminable round, ceaselessly trodden by the same women, and your ears prick up at the clamour rising from the hall saluting the entrance of the conductor, a tall, thin man known for his revolutionary polkas and for his waltzes. A salvo of applause comes from the promenades above and below the boxes in which suspicious glimpses of white female flesh can be seen amid the shadows. The maestro bows, raises his head with its bristle-brush hair, its greying Chinaman moustache and nose complete with pince-nez, and then, his back turned to the stage, he starts to conduct in his black tails and white tie, calmly stirring the music as if bored or overcome by sleep. Then, all of a sudden, turning towards the brass section, he holds out his baton like a fishing-rod, 'playing' the refrain for all it's worth, extracting the notes with a firm gesture as if pulling out teeth, beating the air up and down, pumping out the end of the melody as one pumps on a beer-pull.

# IV

*For Paul Daniel*

THIS SCRAP OF music finished, a silence follows and then the clash of a gong reverberates. The curtain rises: the stage is still deserted, but men dressed in grey cotton overalls with red cuffs and collars, are running to all corners of the house, pulling ropes, undoing clamps, adjusting knots. The confusion continues, two or three men rush about on stage, while a superior keeps an eye on them. They ready themselves to stretch an immense net across the middle of the stage and above the orchestra. The net sways, frees itself from the edge of the balcony where it was rolled up, then, running on rings of copper, it jingles like the sea playing with pebbles.

Applause crackles around the hall. The orchestra grinds out a circus waltz; a man and a woman enter wearing flesh-coloured tights, gorgets and Japanese-style shorts, indigo and turquoise blue with silver spangles and fringes. The woman is English, with over-the-top make-up beneath her yellow hair, and an ample behind projecting over her robust thighs; the man is slimmer by comparison, his hair well-groomed, his moustaches curled. The fixed smile of the barber's revolving dummy plays over their scrubbed, Herculean faces. The man leaps onto a rope, hoists himself up to a trapeze that hangs in front of the curtain between two chandeliers, amid the cables and yards up in the roof, and then, sitting on a bar which presses against the flesh of his thighs, he rapidly executes a few manoeuvres, wiping his hands from time to time on a handkerchief attached to one of the cords.

Next, the woman climbs up onto the net, which sags under her weight, and walks across it from one end to the other, bouncing at each step as if on a trampoline, her sulphur-coloured pigtails dancing against her neck in the light. Then, after having climbed onto a small platform suspended over the balcony opposite the man, separated from her by the length of the hall, she waits. All eyes are fixed on her.

Two beams of electric light projected onto her back from the depths of the Folies envelop her, refracting off the curve of her hips, splashing her from neck to feet, gouache-ing her so to speak, with a silver outline; then, dividing, they pass separately through the chandeliers, almost invisible as they move, reuniting and spreading out when they reach the man on the trapeze in a fan of bluish light that illuminates the fringes of his mica trunks, sparkling like grains of sugar.

The waltz continues more slowly in gentle, hammock-like undulations, its almost imperceptible cradle-like swaying accompanying the soft rhythm of the trapeze and the double shadow of the man projected onto the top of the curtain by the two beams of electric light.

Leaning forward a little, the woman also grabs a trapeze with one hand and restrains herself by a rope held in the other. In the meantime, the man topples over, remaining suspended by his feet on the bar of his trapeze, motionless, upside down, his arms stretched out.

Then, the waltz stops dead. An ominous silence descends, broken suddenly by an explosion from a champagne bottle. A shiver runs through the audience, an 'All right!' resounds around the hall. The woman hurls herself through the air, flies beneath the light of the chandeliers, then, letting go of the trapeze, she falls, feet foremost, into the arms of the man, who to the shattering crash of a cymbal and to the increasingly triumphant and joyful reprise of the waltz swings her for a moment by the feet, then throws her into the net where, with her silver and azure-blue tights, she rebounds like a fish twisting and jumping in a cast-net.

The sound of stamping feet, clapping hands and canes being struck on the floorboards accompanies the acrobats' descent. As they disappear behind a piece of scenery, the shouting becomes even more tumultuous; the man and woman reappear, one bowing very low, the other blowing kisses with both hands, then, with a little, childish jump, they retire once again into the wings.

As the net is gathered up again, the hall is once more filled with the sound of breaking waves.

And then suddenly, I'm thinking of Antwerp, of the great port where, amid a similar rolling sound, you hear the 'All right!' of English sailors about to put to sea. And yet it's in this way that the most disparate places and things come together, through an analogy that seems bizarre at first sight. You evoke in the place you happen to be, the pleasures of the place you are not. This topsy-turvy fact cuts both ways. Like when a fleeting pleasure inspired by the present is diverted just as it's fading and coming to an end, and is renewed and prolonged in another which, seen through the eye of memory, becomes at one and the same time both sweeter and more real.

## V

THE BALLET BEGINS. The scenery vaguely suggests the inside of a seraglio, full of hooded women who waddle about like she-bears. A fancy-dress Ottoman, head wrapped in a turban and mouth furnished with a chibouk, cracks his whip. The hoods fall away, revealing dancing girls, enlisted from the depths of some suburb, who start to skip around to common dance-hall music, enlivened from time to time by the tune of 'Old Bugeaud's Cap', no doubt introduced into this mazurka to justify the arrival of a bevy of women dressed like spahis.

It's at this moment, under the streams of electric light that flood the stage, that a whirlpool of white tulle appears, spattered with blue fire and with naked flesh writhing at the centre; then the *première danseuse*, recognizable by her silk leggings, does a little point work on her toes, shakes the false sequins that surround her like a ring of golden dots, leaps up and collapses into her skirts, simulating a fallen flower, petals on the ground and stalk in the air.

But all this bank-holiday orientalism bursting like a loud *grand finale* cannot distract the connoisseur, who, out of all these great lumps of women rhythmically shaking themselves silly, is interested only in one, the one dressed as a spahi officer, with her large, billowing blue pantaloons, her dainty red boots, her gold-braided spencer, and her little scarlet waistcoat, skin-tight, moulding her breasts and showing off their erect tips. She dances like a goat, but she is adorable and common, with her braided kepi, her wasp waist, her large backside, her retroussé nose, and her look of a pleasantly roguish tom-boy. Such as she is, this girl evokes images of barricades and torn-up streets, exhales a whiff of *trois-six* and gunpowder, calls to mind the epic poem of an armed rabble, the bombast of civil war mixed with drunken debaucheries.

In front of her, you inevitably think of those over-excited periods in our history, of those uprisings in which Marianne of Belleville charges off to save a nation or to stave in a wine-barrel.

# VI

A CEMETERY BACKDROP; to the right, a tombstone with this inscription: *Here lies . . . killed in a duel.* Night time; some muted music; nobody.

Suddenly, from behind scenery 'flats' on the left and right of the stage, two pierrots in black costumes advance slowly, followed by their seconds: the first, tall, thin, recalling the type created by Deburau, a long horse's head, flour-covered, eyes blinking beneath white lids; the other more thick-set, stockier, with a stub nose, his sarcastic, cadaverous face split by the red hole of his mouth.

The impression produced by the entrance of these men is chilling and noble. The comedy drawn from the juxtaposition of their black bodies and plaster faces disappears; this is no longer some sordid theatrical illusion. Life itself rises up before us, breathless and magnificent.

The pierrots read the inscription on the tombstone and step back a pace; trembling, they turn their heads and see a doctor about to unroll some bandages and calmly arranging his medical bag.

The anguish of a face in the process of a breakdown passes over their pale countenances; fear, that terrible nervous sickness, nails them quivering to the spot.

After being placed face to face, one opposite the other, the sight of epées being drawn from serge cloth covers scares them even more. The trembling of their hands increases, their legs wobble, their throats choke, their mouths work in silence, saliva-less tongues beat, searching for breath, their fingers wander and clutch at the cravats they should be untying.

Then their fear increases still more and becomes so imperious and so terrible, that their already rebellious nerves suddenly break down and they go to pieces, no one can hold them. A single idea surges up in their disordered minds, to take flight, and they rush off, knocking over everything; but they are pursued and brought back by the seconds who place them face to face again, epées in hand.

Then, after one final revolt of the flesh which rises up against the carnage awaiting it, the energy of cornered beasts comes to them and they throw themselves, madly, one onto the other, striking and stabbing at random, roused by incredible leaps, unconscious, blinded and deafened by the flashing and chinking of steel, and then suddenly falling, exhausted, like puppets whose strings have broken.

Finishing in a lavish farce, in a disorganized charge, this cruel study of the human machine in the grip of fear has convulsed the hall with guffaws. From a close study of this laughter, it seems to me that the public saw nothing in this admirable pantomime but a parade of grotesques, intended, no doubt, to complete the appearance of a fairground which the Folies-Bergère assumes in those corners in which it sets up gambling wheels, games of *boule*, bearded women and shooting galleries.

For more reflective and more alert minds, though, it's another matter. The whole aesthetics of the English school of caricature is once again brought into play in the scenarios of these side-splitting, yet funereal clowns, the Hanlon-Lees. Their pantomime, so true in its frigid mania, so ferociously comical in its exaggeration, is nothing less than a new and charming incarnation of that lugubrious farce, that sinister buffoonery so unique to that splenetic country, and which has previously been expressed and condensed by those marvellous and forceful artists, Hogarth and Rowlandson, Gillray and Cruikshank.

# VII

AS FAR AS the Folies is concerned, there are two indispensable and delightful types of waltz: one twirling and joyous, expressing the poise of the trapeze, the amazing somersaults of the acrobats, the rhythm of a body that raises and lowers itself by the strength of its own arms, sways, held only by its legs, then up again, head brushing past stomach and abdomen, the arms taking the place of feet which beat the air with their chalk-dusted shoes; the other morbidly voluptuous, displaying the bloodshot eyes and trembling hands of those caught *in flagrante delicto*, of passions stalled by the presence of a third, of debaucheries aborted in full flow for lack of stamina, of bodies contorted and expectant, ending at last with the triumphant crash of cymbals and brasses in the cry of pain and joy of the climax.

It would be meaningless to play, say, *Robert le Diable* in this hall. It would jar like the face of a respectable old man engaged in an illicit *tête-à-tête.* Here, one must have rotten, uncouth music, something that envelops with vulgar caresses, with street kisses, with twenty-franc assignations, the chatter of those who have dined copiously and expensively, people tired of stewing over their murky business affairs, dragging into this theatre promenade their worries about scams that might turn out badly, uneasy about their dubious dealings in shares and in women, but cheered by the high spirits of fraudsters whose tricks have come off and who get tipsy with painted women to the sound of loutish music.

# VIII

WHAT IS TRULY admirable, truly unique, is that this theatre has a real air of the boulevards about it.

It is ugly and it is superb, it is in both exquisitely good and outrageously bad taste. It's also unfinished, like anything that aims to be truly beautiful. The *faux jardin*, with its raised walkways, its arcades of rough wooden latticework with solid lozenges and cut-out trefoils stained red ochre and gold, its canopy of pompommed and tasselled material, striped garnet-red and greyish-brown, its fake Louvois fountains with three women back-to-back sandwiched between two enormous saucers of imitation bronze set amid green tufts, its pathways carpeted with tables, rattan divans and chairs, with bars tended by amply made-up women, resembles at one and the same time the restaurant on the Rue Montesquieu and a Turkish or Algerian bazaar.

Alhambresque *à la* Poyet, Moorish *à la* Duval, with, what's more, the vague smell of those bar-saloons in the old suburbs decorated with oriental columns and mirrors, this theatre, with its auditorium whose faded reds and tarnished golds clash with the brand-new luxury of the *faux jardin*, is the only place in Paris that stinks so deliciously of the make-up of bought caresses and the desperation of depravities that fail to excite.

ALPHONSE ALLAIS

# THE POLYMYTH

*c.* 1890

Translated by Miles Kington

I FIRST SET eyes on him in a café in the Latin Quarter when he came in and sat down at the table next to me. And ordered six cups of coffee.

'Aha,' I thought to myself. 'This gentleman is about to be joined by five friends, if I am not much mistaken.'

I was much mistaken. As soon as the six cups of steaming Mocha had arrived he drank them all himself, one after the other. (Which is much the best way to do it, as you will know if you have ever tried to drink six cups of coffee simultaneously.) When he noticed my air of bafflement, he leant across to enlighten me.

'It's quite simple,' he said. (He spoke in a flat, down-at-heel sort of voice, as if he was talking with his shoe-laces undone.) 'The fact is, I am another Balzac. I, too, drink far too much coffee.'

Fascinated, I waited to see what he would do next. I didn't have to wait long. He called the waiter over and asked him to bring some writing paper. As soon as it came, he scribbled a few words on the first sheet, then crumpled it and threw it under the table. The same happened to the next. And the next. And the next and the next, until the floor was covered in screwed-up pieces of paper.

'You see,' he told me in the same flat voice, 'you see, I am another Flaubert. I find it almost impossible to get a sentence right.'

Such a distinguished man was obviously worth cultivating

and in order to find out more about him, I struck up a conversation. But when I happened to mention that I was a Norman from Honfleur, it brought a deep frown to his face.

'I am sorry to hear that. I am like Charlemagne; I despise the barbarians from the north.'

I hastily explained that we Normans had ceased being Norsemen many years ago, and he looked relieved at the news.

'Ah, I didn't know that. I know nothing about the north – as a matter of fact, I am another Puvis de Chavannes. I too grew up in Lyons.'

Where, it turned out, all his family had been in the meat trade. In fact, his father had insisted on his going into the business for a while.

'I am another Shakespeare. I too started out as a butcher's boy.'

Then he had moved to Paris, fallen in love and got married. He didn't tell me very much about his wife.

'Let's just say that I have much in common with the Emperor Napoleon I. We both married a woman called Josephine.'

Josephine, sad to say, had run off almost immediately with an Englishman, leaving my friend feeling somewhat hurt, not to say rather offended.

'Put it this way,' he put it. 'I am another Molière. I too had an unfaithful wife.'

Part of the trouble seems to have been that he and Josephine were not entirely compatible in some ways. She, apparently, liked very virile, very passionate men. Unfortunately . . .

'You see, I have something else in common with Napoleon. My . . .'

The rest of the sentence was carried away by a sudden gust

of wind. Being very anxious to learn more about a man with so many diverse talents, I was careful not to leave before I had arranged to meet him again, and we agreed to have lunch together soon, fixing our rendezvous for twelve midday precisely.

I arrived at one minute past twelve and found him tapping his watch impatiently.

'You may not have realized that I am another Louis XIV. I cannot bear to be kept waiting.'

He relented sufficiently over lunch to tell me in great detail about a serious eye infection he had been suffering from since I last saw him. Luckily the doctors had found a cure and now it had almost completely cleared up. Or as he put it, with a slight variation on the normal theme:

'I have no wish to be another Homer or Milton.'

The other news he had at this, our second meeting, was that he had managed to shake off the memory of Josephine by falling in love with another woman.

Alas, I heard some time later that she had not returned his feelings and had rejected all his overtures.

So he had shot her dead.

And they had arrested him for murder.

When he first came to court, he refused to answer any of the examining magistrate's questions.

'I am very sorry,' he told him. 'I am afraid I am another Louis XV. I do not recognize the authority of this court.'

Which did not prevent him, in due course, from coming up for trial.

I'm glad to say that this time he did speak up for himself.

'I wish to say in my defence that I am a second Attila the Hun. I am a law unto myself.'

The jury did not consider this to be an extenuating circumstance and passed sentence of death on him. The only thing that could have saved him then was a Presidential reprieve but, as usual, our head of state was surrounded by incompetent advisers and no Presidential reprieve was forthcoming.

Poor boy. I can still remember clearly the third and last time I saw him. He came through the prison gates at dawn like a pale Pierrot, with his hands tied behind his back, his feet bound and his shirt slashed at the top in a conveniently guillotine-shaped cut. I was standing among the onlookers, and he turned round and saw me.

He smiled then, and spoke the last words I ever heard him say in that flat voice which sounded as if he were talking with his shoe-laces undone.

'I am another Jesus Christ. We were both fated to die at the age of thirty-three.'

COLETTE

From

# CLAUDINE IN PARIS

1901

Translated by Antonia White

WELL, AFTER ALL, it's not so terrible going out alone in Paris. I brought back some very interesting observations from my little walk: (1) it's much warmer than in Montigny; (2) your nose is all black inside when you get home; (3) people stare at you if you stand still in front of a newspaper kiosk; (4) people also stare at you when you don't let yourself be disrespectfully treated on the pavement.

Let me narrate the incident that gave rise to observation (4). A very good-looking gentleman followed me in the Rue des Saints-Pères. During the first quarter of an hour, inner jubilation of Claudine. Followed by a very good-looking gentleman, just like in Albert Guillaume's pictures! Second quarter of an hour … the gentleman's step came closer; I hastened mine, but he kept his distance. Third quarter of an hour; the gentleman passed me, pinching my behind with a detached expression. A leap in the air from Claudine who raised her umbrella and brought it down on the gentleman's head with typical Fresnois vigour. Gentleman's hat in the gutter, immense delight of passers-by, disappearance of Claudine, overwhelmed by her too sensational success.

Aunt Coeur is very nice. She's sent me, with a friendly note, a necklace, a thin gold chain with little round pearls strung on it at intervals of ten centimetres. Fanchette thinks this piece of jewellery is charming; she has already flattened two of the links and she bites the pearls with her big teeth, like an expert in precious stones.

*

While I was getting ready for the Thursday dinner-party, I thought about my décolletage. It was very, very modest but suppose I was going to look too thin? Sitting in my tub, quite naked, I noticed that I had put on a little flesh, but I still needed to put on more. What luck that my neck had stayed round and firm! That saved me. It was a pity about the two little salt-cellars at the base, but they couldn't be helped! I wasted time in the hot water, counting the little bones in my back, measuring whether I was the same length from my groin to my feet as from my groin to my forehead, pinching my right calf because I could feel it in my left shoulder bladc. (At every pinch, a funny little sting behind one's shoulder.) And what sheer bliss to be able to hook my feet behind my neck! As that dirty great gangling Anaïs used to say: 'It must be frightfully amusing to be able to bite one's toenails!'

Good heavens, how tiny my breasts were! (At school, we called them bubs and Mélie says titties.) I thought of our 'Competitions' of three years ago, during our rare Thursday walks.

In a clearing of the wood, in a sunken path, we used to sit in a circle – we four big ones – and we used to open our bodices. Anaïs (what cheek!) used to display a morsel of lemon-coloured skin, swell out her stomach and say impudently: '*They've* come on like anything since last month!' Nothing of the sort! The Sahara desert! Luce, pink and white in her coarse schoolgirl chemise – long-sleeved chemises without so much as a scallop, that's the rule – uncovered a hardly discernible 'centre valley' and two small pink points like Fanchette's nipples. And Claudine? A little arched chest but about as much breasts as a slightly plump boy. Well, after all, at fourteen! The exhibition over, we fastened up our bodices again, each of us with the inner conviction that we had much more of *them* than the three others.

My white muslin dress, well-ironed by Mélie, still seemed attractive enough to me not to feel peevish when I put it on. My poor beautiful hair no longer cascaded over it right down to my hips, but it stood out so amusingly round my head that I didn't languish too much over my vanished mane, that night. Ten thousand herds of swine! – to use Papa's pet expression – at all costs, I mustn't forget my gold chain!

'Mélie, is Papa getting dressed?'

'He's getting dressed all right. Overdoing it, if you ask me. He's bust three stiff collars already. Run along and tie his tie.'

I hurried to do so. My noble father had got himself up in a slightly, in fact a *very*, old-fashioned evening suit, but it was impossible for him not to look imposing.

'Hurry up, hurry up, Papa, it's half-past seven. Mélie, you give Fanchette her dinner. My red cloak, and let's be off!'

The white drawing-room, with electric bulbs in all the corners, made me feel that, any moment, I might have an epileptic fit. Papa thinks as I do; he loathes this iced-cake décor so dear to his sister Wilhelmine and said so in no uncertain manner.

'Believe it or not, I'd have myself flogged in public rather than sleep inside this cream bun.'

But the pretty Marcel appeared and beautified everything with his presence. How charming he looked! Light and slim in a dinner-jacket, his hair moonlight fair, his translucent skin velvety under the lights like the inside of a convolvulus. While he was saying good evening to us, I noticed that his pale blue eyes were giving me a swift inspection.

Aunt Coeur followed him, dazzling. That dress of pearl-grey silk with flounces of black Chantilly lace, was its date

1867 or 1900? 1867, more likely, only a household-cavalryman must have sat on the crinoline and flattened it somewhat. The two grey bandeaux were very thick and very smooth; in the old days, she must have studied that pale blue gaze under the drooping, worn eyelids so thoroughly from the Comtesse de Téba that it had become second nature. She had a gliding walk, she wore sleeves set into deep armholes and she showed herself full of . . . urbanity. 'Urbanity' is a noun that suits her as well as her bandeaux.

No other guests beside ourselves. But, goodness me, how they dress up at Aunt Coeur's! At Montigny, I used to dine in my school pinafore and Papa used to keep on the indescribable garment – cloak, overcoat, coachman's cape, a mongrel product of all three – that he'd put on first thing in the morning to feed his slugs in. If one wears low necks for an intimate family meal, what on earth shall I put on for big dinner-parties? Perhaps my chemise with the pink ribbon shoulder straps . . .

(Claudine, old thing, enough of these digressions! You must try and eat correctly and not say, when you're handed a dish you don't like: 'Take it away, I think it's disgusting!')

Naturally, I was seated beside Marcel. Oh horror, oh misery! The dining-room was white too! White and yellow, but the effect was just as bad. And the crystal and the flowers and the electric light . . . it all made such a shindy on the table, you could positively *hear* it. Honestly, all those sparkles of light gave me an impression of noise.

Marcel, under Aunt Coeur's adoring eye, behaved like a society debutante and asked if I was enjoying myself in Paris. At first, a savage 'no' was all he got in reply. But soon I became a little more human, because I was eating a little patty with truffles that would have consoled a widow the day after her bereavement, so I condescended to explain myself.

'You see, I'm quite sure I shall enjoy myself later on. But, up to now, I find it terribly hard to get used to not seeing any leaves. Third floors in Paris don't exactly abound in green "tillers".'

'In green . . . *what*?'

'In "tillers". It's what we call them in Fresnois,' I added with a certain pride.

'Oh, it's a Fresnois word, is it? Rather unusual! Gr-r-reen tillers,' he repeated teasingly, rolling the *r*.

'I forbid you to mimic me! If you imagine it's more elegant, your Parisian *r* that you rumble in the depths of your throat as if you were gargling!'

'Ugh, you dirty little thing! Are your girl friends like you?'

'I didn't have any girl friends. I don't much care for having girl friends. Luce had a soft skin, but that isn't enough.'

'Luce had a soft skin . . . What a funny way of judging people!'

'Why funny? From the moral point of view, Luce simply doesn't exist. I'm considering her from the physical point of view and I tell you she has green eyes and a soft skin.'

'Did you love each other very much?'

(That pretty, vicious face! What wouldn't one say to him to see those eyes light up! Shame on you, you naughty little boy!)

'No, I didn't love her in the least. *She* did, yes. She cried like anything when I went away.'

'But, then, which one did you like better?'

My calmness emboldened Marcel. Perhaps he took me for a goose and would gladly have asked me more definite questions but the grown-ups stopped talking for a moment while a manservant with a clerical face changed the plates and we stopped, too. There was already a touch of complicity between us.

Aunt Coeur's tired blue gaze wandered from Marcel to myself.

'Claude,' she said to Papa, 'look how those two children set each other off. Your daughter's ivory skin and her hair with those bronze lights in it and her deep eyes – all that brunette look some little girls have who aren't really brunettes – make my cherub look fairer than ever. Don't you agree?'

'Yes,' replied Papa with conviction. 'He's much more of a girl than she is.'

Her cherub and I lowered our eyes as becomes children bursting at once with pride and with a desperate desire to giggle. And the dinner pursued its course without further confidences. Moreover, a delicious tangerine ice detached me from all other preoccupations.

I returned to the drawing-room on Marcel's arm. And all at once, no one seemed to know what to do. Aunt Coeur appeared to have some serious things to say to Papa and got rid of us.

'Marcel, my darling, go and show Claudine over the flat. Be nice – try and make her feel a little at home.'

'Come along,' said the 'darling', 'I'll take you to see my room.'

It was white, too, just as I had expected. White and green, with slender reeds on a white ground. But so much whiteness eventually aroused in me a secret desire to upset inkpots – heaps of inkpots – over it, to scribble in charcoal all over the walls, to dirty that distemper with blood from a cut finger ... Heavens, how perverse I'd become in an all-white flat!

I went straight to the chimneypiece on which I saw a photograph-frame. Excitedly, Marcel switched on an electric light just over our heads.

'That's my best friend ... Charlie ... Almost like a brother. Isn't he good-looking?'

Much too good-looking, in fact. Dark eyes, with curving lashes, the merest hint of a black moustache above a tender mouth, hair parted at the side, like Marcel's.

'I certainly agree he's handsome! Nearly as good-looking as you are,' I said sincerely.

'Oh, *much* better!' he exclaimed fervently. 'The photograph can't do justice to his white skin and his black hair. And he's such a charming *person* ...'

And so on and so on. That pretty Dresden china figure was coming to life at last. I listened, without flinching, to the panegyric of the magnificent Charlie and when Marcel, slightly embarrassed, regained his self-possession, I looked completely convinced and answered quite naturally: 'I understand perfectly. You're his Luce.'

He took a step backwards and, under the light, I saw his pretty features harden and his sensitive skin turn imperceptibly paler.

'His Luce? Claudine, what do you mean by that?'

With the boldness derived from two glasses of champagne, I shrugged my shoulders and said:

'But, of course. His Luce, his pet, his darling, whatever you call it! One's only got to look at you – do you *look* like a man? That's just why I found you so pretty!'

And as he stood there, perfectly still, staring at me almost icily, I went up closer to him and added, smiling right into his face:

'Marcel, I find you just as pretty at this very moment, believe me. Now, do I look like someone who wants to upset you? I tease you, but I'm not spiteful and there are lots of things I know perfectly well how to keep quiet about – and to listen to without telling anyone else. I shall never be the little female cousin whose unfortunate male cousin feels he's forced to make love to her as they do in books. May I remind you,' I went on, laughing, 'that you're the grandson of my aunt, what's called my "Breton nephew"? Marcel, it would be practically incest!'

My 'nephew' decided to laugh, but he didn't really want to.

'My dear Claudine, I quite agree that you're not like the little female cousins in "nice" novels. But I'm afraid that, at Montigny, you've got into the habit of making rather, well – risky – jokes. Suppose there'd been someone listening to us. Grandmother, for example – or your father . . .'

'I was only giving you tit for tat,' I said very sweetly. 'And I didn't think it necessary to attract the family's attention when you kept plying me with questions about Luce.'

'You had more to lose than I had, if you *had* attracted their attention!'

'Do you think so? I very much doubt it. In the case of girls, those little diversions are just called "schoolgirls' nonsense". But when it comes to boys of seventeen, it's almost a disease . . .'

He made a violent gesture with his hand.

'You read too much! Young girls have too much imagination to really understand what they read, even if they do come from Montigny.'

I'd managed things badly. That wasn't in the least what I was driving at.

'Have I made you angry, Marcel? I'm a clumsy idiot! All I wanted to do was to prove to you that I wasn't a goose, that I could understand – how can I put it? – *appreciate* certain things. Look, Marcel, you can't really expect me to see you as a great raw-boned schoolboy with enormous feet who'll turn into the perfect type of N.C.O. one day. Just look at yourself! Aren't you, thank heaven, almost exactly like the very prettiest of my schoolfriends? Give me your hand . . .'

He really ought to have been a girl! All he did was to smile furtively at my over-enthusiastic compliments. He held out his little manicured paw with quite a good grace.

'Claudine, you wicked Claudine, let's get back to them quickly. We'll go through Grandmother's bedroom. I'm not angry any more, only a little flabbergasted still. Let me think things over . . . It seems to me you aren't too bad a *boy* . . .'

His sarcasm didn't upset me a bit! To see him sulking and then smiling again, was pure pleasure. I didn't pity his friend with the sweeping eyelashes in the least and I wished them plenty of quarrels with my blessing.

Looking extremely natural – almost unnaturally natural – we continued the tour of the estate. What joy, Aunt Coeur's room was adequate (ghastly word!) to its owner! In it, she had assembled – or exiled – all the furniture that must have been in her room when she was a girl, all the souvenirs of her heyday. The carved rosewood bed, the red damask armchairs that all looked like Their Imperial Majesties' thrones, the tapestry prie-Dieu bristling with oak carvings, the flashy imitation of a Boule desk, console tables galore – they were all there. Damask curtains dripped from the canopy of the bed and the ornate chimneypiece, a shapeless, complicated mass of cupids and acanthus leaves and gilded bronze wreaths, filled me with admiration. Marcel had a supreme contempt for this room and we disputed hotly about the modern style and the merits of beaten egg-white in interior decoration. This aesthetic wrangle allowed us to return, in a calmer frame of mind, to the drawing-room where Papa was yawning like a lion in a cage under the gentle, relentless rain of Aunt Coeur's good advice.

'Grandmother!' cried Marcel, 'Claudine's priceless! She likes your bedroom better than all the rest of the flat.'

'Funny little girl,' said my aunt, caressing me with her languid smile. 'My room's very ugly, really . . .'

'. . . But it suits you, Aunt. Don't you think your bandeaux "clash" with this drawing-room? Thank goodness, you know that perfectly well, because you've kept one little corner of your proper setting!'

It wasn't exactly a compliment perhaps, but she got up and came over and kissed me very sweetly. Suddenly Papa leapt to his feet and consulted his watch.

'Ten thousand herds of . . .! Sorry, Wilhelmine, but it's five minutes to ten and it's the first time this child has been out since her illness . . . Young man, go and order us a cab!'

Marcel went out, and quickly returned, with that quick, supple way of swinging round as he went through a doorway, bringing me my red cloak that he dropped deftly on my shoulders.

'Goodbye, Aunt.'

'Goodbye, my child. I'm at home on Sundays. It would be too charming of you to come and hand round my tea at five o'clock with your friend Marcel.'

Inwardly, I curled up like a prickly hedgehog.

'I don't know how to, Aunt, I've never . . .'

'Now, now, I won't take no for an answer. I must make you into a little person who's as charming as she's pretty! Goodbye, Claude, don't shut yourself up too much in your lair – give a thought now and then to your old sister!'

At the front door, my 'nephew' kissed my wrist a little more lingeringly and accompanied his 'Till Sunday' with a knowing smile and a delicious pout and . . . that was that.

All the same, I'd been on the very verge of quarrelling with that boy! Claudine, old thing, will you never cure yourself of that itch to meddle in things that don't concern you, that rather despicable little wish to show that you're artful and knowledgeable and understand heaps of things beyond your age? This urge to astonish people, this craving to disturb people's peace of mind and upset too-placid lives will play you a nasty trick one of these days.

I felt much more at home, back in my own room, squatting on my four-poster bed and stroking Fanchette who had begun her night without waiting for me and lay there trustingly, with her stomach upturned. But – begging your pardon, Fanchette – I recognized those smiling slumbers, those blissful hours of perpetual purring. And I also recognized that filling-out of the flanks and that exceptionally well-licked belly along which the little pink nipples stood out. Fanchette, you had fallen from virtue! But with whom? Good heavens, it was like running one's head against a brick wall! A female cat who didn't go out-of-doors, the concierge's neutered tom ... who, who could it have been? All the same, I was simply delighted. Kittens in prospect! Compared with this joyous future, even the prestige of Marcel paled.

I asked Mélie for explanations of this mysterious pregnancy. She owned up to everything.

'My lamby, this last time the poor darling did want it so cruel. Three whole days, she was in such a state, she was quite beside herself. So I asked round among the neighbours. The maid downstairs lent me a lovely husband for her, a fine striped grey. I gave him lots of milk to encourage him and our poor darling didn't have to be asked twice ... they got together straight away.'

How she must have been pining, poor Mélie, to act as Cupid's messenger for someone, if only for the cat! She did absolutely right.

*

Our home has become a meeting-place for various odd people, each more astonishing and more scientific than the last. Monsieur Maria, the Cantal caves one, frequently comes along with that shy man's beard of his. When we meet in the book-lair, he bows awkwardly and makes stammering enquiries about my health, which I lugubriously assure him is 'very bad, very bad, Monsieur Maria'. I've made the acquaintance of various fat, untidy men with ribbons in their buttonholes whose lives are devoted, I understand, to the cultivation of fossils . . . Anything but exciting, Papa's friends!

LOUIS ARAGON

# THE PASSAGE DE L'OPÉRA

1926

From

# PARIS PEASANT

Translated by Simon Watson-Taylor

## 1924

MAN NO LONGER worships the gods on their heights. Solomon's temple has slid into a world of metaphor where it harbours swallows' nests and corpse-white lizards. The spirit of religions, coming down to dwell in the dust, has abandoned the sacred places. But there are other places which flourish among mankind, places where men go calmly about their mysterious lives and in which a profound religion is very gradually taking shape. These sites are not yet inhabited by a divinity. It is forming there, a new godhead precipitating in these re-creations of Ephesus like acid-gnawed metal at the bottom of a glass.

Life itself has summoned into being this poetic deity which thousands will pass blindly by, but which suddenly becomes palpable and terribly haunting for those who have at last caught a confused glimpse of it. It is you, metaphysical entity of places, who lull children to sleep, it is you who people their dreams. These shores of the unknown, sands shivering with anguish or anticipation, are fringed by the very substance of our minds. A single step into the past is enough for me to rediscover this sensation of strangeness which filled me when I was still a creature of pure wonder, in a setting where I first became aware of the presence of a coherence for which I could not account but which sent its roots into my heart.

The whole fauna of human fantasies, their marine vegetation, drifts and luxuriates in the dimly lit zones of human activity, as though plaiting thick tresses of darkness. Here, too, appear the great lighthouses of the mind, with their outward resemblance to less pure symbols. The gateway to mystery swings open at the touch of human weakness and we have entered the realms of darkness. One false step, one slurred syllable together reveal a man's thoughts. The disquieting atmosphere of places contains similar locks which cannot be bolted fast against infinity. Wherever the living pursue particularly ambiguous activities, the inanimate may sometimes assume the reflection of their most secret motives: and thus our cities are peopled with unrecognized sphinxes which will never stop the passing dreamer and ask him mortal questions unless he first projects his meditation, his absence of mind, towards them. But if this wise man has the power to guess their secret, and interrogates them in his turn, all that these faceless monsters will grant is that he shall once again plumb his own depths. Henceforth, it is the modern light radiating from the unusual that will rivet his attention.

How oddly this light suffuses the covered arcades which abound in Paris in the vicinity of the main boulevards and which are rather disturbingly named *passages*, as though no one had the right to linger for more than an instant in those sunless corridors. A glaucous gleam, seemingly filtered through deep water, with the special quality of pale brilliance of a leg suddenly revealed under a lifted skirt. The great American passion for city planning, imported into Paris by a prefect of police during the Second Empire and now being applied to the task of redrawing the map of our capital in straight lines, will soon spell the doom of these human aquariums. Although the life that originally quickened them has drained away, they deserve, nevertheless, to be regarded as the secret repositories of several modern myths: it is only today, when the pickaxe menaces them, that they have at last become the true sanctuaries of a cult of the ephemeral, the ghostly landscape of damnable pleasures and professions. Places that were incomprehensible yesterday, and that tomorrow will never know.

'Today, the Boulevard Haussmann has reached the Rue Lafitte,' remarked *L'Intransigeant* the other day. A few more paces forward by this giant rodent and, after it has devoured the block of houses separating it from the Rue Le Peletier, it will inexorably gash open the thicket whose twin arcades run through the Passage de l'Opéra, before finally emerging diagonally on to the Boulevard des Italiens. It will unite itself to that broad avenue somewhere near where the Café Louis XVI now stands, with a singular kind of kiss whose cumulative effect on the vast body of Paris is quite unpredictable. It seems possible, though, that a good part of the human river which carries incredible floods of dreamers and dawdlers from the Bastille to the Madeleine may divert itself through this new channel, and thus modify the ways of thought of a whole district, perhaps of a whole world. We are doubtless about to witness a complete upheaval of the established fashions in casual strolling and prostitution, and it may well be that this thoroughfare, which is bound to make the boulevards and the Quartier Saint-Lazare far more easily accessible to each other, will see entirely new types of person saunter along its pavements, hitherto unknown specimens whose whole lives will hesitate between the two zones of attraction in which they are equally involved, and who will be the chief protagonists of tomorrow's mysteries.

Future mysteries will arise from the ruins of today's. Let us take a stroll along this Passage de l'Opéra, and have a closer look at it. It is a double tunnel, with a single gateway opening to the north on to the Rue Chauchat, and two gateways opening to the south on to the boulevard. Its two arcades, the western one, called the Galerie du Baromètre, and the eastern one, called the Galerie du Thermomètre, are joined by two short cuts, the first of which runs across the passage at its northern end, while the second is at the boulevard end, just behind the bookshop and café which occupy the space between the two southern gateways. If we enter the Galerie du Thermomètre through its opening between the café I have just mentioned and a bookshop, the Librairie Eugène Rey, having passed through the iron gates which at night-time bar the passage to all yearnings deemed contrary to public morals, we can see that whereas practically the whole length of the right-hand façade is taken up, at ground-floor level, by window displays of all kinds, a café, and so on, the upper storeys seem to be occupied by one single building. It is indeed a single edifice, stretching along the entire frontage: a hotel whose rooms possess precisely the atmosphere and lighting appropriate to the laboratory of pleasures which the hotel offers as its sole justification for existence.

I remember that my attention was first drawn to this establishment by the unfavourable publicity accorded it in a notice put up by the Hôtel de Monte-Carlo (whose lobby entrance is in the Galerie du Baromètre) on its wall forming the last sector of the Rue Chauchat: a notice proclaiming proudly that it has *no connection whatsoever with the lodging-house in the passage.* At first-floor level, this lodging-house is a place where couples book by the hour, but on the rather low-ceilinged second floor it is simply a hotel where damp, shabby rooms boasting hot and cold running water and electricity can be rented by the week or month.

Such hotels for transients of various kinds are rather pleasant to live in: an atmosphere of freedom reigns in them, and one does not have the feeling, as in most ordinary lodgings, of being spied on all the time. When I was in Berlin I used to stay at a similar place, in the Joachimstalerstrasse in Charlottenburg, where I paid for my room in advance each evening before going up, even though it already contained my baggage. Picabia, too, occasionally puts up at a hotel for transients, in the Rue Darcet, basing his affection for it on the fact that shoes are never to be seen standing outside the bedroom doors. At the present moment, I can count two friends among the second-floor tenants of the lodging-house in the Passage de l'Opéra. First, there is Marcel Noll, who brought with him from Strasbourg to Paris last year an enormous capacity to promote confusion, a quality which I find entirely admirable. Then there is Charles Baron, the brother of the poet Jacques Baron and a poet himself (more people should realize the fact), although those who do not know him well distinguish him from his brother by calling him *Baron the Boxer*, on account of some vague boxing lessons he once took, and perhaps because at that time he used to go around with a group of boxers which included at least one, Fred Bretonnel, who achieved some success in the ring; Charles Baron, who has taken this stark room so as to live there with a charming girl-friend about whom I will take the liberty of saying only that on certain days she looks strangely like a stabbed dove.

In this romantic lodging-house, whose doors sometimes gape open, revealing interiors like the empty carapaces of weird shellfish, the way the premises are arranged reinforces the already dubious air given it by the rather commonplace uses to which a floating population is capable of putting it. Long corridors, like theatre wings, are strung with boxes, I mean rooms, all on the same side overlooking the passage. A dual system of stairways provides access to the passage at two separate points. Everything is contrived to facilitate hasty departures, to conceal from casual observers the trysts which will muffle some huge secret behind the faded sky-blue wallpaper of a banal decor. On the first floor, someone has had the idea of fixing up a door at the top of the farther staircase, so that if required this exit can be closed, although since the door is framed by nothing more than side posts all that need be done to get past it is to clamber over the banister at that point. This menace, swinging on its hinges, can provoke flights of dizzy speculation in the mind of anyone contemplating it. What can possibly be the hidden significance of this door? Its presence evokes the most ignoble police operations, the pursuit to the very heartland of their loves of those sentimental murderers betrayed by weakness of intellect, encircled at dawn in the voluptuous labyrinths where they are hiding, the search narrowing while these doomed heroes stand on tiptoe, hand on pounding heart, still listening to the involuntary sighs of pleasure filtering through the closed doors. At odd intervals the corridors light up, but semidarkness is their favourite colour. A half-opened door releases a flash of négligée, a trill of song. Then a happiness unravels, fingers unlace, and an overcoat makes its way down towards the anonymous day, towards the country of respectability.

This place is ruled over by two women. One of them is a crotchety old thing who sits nursing her rheumatics beside the fireplace in the hotel office, next to the keyboard. The other one, though no longer very young either, is sweet and gentle, and still dark-haired, through habit, no doubt. She is the real landlady of this establishment, and I often wonder what will happen to her when the demolition men finally drive her out of here. Garrulous and easygoing by nature, she has acquired from her job a liking for anything dubious or chancy. Reluctant to press her tenants for payment, it is only sheer necessity that drives her to do so in the long run. She not only expects even the most regular among them to be involved in some kind of irregularity as a matter of course, she takes a positive interest in the goings on. Well, doubtless she tips off the police, like all the landladies around, but if she talks about them at all it is with a scared note in her voice, as though she were apprehensive of some shadowy misfortune. I remember, one day, my friend Noll was arrested on a perfectly trivial charge, something to do with disturbing the peace at night and yelling seditious slogans. The first thing I knew about it was when the police phoned up from the central station to check on the address he had given. I found his landlady in a terrible state: 'Whatever can have happened to him, Sir? It's so silly to get into trouble like that. At least they won't keep him for long now. Only last month I had a tenant here who was in trouble with them.' She heaved sighs of genuine relief when he appeared a few minutes later.

Between the boulevards and the hotel's first entrance, the building's street-level frontage is taken up by the Librairie Rey, with its window displays of magazines, popular novels and scientific publications. It is one of the four or five places in Paris where one can glance through magazines at leisure without buying them. So it usually has its quota of young people reading busily, making a little tent of the uncut pages to squint inside, and others for whom this illusory occupation provides a screen from behind which they can keep an eye on the comings and goings in the passage, for various reasons which go straight to my heart. A single cashier surveys the bookshelves, from his perch in a little glass-panelled booth equipped with a frontal grille through which business is transacted. The theft rate here is almost as high as at the

Librairie Crès in the Boulevard Saint-Germain, where in 1920 twenty thousand francs worth of books and periodicals were stolen in a single year.

The door of building no. 2 gives access to the staircase leading up to the two floors of furnished rooms. A glance through it will reveal, set back a little from the foot of these stairs, the glass-fronted lodge occupied by the passage's concierge. And to think that these glass panes guard a dual existence of complete passivity, at the very limits of adventure, of the unknown! For years and years the gatekeeper and his wife have been holed up in this retreat, watching skirts and trousers pass by as they climb up towards their assignations. For years now these two old people have been ineluctably moulded to the shape of this absurd place fringing the arcades, visibly consuming their lives, he smoking it away, she sewing, eternally sewing as though the fate of the universe hinged upon her needlework. Some fairly curious fluorescent growths must surely decorate these twin skulls. During the long hours and the darkness, a darkness which spares the exaggerated cost of an electric lamp, beautiful natural formations must build up easily and expansively behind this married couple of foreheads: he and she are so used to each other that their conventional gossip has at last spaced itself out into silence, so that their mechanical gestures of pipe and needle are now accompanied solely by those magnificent confusions of the imagination which are the prerogative of poets. Sedentary, eaten away by age and spiritual sloth, rummaging through their minds at the sight of the footsteps of mystery crossing those of whorishness just the other side of their window, what are they likely to find? A whole pack of obscene playing cards, which I take pleasure in visualizing. The queen of clubs ... but one day I did as the notice suggested, and spoke to the concierge.

It was at the counter of the Café Louis XVI, where he used to treat himself to abbreviated holidays, cap tilted over one ear, nose buried in his drink.

MYSELF. Please forgive me for troubling you, but am I right in thinking you are the concierge of the passage?

HE. Since twenty years and more, Sir. What can I do for you?

MYSELF. Would you care to join me . . .

HE. A small *marc* . . . A real thirsty job I've got . . . All that toing and froing in there, raising a dust . . . Ah, you see some strange customers, pretty women too, and some not so pretty . . . I look at them as little as possible: none of my business, know what I mean? The concierge. Yes, I wouldn't say no to another small *marc*, very good of you, Sir, thank you. Some of them come and tell me their little problems. I give them advice. People, they make mountains out of molehills, you know . . .

MYSELF. You have all sorts and kinds of tenant, in your passage.

HE. (*becomes circumspect*).

I wanted to know if there still existed in his domain a bizarre establishment which Valéry had once described to me: an agency which accepted unstamped letters and arranged to have them posted from any desired point of the globe to the address written on the envelope, a facility that would allow the customer to feign a voyage to the far east, for example, without moving an inch from the far west of some secret adventure. Impossible to find out anything, the concierge had never heard such a place mentioned . . . Anyhow, what does a concierge know? And it was perhaps more than twenty years since Valéry had indulged in such pranks.

A shop selling canes and walking-sticks separates the Café du Petit Grillon from the lodging-house entrance. A perfectly honourable salesman offers to a questionable clientèle a wide choice of luxurious examples of these canes, displayed so as to show both stems and handles to their best advantage. A whole art of spatial panoply is at play here: the canes lower down form fans, while those higher up are crossed like Xs and, as the result of a strange tropism, incline towards the beholder their bouquets of pommels: ivory roses, dogs' heads with jewelled eyes, damascened semidarkness from Toledo, niello inlays of delicate sentimental foliage, cats, women, hooked beaks, countless materials ranging from twisted rattan to rhinoceros horn and the blond charm of cornelians.

JEAN RHYS

From

# QUARTET

1928

# I

IT WAS ABOUT half-past five on an October afternoon when Marya Zelli came out of the Café Lavenue, which is a dignified and comparatively expensive establishment on the Boulevard du Montparnasse. She had been sitting there for nearly an hour and a half, and during that time she had drunk two glasses of black coffee, smoked six caporal cigarettes and read the week's *Candide*.

Marya was a blonde girl, not very tall, slender-waisted. Her face was short, high cheek-boned, full-lipped; her long eyes slanted upwards towards the temples and were gentle and oddly remote in expression. Often on the Boulevards St Michel and Montparnasse shabby youths would glide up to her and address her hopefully in unknown and spitting tongues. When they were very shabby she would smile in a distant manner and answer in English:

'I'm very sorry; I don't understand what you are saying.'

She crossed the boulevard and turned down the Rue de Rennes. As she walked along she was thinking: 'This street is very like the Tottenham Court Road – own sister to the Tottenham Court Road.'

The idea depressed her, and to distract herself she stopped to look at a red felt hat in a shop window. Someone behind her said:

'Hello, Madame Zelli, what are you doing in this part of the world?'

Miss Esther De Solla, tall, gaunt, broad-shouldered, stood looking downwards at her with a protective expression.

When Marya answered: 'Hello! Nothing. I was feeling melancholy, to tell you the truth,' she proposed:

'Come along to my studio for a bit.'

Miss De Solla, who was a painter and ascetic to the point of fanaticism, lived in a street at the back of the Lion de Belfort. Her studio was hidden behind a grim building where the housewives of the neighbourhood came to wash their clothes. It was a peaceful place, white-walled, smelling strongly of decayed vegetables. The artist explained that a *marchande des quatre saisons* kept her stock in the courtyard, and that as the woman was the concierge's sister-in-law, complaints were useless.

'Though the smell's pretty awful sometimes. Sit near the stove. It's cold today.'

She opened a massive cupboard and produced a bottle of gin, another of vermouth, two glasses and a cardboard case containing drawings.

'I bought these this morning. What do you think of them?'

Marya, helped by the alcohol, realized that the drawings were beautiful. Groups of women. Masses of flesh arranged to form intricate and absorbing patterns.

'That man's a Hungarian,' explained Miss De Solla. 'He's just over the way in the house where Trotzky used to live. He's a discovery of Heidler's. You know Heidler, the English picture-dealer man, of course.'

Marya answered, 'I don't know any of the English people in Paris.'

'Don't you?' said Miss De Solla, shocked. Then she added hastily: 'How perfectly lovely for you!'

'D'you think so?' asked Marya dubiously.

Miss De Solla assured her that it was.

'I do think that one ought to make an effort to get away

from the Anglo-Saxons in Paris, or what on earth is the good of being here at all? And it isn't an easy thing to do, either. Not easy for a woman, anyhow. But, of course, your husbands's French, isn't he?'

'No,' said Marya. 'He's a Pole.'

The other looked across at her and thought: 'Is she really married to the Zelli man, I wonder? She's a decorative little person – decorative but strangely pathetic. I must get her to sit for me.'

She began to argue that there was something unreal about most English people.

'They touch life with gloves on. They're pretending about something all the time. Pretending quite nice and decent things, of course. But still . . .'

'Everybody pretends,' Marya was thinking. 'French people pretend every bit as much, only about different things and not so obviously. She'll know that when she's been here as long as I have.'

'As long as I have.' The four years she had spent in Paris seemed to stretch into infinity.

'English people . . .' continued Miss De Solla in a dogmatic voice.

The drone of a concertina sounded from the courtyard of the studio. The man was really trying to play 'Yes, we have no bananas'. But it was an unrecognizable version, and listening to it gave Marya the same feeling of melancholy pleasure as she had when walking along the shadowed side of one of those narrow streets full of shabby *parfumeries*, second-hand book-stalls, cheap hat-shops, bars frequented by gaily-painted ladies and loud-voiced men, midwives' premises . . .

Montparnasse was full of these streets and they were often inordinately long. You could walk for hours. The Rue Vaugirard, for instance. Marya had never yet managed to reach the end of the Rue Vaugirard, which was a very respectable thoroughfare on the whole. But if you went far enough towards Grenelle and then turned down side streets . . .

Only the day before she had discovered, in this way, a most attractive restaurant. There was no *patronne*, but the *patron* was beautifully made up. Crimson was where crimson should be, and rose-colour where rose-colour. He talked with a lisp. The room was full of men in caps who bawled intimacies at each other; a gramophone played without ceasing; a beautiful white dog under the counter, which everybody called Zaza and threw bones to, barked madly.

But Stephan objected with violence to these wanderings in sordid streets. And though Marya considered that he was extremely inconsistent, she generally gave way to his inconsistencies and spent hours alone in the bedroom of the Hôtel de l'Univers. Not that she objected to solitude. Quite the contrary. She had books, thank Heaven, quantities of books. All sorts of books.

Still, there were moments when she realized that her existence, though delightful, was haphazard. It lacked, as it were, solidity; it lacked the necessary fixed background. A bedroom, balcony and *cabinet de toilette* in a cheap Montmartre hotel cannot possibly be called a solid background.

Miss De Solla, who had by this time pretty well exhausted her fascinating subject, stopped talking.

Marya said: 'Yes, but it's pretty lonely, not knowing any English people.'

'Well,' Miss De Solla answered, 'if that's what you're pining for. What are you doing this evening? Come along to Lefranc's and meet the Heidlers. You must have heard of Heidler.'

'Never.'

'Hugh Heidler?' protested Miss De Solla.

She proceeded to explain Mr. Heidler, who was a very

important person in his way, it seemed. He made discoveries, he helped the young men, he had a flair.

'I believe they intend to settle in France for good now – Provence in the winter and Montparnasse for the rest of the year – you know the sort of thing. He's had a kind of nervous breakdown. Of course, people say –'

Miss De Solla stopped.

'I like Mrs. Heidler anyway; she's a very sensible woman; no nonsense there. She's one of the few people in Montparnasse whom I do like. Most of them . . . But abuse isn't any good, and it's better to be clean than kind.'

'Much better!' agreed Marya.

'Not that they are mad on baths or nailbrushes, either,' said the other. 'Never mind.' She got up and lit a cigarette. 'Mrs. Heidler paints, too. It's pretty awful to think of the hundreds of women round here painting away, and all that, isn't it?'

She looked round her austere studio, and the Jewess's hunger for the softness and warmth of life was naked in her eyes.

'Well,' said Marya, 'I'd like to come, but I must telephone to Stephan, to my husband. Where can I telephone from?'

'From the Café Buffalo. Wait a minute, I've got to stand on a chair to put my gas out. My shark of a landlady won't put in electric light. Mind you, I'm fond of this place, though the smell is really awful sometimes. That head over there doesn't look so bad in this light, does it?' said Miss De Solla, wistfully.

Lefranc's is a small restaurant half-way up the Boulevard du Montparnasse. It is much frequented by the Anglo-Saxons of the quarter, and by a meagre sprinkling of Scandinavians and Dutch.

The *patron* is provincial and affable. The *patronne*, who

sits beaming behind the counter, possesses a mildly robust expression and the figure and coiffure of the nineties; her waist goes in, her hips come out, her long black hair is coiled into a smooth bun on the top of her round head. She is very restful to the tired eye.

The Heidlers were sitting at a table at the end of the room.

'Good evening,' said Mrs. Heidler in the voice of a well-educated young male. Her expression was non-committal.

'*Encore deux vermouths-cassis!*' said Mr. Heidler to the waitress.

They were fresh, sturdy people. Mr. Heidler, indeed, was so very sturdy that it was difficult to imagine him suffering from a nervous breakdown of any kind whatever. He looked as if nothing could break him down. He was a tall, fair man of perhaps forty-five. His shoulders were tremendous, his nose arrogant, his hands short, broad and so plump that the knuckles were dimpled. The wooden expression of his face was carefully striven for. His eyes were light blue and intelligent, but with a curious underlying expression of obtuseness – even of brutality.

'I expect he's awfully fussy,' thought Marya.

Mrs. Heidler was a good deal younger than her husband, plump and dark, country with a careful dash of Chelsea, and wore with assurance a drooping felt hat which entirely hid the upper part of her face. She sat in silence for some time listening to Miss De Solla's conversation about the dearth of studios, and then suddenly remarked to Marya:

'H. J. and I have quite made up our minds that eating is the greatest pleasure in life. Well, I mean, it is, isn't it? At any rate, it's one of the few pleasures that never let you down.'

Her eyes were beautiful, clearly brown, the long lashes curving upwards, but there was a suspicious, almost a deadened look in them.

'I'm a well-behaved young woman,' they said, 'and you're not going to catch me out, so don't think it.' Or perhaps, thought Marya, she's just thoroughly enjoying her pilaff.

Miss De Solla, looking more ascetic than ever, agreed that eating was jolly. They discussed eating, cooking, England and, finally, Marya, whom they spoke of in the third person as if she were a strange animal or at any rate a strayed animal – one not quite of the fold.

'But you are English – or aren't you?' asked Heidler.

He was walking along the boulevard by her side, his head carefully thrown back.

Marya assured him that she was. 'But I left England four years ago.'

He asked: 'And you've been all the time in Paris?' Then, without waiting for her to answer, he added fussily: 'Where have Lois and Miss De Solla got to? Oh, there they are! I'll just go and see if Guy is in here, Lois.'

He disappeared into the Café du Dôme.

'It's a dreadful place, isn't it?' said Mrs. Heidler.

Marya, looking through the door at the mournful and tightly packed assembly, agreed that it was rather dreadful.

Heidler emerged, puffing slightly, and announced in a worried tone:

'He's not here. We'll sit on the terrace and wait for him.'

The terrace was empty and cold, but without argument they all sat down and ordered coffee and liqueur brandies.

Marya, who was beginning to shiver, drank her brandy and found herself staring eagerly and curiously at Mrs. Heidler.

A strong, dark woman, her body would be duskily solid like her face. There was something of the earth about her, something of the peasant. Her mouth was large and thick-lipped, but not insensitive, and she had an odd habit of wincing when Heidler spoke to her sharply. A tremor would screw up one side of her face so that for an instant she looked like a hurt animal.

'I bet that man is a bit of a brute sometimes,' thought Marya. And as she thought it, she felt his hand lying heavily on her knee.

He looked kind, peaceful and exceedingly healthy. His light, calm eyes searched the faces of the people passing on the Boulevard Montparnasse, and his huge hand lay possessively, heavy as lead, on her knee.

Ridiculous sort of thing to do. Ridiculous, not frightening. Why frightening?

She made a cautious but decided movement and the hand was withdrawn.

'It's very cold here,' said Heidler in his gentle voice. 'Let's go on to the Select Bar, shall we?'

At a little after midnight Marya got back to the Hôtel de l'Univers, Rue Cauchois. She mounted five flights of steep, uncarpeted stairs, felt her way along an unlighted passage, flung her bedroom door open and embraced her husband violently. He looked so thin after the well-fed Heidlers.

'*Tiens, Mado*,' he said. 'You're very late.'

The room was large and low-ceilinged, the striped wallpaper faded to inoffensiveness. A huge dark wardrobe faced a huge dark bed. The rest of the furniture shrank away into corners, battered and apologetic. A narrow door on the left led into a small, very dark dressing-room. There was no carpet on the floor.

'I've just this minute got back,' remarked Stephan.

Marya said: 'Well, was everything all right?' And when he answered, 'Yes,' she asked no further questions.

Stephan disliked being questioned and, when closely pressed, he lied. He just lied. Not plausibly or craftily, but impatiently and absent-mindedly. So Marya had long ago stopped questioning. For she was reckless, lazy, a vagabond by nature, and for the first time in her life she was very near to being happy.

## II

MARYA, YOU MUST understand, had not been suddenly and ruthlessly transplanted from solid comfort to the hazards of Montmartre. Nothing like that. Truth to say, she was used to a lack of solidity and of fixed backgrounds.

Before her marriage she had spent several years as a member of Mr. Albert Prance's No. 1 touring company. An odd life. Morose landladies, boiled onion suppers. Bottles of gin in the dressing-room. Perpetual manicuring of one's nails in the Sunday train. Perpetual discussions about men. ('Swine, deary, swine.') The chorus knew all about men, judged them with a rapid and terrible accuracy.

Marya had longed to play a glittering part – she was nineteen then – against the sombre and wonderful background of London. She had visited a theatrical agent; she had sung – something – anything – in a quavering voice, and the agent, a stout and weary gentleman, had run his eyes upwards and downwards and remarked in a hopeless voice: 'Well, you're no Tetrazzini, are you, deary? Never mind, do a few steps.'

She had done a few steps. The stout gentleman had glanced at another gentleman standing behind the piano, who was, it seemed, Mr. Albert Prance's manager. Both nodded slightly. A contract was produced. The thing was done.

'Miss – I say, what d'you call yourself? – Miss Marya Hughes, hereinafter called the artist.'

Clause 28: no play, no pay.

'Ladies and gentlemen. This play wants guts!'

He terrified Marya; her knees shook whenever he came anywhere near her.

Sometimes she would reflect that the way she had been left to all this was astonishing, even alarming. When she had pointed out that, without expensive preliminaries, she would be earning her own living, everybody had stopped protesting and had agreed that this was a good argument. A very good argument indeed. For Marya's relatives, though respectable people, presentable people (one might even go so far as to say quite good people), were poverty-stricken and poverty is the cause of many compromises.

There she was and there she stayed. Gradually passivity replaced her early adventurousness. She learned, after long and painstaking effort, to talk like a chorus girl, to dress like a chorus girl and to think like a chorus girl – up to a point. Beyond that point she remained apart, lonely, frightened of her loneliness, resenting it passionately. She grew thin. She began to live her hard and monotonous life very mechanically and listlessly.

A vague procession of towns all exactly alike, a vague procession of men also exactly alike. One can drift like that for a long time, she found, carefully hiding the fact that this wasn't what one had expected of life. Not in the very least.

At twenty-four she imagined with dread that she was growing old. Then, during a period of unemployment spent in London, she met Monsieur Stephan Zelli.

He was a short, slim, supple young man of thirty-three or -four, with very quick, brown eyes and an eager but secretive expression. He spoke English fairly well in a harsh voice and (when he was nervous) with an American accent.

He told Marya that he was of Polish nationality, that he lived in Paris, that he considered her beautiful and wished to marry her. Also that he was a *commissionaire d'objets d'art*.

'Oh, you sell pictures,' she said.

'Pictures and other things.'

Marya, who had painfully learnt a certain amount of caution, told herself that this stranger and alien was probably a bad lot. But she felt strangely peaceful when she was with him, as if life were not such an extraordinary muddle after all, as if he were telling her: 'Now then, look here, I know all about you. I know you far better than you know yourself, I know why you aren't happy. I can make you happy.'

And he was so sure of himself, so definite, with such a clean-cut mind. It was a hard mind, perhaps, disconcertingly and disquietingly sceptical. But at any rate it didn't bulge out in all sorts of unexpected places. Most people hesitated. They fumbled. They were so full of reticences and prejudices and uncertainties and spites and shames, that there was no getting anywhere at all. One felt after a time a blankness and a jar – like trying to walk up a step that wasn't there. But, good or bad, there Monsieur Zelli was. Definite. A person. He criticized her clothes with authority and this enchanted her. He told her that her arms were too thin, that she had a Slav type and a pretty silhouette, that if she were happy and petted she would become charming. Happy, petted, charming – these are magical words. And the man knew what he was talking about, Marya could see that.

As to Monsieur Zelli, he drew his own conclusions from her air of fatigue, disillusion and extreme youth, her shadowed eyes, her pathetic and unconscious lapses into helplessness. But he was without bourgeois prejudices, or he imagined that he was, and he had all his life acted on impulse, though always in a careful and businesslike manner.

It was the end of a luncheon in Soho. Marya finished smoking her cigarette and remarked:

'You know I haven't got any money, not a thing, not a cent.'

She said this because, when he had leaned forward with the lighted match, he had reminded her of China Audley's violinist.

China, also one of Mr. Prance's discoveries, was beloved by a tall, fine-looking young man with a large income and a charming voice. A chivalrous young man. He had fought the good fight with his mother, who considered that honourable intentions were unnecessary when dealing with chorus girls. There the two were – engaged.

Then China had madly jilted this marvel, this paragon, and had secretly married the short, swarthy violinist of a Manchester café. She had spent the rest of the tour getting telegraphic appeals from her husband; 'Please send five pounds at once Antonio,' or something like that. Which entailed putting her wrist watch into various pawnshops and taking it out again. Constantly. 'Well it serves her right, doesn't it?' said all the other girls.

'No money. Nothing at all,' repeated Marya. 'My father and mother are both dead. My aunt . . .'

'I know; you told me,' interrupted Monsieur Zelli, who had long ago asked adroit questions and found out all there was to find out about Marya's relations. He had reflected that they didn't seem to care in the least what became of her and that English ideas of family life were sometimes exceedingly strange. But he had made no remark.

'It's a pity,' said Monsieur Zelli. 'It's better when a woman has some money, I think. It's much safer for her.'

'I owe for the dress I have on,' Marya informed him, for she was determined to make things perfectly clear.

He told her that they would go next day and pay for it. 'How much do you owe?'

'It's not worth that,' he remarked calmly when she told him. 'Not that it is ugly, but it has no chic. I expect your dressmaker cheats you.'

Marya was annoyed but impressed.

'You know – you'll be happy with me,' he continued in a persuasive voice.

And Marya answered that she dared say she would.

On a June afternoon, heavy with heat, they arrived in Paris.

Stephan had lived in Montmartre for fifteen years, he told her, but he had no intimate friends and very few acquaintances. Sometimes he took her with him to some obscure café where he would meet an odd-looking old man or a very smartly-dressed young one. She would sit in the musty-smelling half-light sipping iced beer and listening to long, rapid jabberings: '*La Vierge au coussin vert – Première version – Authentique – Documents – Collier de l'Impératrice Eugénie . . .*'

'An amethyst necklace, the stones as big as a calf's eye and set in gold. The pendant pear-shaped, the size of a pigeon's egg. The necklace is strung on a fine gold chain and set with pearls of an extraordinary purity.' The whole to be hung as quickly as possible round the neck of Mrs. Buckell A. Butcher of something-or-the-other, Pa, or of any lady willing to put up with an old-fashioned piece of jewellery, because *impératrice* is a fine word and even empress isn't so bad.

Stephan seemed to do most of his business in cafés. He explained that he acted as intermediary between Frenchmen who wished to sell and foreigners (invariably foreigners) who wished to buy pictures, fur coats, twelfth-century Madonnas, Madame du Barry's prie-Dieu, anything.

Once he had sold a rocking-horse played with by one of Millet's many children, and that had been a very profitable deal indeed.

One evening she had come home to find Napoleon's sabre lying naked and astonishing on her bed by the side of its cedar-wood case.

('*Oui, parfaitement*,' said Stephan. 'Napoleon's sabre.')

One of his sabres, she supposed. He must have had several of them, of course. A man like Napoleon. Lots. She walked round to the other side of the bed and stared at it, feeling vaguely uneasy. There was a long description of the treasure on the cedar-wood case.

'There are two sheaths, the first of porcelain inlaid with gold, the second of gold set with precious stones. The hilt of the sabre is in gold worked in the Oriental fashion. The blade is of the finest Damascus steel and on it is engraved: "In token of submission, respect and esteem to Napoleon Bonaparte, the hero of Aboukir – Mouhrad Bey."'

That night, long after the cedar-wood case had been packed away in a shabby valise, Marya lay awake thinking.

'Stephan,' she said at last.

'Well?' answered Stephan. He was smoking in front of the open window. 'I thought you were asleep.'

'No,' said Marya. 'Wherever did you get that thing?'

He explained that it belonged to an old French family.

'They're very poor now and they want to sell it. That's all. Why don't they what? The man has to do it on the sly because his mother and his uncle would stop him if they could.'

Marya sat up in bed, put her arms round her knees and said in an unhappy voice:

'He probably has no right to sell it without his mother's consent.'

'His mother has nothing to say,' remarked Stephan sharply. 'But she would bother him if she could.'

Next morning he went out very early, carrying the old valise, and Marya never knew what became of the sabre.

'America,' said Stephan vaguely when she asked. As who should say 'The sea'.

He never explained his doings. He was a secretive person, she considered. Sometimes, without warning or explanation, he would go away for two or three days, and, left alone in the hotel, she dreaded, not desertion, but some vague, dimly-apprehended catastrophe. But nothing happened. It was a fantastic life, but it kept on its legs so to speak. There was no catastrophe. And eventually Marya stopped questioning and was happy.

Stephan was secretive and a liar, but he was a very gentle and expert lover. She was the petted, cherished child, the desired mistress, the worshipped, perfumed goddess. She was all these things to Stephan – or so he made her believe. Marya hadn't known that a man could be as nice as all that to a woman – so gentle in little ways.

And, besides, she liked him. She liked his wild gaieties and his sudden, obstinate silences and the way he sometimes stretched his hands out to her. Groping. Like a little boy, she would think.

Eighteen months later they went to Brussels for a year. By the time they returned to Paris every vestige of suspicion had left her. She felt that her marriage, though risky, had been a success. And that was that. Her life swayed regularly, even monotonously, between two extremes, avoiding the soul-destroying middle. Sometimes they had a good deal of money and immediately spent it. Sometimes they had almost none at all and then they would skip a meal and drink iced white wine on their balcony instead.

From the balcony Marya could see one side of the Place Blanche. Opposite, the Rue Lepic mounted upwards to the rustic heights of Montmartre. It was astonishing how significant, coherent and understandable it all became after a glass of wine on an empty stomach.

The lights winking up at a pallid moon, the slender painted ladies, the wings of the Moulin Rouge, the smell of petrol and perfume and cooking.

The Place Blanche, Paris. Life itself. One realized all sorts of things. The value of an illusion, for instance, and that the shadow can be more important than the substance. All sorts of things.

LOUIS-FERDINAND CÉLINE

From

# JOURNEY TO THE END OF THE NIGHT

1932

Translated by John H. P. Markes

IF ONE WANTED to be respected and decently treated there was no time to be lost in hitting it off with the civilians, because as the war went on they became rapidly more unpleasant. As soon as I got back to Paris I realized this. The women were on heat and the old men had greed written all over them; nothing was safe from their rummaging fingers, either persons or pockets.

Back at home they'd been pretty quick to pick up honour and glory from the boys at the front, and had learnt how to resign themselves to it all bravely and without flinching.

The mothers, all nurses or martyrs, were never without their sombre livery and the little diplomas so promptly presented to them by the War Office. The machine was getting smoothly to work, in fact.

It's just the same at a nicely-run funeral. One's very sad there too, but one thinks of the will, and of next holidays, of the attractive widow (who's good value, so they say) and, by contrast, of going on living oneself quite a time yet, of never dying at all perhaps . . . who knows?

As you follow the bier everybody solemnly takes his hat off to you. That's nice. It's the time to behave very properly, and look respectable, and not to make jokes out loud, to be only inwardly happy. That's allowed. Everything's allowed inside oneself.

In wartime, instead of dancing upstairs, one danced in the cellar. The men on leave put up with that, they even liked it.

In fact, they insisted on it as soon as they came back, and nobody thought it unseemly. The only thing that's really unseemly is bravado. Would you be physically brave? Then ask the maggot to be brave too, he's as pink and pale and soft as you are.

There was nothing for me to complain of. I was winning my freedom with the military medal I'd been given, and my wound and all. They'd brought the medal to me in hospital when I was convalescing. The same day I left the hospital and went to a theatre to show it off to the civvies in the interval. It was a great success. Medals were a novelty in Paris at the time. There was quite a to-do.

It was on this same occasion in the foyer of the Opéra Comique that I met my little American, Lola, and it was due to her that I had my eyes opened completely.

There are certain days which count in that way, after months and months which don't mean a thing. That day of the medal at the Opéra Comique was for me all-important.

It was due to Lola that I became curious about the United States. I immediately asked her a lot of questions about that country which she hardly answered. When you start out on a journey like this you come back as and when you can ...

At the time I'm speaking of, everyone in Paris wanted a nice uniform. Only neutrals and spies hadn't got one and there wasn't much to choose between *them*. Lola had hers and a pretty little thing it was too, all decked out with little red crosses on the sleeves and on the diminutive cap which she always wore at a tilt on her head of wavy hair. She had come to help us save France, as she told the Manager at the hotel, and though she couldn't hope to do much she was ready to do what she could with all her heart. There was understanding between us at once, but it was not quite complete because I'd come to dislike the feelings of the heart very much. I really much preferred the feelings of the body. One should distrust the heart – the war had taught me that, very clearly; and I wasn't likely to forget it.

Lola's heart was tender, weak and enthusiastic. Her body was charming, very attractive, and the only thing to do was to accept her as she was. She was a sweet girl really, but the war was between us, that vast and bloody madness which, whether they wanted it or not, was making one half of humanity drive the other half into the knacker's yard. And of course a thing like that was disturbing to our relationship. To me, who was making my convalescence last as long as possible and who didn't in the least want to take my turn again in the blazing graveyards of the front line, the absurdity of our massacre was startlingly obvious at every step I took in the city. A horrible chicanery pervaded everything.

However, I had little chance of getting out of it, I knew none of the sort of people you need to know in order to get out of it. The only friends I had were poor people, that is to say people whose death was of no interest to anyone. As for Lola it was no good counting on her to help me keep out of it. In spite of the fact that she was a nurse you couldn't imagine a more bellicose creature than that dear child – except perhaps Ortolan. Before I ever went into the muddy hash of heroism myself her little Joan of Arc manner might perhaps have thrilled and converted me, but now, after joining up in the Place Clichy, I was violently ready to reject all forms of patriotism, either verbal or real. I was cured, thoroughly cured.

For the convenience of the ladies of the American Expeditionary Force the group of nurses to which Lola belonged was lodged at the Paritz Hotel, and to make things pleasanter for her in particular, because she had certain connexions, she was given the supervision of a special service of apple fritters, which were delivered from the hotel itself to the hospitals of Paris. Every morning tens of thousands of them were sent out. Lola performed this charitable duty with a devotion which, as a matter of fact, was later to have the very worst effects.

The truth is that Lola had never cooked an apple fritter in her life. So she engaged a number of professional cooks and soon the fritters were produced up to time, beautifully juicy, golden and sweet. All Lola had to do was to taste them before they were sent out to the different hospitals. Every morning she'd get up at ten and after her bath go down to the kitchens, which were below ground near the cellars. Every morning she did that, dressed only in a black and yellow kimono which a friend from San Francisco had given her the day before she left.

Everything was going splendidly, in fact, and we were well on the way to winning the war, when one fine day, at lunch time, I found Lola in a state of prostration and refusing to eat any food. I was seized by anxiety lest some misfortune or sudden illness had overtaken her. I begged her to rely on my loving care.

Thanks to punctiliously tasting confectionery every day for a month, Lola had put on two full pounds. Her little waist bulged in evidence of this disaster. She burst into tears. Wishing to console her as best I could, I took her in a taxi – in the stress of our emotion – to a number of drug-stores in various parts of the town. All the weighing machines, chosen at random, implacably agreed that the two extra pounds had been well and truly added ; they were undeniable. I suggested that she should hand over her job to a colleague who, on the contrary, was eager to gain weight. Lola would not hear of such a compromise, which seemed to her shameful, amounting to a desertion of duty. It was then that she told me of a great-great-great-uncle of hers who had sailed in the glorious and never-to-be-forgotten *Mayflower* and had landed in Plymouth in 1620. In respect to his memory she couldn't dream of neglecting her culinary duties, which were a humble, ah yes, but sacred, trust.

Anyway, from that day onwards she only delicately nibbled her apple fritters, with very even, delightful little teeth. This horror of putting on fat took all the pleasure out of life for her. She languished. Soon she was as afraid of the fritters as I was of shells. We began to go for long healthy walks on the boulevards and by the river because of them, and we stopped going to the Napolitain because ice-creams are so bad for ladies' figures.

I had never dreamed of any place as comfortable to live in as her room, which was all pale blue and had its own bathroom next door. There were signed pictures of her friends all over it, not many women but a great many men, good-looking boys, dark and with curly hair, which was her type. She used to tell me the colour of their eyes and talk about those loving and solemn dedications, every one of them final. At first making love among all these effigies used to worry me, but after a while one gets accustomed to it.

As soon as I finished kissing her she'd go on again about the war and the apple fritters, I couldn't stop her. France came a good deal into our conversations. In Lola's mind France was a sort of chivalrous entity, not very clearly defined either in space or time, but at present grievously wounded and for that very reason extremely exciting. But when people talked to me about France, I thought at once of my guts, so that of course I was rather reserved and not very prone to any access of enthusiasm. Everyone has his own fears. However, as she was kind to me in the matter of sex, I listened without ever contradicting her. But as far as soul was concerned I could scarcely be said to satisfy her. She would have liked to see me keen and eager for the fray, but I for my part could not conceive why I ought to be in that exalted state, and I had on the other hand a hundred irrefutable reasons for remaining in precisely the opposite humour.

After all, Lola was only radiating happiness and optimism in the way that all folk do whose life is easy, privileged and secure, who, enjoying these things and good health, can look forward to living many more years.

She bothered me with her things of the spirit, which she never stopped talking about. The soul is the body's pride and pleasure when in health, but it is also a desire to be rid of the body when one is ill or things are going badly. You choose either the one attitude or the other, whichever suits you best at the particular moment, and that's all there is to it! While you are free to choose between both, all is well. But for me there was no choice, my course was settled. I was up to the neck in reality and could see my own death following me, so to speak, step for step. I found it very difficult to think of anything except a fate of slow assassination which the world seemed to consider the natural thing for me.

During this sort of protracted death-agony, in which your brain is lucid and your body sound, it is impossible to comprehend anything but the absolute truths. You need to have undergone such an experience to have knowledge for ever after of the truth or falsity of the things you say.

I came to the conclusion that even if the Germans were to arrive where we were, slaughtering, pillaging and setting fire to everything, to the hotel, the apple fritters, Lola, the Tuileries, the Cabinet and all their little friends, the Coupole, the Louvre and the big shops, even if they were to overrun the town and let hell loose in this foul fairground, full of every sordidness on earth, still I should have nothing to lose by it and everything to gain.

You don't lose anything much when your landlord's house is burnt down. Another landlord always comes along, if it isn't always the same one, a German or a Frenchman or an Englishman or a Chinaman, and you get your bill just the same . . . whether you pay in marks or francs, it doesn't much matter.

Morals, in fact, were a dirty business. If I had told Lola what I thought of the war she would only have taken me for a depraved freak and she'd deny me all intimate pleasures. So I took good care not to confess these things to her. Besides which, I still had other difficulties and rivalries to contend with. More than one officer was trying to take her from me. Their competition was dangerous, armed as they were with the attraction of their Legions of Honour. And there was beginning to be a lot about this damn Legion of Honour in the American papers. In fact, I think that after she had deceived me two or three times our relationship would have been seriously threatened if just then the minx had not suddenly discovered something more to be said in my favour, which was that I could be used every morning as a substitute taster of fritters.

This last-minute specialization saved me. She could accept *me* as her deputy. Was I not myself a gallant fighting man, and therefore worthy of this confidential post? From then onwards we were partners as well as lovers. A new era had begun.

Her body was an endless source of joy to me. I never tired of caressing its American contours. To tell the truth, I was an appalling lecher – and I went on being one.

Indeed, I came to the very delightful and comforting conclusion that a country capable of producing anatomies of such startling loveliness, and so full of spiritual grace, must have many other revelations of primary importance to offer – biologically speaking, of course.

My little games with Lola led me to decide that I would sooner or later make a journey, or rather a pilgrimage, to the United States; and certainly just as soon as I could manage it. Nor did I ever find respite and quiet (throughout a life fated in any case to be difficult and restless) until I was able to bring off this supremely mystical adventure in anatomical research.

Thus it was in the neighbourhood of Lola's backside that a message from a new world came to me. And she hadn't only a fine body, my Lola – let us get that quite clear at once; she was graced also with a piquant little face and grey-blue eyes, which gave her a slightly cruel look because they were set a wee bit on the upward slant, like those of a wild-cat.

Just to look into her face made my mouth water like a sip of dry wine, of silex, will. Her eyes were hard, and lacking the animation of that charming trademark-vivacity, reminiscent of the Orient and of Fragonard, which one finds in almost all the eyes over here.

We usually met in a café round the corner. Wounded men in increasing numbers hobbled along the streets, in rags as often as not. Collections were made on their behalf. There was a 'Day' for these, a 'Day' for those, Days above all for the people who organized them. Lie, copulate and die. One wasn't allowed to do anything else. People lied fiercely and beyond belief, ridiculously, beyond the limits of absurdity; lies in the papers, lies on the hoardings, lies on foot, on horseback and on wheels. Everybody was doing it, trying to see who could produce a more fantastic lie than his neighbour. There was soon no truth left in town.

And what truth there was one was ashamed of, in 1914.

Everything you touched was faked in some way – the sugar, the aeroplanes, shoe leather, jam, photographs; everything you read, swallowed, sucked, admired, proclaimed, refuted or upheld – it was all an evil myth and masquerade. Even traitors weren't real traitors. A mania for lying and believing lies is as catching as the itch. Little Lola knew only a few phrases in French, but they were all jingo phrases of the 'Up boys, and at 'em!', 'Land of Hope and Glory' type. It was enough to make you weep.

She hovered over the Death which was confronting us, persistently, obscenely – as indeed did all the women now that it had become the fashion to be courageous at other people's expense.

And there was I at that time discovering in myself such a fondness for all the things which kept me apart from the war! I asked her again and again to tell me about America, but she only answered with vague, silly and obviously inaccurate descriptions, which were meant to make a dazzling impression on me.

But I distrusted impressions just then. I'd been had that way once before, I wasn't going to be caught so easily again. Not by anybody.

I believed in her body, I didn't believe in her mind and heart. I considered her charming, and cushily placed in this war, cushily placed in life.

Her attitude towards an existence which for me was horrible, was merely that of the patriotic press: Toodle-loo, pip-pip, Your Country Needs You . . . Meanwhile I made love to her more and more often, having assured her that it would make her slim. But she relied more on our long walks to do that. I hated these long walks myself. But she was adamant.

So for several hours in the afternoon we would stride along in the Bois de Boulogne, round the lakes. Nature is a terrifying thing and even when well domesticated as in the Bois she still inspires a sort of uneasiness in real town-dwellers. They are pretty apt in such surroundings to take you into their confidence. Nothing like the Bois de Boulogne, wet, railed-in, sleek and shorn as it is, for calling up a flock of stubborn memories in the minds of city-folk strolling amid trees. Lola was a prey to this mood of confidential, melancholy unease. As we walked along she'd tell me, more or less truthfully, a hundred and one things about her life in New York and her little friends there.

I couldn't quite disentangle what was convincing from what was doubtful in all this complicated rigmarole of dollars, engagements, dresses and jewellery which seems to have made up her life in America.

That day we were going towards the race-course. At that time one still came across children on donkeys there, and horse-cabs, and more children kicking up the dust and cars full of men on leave hunting all the time in the little paths, as fast as possible, between two trains, for women with nothing to do; they raised even more dust, in their hurry to go off and have dinner and make love, agitated and oily, with roving eyes, worried by the passage of time and the wish to live. They sweated with desire as well as with the heat.

The Bois was less well-kept than usual, temporarily neglected by the authorities.

'This place must have been very pretty before the war,' Lola remarked. 'It must have been awfully smart, wasn't it, Ferdinand? Tell me. Were the races like in New York?'

To tell the truth, I'd never been to the races before the war myself, but I at once made up a colourful description of them for her benefit, basing myself on what I'd often heard about them from other people. Beautiful dresses . . . smart Society women . . . splendid four-in-hands . . . They're off! The gay trumpets . . . the water jump . . . The President of the Republic . . . The excitement of changing odds . . . And so on.

She was so delighted with these idealized vignettes of mine that my remarks brought us closer together. From that moment Lola felt she had discovered a taste which we had in common, a taste, for my part well dissimulated, for the gay social round. She even kissed me there and then in her excitement, a thing which seldom happened with her, I must confess. And then the sadness of fashions dead and gone overcame her. We all mourn the passage of time in our own particular way. For Lola it was the passing of fashion which made her perceive the flight of years.

'Ferdinand,' she asked, 'do you think there will ever be races held here again?'

'I suppose there will, when the war's over, Lola.'

'It's not certain though, is it?'

'No, it's not certain.'

The possibility of there never being any more races at Longchamps upset her. The sadness of life takes hold of people as best it may, but it seems almost always to manage to take hold of them somehow.

'Suppose the war goes on for a long time, Ferdinand, for years perhaps. Then for me it will be too late . . . to come back here . . . Don't you understand, Ferdinand? You see, I'm so fond of lovely places like this, that are so smart and attractive. It'll be too late, I expect. I shall be old then, Ferdinand, when the meetings begin again. I shall be already too old . . . You'll see, Ferdinand, it'll be too late. I feel it will be too late.'

And then once again she was filled with despair, as she had been before about the two pounds' added weight. I said everything I could think of to reassure her and give her hope. After all, she was only twenty-three I told her . . . And the war would be over very soon. Good times would come again.

As good as before, better times than before ... For her at least, an attractive girl like her ... Lost time was nothing: she'd make it up as easily as anything ... There'd be people to admire her, to make a fuss of her, for a long time yet. She put on a less unhappy face, to please me.

'Must we go on walking?' she asked.

'But you want to get slim?'

'Oh, I'd forgotten that ...'

We left Longchamps, the children had gone away. Only the dust was left. The fellows on leave were still looking for Happiness, but out in the open now. Happiness was to be tracked down among the café tables round the Porte Maillot.

We walked towards Saint-Cloud along the river banks hazy with autumn mist. Near the bridge several lighters pressed their bows against the arches, lying deep in the water, loaded with coal to the bulwarks.

The park foliage spread itself like an enormous fan above the railings. These trees are as detached, magnificent and impressive as one's dreams. But I was afraid of trees too, since I had known them conceal an enemy. Every tree meant a dead man. The avenue led uphill towards the fountains flanked by roses. Near the kiosk the old lady who sold refreshments seemed slowly to be gathering all the shadows of evening about her skirts. Farther away in the side-alleys great squares and rectangles of dark-coloured canvas were flapping; the canvas of the tents of a fair which the war had taken by surprise and filled with silence.

'They've been away a whole year now,' the old lady reminded us. 'Nowadays only a couple of people will come along here in all the day. I come still, out of habit ... There used to be such a crowd ...'

The old lady had understood nothing else of what had happened: that was all she knew. Lola had a curious desire to walk past the empty marquees, because she was feeling sad.

We counted about twenty of them, big ones full of mirrors, and a greater number of small ones, sweet-stalls, tombolas, and a small theatre even, full of draughts. There was one to every tree; they were all round us. One in particular near the main avenue had lost its canvas walls altogether and stood empty as an explained mystery.

They leaned over towards the mud and fallen leaves, these tents. We stopped close to the last one, which was farther aslant than the rest, its posts pitching in the rising wind like the masts of a ship with wildly tugging sails about to snap the last of its ropes. The whole tent swayed, its inner canvas flapping towards heaven, flapping above the roof. Its ancient name was written in green and red on a board over the door. It was a shooting-alley. *The Stand of All Nations* it was called.

There was no one to look after it either. He himself was away shooting along with the rest perhaps, the proprietor shooting shoulder to shoulder with his clients.

What a lot of shot had struck the targets of the booth! They were all spotted with little white pellet marks. There was a funny wedding scene, in zinc; there in front the bride with her bouquet, the best man, a soldier, the bridegroom with a big red face, and in the background more guests – they must all have been killed again and again when the fair was on.

'I'm sure you're a good shot, aren't you, Ferdinand? If the fair was still here I'd take you on. You shoot well, don't you, Ferdinand?'

'No. No, I'm not a very good shot . . .'

Farther back, beyond the wedding, was another roughly painted target – the Town Hall with its flag flying. You shot at the Town Hall, when it was working, into the windows, and they opened and a bell rang, and you even shot at the little zinc flag. And you shot too at the regiment of soldiers marching up a hill near by, like mine in the Place Clichy; amid all these discs and uprights, all there to be shot at as much as possible, now it was I who was to be shot at – who had been shot at yesterday and would be shot at tomorrow –

'They shoot at me too, Lola!' I cried out. I couldn't help it.

'Come on,' she said. 'You're being silly, Ferdinand – and we shall catch cold.'

We went on towards Saint-Cloud down the Royal Avenue, avoiding the mud. She held my hand in hers, such a small hand, but I could think of nothing else but the zinc wedding of the *Stand of All Nations* which we had left behind us in the gathering darkness. I even forgot to kiss her, it was all too much for me. I felt very strange.

In fact, I think it must have been from that moment that my head began to be so full of ideas and so difficult to calm.

When we got to the bridge at Saint-Cloud it was quite dark.

'Would you like to eat at Duval's, Ferdinand? You like Duval's . . . It would cheer you up . . . There's always a lot of people there. Unless you'd rather have supper in my room?' She was being very attentive that evening, in fact.

We finally decided on Duval's. But we'd hardly got our table than the place struck me as ludicrous and horrible. All these people sitting in rows all round us seemed to me to be sitting there waiting, they too, to be fired at from all sides as they ate.

'Run, all of you!' I shouted to them. 'Get out! They're going to shoot! They'll kill you. They'll kill us all.'

I was hurried back to Lola's hotel. Everywhere I could see the same thing happening. All the people in the Paritz seemed to be going to get themselves shot and so did the hotel-clerks at the reception desk. There they were, simply asking for it, and the porter man down by the door of the Paritz in his uniform of sky-blue and his braid as golden as the sun, and the soldiers too, the officers who were wandering about, and those Generals – not so grand as he of course but in uniforms nevertheless – it was all one vast shooting-alley from which none of them, not one of them, could possibly escape. 'They're going to shoot!' I shouted to them at the top of my voice, in the middle of the main hall. 'They're going to shoot! Clear out, all of you, run away!' Then I went and shouted it from the window too, I couldn't help myself. There was a terrible scene. 'Poor boy,' people said. The porter took me along very gently to the bar. With great kindness he made me drink, and I drank a Iot and then finally the gendarmes came to fetch me; they were rougher about it. In the *Stand of All Nations* there'd been gendarmes too. I remembered having seen them. Lola kissed me and helped them to handcuff me and lead me away.

After that I was feverish and fell ill; driven insane, they said in hospital, by fear. They may have been right. When one's in this world surely the best thing one can do, isn't it, is to get out of it? Whether one's mad or not, frightened or not.

F. SCOTT FITZGERALD

From

# TENDER IS THE NIGHT

1934

SHE WOKE UP cooled and shamed. The sight of her beauty in the mirror did not reassure her but only awakened the ache of yesterday and a letter, forwarded by her mother, from the boy who had taken her to the Yale prom last fall, which announced his presence in Paris, was no help – all that seemed far away. She emerged from her room for the ordeal of meeting the Divers weighted with a double trouble. But it was hidden by a sheath as impermeable as Nicole's when they met and went together to a series of fittings. It was consoling, though, when Nicole remarked, apropos of a distraught saleswoman: 'Most people think everybody feels about them much more violently than they actually do – they think other people's opinions of them swing through great arcs of approval or disapproval.' Yesterday in her expansiveness Rosemary would have resented that remark – today in her desire to minimize what had happened she welcomed it eagerly. She admired Nicole for her beauty and her wisdom, and also for the first time in her life she was jealous. Just before leaving Gausse's Hôtel her mother had said in that casual tone, which Rosemary knew concealed her most significant opinions, that Nicole was a great beauty, with the frank implication that Rosemary was not. This did not bother Rosemary, who had only recently been allowed to learn that she was even personable; so that her prettiness never seemed exactly her own but rather an acquirement, like her French. Nevertheless, in the taxi she looked at Nicole, matching herself against her. There were all the potentialities for romantic love in that lovely body and in the delicate mouth, sometimes tight, sometimes expectantly half open to the world. Nicole had been a beauty as a young girl and she would be a beauty later when her skin stretched tight over her high cheek-bones – the essential structure was there. She had been white-Saxon-blonde but she was more beautiful now that her hair had darkened than when it had been like a cloud and more beautiful than she.

'We lived there,' Rosemary suddenly pointed to a building in the rue des Saints-Pères.

'That's strange. Because when I was twelve Mother and Baby and I once spent a winter there,' and she pointed to a hotel directly across the street. The two dingy fronts stared at them, gray echoes of girlhood.

'We'd just built our Lake Forest house and we were economizing,' Nicole continued. 'At least Baby and I and the governess economized and Mother travelled.'

'We were economizing too,' said Rosemary, realizing that the word meant different things to them.

'Mother always spoke of it very carefully as a small hotel –' Nicole gave her quick magnetic little laugh, '– I mean instead of saying a "cheap" hotel. If any swanky friends asked us our address we'd never say, "We're in a dingy little hole over in the apache quarter where we're glad of running water," – we'd say "We're in a small hotel." As if all the big ones were too noisy and vulgar for us. Of course the friends always saw through us and told everyone about it, but Mother always said it showed we knew our way around Europe. She did, of course: she was born a German citizen. But her mother was American, and she was brought up in Chicago, and she was more American than European.'

They were meeting the others in two minutes, and

Rosemary reconstructed herself once more as they got out of the taxi in the rue Guynemer, across from the Luxembourg Gardens. They were lunching in the Norths' already dismantled apartment high above the green mass of leaves. The day seemed different to Rosemary from the day before. When she saw him face to face their eyes met and brushed like birds' wings. After that everything was all right, everything was wonderful, she knew that he was beginning to fall in love with her. She felt wildly happy, felt the warm sap of emotion being pumped through her body. A cool, clear confidence deepened and sang in her. She scarcely looked at Dick but she knew everything was all right.

After luncheon the Divers and the Norths and Rosemary went to the Franco-American Films, to be joined by Collis Clay, her young man from New Haven, to whom she had telephoned. He was a Georgian, with the peculiarly regular, even stencilled ideas of Southerners who are educated in the North. Last winter she had thought him attractive – once they held hands in an automobile going from New Haven to New York; now he no longer existed for her.

In the projection room she sat between Collis Clay and Dick while the mechanic mounted the reels of 'Daddy's Girl' and a French executive fluttered about her trying to talk American slang. 'Yes, boy,' he said when there was trouble with the projector, 'I have not any benenas.' Then the lights went out, there was the sudden click and a flickering noise and she was alone with Dick at last. They looked at each other in the half darkness.

'Dear Rosemary,' he murmured. Their shoulders touched. Nicole stirred restlessly at the end of the row and Abe coughed convulsively and blew his nose; then they all settled down and the picture ran.

There she was – the school girl of a year ago, hair down

her back and rippling out stiffly like the solid hair of a Tanagra figure; there she was – *so* young and innocent – the product of her mother's loving care; there she was – embodying all the immaturity of the race, cutting a new cardboard paper doll to pass before its empty harlot's mind. She remembered how she had felt in that dress, especially fresh and new under the fresh young silk.

Daddy's girl. Was it a 'itty-bitty bravekins and did it suffer? Ooo-ooo-tweet, de tweetest thing, wasn't she dest too tweet? Before her tiny fist the forces of lust and corruption rolled away; nay, the very march of destiny stopped; inevitably became evitable, syllogism, dialectic, all rationality fell away. Women would forget the dirty dishes at home and weep, even within the picture one woman wept so long that she almost stole the film away from Rosemary. She wept all over a set that cost a fortune, in a Duncan Phyfe dining-room, in an aviation port, and during a yacht-race that was only used in two flashes, in a subway and finally in a bathroom. But Rosemary triumphed. Her fineness of character, her courage and steadfastness intruded upon by the vulgarity of the world, and Rosemary showing what it took with a face that had not yet become mask-like – yet it was actually so moving that the emotions of the whole row of people went out to her at intervals during the picture. There was a break once and the light went on and after the chatter of applause Dick said to her sincerely: 'I'm simply astounded. You're going to be one of the best actresses on the stage.'

Then back to 'Daddy's Girl': happier days now, and a lovely shot of Rosemary and her parent united at the last in a father complex so apparent that Dick winced for all psychologists at the vicious sentimentality. The screen vanished, the lights went on, the moment had come.

'I've arranged one other thing,' announced Rosemary to the company at large, 'I've arranged a test for Dick.'

'A what?'

'A screen test, they'll take one now.'

There was an awful silence – then an irrepressible chortle from the Norths. Rosemary watched Dick comprehend what she meant, his face moving first in an Irish way; simultaneously she realized that she had made some mistake in the playing of her trump and still she did not suspect that the card was at fault.

'I don't want a test,' said Dick firmly; then, seeing the situation as a whole, he continued lightly, 'Rosemary, I'm disappointed. The pictures make a fine career for a woman – but my God, they can't photograph me. I'm an old scientist all wrapped up in his private life.'

Nicole and Mary urged him ironically to seize the opportunity; they teased him, both faintly annoyed at not having been asked for a sitting. But Dick closed the subject with a somewhat tart discussion of actors: 'The strongest guard is placed at the gateway to nothing,' he said. 'Maybe because the condition of emptiness is too shameful to be divulged.'

In the taxi with Dick and Collis Clay – they were dropping Collis, and Dick was taking Rosemary to a tea from which Nicole and the Norths had resigned in order to do the things Abe had left undone till the last – in the taxi Rosemary reproached him.

'I thought if the test turned out to be good I could take it to California with me. And then maybe if they liked it you'd come out and be my leading man in a picture.'

He was overwhelmed. 'It was a darn sweet thought, but I'd rather look at *you*. You were about the nicest sight I ever looked at.'

'That's a great picture,' said Collis. 'I've seen it four times. I know one boy at New Haven who's seen it a dozen times – he went all the way to Hartford to see it one time. And when I brought Rosemary up to New Haven he was so shy he wouldn't meet her. Can you beat that? This little girl knocks them cold.'

Dick and Rosemary looked at each other, wanting to be alone, but Collis failed to understand.

'I'll drop you where you're going,' he suggested. 'I'm staying at the Lutétia.'

'We'll drop you,' said Dick.

'It'll be easier for me to drop you. No trouble at all.'

'I think it will be better if we drop you.'

'But –' began Collis; he grasped the situation at last and began discussing with Rosemary when he would see her again.

Finally, he was gone, with the shadowy unimportance but the offensive bulk of the third party. The car stopped unexpectedly, unsatisfactorily, at the address Dick had given. He drew a long breath.

'Shall we go in?'

'I don't care,' Rosemary said. 'I'll do anything you want.'

He considered.

'I almost have to go in – she wants to buy some pictures from a friend of mine who needs the money.'

Rosemary smoothed the brief expressive disarray of her hair.

'We'll stay just five minutes,' he decided. 'You're not going to like these people.'

She assumed that they were dull and stereotyped people, or gross and drunken people, or tiresome, insistent people, or any of the sorts of people that the Divers avoided. She was entirely unprepared for the impression that the scene made on her.

IT WAS A house hewn from the frame of Cardinal de Retz's palace in the rue Monsieur, but once inside the door there was nothing of the past, nor of any present that Rosemary knew. The outer shell, the masonry, seemed rather to enclose the future so that it was an electric-like shock, a definite nervous experience, perverted as a breakfast of oatmeal and hashish, to cross that threshold, if it could be so called, into the long hall of blue steel, silver-gilt, and the myriad facets of many oddly bevelled mirrors. The effect was unlike that of any part of the Decorative Arts Exhibition – for there were people *in* it, not in front of it. Rosemary had the detached false-and-exalted feeling of being on a set and she guessed that every one else present had that feeling too.

There were about thirty people, mostly women, and all fashioned by Louisa M. Alcott or Madame de Ségur; and they functioned on this set as cautiously, as precisely, as does a human hand picking up jagged broken glass. Neither individually nor as a crowd could they be said to dominate the environment, as one comes to dominate a work of art he may possess, no matter how esoteric. No one knew what this room meant because it was evolving into something else, becoming everything a room was not; to exist in it was as difficult as walking on a highly polished moving stairway, and no one could succeed at all save with the aforementioned qualities of a hand moving among broken glass – which qualities limited and defined the majority of those present.

These were of two sorts. There were the Americans and English who had been dissipating all spring and summer, so that now everything they did had a purely nervous inspiration. They were very quiet and lethargic at certain hours and then they exploded into sudden quarrels and breakdowns and seductions. The other class, who might be called the exploiters, was formed by the sponges, who were sober, serious people by comparison, with a purpose in life and no time for fooling. These kept their balance best in that environment, and what tone there was, beyond the apartment's novel organization of light values, came from them.

The Frankenstein took down Dick and Rosemary at a gulp – it separated them immediately and Rosemary suddenly discovered herself to be an insincere little person, living all in the upper registers of her throat and wishing the director would come. There was however such a wild beating of wings in the room that she did not feel her position was more incongruous than any one else's. In addition, her training told and after a series of semi-military turns, shifts, and marches she found herself presumably talking to a neat, slick girl with a lovely boy's face, but actually absorbed by a conversation taking place on a sort of gun-metal ladder diagonally opposite her and four feet away.

There was a trio of young women sitting on the bench. They were all tall and slender with small heads groomed like manikins' heads, and as they talked the heads waved gracefully about above their dark tailored suits, rather like long-stemmed flowers and rather like cobras' hoods.

'Oh, they give a good show,' said one of them, in a deep rich voice. 'Practically the best show in Paris – I'd be the last one to deny that. But after all –' She sighed. 'Those phrases he uses over and over – "Oldest inhabitant gnawed by rodents." You laugh once.'

'I prefer people whose lives have more corrugated surfaces,' said the second, 'and I don't like her.'

'I've never really been able to get very excited about them, or their entourage either. Why, for example, the entirely liquid Mr. North?'

'He's out,' said the first girl. 'But you must admit that the party in question can be one of the most charming human beings you have ever met.'

It was the first hint Rosemary had had that they were talking about the Divers, and her body grew tense with indignation. But the girl talking to her, in the starched blue shirt with the bright blue eyes and the red cheeks and the very gray suit, a poster of a girl, had begun to play up. Desperately she kept sweeping things from between them, afraid that Rosemary couldn't see her, sweeping them away until presently there was not so much as a veil of brittle humor hiding the girl, and with distaste Rosemary saw her plain.

'Couldn't you have lunch, or maybe dinner, or lunch the day after?' begged the girl. Rosemary looked about for Dick, finding him with the hostess, to whom he had been talking since they came in. Their eyes met and he nodded slightly, and simultaneously the three cobra women noticed her; their long necks darted toward her and they fixed finely critical glances upon her. She looked back at them defiantly, acknowledging that she had heard what they said. Then she threw off her exigent vis-à-vis with a polite but clipped parting that she had just learned from Dick, and went over to join him. The hostess – she was another tall rich American girl, promenading insouciantly upon the national prosperity – was asking Dick innumerable questions about Gausse's Hôtel, whither she evidently wanted to come, and battering persistently against his reluctance. Rosemary's presence reminded her that she had been recalcitrant as a hostess and glancing about she said: 'Have you met any one amusing, have you met Mr. –' Her eyes groped for a male who might interest Rosemary, but Dick said they must go. They left immediately, moving over the brief threshold of the future to the sudden past of the stone façade without.

'Wasn't it terrible?' he said.

'Terrible,' she echoed obediently.

'Rosemary?'

She murmured, 'What?' in an awed voice.

'I feel terribly about this.'

She was shaken with audibly painful sobs. 'Have you got a handkerchief?' she faltered. But there was little time to cry, and lovers now they fell ravenously on the quick seconds while outside the taxi windows the green and cream twilight faded, and the fire-red, gas-blue, ghost-green signs began to shine smokily through the tranquil rain. It was nearly six, the streets were in movement, the bistros gleamed, the Place de la Concorde moved by in pink majesty as the cab turned north.

They looked at each other at last, murmuring names that were a spell. Softly the two names lingered on the air, died away more slowly than other words, other names, slower than music in the mind.

'I don't know what came over me last night,' Rosemary said. 'That glass of champagne? I've never done anything like that before.'

'You simply said you loved me.'

'I do love you – I can't change that.' It was time for Rosemary to cry, so she cried a little in her handkerchief.

'I'm afraid I'm in love with you,' said Dick, 'and that's not the best thing that could happen.'

Again the names – then they lurched together as if the taxi had swung them. Her breasts crushed flat against him, her mouth was all new and warm, owned in common. They stopped thinking with an almost painful relief, stopped seeing; they only breathed and sought each other. They were both in the gray gentle world of a mild hangover of fatigue when the nerves relax in bunches like piano strings, and crackle suddenly like wicker chairs. Nerves so raw and tender must surely join other nerves, lips to lips, breast to breast . . .

They were still in the happier stage of love. They were full of brave illusions about each other, tremendous illusions, so that the communion of self with self seemed to be on a plane where no other human relations mattered. They both seemed to have arrived there with an extraordinary innocence as though a series of pure accidents had driven them together, so many accidents that at last they were forced to conclude that they were for each other. They had arrived with clean hands, or so it seemed, after no traffic with the merely curious and clandestine.

But for Dick that portion of the road was short; the turning came before they reached the hotel.

'There's nothing to do about it,' he said, with a feeling of panic. 'I'm in love with you but it doesn't change what I said last night.'

'That doesn't matter now. I just wanted to make you love me – if you love me everything's all right.'

'Unfortunately I do. But Nicole mustn't know – she mustn't suspect even faintly. Nicole and I have got to go on together. In a way that's more important than just wanting to go on.'

'Kiss me once more.'

He kissed her, but momentarily he had left her.

'Nicole mustn't suffer – she loves me and I love her – you understand that.'

She did understand – it was the sort of thing she understood well, not hurting people. She knew the Divers loved each other because it had been her primary assumption. She had thought however that it was a rather cooled relation, and actually rather like the love of herself and her mother. When people have so much for outsiders didn't it indicate a lack of inner intensity?

'And I mean love,' he said, guessing her thoughts. 'Active love – it's more complicated than I can tell you. It was responsible for that crazy duel.'

'How did you know about the duel? I thought we were to keep it from you.'

'Do you think Abe can keep a secret?' He spoke with incisive irony. 'Tell a secret over the radio, publish it in a tabloid, but never tell it to a man who drinks more than three or four a day.'

She laughed in agreement, staying close to him.

'So you understand my relations with Nicole are complicated. She's not very strong – she looks strong but she isn't. And this makes rather a mess.'

'Oh, say that later! But kiss me now – love me now. I'll love you and never let Nicole see.'

'You darling.'

They reached the hotel and Rosemary walked a little behind him, to admire him, to adore him. His step was alert as if he had just come from some great doings and was hurrying on toward others. Organizer of private gaiety, curator of a richly incrusted happiness. His hat was a perfect hat and he carried a heavy stick and yellow gloves. She thought what a good time they would all have being with him tonight.

They walked upstairs – five flights. At the first landing they stopped and kissed; she was careful on the next landing, on the third more careful still. On the next – there were two more – she stopped half way and kissed him fleetingly good-by. At his urgency she walked down with him to the one below for a minute – and then up and up. Finally it was good-by with their hands stretching to touch along the diagonal of the banister and then the fingers slipping apart. Dick went back downstairs to make some arrangements for the evening – Rosemary ran to her room and wrote a letter to her mother; she was conscience-stricken because she did not miss her mother at all.

GEORGES SIMENON

# IN THE RUE PIGALLE

1936

Translated by Jean Stewart

A CHANCE VISITOR to Marina's might well have been misled. Lucien, the proprietor, wearing a thick beige sweater that made him look even shorter and broader, was fiddling with his bottles behind the bar, decanting, re-corking, carefully changing the washer on his tap, and his sullenness might well have been put down to the time of day and the weather.

For it was a grey morning, colder than usual, the sort of morning when snow seems imminent and you want to stay in bed. It was barely nine o'clock, and there was little activity in the Rue Pigalle.

The casual visitor would probably have wondered about the identity of the thickset man in a heavy overcoat, who stood with his back to the stove, smoking a pipe and nursing a glass of spirits in his hand; he would certainly not have expected to find here Superintendent Maigret of the Police Judiciaire.

He would also have seen a slatternly Breton servant girl, Julie, with a permanently scared look on her freckled face, kneeling on the floor and wiping the legs of the table.

In the restaurants of the Pigalle district, things seldom start very early. The place had not been cleaned; dirty glasses were still lying around, and in the kitchen, through the open door, the *patronne*, Marina herself, could be seen, looking even grubbier and more ungainly than her maid.

The general effect was quiet and homely. At the farthest

table there were two men who although they were unshaven and their rumpled suits had clearly been slept in, didn't look in too bad shape.

In fact, the casual visitor would just have thought the place a modest restaurant like any other, with its regular customers, a place not of the cleanest, to be sure, but not unattractive on this chilly morning.

He would doubtless have changed his mind on seeing Maigret suddenly glance at the camelhair overcoat belonging to one of the customers and hanging on the coat-rack, go up to it, thrust his hand into the pockets and pull out a knuckle-duster; and then on hearing the Superintendent remark goodhumouredly:

'Hey, Christiani . . . Is this the one that knocked me out?'

Half an hour earlier, on his arrival at the Quai des Orfèvres, Maigret had been called to the phone by somebody who insisted on speaking to him personally, and who was obviously making an effort to disguise his voice.

'That you, Superintendent? . . . Look here, there was a row going on last night at Marina's . . . If you were to look in there you might meet your old friend Christiani . . . And it might occur to you to ask him for news of Martino . . . You know, the kid from Antibes, whose brother has just been shipped off to Guiana? . . .'

Before five minutes were up, Maigret had learnt from the exchange that the telephone call came from a tobacconist's in the Rue Notre-Dame-de-Lorette. A quarter of an hour later, he alighted from a taxi at the corner of the Rue Pigalle, just as the gutters were carrying their fullest load of refuse alongside the pavement.

Although he was still in the dark, Maigret was convinced that the affair must be taken seriously, indeed very seriously, since such denunciations are seldom unfounded.

He had the proof of this right away, as he walked slowly up the street. Almost opposite Marina's he noticed a small bar, kept by an Auvergnat, unexpectedly wedged between two nightclubs. In this bar, keeping watch close to the window, the Superintendent recognized two men, the Niçois and Pepito, who are not usually seen about so early, particularly in such a place.

The minute after, he pushed open the door of the restaurant across the street, at the far end of which he saw Christiani with a young recruit, René Lecoeur, known as the Accountant because he had formerly been a bank clerk in Marseilles.

In this sort of situation it is better not to be surprised at anything. Raising his hand to his bowler hat, Maigret greeted the assembled company, like any harmless regular dropping in for a drink.

'How goes it, Lucien?'

Which did not prevent him from noticing the way the napkin shook in Lucien's hands, while the maid, looking up with a start, bumped her head against a table.

'Did you have a lot of company last night? . . . Give me a coffee and a small calvados . . .'

Then, entering the kitchen:

'How are things, Marina? . . . I saw you'd had a mirror broken above the bar . . .'

For he had noticed at a glance that a mirror had been smashed by a bullet from a revolver.

'That was done some time ago,' Lucien hurriedly explained. 'Somebody I don't know, who had just bought a gun and didn't know it was loaded . . .'

After that things moved very slowly. Maigret had been there for over a quarter of an hour and they had not exchanged more than a score of remarks. The maid went on with her work, Lucien remained behind the bar, and Marina busied herself in the kitchen. Meanwhile the Superintendent smoked his pipe and drank his calvados, going from time to time to glance out at the bistro over the way and then returning to stand by the stove.

He knew the household like the back of his hand. Lucien, who had been in trouble in Marseilles, had subsequently gone straight and opened this little restaurant in Montmartre with his wife. His customers were chiefly old acquaintances, people from the underworld of course but who had settled down, for the most part, and become almost respectable.

This was the case with Christiani who, ten years previously, when arrested, had promptly struck Maigret with his knuckle-duster and who was now owner of a couple of 'houses' in Paris and another at Barcelonnette.

It was more or less the case, too, with the men in the bistro over the way, particularly the Niçois, who also owned 'houses' like Christiani's and unfortunately in competition with his.

'Say, how long has your pal been staying at the Auvergnat's across the street?'

'I'm not interested in such people!' retorted Christiani with contempt.

'That may be. But he certainly seems to be interested in you, and if I didn't know you're a stout fellow I'd think that it's his presence in the little bistro that keeps you from going out . . .'

A pause, and another sip of calvados.

'Yes . . . That's how I'd picture things . . . Last night, for one reason or another, there could have been some unpleasantness. And since then, Pepito and the Niçois could have been waiting for you outside, so that the two of you had to sleep on the restaurant benches.'

As he spoke he went up to the Accountant and fingered the creases on the young man's jacket.

'Only I wonder what could have happened, seeing that everyone knows Lucien doesn't like trouble and that you're no longer the sort to take risks. By the way, Martino's brother, who set off yesterday from the Île de Ré, sends you his greetings . . .'

All very friendly, almost goodhumoured. Nevertheless Christiani had given a start, and since the Accountant was standing there Maigret took the opportunity to feel his pockets and extract a stout knife with a safety-catch.

'That's dangerous, son! You shouldn't go about carrying that kind of toy. What about you, Christiani? Haven't you anything for me in your pockets?'

Christiani, with a shrug, pulled out a Smith and Wesson revolver which he handed over to the Superintendent.

'Why, hello, there's one bullet missing . . . Maybe the one that smashed the mirror . . . What surprises me, by the way, is that you didn't reload it and that you didn't bother to clean the barrel . . .'

He slipped the knife, the knuckle-duster and the revolver into his overcoat pocket, and with apparent unconcern searched in every corner of the place, even opening the ice-box and the telephone booth. Meanwhile his mind was hard at work; he was trying to understand. He built up hypotheses which he rejected one after the other.

'Did you know that the Niçois told Martino that someone had informed on his brother? At any rate, that's the story I've just heard. If I let you go, it's so that you may avoid him, for he might hold it against you and he generally carries a gun.'

'What are you getting at?' growled Christiani, who to all appearances was just as calm as Maigret.

'Nothing . . . I'd like to see Martino . . . I don't know why, but I'd be interested to see him.'

Meanwhile he had made sure that nobody, alive or dead, was hidden in the restaurant, or in the kitchen, or in the adjoining bedroom where Lucien and Marina slept.

At half past nine a messenger brought in a case of aperitifs, and then, almost immediately afterwards, a huge yellow van belonging to the Voyages Duchemin agency stopped in front of the building, leaving again shortly after.

'I'd like a slice of sausage, Marina, one of your own make . . .'

Then Maigret gave a sudden frown on seeing a new figure emerge from the bedroom, looking as surprised as himself.

'Where have *you* come from?'

'I was . . . I was lying on the bed . . .'

It was Fred, who had been Christiani's accomplice on various occasions; he was lying, since Maigret had just ascertained that the bedroom was empty.

'It seems to me,' muttered the Superintendent, 'that you're all so fond of the house that you won't leave it . . . You give me your gun, too.'

Fred hesitated, then held out his revolver, another Smith and Wesson, from which no cartridge was missing.

'Will you give it me back?'

'Maybe . . . It depends on what Martino has to tell me . . . I'm expecting him at any moment. Yes, I told him to meet me here . . .'

He was watching their faces and he saw René Lecoeur turn pale and gulp down a mouthful of spirits.

Maigret made one more effort. He had to find the answer, at all costs, and he found it just as he was looking out into the street, where a lorry was passing.

'Lift the receiver . . .' he ordered Christiani.

He did not want to go into the phone booth himself, for that would have meant taking his eye off his suspects.

'Ask for Police Headquarters ... Get Lucas on the line ... You've got him? Pass me the receiver ...'

Fortunately the cord was long enough.

'That you, Lucas? ... Ring up the Voyages Duchemin Agency right away ... We must get hold of a van of theirs which has just delivered or collected something in the Rue Pigalle ... Understood ? ... Find out what it was ... Quick as you can! ... Yes, I'm stopping here ...'

Then, turning towards the kitchen:

'What about that sausage, Marina?'

'Coming, Superintendent ... Here you are ...'

'I don't expect these gentlemen want any ... Unless I'm very much mistaken, they can't be feeling very hungry ...'

At ten minutes past eleven, they were all still in their places, including the Niçois and his companion at the Auvergnat's over the way. At eleven minutes past eleven, Lucas jumped out of a taxi in a state of great excitement, pushed open the door and signalled to Maigret that he had something important to tell him.

'You can speak in front of these gentlemen, they're all friends.'

'I got hold of the van, in the Boulevard Rochechouart ... They collected a trunk. They'd had a phone call from this house ... A third-floor tenant, Monsieur Béchevel ... It was a huge trunk, or rather a chest, to be sent by goods train to Quimper ...'

'You let it go, I hope!' teased Maigret.

'I had it opened ... There was a body in it, Martino's, the man whose brother ...'

'I know ... And then ...'

'Dr. Paul was at home and he came round right away. I've got the bullet, which was still embedded in the wound . . .'

Maigret fingered it nonchalantly, and muttered as though to himself:

'A Browning, 6 mm. 35 . . . You see how it is: these gentlemen, who spent the night here, only have Smith and Wessons . . .'

Nobody could foresee what he was going to do. Even now, a casual visitor would not have realized the tenseness of the situation. Lucien was exercising all his ingenuity finding things to do behind the bar.

'Shall I tell you what I think happened? . . . Strictly between ourselves, of course . . . Last night Martino, who'd had too much to drink, got it into his head that Christiani was responsible for his brother's arrest. He came to settle accounts with him. And then, as he was a bit over-excited, he had an accident . . . You get my meaning?'

Lucas, too, was wondering what his chief was getting at. Christiani had lit a cigarette and was blowing out the smoke with assumed indifference.

'Only, the Niçois and Pepito were waiting in the street . . . They dared not come in, but they thought they'd wait for the others outside.

'Are you with me now? . . . That's why these friends of ours slept on the restaurant benches while the Niçois kept watch outside, and then, at daybreak, settled down at the Auvergnat's . . . The trickiest part was what to do with that wretched corpse; they couldn't really leave it on Lucien's hands. What would *you* have done, Christiani? . . . You're an intelligent fellow . . .'

Christiani gave a disdainful shrug.

'You tell me, Lucien . . . Who's this Béchevel on the third floor?'

'An old gentleman, an invalid . . .'

'Just what I thought . . . Someone went up there in the small hours and made it clear to him that he'd got to keep quiet . . . Before anyone was awake in the house they took the body up there by the back stairs and put it into a chest belonging to the old man. Then they rang up the Voyages Duchemin. Go up to the third floor and see if I'm right . . . I'm sure you'll be given the description of our friend Fred, who was in charge of the job . . .'

So far there was nothing sensational about the scene. In fact a bank messenger who had called was able to settle his business with Lucien without noticing anything untoward.

'You've still got nothing to tell me, Christiani?'

'Nothing . . .'

'And you, Lecoeur? After all, it's the first time I've seen you involved in serious trouble . . .'

'I don't know what you're talking about,' the boy said in a tense voice.

'Then we shall just have to wait for Lucas . . .'

They waited. And the other lot, across the street, waited too. And the street grew busier, while the clouds lifted a little and the light became brighter.

'Too bad it had to happen here, Lucien! . . . Never let anyone break a mirror . . . It brings bad luck . . .'

Lucas was soon back, announcing:

'You were quite right! . . . I found the poor fellow bound and gagged. He described Fred, but there was somebody else there last night whom he didn't see. They jumped on him while he was still asleep.'

'That'll do! Ring for a taxi . . . Wait! . . . Call Headquarters too, and get them to send somebody to watch the fellows over the way, and see that they don't make trouble.'

Maigret, scratching his head, looked at his three toughs and said with a sigh:

'In the meantime, perhaps we shall find out which of you fired the shot . . .'

As if he had all the time in the world and didn't know how to spend it, Maigret selected one of the tables and spread out on it a regular panoply of weapons, setting Christiani's knuckle-duster by the side of his revolver and Fred's, then putting Lecoeur's knife a little further off.

'Don't panic about what I'm going to tell you, kid,' he said to the young man, who seemed about to faint. 'This is the first time you've been in trouble, but it probably won't be the last . . . This gun, you see, undoubtedly belongs to Christiani, who's been too long in the business to play about with a little Browning like the one that killed Martino. Fred, too, is an old hand who likes serious weapons. When the row broke out, Christiani fired and someone must have knocked his arm, for he only hit the mirror. Then you, with your little Browning . . .'

'I haven't got a Browning,' the Accountant managed to stammer out.

'Exactly! *It's the fact that you haven't got one that proves you fired the shot.* Fred kept his gun because he knew it would prove his innocence. Christiani didn't even clean his to show that he had only fired one shot which hit nobody . . . They both know all about experts' reports and they played the game accordingly. Whereas you had to get rid of your revolver because it would have proved you were the murderer. Where did you put it?'

'I didn't kill him!'

'I'm asking you where you put it . . . Ask Christiani . . . It's too late to play the clever boy . . .'

'You won't find any Browning . . .'

Maigret looked at him with pity and muttered under his breath:

'You poor sucker!'

The more of a sucker, the more to be pitied since Martino had borne him no grudge and he had only fired to prove to the others that he had guts.

When Lucas returned, Maigret whispered to him:

'Look everywhere . . . specially on the roof . . . They won't have been such fools as to hide the gun in Lucien's place or in the old man's. See if, at the top of the stairs, there's a window opening on to the roof . . .'

He took his lot with him, while two or three harmless-looking strollers kept watch on the bistro across the street.

Christiani, in his camelhair overcoat, looked like some respectable citizen who has been arrested by mistake and who will promptly be released with apologies. Fred had assumed a jaunty air. The Accountant was tense in every nerve.

The case was an absolutely classic one. Maigret had always claimed that, but for chance, fifty per cent of criminals would escape punishment and that, but for informers, another fifty per cent would remain at liberty.

It sounded like a wisecrack, particularly when uttered in his cheerful gruff voice.

All the same an informer had played a part here, and so had chance, which had enabled him to notice the yellow van of the Voyages Duchemin.

But was there not also a considerable factor due to professional skill, knowledge of human nature and even what is known as flair?

At three o'clock that afternoon the Browning was discovered on the roof, where it had been thrown through the skylight.

At half past three the Accountant had confessed with tears, while Christiani, giving the address of a celebrated lawyer, asserted:

'You'll see, it'll get me about six months!'

At which Maigret sighed, without looking at him:

'And your knuckle-duster only cost me a couple of teeth . . .'

DJUNA BARNES

# LA SOMNAMBULE

1937

From

# NIGHTWOOD

CLOSE TO THE church of *St. Sulpice*, around the corner in the *rue Servandoni*, lived the doctor. His small slouching figure was a feature of the *Place*. To the proprietor of the *Café de la Mairie du VI*[e] he was almost a son. This relatively small square, through which tram lines ran in several directions, bounded on the one side by the church and on the other by the court, was the doctor's 'city'. What he could not find here to answer to his needs, could be found in the narrow streets that ran into it. Here he had been seen ordering details for funerals in the *parlour* with its black broadcloth curtains and mounted pictures of hearses; buying holy pictures and *petits Jésus* in the *boutique* displaying vestments and flowering candles. He had shouted down at least one judge in the *Mairie du Luxembourg* after a dozen cigars had failed to bring about his ends.

He walked, pathetic and alone, among the pasteboard booths of the *Foire St. Germain* when for a time its imitation castles squatted in the square. He was seen coming at a smart pace down the left side of the church to go into Mass; bathing in the holy water stoup as if he were its single and beholden bird, pushing aside weary French maids and local tradespeople with the impatience of a soul in physical stress.

Sometimes, late at night, before turning into the *Café de la Mairie du VI*[e], he would be observed staring up at the huge towers of the church which rose into the sky, unlovely but reassuring, running a thick warm finger around his throat, where, in spite of its custom, his hair surprised him, lifting along his back and creeping up over his collar. Standing small and insubordinate, he would watch the basins of the fountain loosing their skirts of water in a ragged and flowing hem, sometimes crying to a man's departing shadow: 'Aren't you the beauty!'

To the *Café de la Mairie du VI*^e^ he brought Felix, who turned up in Paris some weeks after the encounter in Berlin. Felix thought to himself that undoubtedly the doctor was a great liar, but a valuable liar. His fabrications seemed to be the framework of a forgotten but imposing plan; some condition of life of which he was the sole surviving retainer. His manner was that of a servant of a defunct noble family, whose movements recall, though in a degraded form, those of a late master. Even the doctor's favourite gesture – plucking hairs out of his nostrils – seemed the 'vulgarization' of what was once a thoughtful plucking of the beard.

As the altar of a church would present but a barren stylization but for the uncalculated offerings of the confused and humble; as the *corsage* of a woman is made suddenly martial and sorrowful by the rose thrust among the more decorous blooms by the hand of a lover suffering the violence of the overlapping of the permission to bestow a last embrace, and its withdrawal: making a vanishing and infinitesimal bull's eye of that which had a moment before been a buoyant and showy bosom, by dragging time out of his bowels (for a lover knows two times, that which he is given, and that which he must make) – so Felix was astonished to find that the most touching flowers laid on the altar he had raised to his imagination were placed there by the people of the underworld, and that the reddest was to be the rose of the doctor.

After a long silence in which the doctor had ordered and consumed a *Chambéry fraise* and the Baron a coffee, the doctor remarked that the Jew and the Irish, the one moving upward and the other down, often meet, spade to spade in the same acre.

'The Irish may be as common as whale-shit – excuse me – on the bottom of the ocean – forgive me – but they do have imagination and,' he added, 'creative misery, which comes from being smacked down by the devil, and lifted up again by the angels. *Misericordioso!* Save me, Mother Mary, and never mind the other fellow! But the Jew, what is he at his best? Never anything higher than a meddler – pardon my wet glove – a supreme and marvellous meddler often, but a meddler nevertheless.' He bowed slightly from the hips. 'All right, Jews meddle and we lie, that's the difference, the fine difference. We say someone is pretty for instance, whereas, if the truth were known, they are probably as ugly as Smith going backward, but by our lie we have made that very party powerful, such is the power of the charlatan, the great strong! They drop on anything at any moment, and that sort of thing makes the mystic in the end, and,' he added, 'it makes the great doctor. The only people who really *know* anything about medical science are the nurses, and they never tell, they'd get slapped if they did. But the great doctor, he's a divine idiot and a wise man. He closes one eye, the eye that he studied with, and putting his fingers on the arteries of the body says: "God, whose roadway this is, has given me permission to travel on it also," which, heaven help the patient, is true; in this manner he comes on great cures, and sometimes upon that road is disconcerted by that Little Man.' The doctor ordered another *Chambéry*, and asked the Baron what he would have; being told that he wished nothing for the moment, the doctor added: 'No man needs curing of his individual sickness, his universal malady is what he should look to.'

The Baron remarked that this sounded like dogma.

The doctor grinned. 'Does it? Well, when you see that Little Man you know you will be shouldered from the path.

'I also know this,' he went on: 'One cup poured into another makes different water; tears shed by one eye would blind if wept into another's eye. The breast we strike in joy is not the breast we strike in pain; any man's smile would be consternation on another's mouth. Rear up eternal river, here comes grief! Man has no foothold that is not also a bargain. So be it! Laughing I came into Pacific Street, and laughing I'm going out of it; laughter is the pauper's money. I like paupers and bums,' he added, 'because they are impersonal with misery, but me – me, I'm taken most and chiefly for a vexatious bastard and gum on the bow, the wax that clots the gall or middle blood of man known at the heart or Bundle of Hiss. May my dilator burst and my speculum rust, may panic seize my index finger before I point out my man.'

His hands (which he always carried like a dog who is walking on his hind legs) seemed to be holding his attention, then he said, raising his large melancholy eyes with the bright twinkle that often came into them: 'Why is it that whenever I hear music I think I'm a bride?'

'Neurasthenia,' said Felix.

He shook his head. 'No, I'm not neurasthenic, I haven't that much respect for people – the basis, by the way, of all neurasthenia.'

'Impatience.'

The doctor nodded. 'The Irish are impatient for eternity, they lie to hurry it up, and they maintain their balance by the dexterity of God, God and the Father.'

'In 1685,' the Baron said, with dry humour, 'the Turks

brought coffee into Vienna, and from that day Vienna, like a woman, had one impatience, something she liked. You know, of course, that Pitt the younger was refused alliance because he was foolish enough to proffer tea; Austria and tea could never go together. All cities have a particular and special beverage suited to them. As for God and the Father – in Austria they were the Emperor.' The doctor looked up. The *chasseur* of the *Hôtel Récamier* (whom he knew far too well) was approaching them at a run.

'Eh!' said the doctor, who always expected anything at any hour, 'Now what?' The boy, standing before him in a red and black striped vest and flapping soiled apron, exclaimed in Midi French that a lady in twenty-nine had fainted and could not be brought out of it.

The doctor got up slowly, sighing. 'Pay,' he said to Felix, 'and follow me.' None of the doctor's methods being orthodox, Felix was not surprised at the invitation, but did as he was told.

On the second landing of the hotel (it was one of those middle-class hostelries which can be found in almost any corner of Paris, neither good nor bad, but so typical that it might have been moved every night and not have been out of place) a door was standing open, exposing a red carpeted floor, and at the further end two narrow windows overlooking the square.

On a bed, surrounded by a confusion of potted plants, exotic palms and cut flowers, faintly over-sung by the notes of unseen birds, which seemed to have been forgotten – left without the usual silencing cover, which, like cloaks on funeral urns, are cast over their cages at night by good housewives) – half flung off the support of the cushions from which, in a moment of threatened consciousness she had turned her head, lay the young woman, heavy and dishevelled. Her legs, in white flannel trousers, were spread as in a dance, the thick lacquered pumps looking too lively for the arrested step. Her hands, long and beautiful, lay on either side of her face.

The perfume that her body exhaled was of the quality of that earth-flesh, fungi, which smells of captured dampness and yet is so dry, overcast with the odour of oil of amber, which is an inner malady of the sea, making her seem as if she had invaded a sleep incautious and entire. Her flesh was the texture of plant life, and beneath it one sensed a frame, broad, porous and sleep-worn, as if sleep were a decay fishing her beneath the visible surface. About her head there was an effulgence as of phosphorus glowing about the circumference of a body of water – as if her life lay through her in ungainly luminous deteriorations – the troubling structure of the born somnambule, who lives in two worlds – meet of child and desperado.

Like a painting by the *douanier* Rousseau, she seemed to lie in a jungle trapped in a drawing room (in the apprehension of which the walls have made their escape), thrown in among the carnivorous flowers as their ration; the set, the property of an unseen *dompteur*, half lord, half promoter, over which one expects to hear the strains of an orchestra of wood-wind render a serenade which will popularize the wilderness.

Felix, out of delicacy, stepped behind the palms. The doctor with professional roughness, brought to a pitch by his eternal fear of meeting with the Law (he was not a licensed practitioner) said: 'Slap her wrists, for Christ's sake. Where in hell is the water pitcher!'

He found it, and with amiable heartiness flung a handful against her face.

A series of almost invisible shudders wrinkled her skin as

the water dripped from her lashes, over her mouth and on to the bed. A spasm of waking moved upward from some deep shocked realm, and she opened her eyes. Instantly she tried to get to her feet. She said: 'I was all right;' and fell back into the pose of her annihilation.

Experiencing a double confusion, Felix now saw the doctor partially hidden by the screen beside the bed, make the movements common to the 'dumbfounder', or man of magic; the gestures of one who, in preparing the audience for a miracle, must pretend that there is nothing to hide; the whole purpose that of making the back and elbows move in a series of 'honesties', while in reality the most flagrant part of the hoax is being prepared.

Felix saw that this was for the purpose of snatching a few drops from a perfume bottle picked up from the night table; of dusting his darkly bristled chin with a puff, and drawing a line of rouge across his lips, his upper lip compressed on his lower, in order to have it seem that their sudden embellishment was a visitation of nature; still thinking himself unobserved, as if the whole fabric of magic had begun to decompose, as if the mechanics of machination were indeed out of control and were simplifying themselves back to their origin; the doctor's hand reached out and covered a loose hundred-franc note lying on the table.

With a tension in his stomach, such as one suffers when watching an acrobat leaving the virtuosity of his safety in a mad unravelling whirl into probable death, Felix watched the hand descend, take up the note, and disappear into the limbo of the doctor's pocket. He knew that he would continue to like the doctor, though he was aware that it would be in spite of a long series of convulsions of the spirit, analogous to the displacement in the fluids of the oyster, that must cover its itch with a pearl; so he would have to cover the doctor. He knew at the same time that this stricture of acceptance (by which what we must love is made into what we can love) would eventually be a part of himself, though originally brought on by no will of his own.

Engrossed in the coils of this new disquiet, Felix turned about. The girl was sitting up. She recognized the doctor. She had seen him somewhere. But, as one may trade ten years at a certain shop and be unable to place the shopkeeper if he is met in the street or in the *promenoir* of a theatre, the shop being a portion of his identity, she struggled to place him now that he had moved out of his frame.

'*Café de la Mairie du VI*$^{e}$,' said the doctor, taking a chance in order to have a hand in her awakening.

She did not smile, though the moment he spoke she placed him. She closed her eyes and Felix, who had been looking into them intently because of their mysterious and shocking blue, found himself seeing them still faintly clear and timeless behind the lids – the long unqualified range in the iris of wild beasts who have not tamed the focus down to meet the human eye.

The woman who presents herself to the spectator as a 'picture' forever arranged, is, for the contemplative mind, the chiefest danger. Sometimes one meets a woman who is beast turning human. Such a person's every movement will reduce to an image of a forgotten experience; a mirage of an eternal wedding cast on the racial memory; as insupportable a joy as would be the vision of an eland coming down an aisle of trees, chapleted with orange blossoms and bridal veil, a hoof raised in the economy of fear, stepping in the trepidation of flesh that will become myth; as the unicorn is neither man nor beast deprived, but human hunger pressing its breast to its prey.

Such a woman is the infected carrier of the past: before her the structure of our head and jaws ache – we feel that we could eat her, she who is eaten death returning, for only then do we put our face close to the blood on the lips of our forefathers.

Something of this emotion came over Felix, but being racially incapable of abandon, he felt that he was looking upon a figurehead in a museum, which though static, no longer roosting on its cutwater, seemed yet to be going against the wind; as if this girl were the converging halves of a broken fate, setting face, in sleep, toward itself in time, as an image and its reflection in a lake seem parted only by the hesitation in the hour.

In the tones of this girl's voice was the pitch of one enchanted with the gift of postponed abandon: the low drawling 'aside' voice of the actor who, in the soft usury of his speech, withholds a vocabulary until the profitable moment when he shall be facing his audience – in her case a guarded extempore to the body of what would be said at some later period when she would be able to 'see' them. What she now said was merely the longest way to a quick dismissal. She asked them to come to see her when she would be 'able to feel better'.

Pinching the *chasseur*, the doctor inquired the girl's name. 'Mademoiselle Robin Vote,' the *chasseur* answered.

Descending into the street, the doctor, desiring 'one last before bed' directed his steps back to the café. After a short silence he asked the Baron if he had ever thought about women and marriage. He kept his eyes fixed on the marble of the table before him, knowing that Felix had experienced something unusual.

The Baron admitted that he had, he wished a son who

would feel as he felt about the 'great past'. The doctor then inquired, with feigned indifference, of what nation he would choose the boy's mother.

'The American,' the Baron answered instantly. 'With an American anything can be done.'

The doctor laughed. He brought his soft fist down on the table – now he was sure. 'Fate and entanglement,' he said, 'have begun again – the dung beetle rolling his burden uphill – oh the hard climb! Nobility, very well, but what is it?' The Baron started to answer him, the doctor held up his hand. 'Wait a minute! I know – the few that the many have lied about well and long enough to make them deathless. So you must have a son,' he paused. 'A king is the peasant's actor, who becomes so scandalous that he has to be bowed down to – scandalous in the higher sense naturally. And why must he be bowed down to? Because he has been set apart as the one dog who need not regard the rules of the house, they are so high that they can defame God and foul their rafters! But the people – that's different – they are church-broken, nation-broken – they drink and pray and piss in the one place. Every man has a house-broken heart except the great man. The people love their church and know it, as a dog knows where he was made to conform, and there he returns by his instinct. But to the graver permission, the king, the tsar, the emperor, who may relieve themselves on high heaven – to them they bow down – only.' The Baron, who was always troubled by obscenity, would never, in the case of the doctor, resent it; he felt the seriousness, the melancholy hidden beneath every jest and malediction that the doctor uttered, therefore he answered him seriously. 'To pay homage to our past is the only gesture that also includes the future.'

'And so a son?'

'For that reason. The modern child has nothing left to hold to, or to put it better, he has nothing to hold with. We are adhering to life now with our last muscle – the heart.'

'The last muscle of aristocracy is madness – remember that –' the doctor leaned forward, 'the last child born to aristocracy is sometimes an idiot, out of respect – we go up – but we come down.'

The Baron dropped his monocle, the unarmed eye looked straight ahead. 'It's not necessary,' he said, then he added, 'But you are American, so you don't believe.'

'Ho!' hooted the doctor, 'because I'm American I believe anything, so I say beware! In the king's bed is always found, just before it becomes a museum piece, the droppings of the black sheep' – he raised his glass, 'To Robin Vote.' He grinned. 'She can't be more than twenty.'

With a roar the steel blind came down over the window of the *Café de la Mairie du VI*[e].

Felix, carrying two volumes on the life of the Bourbons, called the next day at the *Hôtel Récamier.* Miss Vote was not in. Four afternoons in succession he called, only to be told that she had just left. On the fifth, turning the corner of the *rue Bonaparte*, he ran into her.

Removed from her setting – the plants that had surrounded her, the melancholy red velvet of the chairs and the curtains, the sound, weak and nocturnal, of the birds – she yet carried the quality of the 'way back' as animals do. She suggested that they should walk together in the gardens of the *Luxembourg* toward which her steps had been dirrected when he addressed her. They walked in the bare chilly gardens and Felix was happy. He felt that he could talk to her, tell her anything, though she herself was so silent. He told her he had a post in the *Crédit Lyonnais*, earning two thousand five hundred francs a week; a master of seven tongues, he was useful to the bank, and, he added, he had a trifle saved up, gained in speculations.

He walked a little short of her. Her movements were slightly headlong and sideways; slow, clumsy and yet graceful, the ample gait of the night-watch. She wore no hat, and her pale head, with its short hair growing flat on the forehead made still narrower by the hanging curls almost on a level with the finely arched eyebrows, gave her the look of cherubs in renaissance theatres; the eye-balls showing slightly rounded in profile, the temples low and square. She was gracious and yet fading, like an old statue in a garden, that symbolizes the weather through which it has endured, and is not so much the work of man as the work of wind and rain and the herd of the seasons, and though formed in man's image is a figure of doom. Because of this, Felix found her presence painful, and yet a happiness. Thinking of her, visualizing her, was an extreme act of the will; to recall her after she had gone, however, was as easy as the recollection of a sensation of beauty, without its details. When she smiled the smile was only in the mouth, and a little bitter: the face of an incurable yet to be stricken with its malady.

As the days passed they spent many hours in museums, and while this pleased Felix immeasurably, he was surprised that often her taste, turning from an appreciation of the most beautiful, would also include the cheaper and debased, with an emotion as real. When she touched a thing, her hands seemed to take the place of the eye. He thought: 'She has the touch of the blind who, because they see more with their fingers, forget more in their minds.' Her fingers would go forward, hesitate, tremble, as if they had found a face in the dark. When her hand finally came to rest, the palm closed, it was as if she had stopped a crying mouth. Her hand lay still and she would turn away. At such moments Felix experienced an unaccountable apprehension. The sensuality in her hands frightened him.

Her clothes were of a period that he could not quite place. She wore feathers of the kind his mother had worn, flattened sharply to the face. Her skirts were moulded to her hips and fell downward and out, wider and longer than those of other women, heavy silks that made her seem newly ancient. One day he learned the secret. Pricing a small tapestry in an antique shop facing the *Seine*, he saw Robin reflected in a door mirror of a back room, dressed in a heavy brocaded gown which time had stained in places, in others split, yet which was so voluminous that there were yards enough to refashion.

He found that his love for Robin was not in truth a selection; it was as if the weight of his life had amassed one precipitation. He had thought of making a destiny for himself, through laborious and untiring travail. Then with Robin it seemed to stand before him, without effort. When he asked her to marry him it was with such an unplanned eagerness that he was taken aback to find himself accepted as if Robin's life held no volition for refusal.

He took her first to Vienna. To reassure himself he showed her all the historic buildings. He kept saying to himself that sooner or later, in this garden or that palace, she would suddenly be moved as he was moved. Yet it seemed to him that he too was a sightseer. He tried to explain to her what Vienna had been before the war; what it must have been before he was born; yet his memory was confused and hazy, and he found himself repeating what he had read, for it was what he knew best. With methodic anxiety he took her over the city. He said, 'You are a *Baronin* now.' He spoke to her in German as she ate the heavy *Schnitzel* and dumplings, clasping her hand about the thick handle of the beer mug. He said: '*Das Leben ist ewig, darin liegt seine Schönheit.*'

They walked before the Imperial Palace in a fine hot sun that fell about the clipped hedges and the statues warm and clear. He went into the *Kammergarten* with her and talked, and on into the *Gloriette*, and sat on first one bench, and then another. Brought up short, he realized that he had been hurrying from one to the other as if they were orchestra chairs, as if he himself were trying not to miss anything; now, at the extremity of the garden, he was aware that he had been anxious to see every tree, every statue at a different angle.

In their hotel, she went to the window and pulled aside the heavy velvet hangings, threw down the bolster that Vienna uses against the wind at the ledge, and opened the window, though the night air was cold. He began speaking of Emperor Francis Joseph and of the whereabouts of Charles the First. And as he spoke, Felix laboured under the weight of his own remorseless re-creation of the great, generals and statesmen and emperors. His chest was as heavy as if it were supporting the combined weight of their apparel and their destiny. Looking up after an interminable flow of fact and fancy, he saw Robin sitting with her legs thrust out, her head thrown back against the embossed cushion of the chair, sleeping, one arm fallen over the chair's side, the hand somehow older ancl wiser than her body; and looking at her he knew that he was not sufficient to make her what he had hoped; it would require more than his own argument. It would require contact with persons exonerated of their earthly condition by some strong spiritual bias, someone of that old régime, some old lady of the past courts, who only remembered others when trying to think of herself.

On the tenth day, therefore, Felix turned about and reentered Paris. In the following months he put his faith in the fact that Robin had Christian proclivities, and his hope in the discovery that she was an enigma. He said to himself that possibly she had greatness hidden in the non-committal. He felt that her attention, somehow in spite of him, had already been taken by something not yet in history. Always she seemed to be listening to the echo of some foray in the blood, that had no known setting; and when he came to know her this was all he could base his intimacy upon. There was something pathetic in the spectacle: Felix reiterating the tragedy of his father. Attired like some haphazard in the mind of a tailor, again in the ambit of his father's futile attempt to encompass the rhythm of his wife's stride, Felix, with tightly held monocle, walked beside Robin, talking to her, drawing her attention to this and that, wrecking himself and his peace of mind in an effort to acquaint her with the destiny for which he had chosen her; that she might bear sons who would recognize and honour the past. For without such love, the past as he understood it, would die away from the world. She was not listening and he said in an angry mood, though he said it calmly, 'I am deceiving you!' And he wondered what he meant, and why she did not hear.

'A child,' he pondered. 'Yes, a child!' and then he said to himself, 'Why has it not come about?' The thought took him abruptly in the middle of his accounting. He hurried home in a flurry of anxiety, as a boy who has heard a regiment on parade, toward which he cannot run because he has no one from whom to seek permission, and yet runs haltingly nevertheless. Coming face to face with her, all that he could stammer out was: 'Why is there no child? *Wo ist das Kind? Warum? Warum?*'

Robin prepared herself for her child with her only power: a stubborn cataleptic calm, conceiving herself pregnant before she was; and, strangely aware of some lost land in herself, she took to going out; wandering the countryside; to train travel, to other cities, alone and engrossed. Once, not having returned for three days, and Felix nearly beside himself with terror, she walked in late at night and said that she had been half-way to Berlin.

Suddenly she took the Catholic vow. She came into the church silently. The prayers of the suppliants had not ceased nor had anyone been broken of their meditation. Then, as if some inscrutable wish for salvation, something yet more monstrously unfulfilled than they had suffered, had thrown a shadow, they regarded her, to see her going softly forward and down, a tall girl with the body of a boy.

Many churches saw her: *St. Julien le Pauvre*, the church of *St. Germain des Prés*, *Ste. Clothilde*. Even on the cold tiles of the Russian church, in which there is no pew, she knelt alone, lost and conspicuous, her broad shoulders above her neighbours, her feet large and as earthly as the feet of a monk.

She strayed into the *rue Picpus*, into the gardens of the convent of *L'Adoration Perpétuelle*. She talked to the nuns and they, feeling that they were looking at someone who would never be able to ask for, or receive, mercy, blessed her in their hearts and gave her a sprig of rose from the bush. They showed her where Jean Valjean had kept his rakes, and where the bright little ladies of the *pension* came to quilt their covers; and Robin smiled, taking the spray, and looked down at the tomb of Lafayette and thought her unpeopled thoughts. Kneeling in the chapel, which was never without a nun going over her beads, Robin, trying to bring her mind to this abrupt necessity, found herself worrying about her height. Was she still growing?

She tried to think of the consequence to which her son was to be born and dedicated. She thought of the Emperor Francis Joseph. There was something commensurate in the heavy body with the weight in her mind, where reason was inexact with lack of necessity. She wandered to thoughts of women, women that she had come to connect with women. Strangely enough these were women in history, Louise de la Vallière, Catherine of Russia, Madame de Maintenon, Catherine de Medici, and two women out of literature, Anna Karenina and Catherine Heathcliff; and now there was this woman Austria. She prayed, and her prayer was monstrous, because in it there was no margin left for damnation or forgiveness, for praise or for blame – those who cannot conceive a bargain cannot be saved or damned. She could not offer herself up; she only told of herself, in a preoccupation that was its own predicament.

Leaning her childish face and full chin on the shelf of the *prie-Dieu*, her eyes fixed, she laughed, out of some hidden capacity, some lost subterranean humour; as it ceased, she leaned still further forward in a swoon, waking and yet heavy, like one in sleep.

When Felix returned that evening Robin was dozing in a chair, one hand under her cheek and one arm fallen. A book was lying on the floor beneath her hand. The book was the memoirs of the Marquis de Sade; a line was underscored: *Et lit rendit pendant sa captivité les milles services qu'un amour dévoué est seul capable de rendre*, and suddenly into his mind came the question: 'What is wrong?'

She awoke but did not move. He came and took her by the arm and lifted her toward him. She put her hand against his chest and pushed him, she looked frightened, she opened her mouth but no words came. He stepped back, he tried to speak but they moved aside from each other saying nothing.

That night she was taken with pains. She began to curse loudly, a thing that Felix was totally unprepared for; with the most foolish gestures he tried to make her comfortable.

'Go to hell!' she cried. She moved slowly, bent away from him, chair by chair; she was drunk – her hair was swinging in her eyes.

Amid loud and frantic cries of affirmation and despair Robin was delivered. Shuddering in the double pains of birth and fury, cursing like a sailor, she rose up on her elbow in her bloody gown, looking about her in the bed as if she had lost something. 'Oh for Christ's sake, for Christ's sake!' she kept crying like a child who has walked into the commencement of a horror.

A week out of bed she was lost, as if she had done something irreparable, as if this act had caught her attention for the first time.

One night, Felix, having come in unheard, found her standing in the centre of the floor holding the child high in her hand as if she were about to dash it down; but she brought it down gently.

The child was small, a boy, and sad. It slept too much in a quivering palsy of nerves, it made few voluntary movements; it whimpered.

Robin took to wandering again, to intermittent travel from which she came back hours, days later, disinterested. People were uneasy when she spoke to them; confronted with a catastrophe that had yet no beginning.

Felix had each day the sorrow born with him; for the rest, he pretended that he noticed nothing. Robin was almost never home; he did not know how to inquire for her. Sometimes coming into a café he would creep out again, because she stood before the bar – sometimes laughing, but more often silent, her head bent over her glass, her hair swinging; and about her people of every sort.

One night, coming home about three, he found her in the

darkness, standing, back against the window, in the pod of the curtain, her chin so thrust forward that the muscles in her neck stood out. As he came toward her she said in a fury, 'I didn't want him!' Raising her hand she struck him across the face.

He stepped away, he dropped his monocle and caught at it swinging, he took his breath backward. He waited a whole second, trying to appear casual. 'You didn't want him,' he said. He bent down pretending to disentangle his ribbon, 'It seems I could not accomplish that.'

'Why not be secret about him?' she said. 'Why talk?'

Felix turned his body without moving his feet. 'What shall we do?'

She grinned, but it was not a smile. 'I'll get out,' she said. She took up her cloak, she always carried it dragging. She looked about her, about the room, as if she were seeing it for the first time.

For three or four months the people of the quarter asked for her in vain. Where she had gone no one knew. When she was seen again in the quarter, it was with Nora Flood. She did not explain where she had been, she was unable or unwilling to give an account of herself. The doctor said: 'In America, that's where Nora lives. I brought her into the world and I should know.'

BARRY MILES

From

# THE BEAT HOTEL: GINSBERG, BURROUGHS, AND CORSO IN PARIS, 1957–63

ON JUNE 14, they met the Dada poet Tristan Tzara in the Deux Magots. Allen had always thought that his *Dada Manifestos* were good poetry, and he particularly liked the line 'Dada is a virgin microbe.' Tzara invited them to visit his apartment, where he showed Allen and Gregory a long, vituperative letter of denunciation to him from Antonin Artaud accusing him of being a custodian of a museum, an archivist, and not a true Dada poet. The letter was marked with spit and cigarette burns, was stained with some of Artaud's sperm and blood, and was sent from the Rodez Hospital Asylum, where Artaud was hospitalized.

The next day they had been invited by Jean-Jacques Lebel to attend a Surrealist party at his father's house on Avenue President Wilson, near the Trocadero. His father, Robert Lebel, was then working on *Sur Marcel Duchamp*, which was to be published in Paris the next year by Trianon Press, and was a close friend of Duchamp and all of the Surrealists. Jean-Jacques remembers the occasion vividly:

> Duchamp came to Paris and my father said, 'We'll have a party for him, American style, invite some friends.' So we invited Duchamp, Man Ray and their wives, all the surviving Dadaists, Max Ernst and his wife, Breton and his wife, Benjamin Peret, the great Peret. All the people who were still fantastically alive. So my father said, 'Of course you will come?' I said,

'Listen, I would like to bring some American friends.' So my father said, 'Who are they?' He'd never heard of them, of course. 'Well, they're great poets, very great writers and poets.' And my mother said, 'Not that crazy guy who vomits all over the place?' See she had come to my place to visit one day, like mothers do, and there was Gregory puking all over the place. I said, 'No, no, no! Of course not!' When you're a kid you don't want to tell your parents secrets. Of course it was Gregory. William and Gregory and Allen. So I said to my mother, who is a very bourgeois lady, 'Listen. You invite your friends and I'll invite mine and I'm sure they'll get along.' Because I was dying for an occasion to get them together, because my obsession all my life has been to put all the people I love together. To put together these people who didn't know each other and to create a sort of hybrid mix is creating new cultures, it's actually making a dynamite event. So I knew it would be important to put those two generations together.

Allen was the only one who was really interested because he was reading Robert Motherwell's *The Dada Painters and Poets.* He had it in his room. So I said to Allen, 'Hey how would you like to meet some of the guys? Do you like this guy Peret?' He said, 'Peret is a great poet, I've only read one poem of his in a little literary magazine but he's great.' 'What about Man Ray?' 'Man Ray? My dream is meeting Man Ray.' 'What about Duchamp?' And he said, 'Duchamp? Duchamp? I tried to meet him in New York but I couldn't.' So, I said, 'I'll show you how much I love you man, I'm inviting you next week to my parents' house and they'll all be there.' So he actually put on a tie and a white shirt. Put on his wash-and-wear things. He told Gregory,

'Listen man, at least try and comb your hair and don't drink,' of course, when you tell Gregory not to drink, he drinks five times as much. I went to get them because we had to cross Paris and we took two taxis. And the first thing fucking Gregory does is vomit in the staircase. I said, 'One of the historical nights of my life and I'll remember it by Gregory's puking, oh Jesus Christ!' So then I had to wash this puke off the stairs because I didn't want the concierge to have to – so, stupid problems like that.

We walk in, about fifty people were there, everybody's standing. I start introducing people, and Duchamp, Man Ray and Peret were there. Breton's wife was there but Breton was not there that night because he had a flu and was in bed. André Pieyre de Mandiargues, the great writer, was there, and a few fantastic painters such as Jean-Paul Riopelle were there. Friends, friends. And I made the introductions and of course nobody had ever heard of Allen Ginsberg, or Gregory Corso or William Burroughs because their books hadn't been translated, hadn't even been published yet. So it was 'How do you do?' But it wasn't 'I'm glad to meet you,' because they didn't know who they were. So of course what they do is all get piss drunk. And at the end, when people started going away, I see them going up to Duchamp. Gregory holding hands with Allen. Duchamp was sitting in a chair, speaking to people. The first thing goddamn Allen does, he gets down on his knees and starts kissing Duchamp's knees. Thinking he was doing something Surrealistic. And Duchamp was so embarrassed. So embarrassed! Allen being totally drunk, and he was never totally drunk. He made a mix of whiskey and red wine. He was trying to do something that he thought was Dadaistic. But the most embarrassing thing was yet to come. Gregory had found in the kitchen a pair of scissors, and he cuts Duchamp's tie. It's such a corny, childish thing. Knowing Gregory and Allen it's lovely, it's trying to be humble, it's trying to say 'We're children, we're fools, we admire you.' It was a loving thing.

My father comes up to me and he says, 'Hah, your friends huh? Where did you pick up these *clochards*?' He didn't say it but his eyes said it. I was all upset. Here were geniuses on both sides, you know? It was very stupid to have been upset because actually Duchamp loved the guys and Man Ray loved the guys. Every time I'd see them they'd say, 'Where are your American beatniks? I love these beatniks. They are completely drunk but they're childish, they're wonderful, I'm sure they're great poets.' In fact Duchamp spoke excellent English, but they were too drunk to speak. How can you speak to a drunkard who's falling off on the floor everywhere?

Allen told Peter how he kissed Duchamp and made him kiss Bill; how he and Gregory fell to the floor and begged for Duchamp's blessing, as they had done with Auden, tugging on his pants leg, to which Duchamp demurred that he was only human; and how, when Duchamp tried to get away, they crawled after him on all fours between the legs of the well-dressed guests. He didn't mention that Gregory had cut off Duchamp's tie. They were fortunate that the rather formal Breton was not present.

Jean-Jacques continued, 'Two days later Allen said, "I think we fucked up a little bit," and I said, "Forget it, never mind." I said I want you to meet Breton so I gave him Breton's address and Allen wrote him, saying he would like to come to visit him. I helped him translate the letter into French. Breton knew of him through me so he wrote Allen a postcard reply. Breton had an extremely fine, classical literary French handwriting, and he answered Allen saying, "Thank you for your note, J-J told me about you, yes please do come by such and such a day, such and such a time, here's my address." But Allen could not read the handwriting. And I had gone to Italy and he never went. And so I saw Breton when I got back and he said, "Well, your American friend he's not very well behaved." I said, "What do you mean?" He said, "Well I sent him an invitation and he never answered and he never came." I went to Allen, I said, "He sent you an invitation, why didn't you go?" He said, "I got a funny-looking thing, can you translate it for me?" So he missed it. I felt so bad because I wanted those great minds to meet.'

Inspired by meeting so many of the legendary figures of Surrealism and Dada, they all began reading Surrealist texts and went to see Buñuel and Dalí's famous 1928 film *Un Chien Andalou.* The scene of a girl's eye being sliced by a razor had been censored in the United States, but they found it was not as horrifying as they had been expecting.

Allen and Gregory were interviewed by Art Buchwald for his column in the *New York Herald Tribune*, Paris edition. He tried to be sympathetic, but as Allen told Kerouac, 'We were drunk and cuckoo.' The next night Allen wrote Buchwald what he called 'a big prophetic letter' and asked him to use that instead, but of course he didn't.

Gregory recounted his version of things in a letter to poet Gary Snyder, who was now living in Japan. 'Allen and me were interviewed by syndicated funny man for masses newspapers, silly jerky and drunk interview, guy named Art Buchwald who came on simpatico, but his article sounds as if he interviewed two nowhere Bohemian cats, o, well, all is forgivable, next time I know better, Allen says poetry expiates all; he's right but this "beat generation" nonsense lessens the poetic intent, no wonder the academy poets keep aloft, poetry is not for public humor make-fun-of kicks, ridiculous, the whole thing, sardine salesmen, I've been failing my Shelley, it's so easy to jest . . . when asked to talk about poetry and life to interviewers all I can say is fried shoes or something and give them some silly experience, all very nowhere, so now I learn to keep quiet; that interview, in Herald Tribune, really got me wrong and showed me as a talkative idiot, I worry about because I, as a poet, least of all people, should not go novelty on the thing I will die for . . . I think mainly the reason for my silliness and Allen's in interview was because some girl from Frisco came to Paris and showed us articles and clippings of the SF scene that came on so nowhere and gloomy and bullshit and sad, that I felt inclined only to be silly . . . those clippings that girl brought by depressed Allen and me so much, we decided to be jerky, funny, silly, and perhaps change the clime that is threatening gloom.'

Buchwald's column appeared in the *Herald Tribune* every day, so Allen and Gregory must have been familiar with it and should have known what to expect. Buchwald was not unsympathetic; he seems simply to have reported what they said, but that was enough to make them objects of ridicule to many of his readers. His column was actually quite amusing and captured some of the lightheartedness of the Beats:

> When Mr. Ginsberg met Marcel Duchamp, the French painter, he said: 'I ate his shoe.'
> 'Why?'
> 'To show him I even hated his shoe.'

> At the same party Mr. Corso was talking with Man Ray, the photographer and painter.
>
> 'Man Ray was eating a green cookie,' said Mr. Corso, 'and I asked him why he didn't eat the white ones. He said he only ate things the color of his tie. So I ate his tie.'
>
> 'Why?'
>
> 'To show him I dug him. But I got sick.'

Buchwald liked them and visited the hotel. He found Bill very interesting and said that he would introduce them to filmmaker John Huston, who was in Paris. Huston had just completed shooting *The Roots of Heaven*, a film about one man's efforts to stop elephant hunting in Africa and how an American reporter championed him and made him famous. They met for coffee at the Bonaparte and Bill explained his idea for a film about Tangier: episodes seen through the eyes of a junkie looking for a drugstore, junk sick, on Ramadan when everything is closed – a street boy looking to pick up a john; an effeminate tourist sightseeing with his mother. Huston did not think it was quite his sort of movie. Despite his telling Gregory not to call him 'Man,' they got along well and Huston invited them all to a cast party he was giving on a houseboat on the Seine.

It was a glamorous affair with all the stars of the film present: Trevor Howard, Orson Welles, Errol Flynn, and Juliette Greco. Huston introduced them to the film's producer, Darryl Zanuck, and to the stars. They brought B.J. along with them, which turned out to be a mistake. After drinking a great deal of champagne, B.J. asked Flynn if it was true that someone had broken a popper under his nose when he was flying a plane. 'Go away sonny,' Flynn responded, whereupon B.J. emptied his glass of champagne over Flynn's head.

Two security guards immediately seized B.J. and threw him overboard into the murky water of the Seine. Huston was probably expecting bohemian irreverence when he invited them and it did not spoil the party. The actors particularly liked Gregory, with all his energy and his 'fire-engine mouth.'

Gregory had a new girlfriend, a nineteen-year-old Russian girl who paid for his typewriter to be retrieved from the repair shop. She told them she had a house on the Riviera, and invited them all down, but she and Gregory broke up before the plan could materialize. As Gregory told Buchwald, 'I get money from girls. Everytime I meet a girl I ask her how much money she has and then I demand half of it. I'm not doing anything wrong with money. I just use it to buy food.'

One evening Harry Phipps slipped an envelope stuffed full of hundreds of dollars' worth of cocaine under Allen's door, so he and Bill spent the weekend sniffing it. Bill and Allen had a date for an interview at *Figaro Littéraire* with Michel Mohrt, an editor at *La Nouvelle Revue Française*, and one of the very few French people at that time to take the Beats seriously. Both of them kept leaving the room every ten minutes or so to go and sniff another line in the bathroom, so the interview was not a success. The most important thing to come from the interview was that Mohrt knew Louis-Ferdinand Céline and promised that he would arrange a meeting.

It was Burroughs who first introduced Ginsberg and Kerouac to Céline's work. Bill had given Allen a copy of his first novel, *Journey to the End of the Night*, in 1944 and Kerouac read it the next year when Allen, Bill, and Jack were all living together in Joan Vollmer's apartment near Columbia

University. 'That had a big influence on Kerouac, and Bill,' said Allen. 'Mentally on me, more on their prose. Kerouac's famous quote from it was, "We are all going forward in the silence of facts to die." Kerouac liked that. And Céline's humor is like Bill's. Bill gets a lot of that from him. That's one of the strongest influences on Bill I'm sure, literally.'

Bill felt that Céline's work was episodic rather than straightforward narrative, much like his own. Burroughs stated, 'I think [Céline] is in a very old tradition, and I myself am in a very old tradition, namely, that of the picaresque novel. People complain that my novels have no plot. Well, a picaresque novel has no plot. It is simply a series of incidents. And that tradition dates back to the *Satyricon* of Petronius Arbiter, and to one of the very early novels, *The Unfortunate Traveller* by Thomas Nashe. And I think Céline belongs to this same tradition ... Interesting about Céline, I find the same critical misconceptions put forth by critics with regard to his work are put forth to mine: they said it was a chronicle of despair, etc.; *I* thought it was very funny! I think he is primarily a humorous writer. And a picaresque novel should be very lively and very funny.'

Michel Mohrt made the arrangements so that all they had to do was telephone and fix a time. Allen made the call. Céline had a shy, delicate, young-sounding voice on the telephone, which almost quavered, making Allen exclaim, 'How lovely to hear your voice.' Céline, speaking hesitantly, told him, 'Anytime Tuesday after four.' On July 8, 1958, Allen and Bill – Gregory had a new girlfriend to see – took the train to Bas Meudon, a distant suburb to the southwest of Paris, about halfway to Versailles. Here Céline and his wife, Lucette Almanzor, lived at 25 terre, route de Gardes, Meudon, in a Louis-Philippe villa owned by Lucette. It was built on the cliff where the Seine curved around to Billancourt and St.

Cloud. The house overlooked the road and railway below, then the two channels of the Seine. At his gate Céline could look out over Paris in the far distance, with the Eiffel Tower on the horizon. It was a freestanding three-floor, wood-and-mortar house with a mansard roof. Bill and Allen reached the front gate and rang the bell. Big dogs ran to it, barking. Céline came to the gate to welcome them.

Céline was a large man, sixty-seven years old, tall but stooped, with gaunt features, gray skin, and burning eyes. He was wrapped in scarves, though it was summer. Despite his age he continued his practice as a family doctor – he had few patients – and his wife gave ballet lessons. As a writer he was experiencing something of a revival. He had recently completed *D'un Château l'autre*, which was published in June 1957, and was working on *Nord.* Earlier that year Plon had published his *Entretiens familiers* (*Casual Conversations*) with Robert Poulet. He had been interviewed in all the magazines and even had a spoken-word record released on the Festival label in their '*Leurs oeuvres et leurs voix*' series, which was recorded in October 1957. He had become a literary personality, with journalists asking his opinion about everything from the conquest of the moon to *Don Quixote*.

Not everyone was pleased with this new development. After the war Céline had been accused of collaboration and anti-Semitism, but his books had also been banned in Nazi Germany and his opinion of the Germans was no higher than his opinion of his fellow Frenchmen. During the war a Resistance raiding party had destroyed his Paris apartment and all of his papers; his neighbors shunned him. Understanding he was not welcome, he moved to Denmark, where he had a little money set aside. He returned to France in 1950 after six years in Denmark, two of which he spent in jail while the French authorities prepared a case for his extradition for collaborationist activity. The charges were dropped but the collaborationist tag and charges of anti-Semitism continued to pursue him.

Céline, Allen, and Bill sat in a little courtyard behind the house on old, rusty garden chairs, around an old, rusty table, with rusty bedsprings poking up from the overgrown garden, and Lucette brought them wine. About half a dozen dogs roamed the grounds, making Bill very paranoid, as he hated dogs. Allen asked in French if the dogs were dangerous and Céline replied in English that, no, they just made a lot of noise, in order to annoy and scare people away. 'I just take them with me to the post office, to protect me from the Jews,' he said, looking at Allen. He was referring to the death threats and hate mail that he still received from people who believed he had been a collaborator. He told them that his neighbors put out poisoned meat for the dogs.

Céline and Bill had a long talk about the various jails they had been in and Céline made the point that you can only know a country when you have seen its prisons. He described his incarceration in Denmark and told them, 'One great brute simply butted me in the stomach without a word.' His opinion of the Danes was not high: awful sniveling cowardly people. They talked about Bill's drug habits and Céline told them he had once calmed panic on a ship that was supposed to be sinking by injecting everyone with morphine, a story he had used in a book. They discussed Jean-Paul Sartre, Samuel Beckett, Henri Michaux, and Jean Genet, but Céline dismissed them all as little fish in the literary pond. They gave him copies of *Howl*, *Gasoline*, and *Junkie* and told him that they were all influenced by him. His English was no longer very good but he told them he could still read it. 'I'll glance at them,' he said. They conversed in a mixture of broken French and English.

Allen later described the visit. 'He was friendly. And he stayed with us for a couple of hours. I don't think he had many visitors. I asked about his practice and he said, "Ahhh, don't have much of a practice, all these young women want young doctors to look at 'em. Also . . . all the older women want to get naked in front of a young doctor. It's too filthy here to practice." He took us in the house and showed us the room where he writes.' This was a large room on the ground floor, which was a combination kitchen and dining area with piles of books and magazines and papers on the large round table. He showed them his books. 'We were totally friendly, in a respectful way, we really appreciated him,' Allen continued. 'So we reported in as young American geniuses who were coming to salute him and I remember at the gate when we left, he and his wife had brought us to the gate, I said, "We salute you from America to the greatest writer in France." And she said, "In the universe!" So they were playful, they weren't sour.'

When he returned to New York, Allen described his visit to an interviewer from the *Village Voice*: 'He's an old, gnarled man dressed in black, mad and beautiful, and he thought we were newspapermen – "Ah, the press!" – until we told him we were poets.'

Nine months later, on March 31, 1959, Céline gave up his medical practice, had himself taken off the roster of practicing doctors in Seine-et-Oise, and claimed his state pension. He died on July 1, 1961, of a ruptured aneurysm.

JAMES BALDWIN

From

# GIOVANNI'S ROOM

1956

AT FIVE O'CLOCK in the morning Guillaume locked the door of the bar behind us. The streets were empty and grey. On a corner near the bar a butcher had already opened his shop and one could see him within, already bloody, hacking at the meat. One of the great, green Paris buses lumbered past, nearly empty, its bright electric flag waving fiercely to indicate a turn. A *garçon de café* spilled water on the sidewalk before his establishment and swept it into the gutter. At the end of the long, curving street which faced us were the trees of the boulevard and straw chairs piled high before cafés and the great stone spire of Saint-Germain-des-Prés – the most magnificent spire, as Hella and I believed, in Paris. The street beyond the *place* stretched before us to the river and, hidden beside and behind us, meandered to Montparnasse. It was named for an adventurer who sowed a crop in Europe which is being harvested until today. I had often walked this street, sometimes, with Hella, towards the river, often, without her, towards the girls of Montparnasse. Not very long ago either, though it seemed, that morning, to have occurred in another life.

We were going to Les Halles for breakfast. We piled into a taxi, the four of us, unpleasantly crowded together, a circumstance which elicited from Jacques and Guillaume a series of lewd speculations. This lewdness was particularly revolting in that it not only failed of wit, it was so clearly an expression of contempt and self-contempt; it bubbled upward out of them like a fountain of black water. It was clear that they were tantalizing themselves with Giovanni and me and this set my teeth on edge. But Giovanni leaned back against the taxi window, allowing his arm to press my shoulder lightly, seeming to say that we should soon be rid of these old men and should not be distressed that their dirty water splashed – we would have no trouble washing it away.

'Look,' said Giovanni, as we crossed the river. 'This old whore, Paris, as she turns in bed, is very moving.'

I looked out, beyond his heavy profile, which was grey – from fatigue and from the light of the sky above us. The river was swollen and yellow. Nothing moved on the river. Barges were tied up along the banks. The island of the city widened away from us, bearing the weight of the cathedral; beyond this, dimly, through speed and mist, one made out the individual roofs of Paris, their myriad, squat chimney stacks very beautiful and varicolored under the pearly sky. Mist clung to the river, softening that army of trees, softening those stones, hiding the city's dreadful corkscrew alleys and dead-end streets, clinging like a curse to the men who slept beneath the bridges – one of whom flashed by beneath us, very black and lone, walking along the river.

'Some rats have gone in,' said Giovanni, 'and now other rats come out.' He smiled bleakly and looked at me; to my surprise, he took my hand and held it. 'Have you ever slept under a bridge?' he asked. 'Or perhaps they have soft beds with warm blankets under the bridges in your country?'

I did not know what to do about my hand; it seemed better to do nothing. 'Not yet,' I said, 'but I may. My hotel wants to throw me out.'

I had said it lightly, with a smile, out of a desire to put myself, in terms of an acquaintance with wintry things, on an equal footing with him. But the fact that I had said it as he held my hand made it sound to me unutterably helpless and soft and coy. But I could not say anything to counteract this impression: to say anything more would confirm it. I pulled my hand away, pretending that I had done so in order to search for a cigarette.

Jacques lit it for me.

'Where do you live?' he asked Giovanni.

'Oh,' said Giovanni, 'out. Far out. It is almost not Paris.'

'He lives in a dreadful street, near *Nation*,' said Guillaume, 'among all the dreadful bourgeoisie and their piglike children.'

'You failed to catch the children at the right age,' said Jacques. 'They go through a period, all too brief, *hélas!* when a pig is perhaps the *only* animal they do not call to mind.' And, again to Giovanni: 'In a hotel?'

'No,' said Giovanni, and for the first time he seemed slightly uncomfortable. 'I live in a maid's room.'

'With the maid?'

'No,' said Giovanni, and smiled, 'the maid is I don't know where. You could certainly tell that there was no maid if you ever saw my room.'

'I would love to,' said Jacques.

'Then we will give a party for you one day,' said Giovanni.

This, too courteous and too bald to permit any further questioning, nearly forced, nevertheless, a question from my lips. Guillaume looked briefly at Giovanni, who did not look at him but out into the morning, whistling. I had been making resolutions for the last six hours and now I made another one: to have this whole thing 'out' with Giovanni as soon as I got him alone at Les Halles. I was going to have to tell him that he had made a mistake but that we could still be friends. But I could not be certain, really, that it might not be I who was making a mistake, blindly misreading everything – and out of necessities, then, too shameful to be uttered. I was in a box for I could see that, no matter how I turned, the hour of confession was upon me and could scarcely be averted; unless, of course, I leaped out of the cab, which would be the most terrible confession of all.

Now the cabdriver asked us where we wanted to go, for we had arrived at the choked boulevards and impassable side-streets of Les Halles. Leeks, onions, cabbages, oranges, apples, potatoes, cauliflowers, stood gleaming in mounds all over, on the sidewalks, in the streets, before great metal sheds. The sheds were blocks long and within the sheds were piled more fruit, more vegetables, in some sheds, fish, in some sheds, cheese, in some whole animals, lately slaughtered. It scarcely seemed possible that all of this could ever be eaten. But in a few hours it would all be gone and trucks would be arriving from all corners of France – and making their way, to the great profit of a beehive of middlemen, across the city of Paris – to feed the roaring multitude. Who were roaring now, at once wounding and charming the ear, before and behind, and on either side of our taxi – our taxi driver, and Giovanni, too, roared back. The multitude of Paris seems to be dressed in blue every day but Sunday, when, for the most part, they put on an unbelievably festive black. Here they were now, in blue, disputing, every inch, our passage, with their wagons, handtrucks, camions, their bursting baskets carried at an angle steeply self-confident on the back. A red-faced woman, burdened with fruit, shouted – to Giovanni, the driver, to the world – a particularly vivid *cochonnerie*, to which the driver and Giovanni, at once, at the top of their lungs, responded, though the fruit lady had already passed beyond our sight and perhaps no longer even remembered her precisely obscene conjectures. We crawled along, for no one had yet told the driver where to stop, and

Giovanni and the driver, who had, it appeared, immediately upon entering Les Halles, been transformed into brothers, exchanged speculations, unflattering in the extreme, concerning the hygiene, language, private parts, and habits, of the citizens of Paris. (Jacques and Guillaume were exchanging speculations, unspeakably less good-natured, concerning every passing male.) The pavements were slick with leavings, mainly cast-off, rotten leaves, flowers, fruit, and vegetables which had met with disaster natural and slow, or abrupt. And the walls and corners were combed with *pissoirs*, dull-burning, make-shift braziers, cafés, restaurants, and smoky yellow bistros – of these last, some so small that they were little more than diamond-shaped, enclosed corners holding bottles and a zinc-covered counter. At all these points, men, young, old, middle-aged, powerful, powerful even in the various fashions in which they had met, or were meeting, their various ruin; and women, more than making up in shrewdness and patience, in an ability to count and weigh – and shout – whatever they might lack in muscle; though they did not, really, seem to lack much. Nothing here reminded me of home, though Giovanni recognized, revelled in it all.

'I know a place,' he told the driver, '*très bon marché*' – and told the driver where it was. It developed that it was one of the driver's favorite rendezvous.

'Where is this place?' asked Jacques, petulantly. 'I thought we were going to' – and he named another place.

'You are joking,' said Giovanni, with contempt. 'That place is *very* bad and *very* expensive, it is only for tourists. We are not tourists,' and he added, to me, 'When I first came to Paris I worked in Les Halles – a long time, too. *Nom de Dieu, quel boulot!* I pray always never to do that again.' And he regarded the streets through which we passed with a sadness which was not less real for being a little theatrical and self-mocking.

Guillaume said, from his corner of the cab: 'Tell him who rescued you.'

'Ah, yes,' said Giovanni, 'behold my savior, my *patron*.' He was silent a moment. Then: 'You do not regret it, do you? I have not done you any harm? You are pleased with my work?'

'*Mais oui*,' said Guillaume.

Giovanni sighed. '*Bien sûr*.' He looked out of the window again, again whistling. We came to a corner remarkably clear. The taxi stopped.

'*Ici*,' said the driver.

'*Ici*,' Giovanni echoed.

I reached for my wallet but Giovanni sharply caught my hand, conveying to me with an angry flick of his eyelash the intelligence that the least these dirty old men could do was *pay*. He opened the door and stepped out into the street. Guillaume had not reached for his wallet and Jacques paid for the cab.

'Ugh,' said Guillaume, staring at the door of the café before which we stood, 'I am sure this place is infested with vermin. Do you want to poison us?'

'It's not the outside you're going to eat,' said Giovanni. 'You are in much more danger of being poisoned in those dreadful, chic places you always go to, where they always have the face clean, *mais, mon Dieu, les fesses!*' He grinned. '*Fais-moi confiance*. Why would I want to poison you? Then I would have no job and I have only just found out that I want to live.'

He and Guillaume, Giovanni still smiling, exchanged a look which I would not have been able to read even if I had dared to try; and Jacques, pushing all of us before him as though we were his chickens, said, with that grin: 'We can't stand here in the cold and argue. If we can't eat inside, we can drink. Alcohol kills all microbes.'

And Guillaume brightened suddenly – he was really remarkable, as though he carried, hidden somewhere on his person, a needle filled with vitamins, which, automatically, at the blackening hour, discharged itself into his veins. '*Il y a les jeunes dedans*,' he said, and we went in.

Indeed there were young people, half a dozen at the zinc counter before glasses of red and white wine, along with others not young at all. A pockmarked boy and a very rough-looking girl were playing the pinball machine near the window. There were a few people sitting at the tables in the back, served by an astonishingly clean-looking waiter. In the gloom, the dirty walls, the sawdust-covered floor, his white jacket gleamed like snow. Behind these tables one caught a glimpse of the kitchen and the surly, obese cook. He lumbered about like one of those overloaded trucks outside, wearing one of those high, white hats, and with a dead cigar stuck between his lips.

Behind the counter sat one of those absolutely inimitable and indomitable ladies, produced only in the city of Paris, but produced there in great numbers, who would be as outrageous and unsettling in any other city as a mermaid on a mountaintop. All over Paris they sit behind their counters like a mother bird in a nest and brood over the cash register as though it were an egg. Nothing occurring under the circle of heaven where they sit escapes their eye, if they have ever been surprised by anything, it was only in a dream – a dream they long ago ceased having. They are neither ill- nor good-natured, though they have their days and styles, and they know, in the way, apparently, that other people know when they have to go to the bathroom, everything about everyone who enters their domain. Though some are white-haired and some not, some fat, some thin, some grandmothers and some but lately virgins, they all have exactly the same, shrewd, vacant, all-registering eye; it is difficult to believe that they ever cried for milk or looked at the sun; it seems they must have come into the world hungry for banknotes, and squinting helplessly, unable to focus their eyes until they came to rest on a cash register.

This one's hair is black and grey, and she has a face which comes from Brittany; and she, like almost everyone else standing at the bar, knows Giovanni and, after her fashion, likes him. She has a big, deep bosom and she clasps Giovanni to it; and a big, deep voice.

'*Ah, mon pote!*' she cries. '*Tu es revenu!* You have come back at last! *Salaud!* Now that you are rich and have found rich friends, you never come to see us anymore! *Canaille!*'

And she beams at us, the 'rich' friends, with a friendliness deliciously, deliberately vague; she would have no trouble reconstructing every instant of our biographies from the moment we were born until this morning. She knows exactly who is rich – and how rich – and she knows it isn't me. For this reason, perhaps, there was a click of speculation infinitesimally double behind her eyes when she looked at me. In a moment, however, she knows that she will understand it all.

'You know how it is,' says Giovanni, extricating himself and throwing back his hair, 'when you work, when you become serious, you have no time to play.'

'*Tiens,*' says she, with mockery. '*Sans blague?*'

'But I assure you,' says Giovanni, 'even when you are a young man like me, you get very tired' – she laughs – 'and you go to sleep early' – she laughs again – 'and *alone,*' says Giovanni, as though this proved everything, and she clicks her teeth in sympathy and laughs again.

'And now,' she says, 'are you coming or going? Have you come for breakfast or have you come for a nightcap? *Nom de Dieu*, you do not *look* very serious; I believe you need a drink.'

'*Bien sûr*,' says someone at the bar, 'after such hard work he needs a bottle of white wine – and perhaps a few dozen oysters.'

Everybody laughs. Everybody, without seeming to, is looking at us and I am beginning to feel like part of a travelling circus. Everybody, also, seems very proud of Giovanni.

Giovanni turns to the voice at the bar. 'An excellent idea, friend,' he says, 'and exactly what I had in mind.' Now he turns to us. 'You have not met my friends,' he says, looking at me, then at the woman. 'This is Monsieur Guillaume,' he tells her, and with the most subtle flattening of his voice, 'my *patron*. He can tell you if I am serious.'

'Ah,' she dares to say, 'but I cannot tell if *he* is,' and covers this daring with a laugh.

Guillaume, raising his eyes with difficulty from the young men at the bar, stretches out his hand and smiles. 'But you are right, Madame,' he says. 'He is so much more serious than I am that I fear he will own my bar one day.'

He will when lions fly, she is thinking, but professes herself enchanted by him and shakes his hand with energy.

'And Monsieur Jacques,' says Giovanni, 'one of our finest customers.'

'*Enchanté, Madame*,' says Jacques, with his most dazzling smile, of which she, in responding, produces the most artless parody.

'And this is *monsieur l'américain*,' says Giovanni, 'otherwise known as: *Monsieur David. Madame Clothilde*.'

And he stands back slightly. Something is burning in his eyes and it lights up all his face, it is joy and pride.

'*Je suis ravie, monsieur,*' she tells me and looks at me and shakes my hand and smiles.

I am smiling too, I scarcely know why; everything in me is jumping up and down. Giovanni carelessly puts an arm around my shoulder. 'What have you got good to eat?' he cried. 'We are hungry.'

'But we must have a drink first!' cried Jacques.

'But we can drink sitting down,' said Giovanni, 'no?'

'No,' said Guillaume, to whom leaving the bar, at the moment, would have seemed like being driven from the promised land, 'let us first have a drink, here at the bar, with Madame.'

Guillaume's suggestion had the effect – but subtly, as though a wind had blown over everything or a light been imperceptibly intensified – of creating among the people at the bar, a *troupe*, who would now play various roles in a play they knew very well. Madame Clothilde would demur, as, indeed, she instantly did, but only for a moment; then she would accept, it would be something expensive; it turned out to be champagne. She would sip it, making the most noncommittal conversation, so that she could vanish out of it a split second before Guillaume had established contact with one of the boys at the bar. As for the boys at the bar, they were each invisibly preening, having already calculated how much money he and his *copain* would need for the next few days, having already appraised Guillaume to within a decimal of that figure, and having already estimated how long Guillaume, as a fountainhead, would last, and also how long they would be able to endure him. The only question left was whether they would be *vache* with him, or *chic*, but they knew that they would probably be *vache*. There was also Jacques, who might turn out to be a bonus, or merely a consolation prize. There was me, of course, another matter altogether, innocent of apartments, soft beds, or food, a candidate, therefore, for affection, but, as Giovanni's *môme*, out of honorable reach. Their only means, practically at least, of conveying their affection for Giovanni and me was to relieve us of these two old men. So that there was added, to the roles they were about to play, a certain jolly aura of conviction and, to self-interest, an altruistic glow.

I ordered black coffee and a cognac, a large one. Giovanni was far from me, drinking *marc* between an old man, who looked like a receptacle of all the world's dirt and disease, and a young boy, a redhead, who would look like that man one day, if one could read, in the dullness of his eye, anything so real as a future. Now, however, he had something of a horse's dreadful beauty; some suggestion, too, of the storm trooper; covertly, he was watching Guillaume; he knew that both Guillaume and Jacques were watching him. Guillaume chatted, meanwhile, with Madame Clothilde; they were agreeing that business was awful, that all standards had been debased by the *nouveau riche*, and that the country needed de Gaulle. Luckily, they had both had this conversation so many times before that it ran, so to speak, all by itself, demanding of them nothing in the way of concentration. Jacques would shortly offer one of the boys a drink but, for the moment, he wished to play uncle to me.

'How do you feel?' he asked me. 'This is a very important day for you.'

'I feel fine,' I said. 'How do you feel?'

'Like a man,' he said, 'who has seen a vision.'

'Yes?' I said. 'Tell me about this vision.'

'I am not joking,' he said. 'I am talking about you. *You* were the vision. You should have seen yourself tonight. You should see yourself now.'

I looked at him and said nothing.

'You are – how old? Twenty-six or -seven? I am nearly twice that and, let me tell you, you are lucky. You are lucky that what is happening to you now is happening *now* and not when you are forty, or something like that, when there would be no hope for you and you would simply be destroyed.'

'What is happening to me?' I asked. I had meant to sound sardonic, but I did not sound sardonic at all.

He did not answer this, but sighed, looking briefly in the direction of the redhead. Then he turned to me. 'Are you going to write to Hella?'

'I very often do,' I said. 'I suppose I will again.'

'That does not answer my question.'

'Oh. I was under the impression that you had asked me if I was going to write to Hella.'

'Well. Let's put it another way. Are you going to write to Hella about this night and this morning?'

'I really don't see what there is to write about. But what's it to you if I do or I don't?'

He gave me a look full of a certain despair which I had not, till that moment, known was in him. It frightened me. 'It's not,' he said, 'what it is to *me*. It's what it is to *you*. And to her. And to that poor boy, yonder, who doesn't know that when he looks at you the way he does, he is simply putting his head in the lion's mouth. Are you going to treat them as you've treated me?'

'*You?* What have *you* to do with all this? How have I treated *you*?'

'You have been very unfair to me,' he said. 'You have been very dishonest.'

This time I did sound sardonic. 'I suppose you mean that I would have been fair, I would have been honest if I had – if –'

'I mean you could have been fair to me by despising me a little less.'

'I'm sorry. But I think, since you bring it up, that a lot of your life *is* despicable.'

'I could say the same about yours,' said Jacques. 'There are so many ways of being despicable it quite makes one's head spin. But the way to be really despicable is to be contemptuous of other people's pain. You ought to have some apprehension that the man you see before you was once even younger than you are now and arrived at his present wretchedness by imperceptible degrees.'

There was silence for a moment, threatened, from a distance, by that laugh of Giovanni's.

'Tell me,' I said at last, 'is there really no other way for you but this? To kneel down forever before an army of boys for just five dirty minutes in the dark?'

'Think,' said Jacques, 'of the men who have kneeled before you while you thought of something else and pretended that nothing was happening down there in the dark between your legs.'

I stared at the amber cognac and at the wet rings on the metal. Deep below, trapped in the metal, the outline of my own face looked upward hopelessly at me.

'You think,' he persisted, 'that my life is shameful because my encounters are. And they are. But you should ask yourself *why* they are.'

'Why are they – shameful?' I asked him.

'Because there is no affection in them, and no joy. It's like putting an electric plug in a dead socket. Touch, but no contact. All touch, but no contact and no light.'

I asked him: 'Why?'

'That you must ask yourself,' he told me, 'and perhaps one day, this morning will not be ashes in your mouth.'

I looked over at Giovanni, who now had one arm around the ruined-looking girl, who could have once been very beautiful but who never would be now.

Jacques followed my look. 'He is very fond of you,' he said, 'already. But this doesn't make you happy or proud, as it should. It makes you frightened and ashamed. Why?'

'I don't understand him,' I said at last. 'I don't know what his friendship means; I don't know what he means by friendship.'

Jacques laughed. 'You don't know what he means by friendship but you have the feeling it may not be safe. You are afraid it may change you. What kind of friendships have you had?'

I said nothing.

'Or for that matter,' he continued, 'what kind of love affairs?'

I was silent for so long that he teased me, saying, 'Come out, come out, wherever you are!'

And I grinned, feeling chilled.

'Love him,' said Jacques, with vehemence, 'love him and let him love you. Do you think anything else under heaven really matters? And how long, at the best, can it last? since you are both men and still have everywhere to go? Only five minutes, I assure you, only five minutes, and most of that, *hélas!* in the dark. And if you think of them as dirty, then they *will* be dirty – they will be dirty because you will be giving nothing, you will be despising your flesh and his. But you can make your time together anything but dirty; you can give each other something which will make both of you better – forever – if you will *not* be ashamed, if you will only *not* play it safe.' He paused, watching me, and then looked down to his cognac. 'You play it safe long enough,' he said, in a different tone, 'and you'll end up trapped in your own dirty body, forever and forever and forever – like me.' And he finished his cognac, ringing his glass slightly on the bar to attract the attention of Madame Clothilde.

She came at once, beaming; and in that moment Guillaume dared to smile at the redhead. Madame Clothilde poured Jacques a fresh cognac and looked questioningly at me, the bottle poised over my half-full glass. I hesitated.

'*Et pourquoi pas?*' she asked, with a smile.

So I finished my glass and she filled it. Then, for the briefest of seconds, she glanced at Guillaume; who cried, '*Et le rouquin là!* What's the redhead drinking?'

Madame Clothilde turned with the air of an actress about to deliver the severely restrained last lines of an exhausting and mighty part. '*On t'offre, Pierre,*' she said, majestically. 'What will you have?' – holding slightly aloft meanwhile the bottle containing the most expensive cognac in the house.

'*Je prendrai un petit cognac,*' Pierre mumbled after a moment and, oddly enough, he blushed, which made him, in the light of the pale, just-rising sun, resemble a freshly fallen angel.

Madame Clothilde filled Pierre's glass and, amid a beautifully resolving tension, as of slowly dimming lights, replaced the bottle on the shelf and walked back to the cash register; offstage, in effect, into the wings, where she began to recover herself by finishing the last of the champagne. She sighed and sipped and looked outward contentedly into the slowly rising morning. Guillaume had murmured a '*Je m'excuse un instant, Madame,*' and now passed behind us on his way to the redhead.

I smiled. 'Things my father never told me.'

'*Somebody,*' said Jacques, 'your father or mine, should have told us that not many people have ever died of love. But multitudes have perished, and are perishing every hour – and in the oddest places! – for the lack of it.' And then: 'Here comes your baby. *Sois sage. Sois chic.*'

He moved slightly away and began talking to the boy next to him.

And here my baby came indeed, through all that sunlight, his face flushed and his hair flying, his eyes, unbelievably, like morning stars. 'It was not very nice of me to go off for so long,' he said, 'I hope you have not been too bored.'

'*You* certainly haven't been,' I told him. 'You look like a kid about five years old waking up on Christmas morning.'

This delighted, even flattered him, as I could see from the way he now humorously pursed his lips. 'I am sure I cannot look like that,' he said. 'I was always disappointed on Christmas morning.'

'Well, I mean very *early* on Christmas morning, before you saw what was under the tree.' But his eyes have somehow made of my last statement a *double entendre*, and we are both laughing.

'Are you hungry?' he asked.

'Perhaps I would be if I were alive and sober. I don't know. Are you?'

'I think we should eat,' he said with no conviction whatever, and we began to laugh again.

'Well,' I said, 'what shall we eat?'

'I scarcely dare suggest white wine and oysters,' said Giovanni, 'but that is really the best thing after such a night.'

'Well, let's do that,' I said, 'while we can still walk to the dining room.' I looked beyond him to Guillaume and the redhead. They had apparently found something to talk about; I could not imagine what it was. And Jacques was deep in conversation with the tall, very young, pockmarked boy, whose turtleneck black sweater made him seem even paler and thinner than he actually was. He had been playing the pinball machine when we came in; his name appeared to be Yves. 'Are they going to eat now?' I asked Giovanni.

'Perhaps not now,' said Giovanni, 'but they are certainly going to eat. Everyone is very hungry.' I took this to refer more to the boys than to our friends, and we passed into the dining room, which was now empty, the waiter nowhere in sight.

'Madame Clothilde!' shouted Giovanni, '*On mange ici, non?*'

This shout produced an answering shout from Madame Clothilde and also produced the waiter, whose jacket was less spotless, seen in closeup, than it had seemed from a distance. It also officially announced our presence in the dining room to Jacques and Guillaume and must have definitely increased, in the eyes of the boys they were talking to, a certain tigerish intensity of affection.

'We'll eat quickly and go,' said Giovanni. 'After all, I have to work tonight.'

'Did you meet Guillaume here?' I asked him.

He grimaced, looking down. 'No. That is a long story.' He grinned. 'No, I did not meet him here. I met him' – he laughed – 'in a cinema.' We both laughed. '*C'était un film du far west, avec Gary Cooper.*' This seemed terribly funny, too; we kept laughing until the waiter came with our bottle of white wine.

'Well,' said Giovanni, sipping the wine, his eyes damp, 'after the last gun shot had been fired and all the music came up to celebrate the triumph of goodness and I came up the aisle, I bumped into this man – Guillaume – and I excused myself and walked into the lobby. Then here he came, after me, with a long story about leaving his scarf in *my* seat because, it appeared, he had been sitting *behind* me, you understand, with his coat and his scarf on the seat *before* him and when I sat down I pulled his scarf down with me. Well, I told him I didn't work for the cinema and I told him what he could do with his scarf – but I did not really get angry because he made me want to laugh. He said that all the people who worked for the cinema were thieves and he was sure that they would keep it if they so much as laid eyes on it, and it was very expensive, and a gift from his mother and – oh, I assure you, not even Garbo ever gave such a performance. So I went back and of course there was no scarf there and when I told him this it seemed he would fall dead right there in the lobby. And by this time, you understand, everybody thought we were together and I didn't know whether to kick him or the people who were looking at us; but he was very well dressed, of course, and I was not and so I thought, well, we had better get out of this lobby. So we went to a café and sat on the terrace and when he had got over his grief about the scarf and what his mother would say and so on and so on, he asked me to have supper with him. Well, naturally, I said no; I had certainly had enough of him by that time, but the only way I could prevent another scene, right there on the terrace, was to promise to have supper with him a few days later – I did not intend to go,' he said, with a shy grin, 'but when the day came, I had not eaten for a long time and I was very hungry.' He looked at me and I saw in his face again something which I have fleetingly seen there during these hours: under his beauty and his bravado, terror, and a terrible desire to please; dreadfully, dreadfully moving, and it made me want, in anguish, to reach out and comfort him.

Our oysters came and we began to eat. Giovanni sat in the sun, his black hair gathering to itself the yellow glow of the wine and the many dull colors of the oyster where the sun struck it.

'Well' – with his mouth turned down – 'dinner was awful, of course, since he can make scenes in his apartment, too. But by this time I knew he owned a bar and was a French citizen. I am not and I had no job and no *carte de travail.* So I saw that he could be useful if I could only find some way to make him keep his hands off me. I did not, I must say' – this with that look at me – 'altogether succeed in remaining untouched by him; he has more hands than an octopus, and no dignity whatever, *but*' – grimly throwing down another oyster and refilling our glasses of wine – 'I *do* now have a *carte de travail* and I have a job. Which pays very well,' he grinned. 'It appears that I am good for business. For this reason, he leaves me mostly alone.' He looked out into the bar. 'He is really not a man at all,' he said, with a sorrow and bewilderment at once childlike and ancient, 'I do not know what he is, he is horrible. But I will keep my *carte de travail.* The job is another matter, but' – he knocked wood – 'we have had no trouble now for nearly three weeks.'

'But you think that trouble is coming,' I said.

'Oh, yes,' said Giovanni, with a quick, startled look at me, as if he were wondering if I had understood a word of what he had said, 'we are certainly going to have a little trouble soon again. Not right away, of course; that is not his style. But he will invent something to be angry at me about.'

Then we sat in silence for awhile, smoking cigarettes, surrounded by oyster shells, and finishing the wine. I was all at once very tired. I looked out into the narrow street, this strange, crooked corner where we sat, which was brazen now with the sunlight and heavy with people – people I would never understand. I ached abruptly, intolerably, with a longing to go home; not to that hotel, in one of the alleys of Paris, where the concierge barred the way with my unpaid bill; but home, home across the ocean, to things and people I knew and understood; to those things, those places, those people which I would always, helplessly, and in whatever bitterness of spirit, love above all else. I had never realized such a sentiment in myself before, and it frightened me. I saw myself, sharply, as a wanderer, an adventurer, rocking through the world, unanchored. I looked at Giovanni's face, which did not help me. He belonged to this strange city, which did not belong to me. I began to see that, while what was happening to me was not so strange as it would have comforted me to believe, yet it was strange beyond belief. It was not really so strange, so unprecedented, though voices deep within me boomed, For shame! For shame! that I should be so abruptly, so hideously entangled with a boy; what was strange was that this was but one tiny aspect of the dreadful human tangle occurring everywhere, without end, forever.

'*Viens*,' said Giovanni.

We rose and walked back into the bar and Giovanni paid our bill. Another bottle of champagne had been opened and Jacques and Guillaume were now really beginning to be drunk. It was going to be ghastly and I wondered if those poor, patient boys were ever going to get anything to eat. Giovanni talked to Guillaume for a moment, agreeing to open up the bar; Jacques was too busy with the pale tall boy to have much time for me; we said good-morning and left them.

'I must go home,' I said to Giovanni when we were in the street. 'I must pay my hotel bill.'

Giovanni stared. '*Mais tu es fou*,' he said mildly. 'There is certainly no point in going home now, to face an ugly concierge and then go to sleep in that room all by yourself and then wake up later, with a terrible stomach and a sour mouth, wanting to commit suicide. Come with me; we will rise at a civilized hour and have a gentle aperitif somewhere and then a little dinner. It will be much more cheerful like that,' he said with a smile, 'you will see.'

'But I must get my clothes,' I said.

He took my arm. '*Bien sûr.* But you do not have to get them *now.*' I held back. He stopped. 'Come. I am sure that I am much prettier than your wallpaper – or your concierge. I will smile at you when you wake up. They will not.'

'Ah,' I could only say, '*tu es vache.*'

'It is you who are *vache,*' he said, 'to want to leave me alone in this lonely place when you know that I am far too drunk to reach my home unaided.'

We laughed together, both caught up in a stinging, teasing sort of game. We reached the Boulevard de Sébastopol. 'But we will not any longer discuss the painful subject of how you desired to desert Giovanni, at so dangerous an hour, in the middle of a hostile city.' I began to realize that he, too, was nervous. Far down the boulevard a cab meandered toward us, and he put up his hand. 'I will show you my room,' he said. 'It is perfectly clear that you would have to see it one of these days, anyway.' The taxi stopped beside us, and Giovanni, as though he were suddenly afraid that I would really turn and run, pushed me in before him. He got in beside me and told the driver: '*Nation.*'

The street he lived on was wide, respectable rather than elegant, and massive with fairly recent apartment buildings; the street ended in a small park. His room was in the back, on the ground floor of the last building on this street. We passed the vestibule and the elevator into a short, dark corridor which led to his room. The room was small, I only made out the outlines of clutter and disorder, there was the smell of the alcohol he burned in his stove. He locked the door behind us, and then for a moment, in the gloom, we simply stared at each other – with dismay, with relief, and breathing hard. I was trembling. I thought, if I do not open the door at once and get out of here, I am lost. But I knew I could not open the door, I knew it was too late; soon it was too late to do anything but moan. He pulled me against him, putting himself into my arms as though he were giving me himself to carry, and slowly pulled me down with him to that bed. With everything in me screaming *No!* yet the sum of me sighed *Yes*.

JULIO CORTÁZAR

# BLOW-UP

1959

Translated by Paul Blackburn

IT'LL NEVER BE known how this has to be told, in the first person or in the second, using the third person plural or continually inventing modes that will serve for nothing. If one might say: I will see the moon rose, or: we hurt me at the back of my eyes, and especially: you the blond woman was the clouds that race before my your his our yours their faces. What the hell.

Seated ready to tell it, if one might go to drink a bock over there, and the typewriter continue by itself (because I use the machine), that would be perfection. And that's not just a manner of speaking. Perfection, yes, because here is the aperture which must be counted also as a machine (of another sort, a Contax 1.1.2) and it is possible that one machine may know more about another machine than I, you, she – the blond – and the clouds. But I have the dumb luck to know that if I go this Remington will sit turned to stone on top of the table with the air of being twice as quiet that mobile things have when they are not moving. So, I have to write. One of us all has to write, if this is going to get told. Better that it be me who am dead, for I'm less compromised than the rest; I who see only the clouds and can think without being distracted, write without being distracted (there goes another, with a gray edge) and remember without being distracted, I who am dead (and I'm alive, I'm not trying to fool anybody, you'll see when we get to the moment, because I have to begin some way and I've begun with this period, the last one back, the one at the beginning, which in the end is the best of the periods when you want to tell something).

All of a sudden I wonder why I have to tell this, but if one begins to wonder why he does all he does do, if one wonders why he accepts an invitation to lunch (now a pigeon's flying by and it seems to me a sparrow), or why when someone has told us a good joke immediately there starts up something like a tickling in the stomach and we are not at peace until we've gone into the office across the hall and told the joke over again; then it feels good immediately, one is fine, happy, and can get back to work. For I imagine that no one has explained this, that really the best thing is to put aside all decorum and tell it, because, after all's done, nobody is ashamed of breathing or of putting on his shoes; they're things that you do, and when something weird happens, when you find a spider in your shoe or if you take a breath and feel like a broken window, then you have to tell what's happening, tell it to the guys at the office or to the doctor. Oh, doctor, every time I take a breath ... Always tell it, always get rid of that tickle in the stomach that bothers you.

And now that we're finally going to tell it, let's put things a little bit in order, we'd be walking down the staircase in this house as far as Sunday, November 7, just a month back. One goes down five floors and stands then in the Sunday sun one would not have suspected of Paris in November, with a large appetite to walk around, to see things, to take photos (because we were photographers, I'm a photographer). I know that the most difficult thing is going to be finding a way to tell it, and I'm not afraid of repeating myself. It's going to be difficult because nobody really knows who it is telling it, if I am I or what actually occurred or what I'm seeing (clouds, and once in a while a pigeon) or if, simply, I'm telling a truth which is only my truth, and then is the truth only for my stomach, for this impulse to go running out and to finish up in some manner with this, whatever it is.

We're going to tell it slowly, what happens in the middle of what I'm writing is coming already. If they replace me, if, so soon, I don't know what to say, if the clouds stop coming and something else starts (because it's impossible that this keep coming, clouds passing continually and occasionally a pigeon), if something out of all this . . . And after the 'if' what am I going to put if I'm going to close the sentence structure correctly? But if I begin to ask questions, I'll never tell anything, maybe to tell would be like an answer, at least for someone who's reading it.

Roberto Michel, French-Chilean, translator and in his spare time an amateur photographer, left number 11, rue Monsieur-le-Prince Sunday, November 7 of the current year (now there're two small ones passing, with silver linings). He had spent three weeks working on the French version of a treatise on challenges and appeals by José Norberto Allende, professor at the University of Santiago. It's rare that there's wind in Paris, and even less seldom a wind like this that swirled around corners and rose up to whip at old wooden venetian blinds behind which astonished ladies commented variously on how unreliable the weather had been these last few years. But the sun was out also, riding the wind and friend of the cats, so there was nothing that would keep me from taking a walk along the docks of the Seine and taking photos of the Conservatoire and Sainte-Chapelle. It was hardly ten o'clock, and I figured that by eleven the light would be good, the best you can get in the fall; to kill some time I detoured around by the Île Saint-Louis and started to walk along the quai d'Anjou, I stared for a bit at the hôtel de Lauzun, I recited bits from Apollinaire which always get into my head whenever I pass in front of the hôtel de Lauzun (and at that I ought to be remembering the other poet, but Michel is an obstinate beggar), and when the wind stopped all at once and the sun came out at least twice as hard (I mean warmer, but really it's the same thing), I sat down on the parapet and felt terribly happy in the Sunday morning.

One of the many ways of contesting level-zero, and one of the best, is to take photographs, an activity in which one should start becoming an adept very early in life, teach it to children since it requires discipline, aesthetic education, a good eye and steady fingers. I'm not talking about waylaying the lie like any old reporter, snapping the stupid silhouette of the VIP leaving number 10 Downing Street, but in all ways when one is walking about with a camera, one has almost a duty to be attentive, to not lose that abrupt and happy rebound of sun's rays off an old stone, or the pigtails-flying run of a small girl going home with a loaf of bread or a bottle of milk. Michel knew that the photographer always worked as a permutation of his personal way of seeing the world as other than the camera insidiously imposed upon it (now a large cloud is going by, almost black), but he lacked no confidence in himself, knowing that he had only to go out without the Contax to recover the keynote of distraction, the sight without a frame around it, light without the diaphragm aperture or 1/250 sec. Right now (what a word, *now*, what a dumb lie) I was able to sit quietly on the railing overlooking the river watching the red and black motorboats passing below without it occurring to me to think photographically of the scenes, nothing more than letting myself go in the letting go of objects, running immobile in the stream of time. And then the wind was not blowing.

After, I wandered down the quai de Bourbon until getting to the end of the isle where the intimate square was (intimate because it was small, not that it was hidden, it offered its whole breast to the river and the sky), I enjoyed it, a lot. Nothing there but a couple and, of course, pigeons; maybe even some of those which are flying past now so that I'm seeing them. A leap up and I settled on the wall, and let myself turn about and be caught and fixed by the sun, giving it my face and ears and hands (I kept my gloves in my pocket). I had no desire to shoot pictures, and lit a cigarette to be doing something; I think it was that moment when the match was about to touch the tobacco that I saw the young boy for the first time.

What I'd thought was a couple seemed much more now a boy with his mother, although at the same time I realized that it was not a kid and his mother, and that it was a couple in the sense that we always give to couples when we see them leaning up against the parapets or embracing on the benches in the squares. As I had nothing else to do, I had more than enough time to wonder why the boy was so nervous, like a young colt or a hare, sticking his hands into his pockets, taking them out immediately, one after the other, running his fingers through his hair, changing his stance, and especially why was he afraid, well, you could guess that from every gesture, a fear suffocated by his shyness, an impulse to step backwards which he telegraphed, his body standing as if it were on the edge of flight, holding itself back in a final, pitiful decorum.

All this was so clear, ten feet away – and we were alone against the parapet at the tip of the island – that at the beginning the boy's fright didn't let me see the blond very well. Now, thinking back on it, I see her much better at that first second when I read her face (she'd turned around suddenly, swinging like a metal weathercock, and the eyes, the eyes were there), when I vaguely understood what might have been occurring to the boy and figured it would be worth the trouble to stay and watch (the wind was blowing their words away and they were speaking in a low murmur). I think that I know how to look, if it's something I know, and also that every looking oozes with mendacity, because it's that which expels us furthest outside ourselves, without the least guarantee, whereas to smell, or (but Michel rambles on to himself easily enough, there's no need to let him harangue on this way). In any case, if the likely inaccuracy can be seen beforehand, it becomes possible again to look; perhaps it suffices to choose between looking and the reality looked at, to strip things of all their unnecessary clothing. And surely all that is difficult besides.

As for the boy I remember the image before his actual body (that will clear itself up later), while now I am sure that I remember the woman's body much better than the image. She was thin and willowy, two unfair words to describe what she was, and was wearing an almost-black fur coat, almost long, almost handsome. All the morning's wind (now it was hardly a breeze and it wasn't cold) had blown through her blond hair which pared away her white, bleak face – two unfair words – and put the world at her feet and horribly alone in front of her dark eyes, her eyes fell on things like two eagles, two leaps into nothingness, two puffs of green slime. I'm not describing anything, it's more a matter of trying to understand it. And I said two puffs of green slime.

Let's be fair, the boy was well enough dressed and was sporting yellow gloves which I would have sworn belonged to his older brother, a student of law or sociology; it was pleasant to see the fingers of the gloves sticking out of his jacket pocket. For a long time I didn't see his face, barely a profile, not stupid – a terrified bird, a Fra Filippo angel, rice pudding with milk – and the back of an adolescent who wants to take up judo and has had a scuffle or two in defense of an idea or his sister. Turning fourteen, perhaps fifteen, one would guess that he was dressed and fed by his parents but without a nickel in his pocket, having to debate with his buddies before making up his mind to buy a coffee, a cognac, a pack of cigarettes. He'd walk through the streets thinking of the girls in his class, about how good it would be to go to the movies and see the latest film, or to buy novels or neckties or bottles of liquor with green and white labels on them. At home (it would be a respectable home, lunch at noon and romantic landscapes on the walls, with a dark entryway and a mahogany umbrella stand inside the door) there'd be the slow rain of time, for studying, for being mama's hope, for looking like dad, for writing to his aunt in Avignon. So that there was a lot of walking the streets, the whole of the river for him (but without a nickel) and the mysterious city of fifteen-year-olds with its signs in doorways, its terrifying cats, a paper of fried potatoes for thirty francs, the pornographic magazine folded four ways, a solitude like the emptiness of his pockets, the eagerness for so much that was incomprehensible but illumined by a total love, by the availability analogous to the wind and the streets.

This biography was of the boy and of any boy whatsoever, but this particular one now, you could see he was insular, surrounded solely by the blond's presence as she continued talking with him. (I'm tired of insisting, but two long ragged ones just went by. That morning I don't think I looked at the sky once, because what was happening with the boy and the woman appeared so soon I could do nothing but look at them and wait, look at them and . . .) To cut it short, the boy was agitated and one could guess without too much trouble what had just occurred a few minutes before, at most half-an-hour. The boy had come onto the tip of the island, seen the woman and thought her marvelous. The woman was waiting for that because she was there waiting for that, or maybe the boy arrived before her and she saw him from one of the balconies or from a car and got out to meet him, starting the conversation with whatever, from the beginning she was sure that he was going to be afraid and want to run off, and that, naturally, he'd stay, stiff and sullen, pretending experience and the pleasure of the adventure. The rest was easy because it was happening ten feet away from me, and anyone could have gauged the stages of the game, the derisive, competitive fencing; its major attraction was not that it was happening but in foreseeing its denouement. The boy would try to end it by pretending a date, an obligation, whatever, and would go stumbling off disconcerted, wishing he were walking with some assurance, but naked under the mocking glance which would follow him until he was out of sight. Or rather, he would stay there, fascinated or simply incapable of taking the initiative, and the woman would begin to touch his face gently, muss his hair, still talking to him voicelessly, and soon would take him by the arm to lead him off, unless he, with an uneasiness beginning to tinge the edge of desire, even his stake in the adventure, would rouse himself to put his arm around her waist and to kiss her. Any of this could have happened, though it did not, and perversely Michel waited, sitting on the railing, making the settings almost without looking at the camera, ready to take a picturesque shot of a corner of the island with an uncommon couple talking and looking at one another.

Strange how the scene (almost nothing: two figures there mismatched in their youth) was taking on a disquieting aura. I thought it was I imposing it, and that my photo, if I shot it, would reconstitute things in their true stupidity. I would have liked to know what he was thinking, a man in a gray hat sitting at the wheel of a car parked on the dock which led up to the footbridge, and whether he was reading the paper or asleep. I had just discovered him because people inside a parked car have a tendency to disappear, they get lost in that wretched, private cage stripped of the beauty that motion and danger give it. And nevertheless, the car had been there the whole time, forming part (or deforming that part) of the isle. A car: like saying a lighted streetlamp, a park bench. Never like saying wind, sunlight, those elements always new to the skin and the eyes, and also the boy and the woman, unique, put there to change the island, to show it to me in another way. Finally, it may have been that the man with the newspaper also became aware of what was happening and would, like me, feel that malicious sensation of waiting for everything to happen. Now the woman had swung around smoothly, putting the young boy between herself and the wall, I saw them almost in profile, and he was taller, though not much taller, and yet she dominated him, it seemed like she was hovering over him (her laugh, all at once, a whip of feathers), crushing him just by being there, smiling, one hand taking a stroll through the air. Why wait any longer? Aperture at sixteen, a sighting which would not include the horrible black car, but yes, that tree, necessary to break up too much gray space...

I raised the camera, pretended to study a focus which did not include them, and waited and watched closely, sure that I would finally catch the revealing expression, one that would sum it all up, life that is rhythmed by movement but which a stiff image destroys, taking time in cross section, if we do not choose the essential imperceptible fraction of it. I did not have to wait long. The woman was getting on with the job of handcuffing the boy smoothly, stripping from him what was left of his freedom a hair at a time, in an incredibly slow and delicious torture. I imagined the possible endings (now a small fluffy cloud appears, almost alone in the sky), I saw their arrival at the house (a basement apartment probably, which she would have filled with large cushions and cats) and conjectured the boy's terror and his desperate decision to play it cool and to be led off pretending there was nothing new in it for him. Closing my eyes, if I did in fact close my eyes, I set the scene: the teasing kisses, the woman mildly repelling the hands which were trying to undress her, like in novels, on a bed that would have a lilac-colored comforter, on the other hand she taking off his clothes, plainly mother and son under a milky yellow light, and everything would end up as usual, perhaps, but maybe everything would go otherwise, and the initiation of the adolescent would not happen, she would not let it happen, after a long prologue wherein the awkwardnesses, the exasperating caresses, the running of hands over bodies would be resolved in who knows what, in a separate and solitary pleasure, in a petulant denial mixed with the art of tiring and disconcerting so much poor innocence. It might go like that, it might very well go like that; that woman was not looking for the boy as a lover, and at the same time she was dominating him toward some end impossible to understand if you do not imagine it as a cruel game, the desire to desire without satisfaction, to excite herself for someone else, someone who in no way could be that kid.

Michel is guilty of making literature, of indulging in fabricated unrealities. Nothing pleases him more than to imagine exceptions to the rule, individuals outside the species, not-always-repugnant monsters. But that woman invited speculation, perhaps giving clues enough for the fantasy to hit the bullseye. Before she left, and now that she would fill my imaginings for several days, for I'm given to ruminating, I decided not to lose a moment more. I got it all into the view-finder (with the tree, the railing, the eleven-o'clock sun) and took the shot. In time to realize that they both had noticed and stood there looking at me, the boy surprised and as though questioning, but she was irritated, her face and body flat-footedly hostile, feeling robbed, ignominiously recorded on a small chemical image.

I might be able to tell it in much greater detail but it's not worth the trouble. The woman said that no one had the right to take a picture without permission, and demanded that I hand her over the film. All this in a dry, clear voice with a good Parisian accent, which rose in color and tone with every phrase. For my part, it hardly mattered whether she got the roll of film or not, but anyone who knows me will tell you, if you want anything from me, ask nicely. With the result that I restricted myself to formulating the opinion that not only was photography in public places not prohibited, but it was looked upon with decided favor, both private and official. And while that was getting said, I noticed on the sly how the boy was falling back, sort of actively backing up though without moving, and all at once (it seemed almost incredible) he turned and broke into a run, the poor kid, thinking that he was walking off and in fact in full flight, running past the side of the car, disappearing like a gossamer filament of angel-spit in the morning air.

But filaments of angel-spittle are also called devil-spit, and Michel had to endure rather particular curses, to hear himself called meddler and imbecile, taking great pains meanwhile to smile and to abate with simple movements of his head such a hard sell. As I was beginning to get tired, I heard the car door slam. The man in the gray hat was there, looking at us. It was only at that point that I realized he was playing a part in the comedy.

He began to walk toward us, carrying in his hand the

paper he had been pretending to read. What I remember best is the grimace that twisted his mouth askew, it covered his face with wrinkles, changed somewhat both in location and shape because his lips trembled and the grimace went from one side of his mouth to the other as though it were on wheels, independent and involuntary. But the rest stayed fixed, a flour-powdered clown or bloodless man, dull dry skin, eyes deepset, the nostrils black and prominently visible, blacker than the eyebrows or hair or the black necktie. Walking cautiously as though the pavement hurt his feet; I saw patent-leather shoes with such thin soles that he must have felt every roughness in the pavement. I don't know why I got down off the railing, nor very well why I decided to not give them the photo, to refuse that demand in which I guessed at their fear and cowardice. The clown and the woman consulted one another in silence: we made a perfect and unbearable triangle, something I felt compelled to break with a crack of a whip. I laughed in their faces and began to walk off, a little more slowly, I imagine, than the boy. At the level of the first houses, beside the iron footbridge, I turned around to look at them. They were not moving, but the man had dropped his newspaper; it seemed to me that the woman, her back to the parapet, ran her hands over the stone with the classical and absurd gesture of someone pursued looking for a way out.

What happened after that happened here, almost just now, in a room on the fifth floor. Several days went by before Michel developed the photos he'd taken on Sunday; his shots of the Conservatoire and of Sainte-Chapelle were all they should be. Then he found two or three proof-shots he'd forgotten, a poor attempt to catch a cat perched astonishingly on the roof of a rambling public urinal, and also the shot of the blond and the kid. The negative was so good that he made an enlargement; the enlargement was so good that he made one very much larger, almost the size of a poster. It did not occur to him (now one wonders and wonders) that only the shots of the Conservatoire were worth so much work. Of the whole series, the snapshot of the tip of the island was the only one which interested him; he tacked up the enlargement on one wall of the room, and the first day he spent some time looking at it and remembering, that gloomy operation of comparing the memory with the gone reality; a frozen memory, like any photo, where nothing is missing, not even, and especially, nothingness, the true solidifier of the scene. There was the woman, there was the boy, the tree rigid above their heads, the sky as sharp as the stone of the parapet, clouds and stones melded into a single substance and inseparable (now one with sharp edges is going by, like a thunderhead). The first two days I accepted what I had done, from the photo itself to the enlargement on the wall, and didn't even question that every once in a while I would interrupt my translation of José Norberto Allende's treatise to encounter once more the woman's face, the dark splotches on the railing. I'm such a jerk; it had never occurred to me that when we look at a photo from the front, the eyes reproduce exactly the position and the vision of the lens; it's these things that are taken for granted and it never occurs to anyone to think about them. From my chair, with the typewriter directly in front of me, I looked at the photo ten feet away, and then it occurred to me that I had hung it exactly at the point of view of the lens. It looked very good that way; no doubt, it was the best way to appreciate a photo, though the angle from the diagonal doubtless has its pleasures and might even divulge different aspects. Every few minutes, for example when I was unable to find the way to say in good French what José Norberto Allende was saying in very good

Spanish, I raised my eyes and looked at the photo; sometimes the woman would catch my eye, sometimes the boy, sometimes the pavement where a dry leaf had fallen admirably situated to heighten a lateral section. Then I rested a bit from my labors, and I enclosed myself again happily in that morning in which the photo was drenched, I recalled ironically the angry picture of the woman demanding I give her the photograph, the boy's pathetic and ridiculous flight, the entrance on the scene of the man with the white face. Basically, I was satisfied with myself; my part had not been too brilliant, and since the French have been given the gift of the sharp response, I did not see very well why I'd chosen to leave without a complete demonstration of the rights, privileges and prerogatives of citizens. The important thing, the really important thing was having helped the kid to escape in time (this in case my theorizing was correct, which was not sufficiently proven, but the running away itself seemed to show it so). Out of plain meddling, I had given him the opportunity finally to take advantage of his fright to do something useful; now he would be regretting it, feeling his honor impaired, his manhood diminished. That was better than the attentions of a woman capable of looking as she had looked at him on that island. Michel is something of a puritan at times, he believes that one should not seduce someone from a position of strength. In the last analysis, taking that photo had been a good act.

Well, it wasn't because of the good act that I looked at it between paragraphs while I was working. At that moment I didn't know the reason, the reason I had tacked the enlargement onto the wall; maybe all fatal acts happen that way, and that is the condition of their fulfillment. I don't think the almost-furtive trembling of the leaves on the tree alarmed me, I was working on a sentence and rounded it out successfully. Habits are like immense herbariums, in the end an enlargement of 32 × 28 looks like a movie screen, where, on the tip of the island, a woman is speaking with a boy and a tree is shaking its dry leaves over their heads.

But her hands were just too much. I had just translated: 'In that case, the second key resides in the intrinsic nature of difficulties which societies . . .' – when I saw the woman's hand beginning to stir slowly, finger by finger. There was nothing left of me, a phrase in French which I would never have to finish, a typewriter on the floor, a chair that squeaked and shook, fog. The kid had ducked his head like boxers do when they've done all they can and are waiting for the final blow to fall; he had turned up the collar of his overcoat and seemed more a prisoner than ever, the perfect victim helping promote the catastrophe. Now the woman was talking into his ear, and her hand opened again to lay itself against his cheekbone, to caress and caress it, burning it, taking her time. The kid was less startled than he was suspicious, once or twice he poked his head over the woman's shoulder and she continued talking, saying something that made him look back every few minutes toward that area where Michel knew the car was parked and the man in the gray hat, carefully eliminated from the photo but present in the boy's eyes (how doubt that now) in the words of the woman, in the woman's hands, in the vicarious presence of the woman. When I saw the man come up, stop near them and look at them, his hands in his pockets and a stance somewhere between disgusted and demanding, the master who is about to whistle in his dog after a frolic in the square, I understood, if that was to understand, what had to happen now, what had to have happened then, what would have to happen at that moment, among these people, just where I had poked my nose in to upset an established order, interfering innocently in that which had not happened, but which was now going to happen, now was going to be fulfilled. And what I had imagined earlier was much less horrible than the reality, that woman, who was not there by herself, she was not caressing or propositioning or encouraging for her own pleasure, to lead the angel away with his tousled hair and play the tease with his terror and his eager grace. The real boss was waiting there, smiling petulantly, already certain of the business; he was not the first to send a woman in the vanguard, to bring him the prisoners manacled with flowers. The rest of it would be so simple, the car, some house or another, drinks, stimulating engravings, tardy tears, the awakening in hell. And there was nothing I could do, this time I could do absolutely nothing. My strength had been a photograph, that, there, where they were taking their revenge on me, demonstrating clearly what was going to happen. The photo had been taken, the time had run out, gone; we were so far from one another, the abusive act had certainly already taken place, the tears already shed, and the rest conjecture and sorrow. All at once the order was inverted, they were alive, moving, they were deciding and had decided, they were going to their future; and I on this side, prisoner of another time, in a room on the fifth floor, to not know who they were, that woman, that man, and that boy, to be only the lens of my camera, something fixed, rigid, incapable of intervention. It was horrible, their mocking me, deciding it before my impotent eye, mocking me, for the boy again was looking at the flour-faced clown and I had to accept the fact that he was going to say yes, that the proposition carried money with it or a gimmick, and I couldn't yell for him to run, or even open the road to him again with a new photo, a small and almost meek intervention which would ruin the framework of drool and perfume. Everything was going to resolve itself right there, at that moment; there was like an immense silence which had nothing to do with physical silence. It was stretching it out, setting itself up. I think I screamed, I screamed terribly, and that at that exact second I realized that I was beginning to move toward them, four inches, a step, another step, the tree swung its branches rhythmically in the foreground, a place where the railing was tarnished emerged from the frame, the woman's face turned toward me as though surprised, was enlarging, and then I turned a bit, I mean that the camera turned a little, and without losing sight of the woman, I began to close in on the man who was looking at me with the black holes he had in place of eyes, surprised and angered both, he looked, wanting to nail me onto the air, and at that instant I happened to see something like a large bird outside the focus that was flying in a single swoop in front of the picture, and I leaned up against the wall of my room and was happy because the boy had just managed to escape, I saw him running off, in focus again, sprinting with his hair flying in the wind, learning finally to fly across the island, to arrive at the footbridge, return to the city. For the second time he'd escaped them, for the second time I was helping him to escape, returning him to his precarious paradise. Out of breath, I stood in front of them; no need to step closer, the game was played out. Of the woman you could see just maybe a shoulder and a bit of the hair, brutally cut off by the frame of the picture; but the man was directly center, his mouth half open, you could see a shaking black tongue, and he lifted his hands slowly, bringing them into the foreground, an instant still in perfect focus, and then all of him a lump that blotted out the island, the tree, and I shut my eyes, I didn't want to see any more, and I covered my face and broke into tears like an idiot.

Now there's a big white cloud, as on all these days, all this untellable time. What remains to be said is always a cloud, two clouds, or long hours of a sky perfectly clear, a very clean, clear rectangle tacked up with pins on the wall of my room. That was what I saw when I opened my eyes and dried them with my fingers: the clear sky, and then a cloud that drifted in from the left, passed gracefully and slowly across and disappeared on the right. And then another, and for a change sometimes, everything gets gray, all one enormous cloud, and suddenly the splotches of rain cracking down, for a long spell you can see it raining over the picture, like a spell of weeping reversed, and little by little, the frame becomes clear, perhaps the sun comes out, and again the clouds begin to come, two at a time, three at a time. And the pigeons once in a while, and a sparrow or two.

RAYMOND QUENEAU

From

# ZAZIE

1959

Translated by Barbara Wright

'AH, PARIS,' CRIED Gabriel with greedy enthusiasm. 'Hey, Zazie,' he added abruptly, pointing at something a long way away, 'look!! the metro!!!'

'The metro?' said she.

She frowned.

'The elevated, of course,' said Gabriel blissfully.

Before Zazie had had time to bellyache he iksclaimed again:

'And that! over there!! look!!! The Panthéon!!!!'

'Tisn't the Panthéon,' said Charles, 'it's the Invalides.'

'You're not going to start all over again,' said Zazie.

'Oh go on,' cried Gabriel, 'so that isn't the Panthéon?'

'No, it's the Invalides,' replied Charles.

Gabriel turned in his direction and looked him in the cornea of the eyes:

'Are you sure about that,' he asks him, 'are you really so sure as all that?'

Charles didn't answer.

'What is there that you're absolutely sure about?' Gabriel insisted.

'I've got it,' Charles then roars, 'that thing there, tisn't the Invalides it's the Sacré-Coeur.'

'And you I suppose,' says Gabriel jovially, 'wouldn't by any chance be the sacred cow?'

'Little humorists your age,' says Zazie, 'give me the willies.'

After which they observed the orama in silence, then Zazie investigated what was going on some 300 metres below as the plumb line falls.

'Tisn't as high as all that,' Zazie remarked.

'All the same,' said Charles, 'you can only just make out the people.'

'Yes,' said Gabriel, sniffing, 'you can hardly see them but you can smell them just the same.'

'Less than in the metro,' said Charles.

'You never go in it,' said Gabriel. 'Nor do I, for that matter.'

Wishing to avoid this painful subject, Zazie said to her uncle:

'You aren't looking. Lean over, it's funny, you know.'

Gabriel made an attempt to cast an eye into the depths.

'Hell,' said he, retreating, 'it makes me giddy.'

He mopped his brow and gave off an aroma.

'Personally,' he adds, 'I'm going down. If you haven't had enough I'll wait for you on the ground floor.'

He's gone before Zazie and Charles can stop him.

'It must be twenty years since I came up it,' says Charles. 'I've driven enough people here though.'

It's all the same to Zazie.

'You don't laugh much,' says she to him. 'How old are you?'

'How old would you say I was?'

'Hm, yaren't young: thirty.'

'And fifteen on top.'

'Hm well then you don't look too old. An unkoo Gabriel?'

'Thirty-two.'

'Hm, well him now he looks older.'

'Goodness sake don't tell him so, it'd make him cry.'

'Why on earth? Because he practises hormosessuality?'

'Where did you dig that one up?'

'It was the chap who said that to uncle Gabriel, the chap who brought me back. That's what he said, the chap, that you could go to jug for that, for hormosessuality. What is it?'

'Tsnot true.'

'*Tis* true that he said that,' retorted Zazie, indignant that anyone should doubt a single one of her words.

'That's not what I mean, I mean that, about Gabriel, tisn't true what the chap said.'

'That he's a hormosessual? But what does it mean? That he uses perfume?'

'That's it. Now you know.'

'Znothing in that to go to prison for.'

'Of course there isn't.'

They mused for a moment in silence as they observed the Sacré-Coeur.

'What about you?' asked Zazie. 'Are you one, a hormosessual?'

'Do I look queer?'

'No, you look pretty ordinary to me.'

'Well then you see.'

'I don't see a thing.'

'Well I'm certainly not going to do you a drawing.'

'Are you good at drawing?'

Charles turned in the other direction and became absorbed in the contemplation of the spires of Sainte-Clotilde, the work of Gau and Ballu, and then suggested:

'Shall we go down?'

'Tell me,' asked Zazie without budging, 'why aren't you married?'

'That's life.'

'Why don't you get married?'

'Haven't found anyone who suits me.'

Zazie whistled admiringly.

'You certainly think a lot of yourself.'

'That's the way it is. But tell me, when you're grown-up, do you think there'll be so many men you'd want to marry?'

'Staminute,' said Zazie, 'what're we talking about? Men or women?'

'Sa question of women for me, and men for you.'

'There's no comparison,' said Zazie.

'Can't say you're wrong.'

'You really are funny,' said Zazie. 'You never really know what you think. It must be exhausting. Is that why you always look so solemn?'

Charles deigns to smile.

'What about me?' says Zazie, 'would I suit you?'

'You're only a brat.'

'There's some girls who get married at fifteen, at fourteen even. There's some men who like that.'

'Well then? tabout me? would I suit you?'

'Of course not,' replied Zazie with simplicity.

Having swallowed this primary truth, Charles resumed the conversation in these terms:

'You've got some funny ideas, you know, for your age.'

'Yes that's true, I even wonder myself where I get them from.'

'Well I certainly couldn't tell you.'

'Why is it that we say some things and not others?'

'If we didn't say what we have to say, we wouldn't make ourselves understood.'

'How about you, do you always say what you have to say to make yourself understood?'

'(gesture)'

'All the same nobody forces us to say anything we do say, we could say something else.'

'(gesture)'

'Well you might answer me!'

'You make me tired. All that's not questions.'

'Of course it's questions. Only it's questions you don't know how to answer.'

'I don't think I'm ready to get married just yet,' said Charles pensively.

'Oh! you know,' said Zazie 'all women don't ask questions like I do.'

'All women, just listen to her, all women. But you're only a little chick.'

'Oh! excuse me, I've already started . . .'

'That's enough. No indecencies.'

'There's nothing indecent about that. That's life.'

'It's a fine thing, life.'

He pulled at his moustache, again squinting morosely at the Sacré-Coeur.

'Life,' said Zazie, 'you ought to know all about it. They say you see some funny things in your trade.'

'Where'd you get that one from?'

'I read it in the Sunday Sanctimontronian, a rag that's pretty up to date even for the provinces, where they write about famous love-affairs, astrology and everything, well, it said there that taxi-drivers, they see it in all its aspects and of all sorts; sessuality. Starting with the customers who want to pay in kind. Zthat often happened to you?'

'Oh that'll do that'll do!'

'That's all you can say: "that'll do that'll do". You must be repressed.'

'God she makes you sick.'

'Oh come on, don't bellyache, it'd be better if you told me about your complexes.'

'Oh Jesus what next.'

'Women frighten you, eh?'

'I'm going down. Because I feel giddy. Not because of that (gesture). But because of a junior doll like you.'

He withdraws and some time later there he is again only a few feet above sea-level. Gabriel, with a dull look in his eye, was waiting, his knees wide apart and his hands resting on them. Seeing Charles without his niece he leaps up, and his face takes on an anxious-green colour.

'Oh even so you haven't done that,' exclaims he.

'You'd have heard her fall,' replies Charles as he sits down, worn out.

'Oh that wouldn't have mattered. But to leave her alone.'

'You can collect her at the exit. She won't fly away.'

'Yes but from now till she gets there, how much more trouble is she going to cause me (sigh). If only I'd known.'

Charles doesn't react.

So Gabriel looks at the tower attentively, lengthily, then comments:

'I wonder why people think of the city of Paris as a woman. With a thing like that. Before they put it up, perhaps. But now. It's like women who turn into men because they're so keen on sport. You read about it in the papers.'

'(silence)'

'Ah well, now you've lost your tongue. What do *you* think about it?'

Charles then utters a long, mournful neighing sound, clutches his head in his two hands and groans.

'Him too,' he says, still groaning, 'him too . . . always the same thing . . . always sessuality . . . always a question of that . . . always . . . all the time . . . putrefaction . . . nauseation . . . they think of nothing else . . .'

Gabriel pats him on the shoulder benevolently.

'You look as if there's something the matter,' he says casually. 'What happened?'

'It's your niece . . . your whore of a niece.'

'Oy oy, careful,' cries Gabriel, removing his hand in order to lift it up towards the heavens, 'my niece is my niece. Moderate your language, or you'll hear plenty about your grandmother.'

Charles makes a despairing gesture, then gets up abruptly.

'Ah well,' says he, 'I'm off. I'd rather not see that brat again. Farewell.'

And he goes off towards his jalopy.

Gabriel runs after him:

'How'll we get back?'

'You can take the metro.'

'Marvellous jokes he thinks up,' Gabriel grunted, giving up his pursuit.

The taks departs.

Left standing, Gabriel meditated, and then pronounced these words:

'Being or nothingness, that is the question. Ascending, descending, coming, going, a man does so much that in the end he disappears. A taxi bears him off, a metro carries him away, the Tower doesn't care, nor the Panthéon. Paris is but a dream, Gabriel is but a reverie (a charming one), Zazie the dream of a reverie (or of a nightmare) and all this story the dream of a dream, the reverie of a reverie, scarcely more than the typewritten delirium of an idiotic novelist (oh! sorry). Over there, farther – a little farther – than the Place de la République, the graves are overflowing with Parisians who were, who ascended and descended the stairs, came and went in the streets, and who did so much that in the end they disappeared. Forceps bore them, a hearse carries them away, and the Tower rusts and the Panthéon cracks more rapidly than the bones of the dead who are too much with us dissolve in the humus of the town impregnated with cares. But *I* am alive, and there ends my knowledge, for of the taxi-mann, fled in his locatory jalopy, or of my niece, suspended a thousand feet up in the atmosphere, or of my spouse the gentle Marceline, left guarding the household gods, I know nothing at this precise moment, here and now, I know nothing but this, alexandrinarily: that they are almost dead because they are not here. But what do I see above the hairy noddles of the good people who surround me?'

Some travellers were standing in a circle round him, having taken him for a supplementary guide. They turned their heads to see what he was looking at.

'And what *do* you see?' asked one of them, particularly versed in the French language.

'Yes,' approved another. 'What is there to see?'

'Indeed,' adds a third, 'what ought we to see?'

'Tweetosee?' asked a fourth, 'tweetosee? tweetosee? tweetosee?'

'Tiutosee?' replied Gabriel, 'why (grand gesture) Zazie, my niece Zazie, who is issuing forth from the ironmongery and wending her way towards us.'

Cameras crepitate, then the travellers make way for the child. Who cackles.

'Well, uncle? doing a good trade?'

'As you see,' replied Gabriel with satisfaction.

Zazie shrugged her shoulders and looked at the audience. She didn't see Charles in their midst and drew attention to that fact.

'He beat it,' said Gabriel.

'Why?'

'No reason.'

'No reason, that's not an answer.'

'Oh wurl, he just went.'

'He must have had a reason.'

'Oh you know, Charles (gesture).'

'You don't want to tell me?'

'You know why as well as I do.'

A traveller intervened:

'Male bonas horas collocamus si non dicis isti puellae weshalb dieser Mann Karl weggegangen ist.'

'My dear little fellow,' replied Gabriel, 'mind your own Geschäft. Sie weiss warum and sie ärgert mich sehr.'

'Oy oy,' exclaimed Zazie. 'Now it seems you can talk ouslandish languages.'

'I didn't do it on purpose,' replied Gabriel modestly, lowering his eyes.

'Höchst interessant,' said one of the travellers.

Zazie returned to her point of departure.

'All this doesn't tell me why Charlesbuggadorff.'

Gabriel got annoyed.

'Because you were talking about things he didn't understand. Things not suitable for someone his age.'

'Well, unkoo Gabriel, supposing I said things to you that you didn't understand, things not suitable for someone your age, what'd you do?'

'Try,' said Gabriel in an apprehensive voice.

'For egzample,' went on Zazie relentlessly, 'if I asked you, are you a hormosessual or aren't you? would you understand? Dthat be suitable for someone your age?'

'Höchst interessant,' said a traveller (same one as before).

'Poor Charles,' sighed Gabriel.

'Are you going to answer, yes or nosepick,' shouted Zazie. 'Do you understand the word: hormosessual?'

'Of course,' yelled Gabriel, 'want me to do you a drawing?'

The crowd, interested, expressed approval. A few applauded.

'Ywouldn't have the guts to,' retorted Zazie.

It was then that Fyodor Balanovitch appeared on the scene.

'Come on, get a move on!' he started to holler. 'Schnell! Schnell! back into the coach, and at the double.'

'Dove andiamo adesso?'

'To the Sainte-Chapelle,' replied Fyodor Balanovitch. 'That gem of Gothic art. Come on, get a move on. Schnell! Schnell!'

But the people didn't get a move on, greatly interested as they were by Gabriel and his niece.

'There,' the latter was saying to the former, who hadn't drawn anything, 'you see you didn't have the guts to.'

'God what a bore she can be,' the former was saying.

Fyodor Balanovitch, having confidently climbed aboard his lugger, perceived that he had only been followed by three or four mental defectives.

'Oy, you lot,' he bawled, 'what's happened to your discipline? What're they bloody well doing, my God!'

He hooted a few times. Which caused no one to budge. But a cop gave him a dirty look. As Fyodor Balanovitch had no desire to engage in vocal conflict with an individual of that species, he climbed down from his driving seat again and directed his steps towards the group formed by his administrees in order to discover what could be luring them into insubordination.

'But it's Gabriella,' he exclaimed. 'What the devil are you doing here?'

'Sh sh,' said Gabriel, while the circle of his admirers went into naïve raptures at the sight of this encounter.

'No really though,' went on Fyodor Balanovitch, 'you're

surely not going to treat them to *The Dying Swan* in a tutu, are you?'

'Shh shh,' said Gabriel again, very short of conversation.

'And what's this brat you're carting around with you? Where d'you pick her up?'

That's my niece and kindly try and show some respect for my family, minor though it be.'

'And that chap, who's he?' asked Zazie.

'A pal,' said Gabriel. 'Fyodor Balanovitch.'

'You see,' said Fyodor Balanovitch to Gabriel, 'I'm not doing Paris *bâille-naïte* any more, I've gone up in the social hierarchy and I'm taking all these clot-faces to the Sainte-Chapelle.'

'Maybe you could take us home. With this strike of the public transpiration you can't do anything you want to any more. Not a taks to be seen.'

'We're not going home yet,' said Zazie.

'In any case,' said Fyodor Balanovitch, 'we'll have to go to the Sainte-Chapelle first before it closes. After that,' he added, to Gabriel, 'I might possibly take you home.'

'And is it interesting, the Sainte-Chapelle?' asked Gabriel.

'Sainte-Chapelle! Sainte-Chapelle!' such was the touristic clamour and those who uttered it, this touristic clamour, swept Gabriel along with them to the coach with irresistible impetus.

'They've fallen for him,' said Fyodor Balanovitch to Zazie, who, like him, was left behind.

'All the same you needn't,' said Zazie 'think I'm going to let myself be carted round with all those sheep.'

'I,' said Fyodor Balanovitch, 'don't give a bugger.'

And he climbed up again behind the steering wheel and his mike, immediately utilizing this last-mentioned instrument:

'Come on, get a move on,' he loud-spoke jovially. 'Schnell! Schnell!'

Gabriel's admirers had already installed him comfortably and, equipped with adequate apparatuses, were measuring the weight of the light in order to take his portrait with a silhouette effect. Albeit all these attentions flattered him, he enquired nevertheless as to the fate of his niece. Having learnt from Fyodor Balanovitch that said niece refused to follow the crowd, he snatched himself out of the magic circle of xenophonics, got out again and threw himself on Zazie whom he seized by one arm and dragged along to the coach.

The cameras crepitated.

'You're hurting me,' yelped Zazie, mad with rage.

But she too was carried along towards the Sainte- Chapelle by the vehicle with the heavy pneumatic tyres.

GEORGES PEREC

From

# THINGS

1965

Translated by David Bellos

THEY WOULD HAVE liked to be rich. They believed they would have been up to it. They would have known how to dress, how to look and how to smile like rich people. They would have had the requisite tact and discretion. They would have forgotten they were rich, would have grasped how not to flaunt their wealth. They wouldn't have taken pride in it. They would have drunk it into themselves. Their pleasures would have been intense. They would have liked to wander, to dawdle, to choose, to savour. They would have liked to live. Their lives would have been an art of living.

But such things are far from easy. For this young couple, who were not rich but wanted to be, simply because they were not poor, there could be no situation more awkward. They had only what they deserved to have. They were thrown, when already they were dreaming of space, light, silence, back to the reality, which was not even miserable, but simply cramped (and that was perhaps even worse), of their tiny flat, of their everyday meals, of their puny holidays. That was what corresponded to their economic status, to their social situation. That was their reality and they had no other. But beside them, all around them, all along the streets where they could not but walk, existed the fallacious but nonetheless glowing offerings of antique-dealers, delicatessens and stationers. From Palais-Royal to Saint-Germain-des-Prés, from Champ-de-Mars to the Champs-Élysées, from the Luxembourg Gardens to Montparnasse, from Île

Saint-Louis to the Marais, from Place des Ternes to Place de l'Opéra, from Madeleine to the Monceau Gardens, the whole of Paris was a perpetual temptation. They burned with desire to give in to it, passionately, straight away and for ever. But the horizon of their desires was mercilessly blocked; their great impossible dreams belonged only to utopia.

They lived in a quaint, low-ceilinged and tiny flat overlooking a garden. And as they remembered their garret – a gloomy, narrow, overheated corridor with clinging smells – they lived in their flat, to begin with, in a kind of intoxication, refreshed each morning by the sound of chirping birds. They would open the windows and, for many minutes, they would gaze, in utter happiness, at their courtyard. The building was old, not yet at all at the point of collapse, but dowdy and cracked. The corridors and staircases were narrow and dirty, dripping with damp, impregnated with greasy fumes. But in between two large trees and five tiny garden plots of irregular shapes, most of them overgrown but endowed with precious lawn, flowers in pots, bushes, even primitive statues, there wound a path made of rough, large paving stones which gave the whole thing a countryside air. It was one of those rare spots in Paris where it could happen, on some autumn days, after rain, that a smell would rise from the ground, an almost powerful smell of the forest, of earth, of rotting leaves.

They never tired of these charms and they always remained just as naturally responsive to them as they had been on the first day, but it became obvious, after a few care-free, jaunty months, that these attractions could in no way suffice to make them oblivious of the inadequacies of their dwelling. Accustomed to living in squalid rooms where all they did was to sleep, and to spending their days in cafés, they took a long time to notice that the most banal functions of everyday life – sleeping, eating, reading, chatting, washing – each required a specific space, the manifest absence of which then began to make itself felt. They found consolation where they could, congratulated themselves on the excellent neighbourhood they were in, on the proximity of Rue Mouffetard and the Jardin des Plantes, on the quietness of the street, on the stylishness of their low ceilings, and on the magnificence of the trees and the courtyard through all the seasons; but indoors it all began to collapse under the heaps of objects, of furniture, books, plates, papers, empty bottles. A war of attrition began from which they would never emerge victorious.

With a total floor area of thirty-five square metres, which they never dared check, their flat consisted of a minute entrance hall, a cramped kitchen, half of which had been converted into a washroom, a modest-sized bedroom, an all-purpose room – library, living-room or study, spare bedroom – and an ill-defined nook, halfway between a broom-cupboard and a corridor, in which space had somehow been found for a matchbox fridge, an electric water-heater, an improvised wardrobe, a table, at which they ate, and a laundry-box which doubled up as a bench-seat.

On some days the lack of space became overwhelming. They would suffocate. But it was no use pushing back the boundaries of their two-roomed flatlet, no use knocking down walls, calling up corridors, cupboards, openings, no use imagining ideal wardrobes or taking over adjacent flats in their dreams, they would always end up back in what was their lot, their only lot: thirty-five square metres.

Judicious improvements would undoubtedly have been feasible: a partition wall could have been removed, freeing a huge and ill-used corner space, a too-bulky piece of furniture could be replaced advantageously, a set of cupboards could spring up. Doubtless, then, provided it was repainted, stripped, done up with a little love, their dwelling would have been unquestionably charming, with its one red-curtained window and its other window with green curtains, with its long, rather wobbly oak table that had been bought at the flea market filling the whole length of one wall section, beneath the very fine reproduction of a mariner's chart, and which a little roll-top Second Empire *escritoire* made of mahogany with inlaid brass beads, several missing, separated into two working desks – to the left, for Sylvie, to the right, for Jérôme – each signalled by an identical red blotter, an identical glass tile, an identical pencil-box; with its old pewter-rimmed glass jar that had been transformed into a lamp, with its metal-reinforced, wood-veneer seed-measuring jar which did as a wastepaper basket, with its two unmatched armchairs, its rush-seated chairs, its milking stool. And the neat, clean and ingenious whole would emanate friendliness and warmth, a wholesome aura of work and shared living.

But the mere prospect of the work involved scared them. They would have had to borrow, to save, to invest. They could not bring themselves to do it. Their hearts weren't in it: they thought only in terms of all or nothing. The bookcase would be light oak or it would not be. It was not. Books piled up on two dirty wooden shelving stacks, and, in double rows, in cupboards which should never have been used that way. For three years an electric point remained unrepaired, without their making up their minds to call in an electrician, whilst along almost every wall ran crudely spliced and shoddily extended leads. It took them six months to replace a curtain pulley-rope. And the slightest hold-up in regular maintenance resulted within twenty-four hours in a mess which the beneficent presence of trees and gardens so close at hand made even more unbearable.

The temporary, the provisional held absolute sway. They were in wait only of a miracle. They would have summoned architects, contractors, builders, plumbers, decorators and painters. They would have gone on a cruise and on their return would have found a flat transformed, converted, refurbished, a model apartment, miraculously enlarged, full of custom-built details, removable partitions, sliding doors, an efficient and unobtrusive heating system, invisible electrical wiring, good quality furniture.

But between these too grand daydreams in which they wallowed with strange self-indulgence, and their total lack of any actual doing, no rational plan, matching the objective necessities to their financial means, arose to fill the gap. The vastness of their desires paralysed them.

Such a lack of directness, of clear-headedness, almost, was typical. What was probably the most serious thing was that they were cruelly lacking in ease – not material, objective ease, but easiness, or a certain kind of relaxedness. They tended to be on edge, tense, avid, almost jealous. Their love of well-being, of higher living standards, came out most often as an idiotic kind of sermonizing, when they would hold forth, they and their friends, on the sheer genius of a pipe or a low table; they would turn them into *objets d'art*, into museum pieces. They would become passionate about a suitcase – one of those tiny, astonishingly flat cases in slightly grainy black leather you could see on display in shop windows around Madeleine and which seem the quintessence of the alleged pleasures of lightning visits to New York or to London. They would cross all of Paris to see an armchair they'd been told was just perfect. And since they knew their classics they would sometimes even hesitate to put on some new garment, as it seemed so important to them, for it to look its best, that it should first have been worn three times. But the slightly ritualized gestures they would make to show their approval at a tailor's, or a milliner's, or a bootmaker's shop window display only managed, most often, to make them look slightly silly.

Perhaps they were too marked by their past (not they alone, moreover, but their friends, their colleagues, people of their age, the circles they mixed in). Perhaps they were too greedy from the outset: they wanted to go too fast. The world and its things would have had to have always belonged to them, and then they could have imprinted on them myriad signs of their ownership. But they were condemned to conquest; they could become richer and richer, but there was no way they could have always been rich. They would have liked to live in comfort, amidst beauty. But they shrieked, they admired, and that was the surest proof that they were not in it, not amidst it. They lacked tradition – in perhaps the most despicable sense of the word – as well as true enjoyment, implicit and immanent, like a self-evident truth, the enjoyment which involves bodily happiness; their pleasure was cerebral. Too often, what they liked in the things they called luxury was only the money behind them; they loved wealth before they loved life.

In this respect their first sallies outside the student world, their first forays into the universe of high-class shops which was soon to become their Promised Land, were particularly revealing. Their still-wavering taste, their over-hesitant meticulousness, their lack of experience, their rather blinkered respect for what they believed to be the standards of true good taste, brought them some jarring moments, some humiliations. For a time it might have appeared that the sartorial ideal to which Jérôme and his friends aspired was not that of the English gentleman, but the utterly continental caricature of it presented by a recent emigrant on a modest salary. And on the day Jérôme bought his first pair of British shoes, he took great care, after polishing them at length with a woollen rag dipped in a little beeswax of superior quality, rubbing very gently in small concentric circles, he took great care to put them in the sun where they were supposed to acquire an outstanding shine in the least time. Alas, alongside a pair of crepe-soled moccasin ankle-boots which he obstinately refused to wear, they were his only shoes; he misused them, dragged them through rutted tracks, and finished them off in just under seven months.

Then, as time passed, with the help of accumulating experience, it seemed that they were learning how to stand back a little from their most fervent passions. They had learned how to wait, and how to grow accustomed. Their taste matured slowly, became firmer, more balanced. Their desires had time to ripen; their greed became less sour. When on outings around Paris they stopped in villages to look at antiques, they no longer rushed straight towards the china plates, towards the church pews, towards the blown-glass demijohns and the brass candlesticks. To be sure, the somewhat static image they had of the ideal home, of perfect amenity, of the happy life was still imbued with a lot of naivety, a lot of self-indulgence: there was something forced in their liking for objects which only the taste of the day decreed to be beautiful: imitation Epinal pseudo-naive cartoons, English-style etchings, agates, spun-glass tumblers, neo-primitive paste jewellery, para-scientific apparatus, which in no time at all they would come across in all the window displays in Rue Jacob, in Rue Visconti. They still dreamt of possessing such things; they would have assuaged that obvious, instant need to be up-to-date, to be seen to be connoisseurs. But this extreme imitativeness was becoming less and less important, and it was pleasant for them to reflect that the picture they had of life had slowly been stripped of all its more aggressive, showy and occasionally juvenile trappings. They had burnt what they had previously worshipped: the witches' mirrors, the chopping-blocks, those stupid little mobiles, the radio-meters, the multi-coloured pebbles, the hessian panels adorned with expressive squiggles as if by Mathieu. It seemed to them that they were progressively mastering their desires: they knew what they wanted; they had clear ideas. They knew what their happiness, their freedom would be.

But they were wrong all the same. They were beginning to lose their way. Already they were starting to feel they were being propelled along a path of which they knew neither the turns nor the terminus. They did on occasions feel frightened. Most often, however, all they felt was impatience: they felt ready; they were available; they were waiting to live, they were waiting for money.

RICHARD COBB

# PARIS Xe

1980

THERE IS ALWAYS some danger, I think, both in historical terms and in those of literary localism, of confusing regionalism with provincialism, or even with what I would describe as a pseudo-peasant folklore. Those who react most strongly against the narrowness, the deliberate archaism, and the politically motivated reactionary romanticism of a Charles Péguy or of a Jean Giono – you know the sort of thing: the ancient rural values, a happy and unquestioning paternalism, the idealization of *le labeur* by those who have never put their hands to a plough – will identify such a tradition with appeals both against Paris and against the political system established in Paris.

That sort of regionalism can very often be equated with anti-parliamentarianism, and can best be located in just those areas of France in which an aristocratic nostalgia has, to some extent, survived – for instance, in La Varende's Lower Normandy, in the Bessin, the country round Bayeux; and in Michel de Saint-Pierre's west of France, as illustrated in his *Les Aristocrates*, and so on.

But there is also an abundant literature of Paris that, very far from being in any way national, is as firmly set in a local context as Jean-Louis Bory's celebrated semi-autobiographical book, *Mon Village à l'heure allemande*. To look at what appears to be a conflict between Paris and the rest of France in the perspective, for instance, of a very celebrated polemical piece that came out in the late 1940s – *Paris et le désert français* – is merely to equate Paris with a rather faceless authority, with Bureaucracy, and to forget that Paris is itself a whole jumble of quarters and villages, each retaining a very strong sense of identity, even though this is now tending to be lost, each existing in its own right as the framework for childhood, wonder, and exploration.

No literature, in fact, could be more pronouncedly regional than that of Paris and its neighbourhood. And while Léo Larguier's book, *Saint-Germain-des-Prés, mon village*, written in the 1930s, would now appear merely pathetic, as a reminder from a very, very long time back of an innocence and spontaneity long since lost, there is still plenty of life left for the evolution of this or that *arrondissement*, this or that *commune* of the *grande banlieue*. Indeed, Georges Simenon has shown, with great skill, how such a theme as this sudden loss of identity, in personal terms, could still be handled, in his novel *Le Déménagement* – the move from central Paris, from the Marais, to Cachan or Bagneux or Sarcelles or somewhere else farther out, south of Paris on the electric line, *la ligne de Sceaux*: a sociological fact that could be reproduced by thousands and thousands of similar examples.

Even *gauchisme* can readily accommodate the diversity of Parisian geography, and May 1968 was, above all, a phenomenon confined to a couple of *arrondissements* – the Ve and the VIe, on the Left Bank. And it was a phenomenon that brought few enough echoes on the Right Bank, even if many of the most active participants, after revolutionizing all day, were, most nights, in the habit of returning to their homes in the XVIe and XVIIe *arrondissements*, to sleep it off.

Nor could anyone be more provincial and more élitist than *les mandarins*, as described in the memoirs of Simone de Beauvoir: very self-satisfied intellectuals who move in a very narrow physical and social circle. Indeed, they are not all that different from the two *normaliens*, Jallez and Jerphanion, as described in the immense novel *Les Hommes de bonne volonté* of Jules Romains, and from all those who observe the sleeping city from the roof of the rue d'Ulm, which is the street which houses the École Normale Supérieure.

Certainly, *I* have not forgotten Paris, nor its suburbs. I have omitted them so far because I have been speaking mostly of exiles writing in Paris, and writing with the added nostalgia of absence, lost innocence, and death. How, indeed, could one forget such wealth and diversity as are provided by the tumultuous Paris of childhood? – the sunny, silent, empty Paris of June 1940, the Occupied Paris of the ration cards, of the J3, and of the black market, the Front Populaire of 1936, recalled in the suburbs, Villeneuve-Saint-Georges during the Occupation years, in René Fallet's first novel *Banlieue, sud-est*; *Les Enfants d'Aubervilliers*, the title of a very remarkable documentary film of the 1930s about sad, rickety, tubercular children; Charles-Louis Philippe's description of the quartier de la Gaîté, behind the old Montparnasse station, in his novel *Bubu*; the mediocrity and the small-mindedness of the passage des Panoramas, which is where Louis-Ferdinand Céline, Dr Destouches, spent his own rather unhappy childhood and which he exploited both in *Voyage au bout de la nuit* and in *Mort à crédit*.

Paris, on the contrary, must dominate any attempt to explore varieties of regionalism through works of imagination, as indeed it should, for, of all the infinite forms of French and francophone regionalism, that of Paris is the most insistent, imperious, the most cantankerous, the funniest, and, certainly, always the most inventive.

I am very conscious of this and, in my own case, of the strength of my own affiliations, experiences, mishaps, and near disasters, sudden glimpses of absolute happiness, like an April Paris shaft of sunlight all at once lighting up a leprous wall at the top of a house, cut down the side, like a chunk of ice-cream, Utrillo-coloured, and making it appear warm yellow. I remeber the surrealist quality of so many Parisian itineraries: Filles-du-Calvaire to Barbès-Rochechouart; Sèvres-Babylone to Marcadet-Poissonniers; Corentin-Cariou to Corentin-Celton; Château-Rouge to Glacière; Strasbourg-Saint-Denis to Richelieu-Drouot; Château-d'Eau to Levallois; Porte-Brancion to Porte des Lilas; Robespierre to Jasmin; La Motte-Picquet-Grenelle to Sully-Morland; De Gaulle to Convention. I remember, too, the *Métro aérien* on green, raised bridges, clanging along at the level of fourth or sixth storey, opening up façades and giving a sort of running view of a bedroom, a kitchen, a dining-room, the figures silhouetted in activity; *Métro à éclipses* suddenly coming out into the light and just as soon disappearing once more into the semi-darkness of tunnel. And I am old enough to have travelled by tram down the boulevard Saint-Michel in the direction of the Gare de l'Est (and that certainly does date me), and I have, indeed, been so much conditioned by Paris – much more than by any other place, even Ixelles – that I feel it really necessary to place on record my own early subjection to Parisian imperialism.

Whether it is an advantage or a disadvantage I would hesitate to say, but I think there is certainly very much to be said for beginning with the capital of a country, provided one goes round the rest of the country at some later date. In my case, my first exposure to France, its language, its population, its climate, its sudden and terribly alien gusts of violence, and its reassuringly regular movements of work and leisure, of the week and the weekend, the differentiation of class as judged by clothing, came to me in the form of Paris.

My first introduction to Paris was not to the fashionable parts of the city; it was to the Xe *arrondissement*, just where it borders on the IXe, as well as where it borders on the busy quartier du Sentier, the not very reputable rue de la Lune, a steep walk up to vice, almost as steep, but certainly not so long as the climb up to redemption, provided at the top by the hideous Sacré-Coeur, and the ancient theatreland of the boulevard Saint-Martin.

To the north lay a whole maze of *passages*, undetected even by Céline or by Aragon, and so lost to literature. Immediately below the boulevard Bonne-Nouvelle, where I lived, ran a sort of gully that on the day of the execution of Louis XVI, in January 1793, had provided the royalist conspirator, Baron de Batz, with a platform and, as he had hoped, literally a jumping-off ground from which to storm the heavily guarded *berline*, the carriage containing the king and his Irish non-juror confessor, the Abbé Edgeworth.

To the right, a leaden January sky was brightened by the huge black-and-red pennant that flew over the offices of the newspaper *Le Matin*, and by the enormous, apparently fortified Rex, the largest cinema in Paris, a sort of vast, rectangular cube in beige cement that looked like a permanent ice-cream.

Beyond the Rex and beyond *Le Matin* were the salerooms and the offices of auctioneers of the *commissaires-priseurs*, the official valuers, of the Hôtel des Ventes, of the rue Drouot, and their offices in the neighbouring rue Rossini and in the Cité de Trévise, which is partly closed in with glass passages. And there was a female population certainly representative of every province of France and, indeed, pretty well the whole French empire, as well as of francophone Belgium and of Luxembourg, as one approached the Folies-Bergère via the rue du Faubourg-Montmartre.

It was an area of central Paris that had been a *quartier d'agrément* in the time of Baron Haussmann, in the Second Empire, because it was in such convenient proximity to the Bourse, to the Sentier, to the newspaper offices, and to all the theatres of the *grands boulevards*. But, well before 1914, it became an area that was going into a steady social decline. As early as 1900 affluent and middle-class *boursicotiers* and *agents de change*, stockbrokers and so on, and currency speculators had begun moving out from the tall apartment buildings and migrating towards the more fashionable area to the west.

And so at No. 26 boulevard Bonne-Nouvelle, where I lived, the impressive double doors to the flats on the first, second, third, and fourth storeys bore the names of Polish furriers and tailors, of private detective agencies, of doctors, though probably not very good doctors – doctors who played safe by specializing in *la sécurité sociale* and *les accidents de travail*.

From my bedroom window I could hear both the dull rumble of the *Métro* which is very shallow at this point, and the continuous clatter of machinery that sounded as if it might be related to the activities of the Armenian *tapissiers* whom, in a voyage of discovery from fifth to seventh floor, I found to be established towards the top of the house.

The terrible screams and apparent cries for help that had so alarmed me during my first week, inducing me to believe that Paris was undergoing a replay of the September Massacres next door to my bedroom and laid on specially for my benefit, were eventually traced to the presence, on the bottom three floors of the building immediately to the west, of the public baths, the Bains Neptuna.

Immediately below the flat, the pavement widened out so as to include several *kiosques* with elaborate ironwork turrets, selling the newspapers of the world of the 1930s, including *Pravda*, *Izvestia*, and papers from Prague, Warsaw, and so on. At weekends and on public holidays, there were street bands – one or two concertinas, a drum, and a very hoarse singer – selling sheet music of the latest hits.

On Saturdays and Sundays, the very wide *chaussées* were invaded by lugubrious family processions and by noisy cat-calling young men and by girls who had come in from the factory suburbs to the north and the north-east of the city, who were sufficiently ill-informed about the more recent shifts in Parisian fashions to believe that the porte Saint-Denis and the porte Saint-Martin and the *grands boulevards*, from there to Richelieu-Drouot, still constituted the very centre of the capital, the place where all the important things happened and where all the great shops had their frontages.

During the week, the crowds walked fast and humbly, bent down to face the east wind that swept in from the direction of the République. Haussmann, thanks to his east–west grid, succeeded in rendering Paris one of the coldest cities in Western Europe. And when I came to know the Left Bank better, I could appreciate that the area around the *Métro* station Glacière had earned its name doubly.

Crowds poured out of the shallow station Bonne-Nouvelle and headed for the Bourse, the Sentier, the rue Turbigo, the rue Drouot, the newspaper and printing offices of the rue Réaumur, the big shops, the chain restaurants and cafés of the boulevards themselves: *petits employés*, clerks, waiters, shop assistants, tailors, seamstresses, printers, *commissionnaires*, errand boys, armed in the mornings of the 1930s with such papers as *Le Petit Parisien*, *Le Journal*, or *Le Matin*, and armed in the evening with *Paris-Soir* or *L'Intransigeant*. I really never discovered anybody who read *Paris-Midi*, a midday or afternoon paper, apart from those bent either on attending the afternoon races at Vincennes or at Longchamp or on betting on them at the betting-shop, the Pari Mutuel Urbain.

It was an area of what you might call *grand passage*, of work and leisure, a little too far to the east to attract the tourists, whether foreign or provincial, and too far from the Left Bank, from the Palais Bourbon, from the place de la Concorde, the ministries, the embassies, or any of the railway termini, ever to attract a political demonstration or procession. Left-wing processions and demonstrations tended to pack up at the level of the République as their farthest point west. Right-wing demonstrations or processions favoured the boulevard Saint-Michel or the prestigious Champs-Élysées, so that the Xe *arrondissement*, whether by luck or negligence, or as the result of important matters having increasingly tended to pass it by, had consequently fallen into a sort of political apathy.

The family with whom I was staying were survivors from a more prosperous and prestigious period; they had simply not bothered to follow the general current westwards, clinging on to a very commodious flat that had originally been acquired by the maternal grandfather, M. Feuillas, a stockjobber on the Bourse in the lush years of the Third Republic before 1914, and a sufficiently well-known figure in the quartier de la Bourse to have been the subject of several caricatures – bowler hat, spats, long black coat with velvet collar – by famous caricaturists of the turn of the century.

The flat, which was, as I have said, very large, was shaped like an L, with a balconied salon, its two french windows facing on to the boulevard. This room was very seldom used; its furniture, much of the time, was kept under beige covers. There was also a balconied dining-room, round-fronted with a sort of *vue plongeante*, a view from above, right up the boulevard Bonne-Nouvelle past the Bains Neptuna as far as the Théâtre du Gymnase and the Théâtre Sarah Bernhardt. There was a very dark hall which always needed artificial light, and a tiny kitchen facing on to the deep well formed by seven storeys of enclosed *appartements.* Also always lit by electric light was a long, gloomy corridor off which were four bedrooms, themselves equally dark, as only a few feet separated their windows from the tall mass of the building housing the swimming-baths.

The furniture of the salon and of the dining-room, of *faux Louis XVI*, looked as if it had been mostly acquired in one go as a series of sets; *salle à manger, complète*; *entrée, complète*; *chambre à coucher, complète.* And right down to the last detail: *service de table,* several sets of linen, even the bound volumes of the appropriate *grands auteurs*, certainly not designed to be read, but rather to furnish.

Probably, it had all been acquired at the time of Mme. Feuillas' marriage, a suggestion that seemed to be confirmed by the paucity of the kitchen equipment, hinting at a period of purchase many years before the Bazar de l'Hôtel de Ville, the paradise for kitchenware, as far as Paris is concerned, angling for the family unit, began to place the chief emphasis on *la femme au foyer*, and to make its reputation in the furnishing of *les arts ménagers*. When Mme. Feuillas married, the kitchen was still the unvisited prison of the maid, who was exhibited professionally only when she was waiting at table, in her best black silk with white apron.

Later, at Samois-sur-Seine, the village on the Seine where the family had a country house, I discovered something like thirty years of the annual catalogues of the Bon Marché, all of them pre-1914, so my guess would be that the family's furniture, with everything that went with it, had been acquired in a bulk order from that emporium when the young stockjobber and his bride had first set up house.

Certainly, there was little to suggest, in the standard parade of marble-topped tables, wall brackets, and so on, any evidence of personal choice or fantasy. Even the Chinese silk screens looked as though they would have gone with the rest, suggesting a date when Pierre Loti was beginning to seep down to the all-inclusive, regimented tastes of the Bon Marché or of the Grands Magasins du Louvre.

The whole set had seen much better days: the silk screens were torn in innumerable places and, in the salon, most of the arm-rests on the chairs were liable to fall off under the slightest pressure. The bookcases, as I soon discovered, were not designed to be opened. I did manage to prise one of them open, whereupon the whole front came away, revealing, along with the bound Hugos and Balzacs, several bound sets of *Le Petit Journal Illustré.* The chairs themselves were quite safe, but scarcely comfortable.

On the other hand, the silver and table service were both heavy and lavish, and the napkins were the size of the towels in which schoolboys would carry their bathing-trunks to the municipal baths. The glassware was reassuringly abundant, and the dinner-table, when fully laid out, made a very fine late-nineteenth-century showing indeed, under an elaborate cluster of electric lights, which sprouted luxuriantly, like oranges, and were held up by rather dusty, gilt-painted cherubs. There was very little doubt as to what constituted the focal point of an *appartement* that still preserved plenty of mainly unused *signes de grandeur* – fitted corner cupboards, stacked with tureens and flowered plates, much of the ugliest and most massive Sèvres, cut-glass, and fruit-knives.

The maid slept somewhere above the seventh storey, somewhere under the roof, though she seemed to be on call any time from 7:30 a.m. until midnight, save on Saturday afternoons, when she went out with her fiancé, who was a young Alsatian, like herself.

The family had remained in the boulevard Bonne-Nouvelle as a sort of bourgeois enclave in an encroaching sea of *fourreurs*, *tapissiers*, *merciers*, *rubaniers*, *bimbelotiers*, dentistes américains who, whatever their origin, were certainly not American. Many of the tenants, as far as I could make out, did not live on the premises, but simply used the flats as workshops, returning at night to rooms in the XIe, XIIe or the IVe *arrondissements.* Certainly, at night, the *cage d'escalier* was eerily quiet and one never met anyone coming up or going down after about 8 p.m.

The two sons, however, made up for the surrounding silence and stillness by a maximum amount of noise and bustle, taking the stairs at a furious gallop, and endlessly telephoning their friends, male and female, groping for the Bottin in the pitch-black hall, feebly lit by an anaemic yellowish bulb, to the west and south-west of the city (they had quite a few in the VIIe, some among the parishioners of Sainte-Clotilde, rather more in the VIIIe and the XVIe, or in the far-away Ternes, with cousins, the children of Mme. Thullier's artistic sister and a massive barrister, in Saint-Mandé). Édouard was beginning his degree at the Faculty of Medicine; François was preparing to set up in the Hôtel Drouot, as a *commissaire-priseur*, and was thus running through the dreary hoops of a *licence de droit.* Perhaps it was on account of the latter's destined career that they had thus held on to a quarter given over more and more to offices, chain stores, vast cafés, and cinemas, and in the *passages*, alleyways, *cités*, and small streets to the north of the boulevard, small trades: engravers, printers of visiting cards and *faire-parts*, manufacturers of rubber stamps (by no means a declining industry), sign-painters, stamp-traders, and very small haberdashers.

They were the nearest thing to Parisian one was ever likely to encounter. Both sides of the family had originated from the Seine-et-Marne, first as peasants, then as speculators in national lands; and Mme. Thullier still possessed rural properties – a whole street of houses in the Brie, a house in the valley of the Seine, land in that of the Bièvre. But they were rude about most provincials, referred to peasants as *les pecquenots*, employed, often quite unconsciously, a great deal of Paris slang, particularly when describing women and girls: '*bien fringuée*,' '*toute pomponnée*,' '*de jolis châssis*,' and that sort of thing – some of it acquired, I suppose, in hospital wards, much of it also from the shop-girls whom they ran after at weekends – and possessed an outsize packet of Parisian cheek, particularly well employed by François, once he had become established as an auctioneer, his iron voice brilliantly accompanied by his *aboyeurs*: a veritable orchestra in the long vowels of common Parisian. They were certainly not of a philosophical bent, were not given to pure speculation, were never heard to formulate a general idea or theory, were only peripherally interested in politics, but much engaged in football and in chasing girls, of all conditions, though only French ones: they were quite immune to the exoticism and mystery of *l'âme slave*, preferring a typist from Belleville or Bezons any day, though a Russian accent in French sent them off in peals of laughter. Not for them either the smoky delights of *la peau mate* or *les blondeurs* of the Nordics; in fact, they were remarkably unadventurous in this respect, though, much later in life, when he was a doctor with the French Army in Indochina, Édouard seems to have widened his interests. Although they had been to L'École des Roches as boarders, they did not appear to have even a disapproving awareness of homosexuality, and the standard French jokes about antique-dealers and dress designers did not figure in their repertoire. There was then a certain innocence about them even in the totally uninhibited cheek that they displayed in the pursuit of shop-girls or merely female fellow-travellers on *les transports communs.* In this one respect at least I felt myself considerably more worldly-wise than these two hardened and joyful *dragueurs* (there was too a strong element of competitiveness in their sweeping, as in everything else, save, of course, Law and Medicine). They also attached a considerable importance to the joys of eating and drinking; but this certainly did not extend to good behaviour at table; on the contrary, the more important the guests, the worse would be their behaviour. They enjoyed being students, rather than studying, and were complete extroverts. They were sentimental, foolhardy, and potentially very brave. Their courage was not just juvenile *panache*: in 1939, the lawyer volunteered for the Corps Francs, and was probably one of the few soldiers thoroughly to have enjoyed the period of the phoney war, which, for him, was anything but, consisting of almost daily *coups de main* against German outposts in the Forêt de Warndt; the doctor remained behind, in sole charge of a large military hospital, somewhere in the area of the Maginot Line, in June 1940, and was captured by the Germans. In 1935, my own fear was that they would kill us all there and then: themselves, their mother, the maid, and myself, as a result of the utterly reckless manner in which they drove Mme. Thullier's enormous black Panhard-Levassor, on the weekend trips to Samois-sur-Seine.

Although they made rude remarks about peasants, they were also given to boasting about their peasant ancestors – great-grandparents and so on – no doubt as enhancing their own rise to the level of a solid and affluent professional bourgeoisie. They did not often talk about money; but there always seemed to be plenty of it. Clearly, apart from landed and urban property, *le père* Feuillas must have left a substantial fortune in the safer shares. They were certainly not the sort of people who would have fallen in a big way for Russian bonds: *chemins de fer* and *la Rente* were their mother's declared stand-bys.

Both boys much looked forward to the prospect of war, though they did not have any strong ideas as to whom it should be against. As their father had been killed at Gallipoli, they tended on the whole to stick to the Entente system of alliances, mainly out of a sense of family loyalty. But I think that they would have most favoured the Italians as ideal enemies, as they could see themselves giving them a sound trouncing; also *les Ritals* were ridiculous, and their rendering of French represented one of the brothers' favourite party-pieces late on a convivial evening; though I never heard them express any views of Fascism, Ciano was one of their most cherished butts, because he rolled his eyes and brilliantined his hair (they always referred to him as '*le gommeux*'). In fact, *all* Italians were objects of high comedy. Hitler certainly was not that; but he might not have existed, as far as they were concerned, for I cannot recall his name ever having been mentioned in No. 26, though they had a number of Austrian friends. But they were apt to make rude remarks about Jews, and were also given to imitations of Jewish furriers, old-clothes merchants, and so on, as they attempted to wrestle with the ambiguities of French. I do not think, however, that they were truly anti-Semitic, it was not so positive as that. Pretty well *anyone* with a foreign accent in French was something of a joke-figure, though none could compete with '*les macaronis*'. There were others within France, too, mostly Marseillais and other southerners, and Bécassine and other female simpletons (*gourdes*) from where she came in the depths of *la Bretagne bretonnante.*

They also possessed a considerable repertoire of anti-papal and anti-clerical songs and stories. There was one sung saga about the adventures of a Paris prostitute who, repentant, '*est allée voir le Pape à Rome*,' finding him, predictably, in a brothel. They regarded priests as poor, hybrid creatures, skirted men who did not serve any useful function in life and were driven to take sex surreptitiously (they claimed to have a detailed knowledge of the specialized clerical brothels in the quartier Saint-Sulpice). I suspect that their most vigorous and scandalous manifestations of anti-clericalism were directed at their mother, whom they greatly loved and indeed, in important matters, respected, but whose totally non-religious attachment to the proprieties of the religious calendar and to very occasional attendance at Mass they easily saw through. In fact, they were no fools, and were quick to detect pretension and hypocrisy, reserving their very worst manners for the occasional visits to dinner of the various literary and artistic luminaries, some of them aspiring *académiciens*, none actually immortalized – not even later on, which was surprising, such was their common mediocrity – most of them of the long-winded and eloquent sort that one would associate with Alliance Française lectures or with fashionable *conférences* in the faubourg Saint-Honoré, who represented Mme. Thullier's claim to intellectual status. They were genuinely proud of her artistic achievements and of the official recognition that she had received, as Présidente de la Société des Femmes-Peintres, from la Ville de Paris, the arms of which, *fluctuat nec mergitur*, the *Nef*, and the rest, she wore, on such occasions, as an outsize medal pinned on her dress like a *camée*. They also thought, rightly, that her painting, and her standing with *les femmes-peintres*, kept their mother occupied and reasonably happy. They were good sons. But they had little time for intellectuals, male or female; and I never saw either of them, or Mme. Thullier, read a book, whether a novel or the sort of fashionable history dished out by la Maison Hachette.

The brothers were not, however, total philistines, regularly attending each new play at l'Atelier, and having a special admiration for Dullin himself. There was a good deal of theatre – or should it be music-hall? – about their own noisy manner of life, even the simplest gestures being accompanied by the most almighty clatter; and I have never met anyone who derived more genuine pleasure from the sound of breakage, especially that of china or glass, a pleasure which I entirely shared with them, so that I offered a most appreciative audience, and I think the amount of breakage much increased in my time.

I have always believed that François chose the career of *commissaire-priseur* as much for the opportunity it offered him to cut a wonderfully eloquent public figure, from the moment that he made a very rapid and businesslike *entrée* on his rostrum, plunging straight into the sale, with a semi-serious description of some grotesque object held up before him, as if it had been a heraldic symbol, by two of his uniformed acolytes, and acquiring full momentum in the breakneck '*qui dit mieux?*' of the actual bidding, and exercising his machine-gun repartee at the expense of the most faithful attendants, whom he could pick out at a glance, even if they were standing half-hidden right at the back of his *salle*, at that anarchical cult, as to make a lot of money, which he certainly did as well. Each of his appearances at the Hôtel Drouot represented a small masterpiece of Parisian cheek and knock-about humour, with his audience conquered from the start, and the regulars drawn in by name. He also greatly enjoyed the extensive social promiscuity involved in the job, finding himself completely at home with a disparate group ranging from doubtful *brocanteurs*, Greek philatelists, Armenian carpet-dealers, elderly female eccentrics who spent most of their time nosing around the different *salles*, attending every sale of their favourite, Maître Thullier, and never buying anything – their pleasure was purely artistic – to elegant, fastidious, and thin-waisted antique-dealers, and very rough, ill-spoken *ferrailleurs* and *chiffonniers*, in from the flea markets of the porte des Lilas and the porte de Montreuil. He was perhaps the only auctioneer in the place not to have a speciality: carpets, postage stamps, pictures, silver, jewellery, furniture, china, *everything* passed his way, a veritable shower of junk and valuables, the intimacies of past regimes and forbidden, once glorious pleasure-palaces – he put under the hammer a bust of Jean Chiappe, a full-length portrait of Jacques Doriot, standing with his deputy's sash, on a barricade, against a background of red flags, factory chimneys, and clenched fists; at one sale he knocked off, in lots of half a dozen, official photographs of Marshal Pétain, the full uniform of a deceased *immortel* was held up in front of him, commented upon, along with its former wearer, the *bicornes* of *polytechniciens* would be disposed of in company with the shakos of *cyrards*, medals and sashes showered on the table in front of him, immense quantities of female clothing, down to the intimacies of night-wear, knickers, shifts, *soutiens-gorge*, and under-skirts would appear on the anatomical shelves in front of his rostrum, as if this had been an unofficial *morgue*, minus the bodies, with the *clothes* desperately seeking their lost owners, and, in the immediate wake of the *loi Marthe-Richard*, it fell to him to dispose of the entire stock of two of the most celebrated Paris brothels, right down to the erotic lampstands and priapic bathroom fittings: a challenge to his descriptive powers which he met with comfortable brilliance, amidst a perfect uproar of hilarity.

His office in the nearby rue Rossini, a sort of antechamber to the real drama, looked as if it had been contrived to the specifications of Salvador Dalí. Like, so it is said, the last Emperor of Germany, he affected to receive customers while seated on a rocking-horse or any other bizarre mount that had come his way, including elaborately decorated commodes or massively Gothic ecclesiastical furniture; and he seemed to expand in the menacing company of springing tigers and panthers, growling leopards, cheetahs with holes in them and the stuffing coming out, bored-looking owls, and a jaded stuffed pike, *aux yeux glauques*, drinker's eyes as boiled as those of one of his *aboyeurs*. Indeed, I suspect that he secretly preferred *le toc* to the real thing, the fancifully hideous extravaganza, of no conceivable use, to the object of rare beauty and great value; and that he liked to live with objects that were bizarre and big, grimacing and in awful colours, as a sort of perpetual student engaged in an everlasting *Bal des Quat'z'Arts*, a carnival that for him took place thrice daily, three days a week. He threw himself into his sales, his wild performances on the rostrum, spectacularly aided by his choir of *aboyeurs*, whose muscles were as strong as their stentorian Parisian voices, with a frenetic energy worthy of Pierre Brasseur acting *Kean*. But he was alone on the stage, a one-man act, in which every gesture, every *coup d'oeil*, every inflection of the voice was used to maximum effect. No wonder his audience seldom varied; few enough came to buy, a great many came merely to watch, and to be spotted and called out by name.

It was not just the public performance. He enormously

enjoyed the haggling, even if it was over some wretched broken telephone, a chair with a leg missing and the seat giving way, or a family photograph album. He spent much of his time chatting with the odd creatures who brought in their daily haul of impossible objects, and was extremely friendly to such a minor operator as my oldest French friend, Maurice Chauvirey. Perhaps, even more, his occasional *voyages à l'intérieur* took him out of the daily round of dust, noise, and flotsam; entry into closed apartments, to make an inventory of furniture, silver, china, linen, the truly astonishing interiors of elderly recluses: bachelor or spinster couples, survivors of noble lineages, shut away in the faubourg Saint-Germain for thirty or forty years, the light penetrating into a fortress closed and shuttered for as long, the ghastly, pathetic, or comical secrets of families gradually unfolding before the washed-out blue, rather globular eyes – his eyes were strikingly like those of the Bourbons – of the auctioneer, the unbelievable smells of old age, avarice, neglect, loneliness, total sloth. Here was a man who had little need to travel, and who could have written, many hundreds of times, *Voyage à travers ma chambre*, save that, better still, each time it would always be someone else's. He liked the *aristos* best – not out of any *bourbonien* affinity or political sympathy, but because their raped interiors were much more unpredictable, always much filthier, often with layers and layers of dirt, and their contents much more bizarre than in the apartment of a banker or an Inspecteur des Finances, where everything would be neat and in place. He had a theory that some elderly *marquises* and *vicomtesses* must have kept themselves in trim well into their eighties by hurling the heads of deer and moose across the room or throwing Sèvres set pieces at one another. He enjoyed the evidence of such posthumous breakage as much as he had enjoyed smashing things, as a young man, when I first met him, at No. 26, his mother's much-misused flat.

On reflection, I think François was a committed artist, a poet, even a social historian of a kind, endlessly fascinated by breaking into privacy and totting up the balance-sheet of lonely, hidden, and unambitious lives. His favourite customers were those who never bought anything and from whom he never obtained a commission, who came to the Hôtel like gamblers to the green tables, because they had nothing else to do, because they lived in a fantasy world which he helped to create for them. He was not an indifferent man; and his fascination with useless objects came from his own deep humanity, he was not so much interested in the objects as such, but in the people, mostly dead, to whom they had at one time been attached and to whom they had once given pleasure. His curiosity about people was insatiable; and I suppose he will go on in the Hôtel Drouot till he drops, for there is no retiring age in that profession. I have come to understand why he has never felt the urge to read a novel, or even follow the *chronique judiciaire* in a newspaper. It is all there in his *salle* on the second floor: his theatre, his full expression, his realization, to which his chaotic office in the rue Rossini is a *loge*, a place of preparation, meditation, conversation, and, sometimes, rest.

With his brother, a quieter, less flamboyant person, medicine eventually satisfied very different needs. Édouard preferred the quiet parts, away from the limelight, finally setting up as a consultant anaesthetist, on call night and day, as well as in general practice, boulevard Malesherbes, on the fringes of an upper-class and a lower-middle-class quarter, offering then a varied clientele. He was the silent man, the watcher, the giver of sleep. When I first met them, the two boys seemed to have much in common, François being so overpowering that something of him ran off on to his younger brother. But I think Édouard was only making a show of trying to keep up with the spanking pace set by his ebullient elder. Once separated, they developed quite differently, and while François grew in size and in noise and clamour, his brother disappeared to the Far East, only returning at his mother's entreaty. Even so, and though both married, they remained very close. They were in fact very fond of each other and came, in later years, to appreciate one another's differences. Édouard spoke with amused affection of his brother's extraordinary performances on the rostrum. What they did have in common – and retained together – was immense physical courage, a marvellously juvenile irreverence – I had come to the right place early to learn the sense of *épater le bourgeois* – an apparently limitless capacity for enjoyment in such important matters as food, drink, girls, and, as far as François was concerned, in that, related, of war, seen indeed as a sort of prolongation of sport, and a great deal of generosity. Public affairs and politics passed largely beside them, with only muted echoes at No. 26.

The Xe *arrondissement*, as far as I know, possesses no literature, and it has been sung about by no poet. Could it be that people simply walk through it in haste to work, in fatigue at the end of the day, along the regular east–west itinerary described in one of Raymond Queneau's novels, *Le Chiendent*, or noisily hitting this outdated *voie triomphale* of music, vice, and pleasure, all three of very low quality, on Saturday nights? As if, indeed, it were but a *lieu de passage*, a sort of surface *Métro*, just like the one following exactly the same route, reflecting the same street intersections, just below the ground. I wonder.

Yet lovers must have met on its broad pavements,

domestic dramas dragged along its grim, Sunday expanses, friendships been born between prostitutes and clients on the corner of the rue Faubourg-Montmartre or in the little café opposite the porte Saint-Denis.

It was not murder country. That was farther north: Pigalle, place Blanche, la Chapelle. Or it was farther east: in the old, traditional badlands of the rue de Lappe and 'la Bastoche.' Or it was over on the other side of the river, along the deserted *quai* skirting the Jardin des Plantes. Pigalle and 'la Bastoche,' in particular, still attempted to disguise themselves as dangerous territory, certainly convincingly enough to make the tourist on a tour of the *bals musettes* shiver in anticipation of the knives coming out. Nor was it really *faits divers* country, save for the occasional street accident, though I know that suicide often briefly inhabited its loneliness in small hotels situated in side-streets like the rue Mazagran – *voie sans issue.*

For me at least, the Xe *arrondissement* still holds the freshness of relative innocence, of adolescence, and, above all, of discovery and acclimatization, so, perhaps, I am the one who should commemorate it: part of central Paris witnessed both from the fifth floor and at boulevard and *Métro* level. One's home station offers as warmly welcoming a homecoming, as great a sense of belonging, as a return from any familiar itinerary which is regularly followed. For me, the famous *agent à double barbe*, the man who had a huge beard coming down into two points, who was always on traffic duty in the daytime at the porte Saint-Denis, signified the imminence of lunch or dinner. And I could even recognize the man who sold *Paris-Soir* in the long corridor of the *Métro* Bonne-Nouvelle, intoning like a litany, in a voice of monotonous despair, as if the last thing he wanted was ever to sell one of his papers, '*Paris-Soir . . . l'Intran . . . Sport,*' with a voice falling in a sort of death agony on the last word, as if it signified ultimate doom, rather than Longchamp, Vincennes, Compiègne, and Chantilly, the Vélo d'Hiv and the Palais des Sports, Roland-Garros, and Colombes.

I went to sleep to the tired, dawdling sound of the *Métro* heading unhurriedly towards Faubourg-Montmartre and Richelieu-Drouot or the bustling Strasbourg-Saint-Denis. I could distinguish between the wheezing gears of the green bus and the sound of a private car, and I woke to the noise of many heels walking rapidly to work on the wooden boulevard. It was as good an introduction, I think, as one could wish for, offering very few constraints and certainly absolutely no pretensions.

If, indeed, the Xe *arrondissement* has produced any literature, it would not be in French; it would more likely be in Yiddish – a chronicle of lost *Stetl* and of dispersed families from White Russia, Lithuania, Poland, and Romania, populations decimated by the Second World War. I walked up the dark and musty staircase of No. 26 sometime late in the 1960s and could find no Polish, Russian, or Romanian names any more, only the names of Armenian carpet-dealers and of dentists.

And yet it was a district of Paris as much deserving of literature as the fashionable literary quarters of Paris or those patronized by populist writers – Ménilmontant, Belleville, or la Goutte-d'Or. The glass *passages* behind the boulevard Bonne-Nouvelle are as bizarre as those enclosed journeys in glass-covered surrealism explored so lovingly by Aragon, in *Le Paysan de Paris*, in the 1920s, farther west in the quartier de la Bourse and the quartier Saint-Lazare. And for sheer ugliness and monumental bad taste, the monster cheap clothing stores that line the street between Bonne-Nouvelle and Richelieu-Drouot must surely be *hors concours*, at least in the highly competitive terms of purely Parisian ugliness.

The quarter, then, would seem to have been crying out for literary commemoration of the same imaginative sympathy and careful observation as two recent works of that great Paris historian, Louis Chevalier, *Les Parisiens* and *L'Assassinat de Paris*, both of them evocations of a Paris which, as he says, is *le paradis perdu* – a Paris already largely lost.

MICHEL TOURNIER

From

# THE GOLDEN DROPLET

1986

Translated by Barbara Wright

IT WAS STILL dark when Idris left the yard of the Francoeur studios, pulling the haughty, miserable shadow of the Palm Grove camel along on a rope. His memory had recorded the somewhat confused directions lavished on him as to how to get to the Vaugirard horse abattoirs. At all events, he had concluded that he had to cross the whole of Paris from north to south. The distance didn't alarm him, and he had all eternity in front of him. But a camel isn't a bicycle. The ridiculous, woebegone silhouette looming up in the grey, rainy Paris dawn amazed the passers-by and irritated the policemen. Right from the start, one of them told him to get off the pavement and walk in the road, alongside the parked cars. But the double-parked delivery trucks constituted dangerous obstacles. One had a load of vegetables. Idris was alarmed to observe that the camel had plucked a cauliflower as it went by and was carrying its prize high up in the air, which might well have caused a riot among the market gardeners. He preferred to stop and let it eat its cauliflower in the gutter, which it did very slowly, with snorts of satisfaction. Then they set off again. The camel's soft pads kept slipping on the greasy road. The drizzle beaded its coat. And yet Idris felt strangely comforted by this gigantic, ungainly presence. He thought back to the Tabelbala *regs*, the Beni-Abbès sands. Circumventing the cars, stopping at traffic lights, going through underpasses, he heard Zett Zobeida's song singing in him:

The dragonfly flutters low over the water
The cricket creaks on the stone
The dragonfly flutters and wordlessly twitters
The cricket creaks and utters no word
But the dragonfly's wing is a skit
But the cricket's wing is a script
And this skit thwarts the tricks of death
And this script tells the secret of life.

They came to a high wall behind which there seemed to be some trees. After this night of electric lights and cigarette smoke, Idris would have liked to rest in a garden. He found a vast, open gate. He went in. It wasn't really a garden, in spite of the greenery. It was the Montmartre cemetery. At this hour, it was deserted. Side by side with ostentatious chapels, some of the graves were simple rectangular slabs. Idris lay down on one of them and immediately fell asleep. How long did he sleep? A very short time, no doubt, but long enough to be transported into the other cemetery, in Oran, where Lala Ramirez had taken him. The old woman was there, roundly abusing him and shaking her fist with her skinny arm. She was abusing him in French and in a man's voice, and she finally shook him by the shoulders. A man with a moustache, wearing a cap with a shiny peak, was bending over Idris, ordering him roughly to get the hell out of there with his camel. Idris sat up on the tombstone. Only to see the camel devastating a nearby grave that had recently been embellished with flowers. Having finally found a wreath to its taste, it had begun to pull it to pieces, slowly and methodically. The man in the cap was choking with fury; he talked about despoiling of tombs and, being a professional, invoked Article 360 of the Penal Code. Idris had to get up, drag the camel away from its chrysanthemums, and try to find his way out among the labyrinth of monuments. They crossed a square, a market, a bus station. Idris had never before ventured so far out of the Barbès district. Never for a moment, though, did it occur to him to ditch the camel and go back to the hostel in the Rue Myrha. Somehow he felt responsible for the animal. It was compelling him to continue this ridiculous, sinister trek, but it represented a duty for the Saharan nomad he still remained. And anyway, as he began to leave the poorer districts behind and to enter the fashionable ones, it was clear that the passers-by were more and more inclined to pretend not to see him. After the Gare Saint-Lazare, but even more so in the Place de la Madeleine and Rue Royale, nobody seemed to notice this strange couple among the hurrying, early-morning crowds. After a perilous crossing of the Place de la Concorde, he succumbed to the temptation to go down to the banks of the Seine to escape the inferno of the traffic. Patches of haze were drifting over the black water. Under the Pont Alexandre III, tramps, huddled together round a little fire built from street sweepings, called out to him merrily, brandishing empty wine bottles. A woman, hanging her washing out on a barge, stopped what she was doing and went and called a child to show it the camel. A dog came bounding up to it, barking. Once again, as the tissue of social relationships became less compact, the camel had become visible. Idris walked on past the river boats, then went back up to the embankment, crossed the Pont de l'Alma in the direction of the Eiffel Tower, passed under its belly, his head raised, seeing nothing beyond its criss-cross girders. The camel, so far totally indifferent to everything, suddenly shied, with a raucous snarl, at the sight of an old man holding a bunch of multicoloured balloons on a stick.

At last they found the Rue de Vaugirard, whose name rang

in Idris's ears as the key to the labyrinth in which they had been forlornly wandering for several hours. He had in fact been told: Rue de Vaugirard, and then Rue Brancion, and in that street, at number 106, the horse abattoir. He was making his way down the Rue des Morillons when he was surprised to see a herd of cows. The patter of their hooves on the macadam, their subdued lowing, and above all the smell of dung enveloping them, were as surprising in these surroundings as was the presence of the Palm Grove camel. And anyway, it seemed that the camel was sensitive to the animal presence of the cows because it quivered, gathered up its strength and, passing Idris, broke into an awkward little trot and caught them up. In this fashion they came to number 40 Rue des Morillons, whose gate was surmounted by an ox's head made of golden metal. For indeed, if horses enter this place of death by the Rue Brancion, it's by way of the Rue des Morillons that bovines go to hell. A hell, moreover, that at first looks familiar and even reassuring. For Idris found himself in the middle of vast wooden stables full of straw, warm, giving out an agreeable smell of hay and dung, in a pleasant atmosphere of peaceful lowing, sighs, and sleepy movements. True, at the far end of the stalls there was a little door through which the cows were passing calmly, one after the other, without jostling each other, as if they were going to the milking parlour or out to graze. This door opened on to a gangway that led up to a vast room with a guillotine-type door. The cows waited on the gangway, each one's head resting on the rump of the one in front, full of confident resignation. They were like patient housewives, shopping basket in hand, waiting at a shop door.

The guillotine rises. The first cow moves forward. The guillotine falls behind her. She finds herself imprisoned in a cage a little above the ground. The killer waits until the plaintive head is placed in a suitable position. He brings his 'matador' down in the middle of the forehead, between the big, apprehensive eyes gazing up at him. A sharp crack. The animal collapses on to its knees. The left-hand panel of the cage disappears and the huge body, shaken with spasms, topples over on to the grid covering the ground. The slaughterer bends down and cuts the carotid artery. Then he attaches the animal's right back hoof to a chain hanging from an overhead rail. The chain becomes taut and the carcass is raised by one hoof, like a rabbit brandished by a gigantic hunter. The carcass glides along the rail, while a vermilion fountain gushes down on to the grid. The left back leg thrashes the air convulsively. The warm, panting carcass joins its fellow carcasses crowded together in the slaughterhouse on enormous, funereal suspensions. Men enveloped from head to foot in white oilcloth attack them with choppers and electric saws. Stripped of their skin, immense lustrous surfaces appear, all gleaming muscles and mottled slime. Steaming mauve and green viscera cascade down into vats.

An employee was hosing away the organic waste and brown sanies, which went cascading over to the drainage grids. Suddenly, he stopped in amazement. The tall silhouette of the camel had just appeared in the open doorway. He called a colleague.

'Good God! Come and have a look! What d'you think of that! Now we'll have seen it all, here: a Bedouin with his camel. Well, well, now we know that France has had it!'

Three or four knackers came up to Idris and his animal, guffawing.

'So you've brought us a camel, have you. You want us to turn it into steak? You've got a nerve, my lad!'

'Have *you* ever slaughtered a camel?'

'Who, me? What d'you take me for? And can you imagine any butcher wanting to buy that?'

The killer came down from his platform and said to Idris:

'Me, know how kill cows and horses. Me, no know how kill rhinoceroses. Where you hit it, to kill a camel? On its hump?'

'Here – I'll give you some good advice: take it back to Africa, where it comes from. It ought never to have left its own country.'

'Or take it to the lost property office, it's just round the corner in the Rue des Morillons!'

Idris decided to leave. But before he could get out, this shepherd had the misfortune to pass through the room where the sheep were slaughtered. There were about twenty of them, their throats cut, hanging by one foot, and they were swaying like so many censers, projecting their blood on to the walls and the people, a tragic, grotesque aerial ballet.

He didn't know where to go with his camel. All the fatigue of the night descended on to his shoulders. He turned into various streets at random, crossed avenues, crossed the Seine again. He had the vague intention of returning to the hostel in the Rue Myrha, but no idea of which way to go. He was attracted by some trees which were becoming increasingly numerous, a still-distant mass of foliage. It was a relief to be at last walking on the soft ground of a path running alongside the iron gates of sumptuous residences. The camel just managed to avoid a funny little blue and green train with its bell jingling madly. Children were crowding round a door with a pay box window. It was the Zoo. Idris followed them and, thanks to the camel no doubt, he was allowed in without a ticket. He wandered about for a moment between the aviary containing the birds of prey and the 'Enchanted

River'. Then he had a surprise: another camel had appeared, a she-camel to be precise, her little round ears flapping as a sign of welcome. The two animals rubbed flanks. Their morose, disdainful heads met very high up in the sky, and their big, pendulous lips touched. Under a thatched shelter Idris noticed saddled and bridled donkeys and a charming little varnished-wood cart, to which two goats were harnessed. Adolescents dressed as Turks – turbans, baggy silk trousers and Turkish slippers – got to work on Idris's camel. They put an embroidered blanket over its back, a cloth with little bells over its ears, a muzzle over its mouth. Small children pushed and shoved each other up a kind of tall red ladder which was just the right height to enable them to perch on the camel's back.

Idris walked away, drunk with fatigue and happiness. He passed the Palace of Distorting Mirrors, and observed himself puffed up like a balloon, or on the contrary tall and skinny, or cut in half at the waist. He stuck out his tongue at these grotesque images of himself, the latest additions to so many others. A chorus of youthful laughs answered him. He saw his dressed-up camel passing majestically by, on its back a cluster of little girls shrieking with joy. The sun spread fans of light through the foliage. There was music in the air.

Idris remembered the glass-fronted cabinets of the Saharan museum in Beni-Abbès; they were shop windows in miniature. But ever since he had been in Paris he had in fact done nothing but go from shop window to shop window. When he crossed a road, it was almost always because, once his eyes had had their fill of one window display, the goods in the shop opposite had beckoned to him. The small shops in the Barbès district overflow on to the pavement and offer to the hands of passers-by piled-up racks of shoes, underclothes and bottles of perfume. A shop window signifies a better-class establishment. But even then, it mustn't be confined to a single window which gives you immediate access to the shop, where you find its owner, his till, and the customers coming and going. No, a shop window worthy of the name is sealed off by a partition. It forms an enclosed area, at the same time totally exposed to the gaze and inaccessible to the hands, impenetrable and yet without secrets, a world you may only touch with your eyes but which is nevertheless real, in no way illusory like the world of photography or television. A fragile, provocative safe, a shop window is just asking to be broken into.

Idris had not finished with shop windows. That evening, coming from the Boulevard Bonne-Nouvelle, he had turned into the Rue Saint-Denis, and he became aware of the call and smell of sex coming up from all sides. He remembered Marseille and the Rue Thubaneau. And yet the contrast between the two 'hot' streets was immediately apparent. The girls here seemed younger; at all events they were less corpulent, and none was of the African type. But it was above all by its flashing, multicoloured shops, by the heavy curtains concealing their entrances, that the Rue Saint-Denis outclassed the Rue Thubaneau and gave itself an air of feverish, hidden luxury. *Sex Shop. Live Show. Peep Show.* These words kept repeating themselves in flashing lights over the shop fronts. Their triple red grimace promised the young unmarried man, condemned to chastity by solitude and poverty, the satisfaction of his virile needs among showers of obscene images. He passed three small shops, and then pushed aside the curtain over the doorway of the fourth.

At first he thought he was in a bookshop. The walls were covered in books with garish covers and enigmatic titles: *My Wife is a Lesbian*, *Mixed Doubles*, *X Nights*, *Three Vestas for one Cigar, Heads with Tails, Loves, Delights and Orgasms, Woman Descends from Ape, The Hidden Face of the Moon.* With some difficulty, Idris deciphered these words which meant nothing to him. The photos on the covers, on the other hand, displayed a brutal, puerile eroticism that spoke more of abjection and burlesque than of beauty or seduction. Yet Idris could well see what reduced the violence of these images: the more completely the anatomical details of the genitals were revealed, the less the faces appeared. In many of the photographs they were even totally invisible. There was a kind of compensation in this. It seemed that by abandoning only the lower part of their bodies to the photograph, both men and women managed to deprive it of the essence of their real selves. Perhaps these butchers' displays were finally less compromising in their anonymity than the portraits, which were apparently more discreet?

The objects on the stands and shelves aroused few echoes in Idris's imagination. The 'delicate lingerie' with the lace panties, suspender belts, fishnet stockings and bras conjured up no more than vague memories, but he remained totally perplexed by the collections of Japanese vibrators of all shapes and sizes and the simple, grooved, ringed, nodulous or barbed dildos, whose use escaped him. A panoply of 'sado-maso' whips made of plaited cowhide, and which writhed like snakes, seemed to him by comparison more familiar and almost reassuring. A life-sized inflatable doll with buoyant curves and lacking in none of the charms of the feminine anatomy was standing stiffly, rounded and smiling, at the foot of a little staircase leading to the peep show. Idris went up it.

A man sitting behind a counter gave him change in five-franc coins, and pointed to the door of booth number 6, whose red light was not on. It was a tiny room, almost entirely taken up by a huge leather armchair facing a concealed window. Idris sat down and looked round him. The floor, sticky with moist patches, was strewn with crumpled paper handkerchiefs. On the right-hand wall a metal box with a slot bore this laconic inscription: 2 x 5 *francs = 300 seconds.* Idris put the two required coins in the slot. Immediately an indicator lit up, showing the figure 300, which began to decrease second by second. At the same time the light in the booth went out and the screen over the window rose. The crack of a whip rang out against a background of languorous music. The scene was bathed in yellow light. The action took place on a slowly revolving turntable and was reproduced in a series of mirrors, the reverse side of the booth windows, which were made of one-way glass so that the spectators could not see one another. A woman-lioness was lying on her side across the revolving stage. She shook her splendid mane, with a bitter, twisted smile. Her midriff was squeezed into a golden fur garment that left her buttocks and bulging breasts exposed. She held her breasts in her hands and looked at them avidly with her green, slanting eyes, then rubbed their nipples against her cheek and held them up in supplication towards one of the windows, as a mother might hold her children up to a hypothetical saviour. Then she writhed on the ground, a prey either to pain or voluptuousness – to voluptuous pain – still caressed, however, by the syrupy music, under the sightless gaze of the mirrors. At this point a new crack of the whip tore into the music. The lioness shuddered. Her big mouth, with its twisted smile, opened and emitted a silent roar. She arched her back and opened her thighs, revealing the yawning gap of her newly shaved vulva, which she began to claw at with the sharp-pointed red nails of one hand. Then she rolled over on to her stomach, and her buttocks rose and fell violently in time with the music.

The curtain fell over the window and the light in the booth came on again. Idris stood up, trembling with frustrated desire.

'You're crazy to want to meet her,' Achour had told him. 'It's as if that woman didn't exist.'

'But she does exist,' Idris had protested. 'She was on the other side of the window. I could talk to her like I'm talking to you!'

'She existed for your eyes, but not for your hands. Here, everything's for our eyes, nothing's for our hands. Glass windows are like the movies and the television – for the eyes, only for the eyes! You need to understand these things. And the sooner the better!'

But Idris still didn't understand these things, for the very next morning he went back to the Rue Saint-Denis. He had no difficulty in finding the sex shop again, but he didn't notice that the luminous sign advertising the peep show was not lit. He went into the shop. There was no one there to welcome him but the inflatable doll, still stiff, curvaceous and smiling, standing at the foot of the little staircase. He went up. The doors of all the booths were open. In one, he saw the back of a cleaning woman who was wielding a long-handled floor mop. She was dressed in a grey overall which revealed her naked legs, knotted with varicose veins. She stopped mopping and turned round to empty a plastic rubbish bag full of crumpled paper handkerchiefs.

'And what might the young man want?'

Her pepper-and-salt hair was cut very short, her face was a mask hardened by the absence of make-up. She screwed up her eyes to try and get a better look at Idris, who stared at her in amazement. Those slightly slanting green eyes reminded him of something.

'If you've come for the peep, it doesn't start until five,' she added.

And she went back into the booth to fetch her mop and bucket of water.

'These men! It's incredible how filthy they are! They squirt it all over the place. On the chair, on the walls, on the ground! Some even splash it over the window!'

And as she said these last words, her big mouth was distorted into the twisted smile of the whipped lioness.

PATRICK MODIANO

From

# FLOWERS OF RUIN

1991

WHEN I WAS twenty, I would feel relieved when I passed from the Left Bank to the Right Bank of the Seine, crossing via the Pont des Arts. Night had already fallen. I turned back one last time to see the North Star shining above the dome of the Institut de France.

All the neighborhoods on the Left Bank were only provinces of Paris. The moment I reached the Right Bank, the air felt lighter.

Today I wonder what I could have been fleeing by crossing over the Pont des Arts. Perhaps the neighborhood I had known with my brother, which wasn't the same without him: the school on Rue du Pont-de-Lodi; the town hall of the sixth arrondissement, where they handed out the scholastic prizes; the number 63 bus that we waited for in front of the Café de Flore, which took us to the Bois de Boulogne . . . For a long time, I felt uneasy walking on certain streets of the Left Bank. At this point, the area has become indifferent, as if it had been rebuilt stone by stone after a bombardment but had lost its soul. And yet, one summer afternoon, turning onto Rue Cardinale, I rediscovered in a flash something of the Saint-Germain-des-Prés of my childhood, which resembled the old city of Saint-Tropez, without the tourists. From the church square, Rue Bonaparte sloped down toward the sea.

Once across the Pont des Arts, I walked beneath the archway of the Louvre, another domain with which I'd long been familiar. Beneath that archway, a musty odor of mildew, urine, and rotten wood wafted from the left side of the passage, where we'd never dared venture. Light fell from a filthy, cobweb-covered window, leaving in half-shadow heaps of rubble, wooden beams, and old gardening implements. We were sure that rats were hiding in there, and we hastened our steps to emerge into the fresh air of the Louvre courtyard.

In the four corners of that courtyard, grass spurted between the loose cobblestones. There, too, were heaps of rubble, building stones, and rusty iron rods.

The Cour du Carrousel was lined with stone benches, at the foot of the palace wings that framed the two little squares. There was no one on those benches. Except for us. And sometimes a vagrant. In the middle of the first square, on a pedestal so high that you could barely make out the statue, General Lafayette vanished into the stratosphere. The pedestal was surrounded by a lawn that they never trimmed. We could play and lie around in the tall grass without a groundskeeper ever coming to reprimand us.

In the second square, among the copses, were two bronze statues side by side: Cain and Abel. The fence surrounding them dated from the Second Empire. Visitors crowded around the museum entrance, but we were the only children to frequent those abandoned squares.

The most mysterious zone stretched to the left of the Carrousel gardens along the southern wing that ends at the Pavillon de Flore. It was a wide alley, separated from the gardens by a fence and lined with streetlamps. As in the Louvre courtyard, weeds grew among the cobblestones, but most of the stones had disappeared, leaving bare patches of ground. Farther up, in the recess formed by the palace wing, was a clock. And behind that clock, the cell of the Prisoner of Zenda. No stroller in the Carrousel gardens ventured down that alley. We spent entire afternoons playing amid the broken birdbaths and statues, the stones and dead leaves. The hands of the clock never moved. They forever struck five-thirty. Those immobile hands enveloped us in a deep, soothing silence. We only had to stay in the alley and nothing would ever change.

There was a police station in the courtyard of the Louvre, on the right-hand side of the archway that led out to Rue de Rivoli. A Black Maria was parked nearby. Officers in uniform stood in front of the half-open door, through which filtered a yellow light. Under the archway, to the right, was the main entrance to the station. For me, that was the border post that truly marked the passage from the Left Bank to the Right, and I felt my pocket to make sure I was carrying my identity card.

The arcades of Rue de Rivoli, along which ran the Magasins du Louvre. Place du Palais-Royal and its metro entrance. This led to a corridor featuring, in a row, small shoeshine booths with their leather seats, and shop windows displaying junk jewelry and souvenirs. At this point, one had only to choose the journey's end: Montmartre to the north or the affluent neighborhoods to the west.

At Lamarck-Caulaincourt, you had to take an elevator to exit the station. The elevator was the size of a cable car, and in winter, when it had snowed in Paris, you could convince yourself it was taking you to the top of a ski slope.

Once outside, you walked up a flight of steps to reach Rue Caulaincourt. At the level of the first landing, on the flank of the left-hand building, was the door to the San Cristobal.

Inside reigned the silence and half-light of a marine

grotto, on July afternoons when the heat emptied the streets of Montmartre. Windows with multicolored panes projected the sun's rays onto the white walls and dark paneling. San Cristobal . . . The name of an island in the Caribbean, near Barbados and Jamaica? Montmartre, too, is an island that I haven't seen in about fifteen years. I've left it behind me, intact, in the blue of time . . . Nothing has changed: the smell of fresh paint from the walls, and Rue de l'Orient, which will always remind me of the sloping streets of Sidi-Bou-Saïd.

It was with the Danish girl, the evening I ran away from school, that I went for the first time to the San Cristobal. We were sitting at a table in back, near the stained-glass windows.

'What will you have, old top?'

Over dinner, I tried talking to her about my future. Now that they'd no longer want me at school, could I still continue my studies? Or would I now have to find a job?

'Tomorrow is another day . . . Have some dessert.'

She didn't seem to register the gravity of the situation. A tall blond fellow wearing a glen plaid suit came into the San Cristobal and headed for our table.

'Hiya, Tony.'

Hi.'

She seemed delighted to see him. Her face lit up. He sat down next to us.

'Let me introduce you to a friend who was all alone this evening,' she said, pointing to me. 'So I decided to take him to dinner.'

'Well done.'

He smiled at me.

'Does the young gentleman work in music?'

'No, no . . .' she said. 'He ran away from school.'

He knitted his brow.

'That's a bit awkward . . . Doesn't he have any parents?'

'They're traveling,' I stammered.

'Tony is going to call your school,' said the Danish girl. 'He'll tell them he's your father and that you're safely back home.'

'You really think that's a good idea?' asked Tony.

He gently rolled the end of his cigarette along the edge of the ashtray.

'Go do it, Tony.'

She had taken an imperious tone and was threatening him with a wagging index finger.

'Okay . . .'

It was she who called information for the school's telephone number, which she jotted down on a scrap of paper.

'Your turn now, Tony . . .'

'If you insist.'

He stood up and, with a casual gait, walked toward the phone booth.

'You'll see . . . Tony will fix everything . . . '

After a moment, he reappeared at our table.

'Uh, well . . . They said my son had been expelled and that I have to go pick up his things before the end of the week . . .'

He shrugged, looking apologetic. I must suddenly have turned very pale. He laid his hand on my shoulder.

'Don't worry . . . They can't bother you anymore . . . I told them you were home safe and sound.'

The three of us found ourselves on Rue Caulaincourt.

'I won't be able to come to the movies with you,' the Danish girl said to me. 'I have to spend a little time with Tony . . .'

She had planned to take me to the Gaumont-Palace to see *Solomon and Sheba.* She dug into her pocket and handed me a ten-franc bill.

'You'll go to the Gaumont on your own, like a grown-up . . . And afterward, you'll take the metro and come back to sleep at my house . . . Take the line that goes to Porte Dauphine and change at Étoile . . . Then the line to Nation and get off at Trocadéro.'

She gave me a smile. He shook my hand. The two of them got into his blue car, which disappeared around the first corner.

I didn't go to the movies that evening. I walked around the neighborhood. Heading up Rue Junot, I came to the Château des Brouillards. I was sure that one day I would live around there.

I remember a car ride, five years later, from Pigalle to the Champs-Élysées. I had gone to see Claude Bernard in his bookstore on Avenue de Clichy and he offered to take me to the movies to see *Lola* or *Adieu Philippine*, which I remember fondly . . . It seems to me that the clouds, sun, and shadows of my twentieth year miraculously live on in those films. Normally we only spoke about books and movies, but that evening I alluded to my father and his misadventures under the Occupation; the warehouse on the Quai de la Gare, Pagnon, the Rue Lauriston gang . . . He looked over at me.

'A former sentinel from Rue Lauriston is now a doorman at a nightclub.'

How did he know that? I didn't have the presence of mind to ask.

'Would you like to see him?'

We followed Boulevard de Clichy and stopped in Place Pigalle, next to the fountain. It was around nine in the evening.

'That's him . . .'

He pointed out a man in a navy blue suit standing post in front of Les Naturistes.

At around midnight, we were walking up Rue Arsène-Houssaye, at the top of the Champs-Élysées, where Claude Bernard had parked his car. And we saw him again. He was still wearing his navy blue suit. And sunglasses. He stood immobile on the sidewalk, in the space between two neighboring cabarets, so that one couldn't exactly tell which one he worked for.

I would have liked to ask him about Pagnon, but I felt awkward as soon as we passed in front of him. Later, I looked up his name among the other members of the gang. Two young men had served as lookouts on Rue Lauriston: a certain Jacques Labussière and a certain Jean-Damien Lascaux. Labussière, at the time, had lived on Rue de la Ronce in Ville-d'Avray and Lascaux somewhere near Villemomble. They had both been handed life sentences. Which one was he? I didn't recognize him from the blurry photos that had appeared in the newspapers at the time of the trials.

I ran into him again, around 1970, on the sidewalk of Rue Arsène-Houssaye, still standing at the same place, with the same blue suit and the same sunglasses. A sentinel for all Eternity. And I wondered whether he wore those sunglasses because after thirty years his eyes had worn out from seeing so many people go into so many sleazy places . . .

Several days later, Claude Bernard had rummaged in a closet at the back of his bookstore and taken out this letter that he gave me, which dated from the Occupation. I've kept it all these years. Was it addressed to him?

My dearest love, my adored man, it is one in the afternoon; I've woken up very tired. Business not so good. I hooked up with a German officer at the Café de la Paix, brought him to the Chantilly, did two bottles: 140 francs. At midnight he was tired. I told him I lived a long ways away, so he rented me a room. He took one for himself. I got a kickback on both and he gave me 300 francs. That got me my 25 louis. He'd made a date with me for last night in the lobby of the Grand Hôtel, but at seven, when we were supposed to meet, he showed up all apologetic and showed me his orders to ship out to Brest. After my failed date, I said to myself, 'I'll go to Montparnasse to the Café de la Marine and see if Angel Maquignon is there.' I went. No Angel. I was about to take the subway home when two German officers picked me up and asked me to go with them, but I could see they were idiots so gave them the brush. I went back to Café de la Paix. Nothing doing. When Café de la Paix closed, I went to the lobby of the Grand Hôtel. Nada. I went to the bar at the Claridge. Bunch of officers having a staff meeting with their general. Nothing. I returned to Pigalle on foot. On the way, nothing. It was about one in the morning. I went into Pigalle's, after checking in at the Royal and at the Monico, where there wasn't anything. Nothing at Pigalle's either. Heading back out, I ran into two hepcats who took me with them, we sank two bottles at Pigalle's, so 140 francs, then we went to Barbarina, where I got another 140 francs. This morning at six-thirty I staggered home to bed, completely worn out, with 280 francs. I ran into Nicole at Barbarina, you should have seen her get-up . . . If you could have been there, my poor Jeannot, you'd have been ill . . .

Jacqueline

Who was that Angel Maquignon, whom this Jacqueline was going to meet at Café de la Marine? In the same café, a witness claimed to have seen Gisèle and Urbain T., that night in April when they'd mixed with bad company in Montparnasse.

The Champs-Élysées . . . It's like that pond a British novelist talks about, at the bottom of which, in layered deposits, lie the echoes of the voices of every passerby who has daydreamed on its banks. The shimmering water preserves those echoes forever and, on quiet evenings, they all blend together . . . One evening in 1942, near the Biarritz cinema, my father was picked up by Inspector Schweblin and Permilleux's stooges. Much later, toward the end of my childhood, I accompanied him to his meetings in the lobby of the Claridge and the two of us went to have dinner at the Chinese restaurant nearby, whose dining room was upstairs. Did he occasionally glance at the sidewalk across the avenue, where years earlier the Black Maria had been waiting to take him to the holding cell? I remember his office, in the ochre building with large bay windows at 1 Rue Lord-Byron. By following endless corridors, one could exit onto the Champs-Élysées. I suspect he had chosen that office for its double exit. He was always alone up there with a very pretty blonde, Simone Cordier. The telephone would ring. She'd pick up:

'Hello? . . . Who's calling, please?'

Then, turning to my father, she whispered the name. And she added:

'Should I tell him you're here, Albert?'

'No. I'm not here for anyone . . .'

And that's how the afternoons passed. Empty. Simone

Cordier typed letters. My father and I often went to the movies on the Champs-Élysées. He took me to see revivals of films he'd enjoyed. One of them featured the German actress Dita Parlo. After the movie, we walked down the avenue. He had told me in a confiding tone, which was unusual for him:

'Simone was a friend of Dita Parlo's . . . I met the two of them at the same time.'

Then he'd fallen silent, and the silence between us lasted until Place de la Concorde, where he'd asked me about my studies.

Ten years later, I was looking for someone to type up my first novel for me. I had found Simone Cordier's address. I called her. She seemed surprised I should still remember her after all that time, but she made an appointment to see me at her home on Rue de Belloy.

I entered the apartment, my manuscript under my arm. First she asked me for news of my father and I didn't know what to answer, as I didn't have any.

'So, you're writing novels?'

I answered yes in a halting voice. She showed me into a space that must have been the living room, but it no longer had any furniture. The tan paint on the walls was peeling in spots.

'Let's go to the bar,' she said.

And with an abrupt movement she pointed to a small white bar at the back of the room. The gesture had struck me at the time as rather offhanded, but now I realize how much shame and confusion it masked. She went to stand behind the bar. I put my manuscript down on it.

'Shall I pour you a whiskey?' she asked.

I didn't dare say no. We were both standing, on opposite

sides of the bar, in the dim light of a wall lamp. She poured herself a whiskey as well.

'Do you take it the same as me? Neat?'

'Sure.'

I hadn't had whiskey since the Danish girl had given me some at Chez Malafosse, so long before . . .

She downed a large gulp.

'So you want me to type all that for you?'

She pointed to the manuscript.

'You know, I haven't been a typist in a long time . . .'

She hadn't aged. The same green eyes. The beautiful architecture of her face had remained intact: her forehead, the arch of her eyebrows, her straight nose. Only her skin had gone a bit florid.

'I'll have to get back into the swing of it . . . I've gotten kind of rusty.'

I suddenly wondered where she could possibly type anything in that empty room. Standing, with the typewriter resting on the bar?

'If it's a problem,' I said, 'we can forget it . . .'

'No, no, it's no problem . . .'

She poured herself another whiskey.

'I'll get back into the swing of it . . . I'll rent a typewriter.'

She slapped the flat of her hand down on the bar.

'You leave me three pages and come back in two weeks . . . Then you can bring me three more pages . . . And so on and so forth . . . Sound all right to you?'

'Sure.'

'Another whiskey?'

After leaving Simone Cordier's apartment, I didn't immediately take the metro at Boissière. Night had fallen and I wandered aimlessly around the quarter.

I had left her three pages of my manuscript, without harboring much hope that she'd type them. She had shrugged her shoulders when I'd said I hadn't heard from my father in five years. Apparently, nothing could surprise her about 'Albert,' not even his disappearance.

It had rained. A smell of gasoline and wet leaves hovered in the air. Suddenly, I thought of Pacheco. I imagined him walking on the same sidewalk. I had gotten as far as the Hôtel Baltimore. I knew that one evening he'd gone to meet someone at that hotel and I wondered what sort of person he might have seen there. Perhaps Angel Maquignon.

The only information I'd ever gleaned about Pacheco had come by chance, in the course of a conversation, at Claude Bernard's house on the Île des Loups. We were having dinner with an antiques dealer from Brussels whom he'd introduced as his associate. By what circuitous path had we come, that man and I, to speak of the duc de Bellune, then of Philippe de Bellune, alias de Pacheco? The name rang a bell with him. When he was very young, he had known, on a beach in Belgium, at Heist near Zee-brugge, a certain Felipe de Pacheco. The latter lived with his grandparents, in a dilapidated villa on the dike. He claimed to be Peruvian.

Felipe de Pacheco frequented the Hôtel du Phare, where the owner, who had been a diva at the Liège Opera, sometimes gave recitals for the evening clientele. He was in love with her daughter, a very pretty blonde named Lydia. He spent his nights drinking beer with his friends from Brussels. He slept until noon. He had abandoned his studies and was living by his wits. His grandparents were too old to keep an eye on him.

And several years later, in Paris, my interlocutor had again met this boy in a drama class, where he was calling himself Philippe de Bellune. He was taking the course in the company of a girl with light brown hair. He was a dark young man with a spot on one eye. One day, this Philippe de Bellune announced that he'd just found a well-paying job through the want ads.

They had never been seen again. Neither Philippe de Bellune nor the girl with light brown hair. It must have been the winter of 1942.

I scoured the job offers placed in the newspapers that winter:

> Several young persons needed for lucrative work, immediate payment, no special qualifications required. Write to Delbarre or Etève, Hôtel Baltimore, 88-bis Avenue Kléber, 16th. Or come to that address after 7 p.m.

I recall a Hôtel de Belgique on Boulevard Magenta, not far from the Gare du Nord. It's the area where my father spent his childhood. And my mother arrived in Paris for the first time at the Gare du Nord.

Today, I felt like going back to that neighborhood, but the Gare du Nord seemed so far away to me that I gave up. Hôtel de Belgique . . . I was sixteen years old when my mother and I washed up one summer in Knokke-le-Zoute, like two drifters. Some friends of hers were kind enough to take us in.

One evening, the two of us were walking along the large dike at Albert-Plage. We had left behind the casino and an area of dunes past which began the dike of Heist-sur-Mer. Did we pass by the Hôtel du Phare? On our way back, via Avenue Elisabeth, I had noticed several abandoned villas, one of which might have belonged to Felipe de Pacheco's grandparents.

# ACKNOWLEDGMENTS

VILLIERS DE L'ISLE ADAM: 'The Unknown Woman' (1883). Translated by Robert Baldick. Reprinted by permission of Oxford University Press.
LOUIS ARAGON: From *Paris Peasant.* Translated by Simon Watson-Taylor. Published by Picador and Exact Change Publishing. *Le Paysan de Paris,* Louis Aragon © Editions Gallimard, Paris, 1926.
JAMES BALDWIN: Excerpted from *Giovanni's Room* © 1956 by James Baldwin. Copyright renewed. Published by Vintage Books (US) and Penguin Books (UK). Reprinted by arrangement with the James Baldwin Estate.
HONORÉ DE BALZAC: From *A Harlot High and Low* by Honoré de Balzac, translated with an introduction by Rayner Heppenstall (Penguin Classics, 1970). Translation and introduction copyright © Rayner Heppenstall, 1970. Reproduced by permission of Penguin Books Ltd.
DJUNA BARNES: *Nightwood* (1937), Chapter 2, 'La Somnambule'. Published by Houghton Mifflin Harcourt.
LOUIS-FERDINAND CÉLINE: From *Voyage au bout de la nuit,* Louis-Ferdinand Céline © Editions Gallimard, Paris, 1952. Translated by John H. P. Marks as *Journey to the End of the Night*, published by The Random House Group Limited.
RICHARD COBB: Excerpt (Chapter 2: 'Paris Xe') from *Paris and Elsewhere* (John Murray, 1998, then NYRB, 2004). Reprinted by permission of Mr. Christopher Sinclair-Stevenson.
COLETTE: From *Claudine in Paris* by Colette (translated by Antonia White). Published by Secker & Warburg. Reprinted by permission of The Random House Group Limited. Excerpt from *Claudine in Paris* from *The Complete Claudine* by Colette, translated by Antonia White. Translation copyright © 1958 by Martin Secker &

Warburg Ltd. Complete volume copyright © 1976 by Farrar, Straus and Giroux, LLC. Reprinted by permission of Farrar, Straus and Giroux, LLC.

JULIO CORTÁZAR: 'Blow-Up' copyright © 1967 by Random House LLC; from *End of the Game and Other Stories* by Julio Cortázar. Used by permission of Pantheon Books, an imprint of the Knopf Doubleday Publishing Group, a division of Penguin Random House LLC. All rights reserved. Any third party use of this material, outside of this publication, is prohibited. Interested parties must apply directly to Penguin Random House LLC for permission. 'Blow-Up' (original title 'Las Babas') © Heirs of Julio Cortázar, 1959. Reprinted by permission of Agencia Literaria Carmen Balcells.

F. SCOTT FITZGERALD: Reprinted with the permission of Scribner, a division of Simon & Schuster, Inc. from *Tender Is the Night* by F. Scott Fitzgerald. Copyright © 1933, 1934 by Charles Scribner's Sons. Copyright renewed © 1961, 1962 by Frances S. F. Lanahan. All rights reserved.

GUSTAVE FLAUBERT: From *A Sentimental Education* by Gustave Flaubert, translated by Robert Baldick (Penguin Classics, 1970). Translation copyright © Robert Baldick, 1970. Reproduced by permission of Penguin Books Ltd.

GONCOURT BROTHERS: Excerpt from *Journals* (translated by Robert Baldick), OUP 1962, reprinted with permission from David Higham Associates on behalf of the author's estate.

VICTOR HUGO: From *The Wretched* by Victor Hugo, translated by Christine Donougher (Penguin, 2013). Translation © The Folio Society, 1976. Reproduced by permission of Penguin Books Ltd.

JORIS-KARL HUYSMANS: 'The Folies Bergère' (translated by Brendan King), taken from *Paris Sketches* (1880), Dedalus, 1963. Reprinted with the permission of Dedalus Limited.

MILES KINGTON (translator): Alphonse Allais, 'The Polymyth', translated into English by Miles Kington. Copyright © Miles Kington, 1976. Reproduced by permission of the Estate of Miles Kington c/o Rogers, Coleridge & White Ltd., 20 Powis Mews, London W11 1JN.

GUY DE MAUPASSANT: From *A Parisian Affair and Other Stories* by Guy de Maupassant, translated by Siân Miles (Penguin Books,

2004). Translation copyright © Siân Miles, 2004. Reproduced by permission of Penguin Books Ltd.

BARRY MILES: Excerpt from *Beat Hotel* by Barry Miles, copyright © 2000 by Barry Miles. Used by permission of Grove/Atlantic, Inc. Any third party use of this material, outside of this publication, is prohibited.

PATRICK MODIANO: Excerpt from *Flowers of Ruin* from *Suspended Sentences: Three Novellas*, translated by Mark Polizzotti, Yale University Press, 2014. Reprinted with permission.

GEORGES PEREC: From *Things: A Story of the Sixties* by Georges Perec (translated by David Bellos). Published by Harvill Press. Reprinted by permission of The Random House Group Limited. Reprinted in the US by permission of David R. Godine.

RAYMOND QUENEAU: From *Zazie in the Metro* by Raymond Queneau, translated by Barbara Wright, copyright © 1959, 1982 by Librairie Gallimard; translation copyright © 1960, 1982 by Barbara Wright. Used by permission of Penguin Books, an imprint of Penguin Publishing Group, a division of Penguin Random House LLC. Reproduced by permission of Penguin Books Ltd.

JEAN RHYS: From *Quartet* (Chatto & Windus, 1928), chapters 1 and 2.

GEORGES SIMENON: 'In the Rue Pigalle' from *Maigret's Pipe* by Georges Simenon, translated by Jean Stewart (Penguin Books, 1978). Reproduced by permission of Penguin Books Ltd. and Houghton Mifflin Harcourt.

MICHEL TOURNIER: From *The Golden Droplet*, 1986, translated by Barbara Wright, published by Methuen.

EMILE ZOLA: From *L'Assommoir*, translated by Margaret Mauldon (1998), 3870 words from pp.34–43. By permission of Oxford University Press.

Although every effort has been made to trace and contact copyright holders, in a few instances this has not been possible. If notified, the publishers will be pleased to rectify any omission in future editions.